James Freil was born
and at UCNW, Bango
Wales. His first novel, *Left of North*, won a Betty Trask
Award.

Also by James Friel in Abacus:

LEFT OF NORTH

JAMES FRIEL

Taking The Veil

An Abacus Book

First published in Great Britain by Macmillan London Limited, 1989
Published in Abacus by Sphere Books Ltd, 1991

ISBN 0 349 10200 7

Printed and bound in Great Britain by
BPCC Hazell Books
Aylesbury, Bucks, England
Member of BPCC Ltd.

Sphere Books Ltd
A Division of
Macdonald & Co (Publishers) Ltd
165 Great Dover Street
London SE1 4YA

A member of Maxwell Macmillan Publishing Corporation

I

Riot Saint

I

The Fire on Brackley Street

For the past two nights rioters had controlled the southern part of the city. The area known as Radcliffe Park had been sealed off with barricades of burning cars and the night sky was fogged over with smoke, heavy black clouds of it, streaked through with flames and peppered with sparks. The air was thick with the sounds of sirens, and the spit, crackle and shuddering fall of buildings.

There wasn't a road or back alley in Radcliffe Park that wasn't part of the show but Brackley Street was where the fighting and the burning were at their worst. Its houses had been evacuated and most were now gutted, its shops smashed, looted and aflame. The rioters, young men in T-shirts and soccer scarves, jostled each other, waved angry and exultant fists and threw at their enemy insults, stones, railing spikes, bricks and milk-bottles filled with petrol and stoppered with burning rags. Facing them from behind an irregular and uneven wall of quivering plastic shields, the police, four rows deep, tried vainly to encircle and protect the firemen putting out the larger of the fires.

The youths howled, grew braver, and began to advance. Some, growing braver still, cockier, broke from the ranks, running forward to bowl with elegant overarm flaming petrol-bombs at the massed wickets of the policemen's shields before dashing back with a whoop and a leap to be lost in the cheering body of the mob.

The police, too, edged forward but more slowly, cowering behind their shields, only to be beaten back by yet another hail of yells and jeers, bricks and petrol-bombs. Their shields began to buckle under the impact of the bricks or to melt and drip hot plastic on to their hands, helmets, shoulders, faces.

3

The night before, when the police had only dustbin lids with which to protect themselves, the mob had won. The police had fled and Radcliffe Park had been left to the rioters until daylight had brought a fragile semblance of order, which crumbled when darkness returned and with it the rioters. On Dearie Street and Wiley Avenue they had vanquished the police yet again, charging forward and scattering them like a gale through a house of cards. In Brackley Street they were more evenly matched, the police more tenacious, more vicious, and neither side was winning.

What was happening in Brackley Street, in Radcliffe Park, was happening in other streets, in other cities. It was the year for riots and people were just beginning to realise it. Some said it wasn't rioting, it was more like war, and that was how it felt. Some blamed unemployment, the recession, racism or national despair, and some said thugs were thugs and needed no excuse and the riots were a laugh if you were in them and you were winning. Some blamed the weather. Britain wasn't used to heat. It was the highest of hot summers, the middle of July, and it hadn't rained since May.

The firemen hid behind the police, ducking the bricks and the flying glass, their hoses sending up great waving arcs of foam on to the fiery shell of what had once been a mini-supermart. The foam, coloured orange by the flames, splashed over the walls and showered the policemen below. From inside came the soft *pop pop* of exploding cans and aerosols sounding sweet and low and faintly rhythmical against the rush of flames and the noise of pitched battle outside.

The fifty yards or so of no man's land between police and rioters was cluttered with debris and had become a shallow river of water and dirty foam. The shops on either side of the road were dark, their windows broken, their contents looted; television sets, jeans, gardening tools and damaged kitchen units littered the sodden street. What had once been a newsagent's was now a pile of rubble, razed the night before and smoking still. You could clamber over it and reach the milk-coloured canal over which Brackley Street formed a hump back. The canal, like Brackley Street, ran on right through to the centre of the city.

The street-lamps were all broken, smashed, giant daffodils

4

with shattered heads. The power supply to the area had been cut off – water from the firemen's hoses had shorted the circuits – but there was light enough, bright but intermittent, made up of the orange glow of the burning mini-supermart, the spinning white strobe of a battery-powered burglar-alarm and the flashing blue of the fire engines and the police vans.

A woman appeared in the middle of Brackley Street, a tiny doll of an old woman. She appeared suddenly from nowhere or so it seemed; perhaps she'd come along the canal and over the rubble of the newsagent's. A dumpy, frail-looking woman, sixty, maybe seventy, in a heavy cream-coloured coat, ankle-boots and a blue headsquare, she stood on the kerb of the pavement, uncertain, wavering slightly.

Her sudden and inexplicable appearance caused both sides to become momentarily still, gobsmacked. Curiosity caused police and rioters to fall silent and a calm to drop like a knife, a calm broken only by the rasping lick and slurp of the fire and the battery-operated burglar-alarm dying into a faded buzz. They stared at the old woman, watched her as she turned first towards the police and then towards the rioters, watched her, no longer wavering but standing firm, upright, with a conscious, almost comic dignity, straight as a nail holding the road in place.

'Hey,' someone shouted at the police, 'it's your mam. She's come to take you home.'

A sudden guffaw, the rioters began to laugh, to screech even.

'She's come to join the scrap!'

'Hit 'em with your pension book!'

'Get that stupid cow out of here!' someone screamed from the back of the police and a young policeman was pushed out from the ranks to rescue the old woman. Seeing him, the rioters attacked again. Another volley of missiles came flying down the street, right over the old woman's head. She seemed not to notice. A brick caught the young policeman on the shoulder. He fell back with a splash on the wet street. He lay there, flat, until another brick caught him full in the stomach. He screamed, curled into himself and was still. Policemen crawled forward and, dodging another hail of bricks, gripped him by the jacket and dragged him back into the ranks.

The old woman looked on with interest but no real concern.

She put her hand up to the collar of her coat as if for warmth although it was summer, the night muggy, the air thickly warm. She stepped off the pavement, her feet splashing the foam-covered puddles. She moved easily and with a peppy grace over the bricks and broken glass. She looked as if she were out shopping.

'Shops are closed, love!'

This she heard. She turned to look, scowling, a mean little face, pinched, with eyes too large for it. She looked about her, a troubled, faintly suspicious look. Her eyes, smarting and tearful from the smoke, glistened in the light from the fires. The rioters cheered her on and the police beckoned madly at her to move away. She carried on until she reached the middle of the road and then she stopped. She pulled the blue headsquare from her head and let it fall.

'Hey! Hey! She's doing a strip!'

Wolf-whistles from the crowd.

The woman turned and faced the ruined building over which she must have climbed and, as if Brackley Street were suddenly a cathedral and the rubble of the newsagent's its altar, she went down on her knees before it.

A silence fell again but more one of disbelief than of curiosity or respect. The fire crackled and raged on, the alarm a lazy hum. The firemen still worked the hoses, the foam swishing ineffectually against the flaming walls of the mini-supermart, but their attention was on the old woman.

She kneeled there, oblivious of fire, water, riot, intent on some purpose of her own. The flames flapped and thundered, filling her head with the sound of many wings beating against glass. The smoke rose up in rich dark folds and hid the heavens from view. She stretched out her arms, fingers splayed. Leaning forward, she put her palms down on to the surface of the road, deep into the puddle before her, and then cupped them and brought them, dripping, to her face.

'What's she doing?'

She buried her face in her hands.

'She's drinking it! She's drinking that puddle with her hands!'

She took her hands away and her wet face glittered in the firelight. She brought her hands together.

'She's praying!'

'She's bloody praying!'

'The cow, who does she think she is?'

'Bloody Mother Mary of Moss-side!'

'Let her have it!'

Stone upon stone fell on her and she fell face down on the road, jerking and writhing and screaming with each stone that hit her, rippling and wriggling like a firecracker on the wet road. Each scream was one of terror and a plea for mercy. It was as if she were at last awake and knew where she was and what she had walked into. The crowd bayed and she screamed and screamed again as each stone hit its mark. She crawled and struggled in the wet, vainly defending herself with flailing arms. The missiles rained down. The police edged forward in ranks in order to retrieve her.

A milk-bottle filled with petrol, its neck crammed with newspaper and set alight, was thrown with extreme grace and landed on the old woman's back where it burst, covering her instantly in flames. She picked herself up and began to dance wildly, the flames shooting from her back like fiery wings. She twirled, pranced and shimmied madly, her body a black shadow dancing inside the flames, tripped and fell backwards.

The water-sodden street doused her almost immediately. With a hiss that was audible even above the cries and jeers and the tumble of masonry, she was lost to sight in a pillar of smoke and steam.

The police charged at the rioters and the rioters fled further up the street. In the charge the old woman was lifted up by six policemen and carried by her arms and legs with great speed and little care to an ambulance two streets away. All the while she struggled, fighting with the flames that had covered her and which, in her head, burned on.

They laid her in the ambulance face down, an oxygen-mask held over her bruised mouth. She was alive but barely so. She was conscious still and boxing with the flames, feebly hitting out at ambulancemen, kicking with weak and raw-skinned legs. Then she vomited, not food but blood, into the oxygen-mask. They wiped it away. She fell back, mouth biting bits out of the air like a fish out of water. She stiffened then was still, remained paralysed, mouth a pouting 'O' as if offering a kiss, the eyes open but dull, as if this death were neither surprising nor horrifying but a sad fact, a duty wearily but politely to be borne.

They searched the pockets of her coat – or that part of her coat that had not been burned away or melted into her flesh – and found only a library card. It told them only her name but that was enough for there were few in that city of any age who had not heard of Ursula Trench.

II

What the Papers Said

Ursula Trench was buried on 21 July in the grounds of a religious retreat not a mile away from the place where she was burned to death. She had been dead less than a week. Her funeral was attended by eight nuns, two priests and a photographer from the *Daily Star*.

The photographer had not been invited but had climbed over the wall before the burial had begun and had hidden behind a bush some fifteen yards from the open grave.

Ernie Mather took at least thirty photographs that morning but it was the first three that were used in the next morning's paper. The first, taken from behind the bush, was a simple but dramatic study of eight sturdy nuns and two priests standing over the open grave, their figures punched black against the grey morning mist. The second showed the same group but in disarray, one of the nuns lying flat on the ground and the others staring into the camera. The third photograph was of the prostrate nun seen close up, face looking heavenwards, her mouth agape, her expression something close to either ecstasy or indigestion.

This last photograph was the one that filled the front page of the *Daily Star* with the headline beneath it: 'WE HAVE BURIED A SAINT!' : WEIRD NUN'S CLAIM FOR KILLER TRENCH

Inside, on pages two to three, in simple language, the *Daily Star* told its readers of the final instalment of the bizarre life of murderess-cum-martyr, Ursula Trench: how a hoax funeral had been set up to deceive the press; how she had been secretly buried in the early morning by a coven of eccentric nuns and how that funeral, eerie rite that it was, developed into a macabre orgy when one particularly demented nun had hurled herself into the grave, convinced of its occupant's sanctity.

The *Daily Star* did not hesitate to remind its readers how Ursula Riot Saint Trench had met her death and of her long years in prison for the murder of a man called Andreas. Nor was it subtle or retiring in pointing out the morbid irony not only in where she had died but also in where she had been laid to rest – 'that garden of blood'.

'Ursula Trench,' it ended, 'Saint or Satan? What do YOU think?' Readers were encouraged to ring a certain number and let the *Daily Star* know their verdict.

And, of course, they mentioned the weather.

III

The Dummy Funeral

Since the death of Ursula Trench the Cenacle had been surrounded by reporters. The riots had brought them to the city in full strength. Now they pitched camp outside the grand but ugly mansion that housed the Cenacle of the Lancashire Martyrs. They rang the doorbell constantly until the nuns disconnected it. They shouted through the letterbox and tapped relentlessly on all the ground-floor windows, breaking three of them.

The nuns, concerned that even after death Ursula Trench would know no peace, had devised a 'dummy' funeral. With the Bishop's full backing, they arranged with a sympathetic chapel of rest in Mallet that a room be set aside and in it placed a sealed but vacant coffin. The coffin bore no name and no nun ever said it contained the half-charred corpse of Ursula Trench but who expected nuns to flirt so with the truth?

Most of the flowers, wreaths and cards – the pleasant ones – were sent to the Mallet Chapel of Rest. Throughout the week, individual nuns rolled up in taxicabs to pay their respects. Attention shifted to the Mallet Chapel of Rest and away from the Cenacle in the grounds of which the nuns planned to bury Ursula Trench.

There was neither reason nor precedent to distrust a nun; only Ernie Mather of the *Daily Star* did so, out of principle: 'Distrust the world and work alone' was the motto experience had tattooed on his mind.

Ernie, a frail, bleached rodent of a man, had a face so thin it had no business being there and a body so skinny that strangers gave him pitying glances. He looked like a thing kept forever indoors and in the dark but this was not

11

so. He was a veteran of the foot-in-the-door-figure-under-the-lamp-post-sheltering-from-the-rain-under-the-privet journalist. He had found out all about TV Pam and MP David in 'Zombie Sex Slave Love Nest' and had brought to public attention many a soap star's secret shame.

He knew that Ursula's body lay not in the Mallet Chapel of Rest but in the Cenacle itself. If she lay anywhere it was in that house. He knew that the body would be buried in the garden – a juicy bone only he knew how to dig up. He knew it all, if not for a fact then as good as, as good as.

'I've a nose,' he'd muttered to himself.

He had no more nose than anyone else, but what he had was a sense of the fitness of things, of knowing that, no matter how crazy the look of it, life's fabric had a regular pattern to it.

On the morning of 21 July, ten o'clock, the parish priest of Saint Greg's, Mallet, arrived at the chapel of rest. He called the press from out of the snowy drizzle and they clustered about the coffin. Coughing badly and reading from notes he'd made on the back of a packet of Marlboro, he explained to them that Ursula had already been laid to rest some two hours ago.

On hearing that they had been tricked, the majority of the reporters had not waited for explanations or apologies but had rushed to waiting cars, vans or scooters and dashed to the Cenacle in the empty hope of catching the end of the authentic funeral.

Too late: Ernie was waiting for them, perched on the bonnet of his Nissan Micra. When he saw them coming he slid down and got into the car, pausing to brandish his camera, holding it above his head as if it were a trophy and he winning it yet again.

'You won't believe the show I've seen!' he cried, a grin creasing his narrow face. 'What a show! And it's all in here, all of it.'

He waved his camera at them, laughing, and got in his car. They clambered round it and begged Ernie to tell all – or just a bit of all – but Ernie, still laughing, drove off. 'Suckers,' he mouthed at them through the car window.

Ernie-less, story-less, their blood up, they turned to face the Cenacle. The front of the house gave nothing away,

12

the windows blind with pulled curtains. In a herd they rushed forward to bang on the door and windows. What had happened, they wanted to know, what had gone on? They ran round the back. Here, too, the curtains were pulled; there was no sign of a nun. They scampered across the damp lawn to the bottom of the long garden and saw the freshly covered grave of Ursula Trench side by side with the graves of two other nuns who had died over the past five years. They turned back to the house, hungry for explanations. They unscrewed the flap of the letterbox and hollered for someone to talk to but the house seemed as deserted within as it was without.

Some time in the afternoon a taxi came. The door opened and out of the seemingly empty house emerged a young priest, his face dark and unpleasant with barely contained anger. He pushed his way through the reporters who pulled at his sleeves and tried to haul him back by the tail of his soutane. He kicked them off and closed the taxi door.

They followed the taxi to the airport. Once there, they harried him further still with their questions, pushing money into his fists, his pockets and down his dog-collar in the hope that he would answer them and tell them all. They would have followed him on to the plane but the flight to Dublin was fully booked. They learned nothing from him or about him other than his name on the passenger-list: Ayomon Devlin. It told them nothing.

IV

The Funeral Garden

Father Ayomon Devlin, not Irish as his name suggests but locally born of an Irish father and a Mallet mother, watched the snow fall with a gloomy fascination. He was standing in the porch of the small chapel that had been built as an extension to the original house. The nuns inside the chapel were waiting for the funeral to begin as was Father Dunn, the parish priest, who had been invited to say the mass. Devlin felt that he should have been invited to say it considering the distance he'd come. He would have refused to say it but he would have liked to be asked so as to have the pleasure of refusing.

Devlin's face was long, his jaw heavy and square, his eyes shadowy slits, but his skin was as soft and uncreased as an infant's. When a boy and in what his mother called a 'fret', sulks that would last for days, his lips used to protrude sullenly and his chin sink to his chest. 'The wind'll come and your face'll stick like that,' his mother had warned him but he had sulked on. The wind had not come, time had, and his face had stuck. When he most thought himself an angry young man he looked most like a spoiled and tearful child.

He scowled at the snow. It fell in feeble, undernourished flakes and melted instantly on the ground. It was strengthened by a fine drizzle with a satiny sheen to it which dimmed the morning light and misted the garden over, making it spectral, a place for ghosts to haunt. The smooth lawns showed deep green underneath this dingy veil and the scarlet roses showed through like angry wounds dressed in a thin gauze.

One of the nuns had said last night that it had snowed like this every morning since Ursula Trench died. Snow in July and in a heatwave; was it a sign? she had asked. He remembered his answer – 'Only of your stupidity' – and how it had hurt her; her

14

cow eyes had grown milkily tearful. He smiled to recall it.

He had arrived the night before from Dublin and had been greeted warmly by this nun because he was an old friend of Ursula's. She had told him of the Dummy Funeral and of the real one that would take place in the garden.

'It'll be just us and Father Dunn and you,' she had said. 'There were loads who wanted to come, loads and loads, but Ursula would have wanted it to be just us. She wasn't one for crowds. We let you come because, well, you were the only one from her past who asked.'

The Sisters of the Cenacle of the Lancashire Martyrs had a reputation for worldliness. It was said that they grew sleek and plump on the good life for which their customers paid so handsomely. They fed and cosseted the wealthy, mainly Mancunian Catholics who, experiencing spiritual crises, wished to renew their faith in pleasant but local surroundings. The Cenacle was a health farm for the spiritually sick. The sisters did not attend to spiritual ills – local priests and visiting missionaries did that. The nuns kept house, made beds, cooked meals of epic size and famed deliciousness and created about them so congenial an atmosphere that guilt, reproof or any other corrosive of the soul would not dare contaminate it. They were there to make God's word a cheery one and His world comforting to those uneasy in it.

From inside the candle-lit chapel he could hear them shuffling in their pews, the murmur of a prayer or conversation, the odd cough. They were waiting for Mother Tess, who had been called to the phone. Devlin looked up, away from the falling snow, and saw her coming.

'It was the Bishop,' she called out, 'wanted to wish us luck. The plans for the Dummy Funeral are AOK and there'll be an announcement at nine, which gives us an hour.' She bobbed along the path towards him, her grey habit flapping about her as she made absent-minded attempts to pluck a missal from her pocket. 'Snow in July, Father. It could only happen in the North. Did you guess I was a local girl? We all are except Sister Bridget. Irish, but we don't hold it against her and she's not a girl for talking so you can't tell by looking at her. Well, it's not uncommon, is it?'

'What isn't?' Devlin asked guardedly. Mother Tess's rapid

speeches sometimes lost him and, because he was still smarting from a rap over the spiritual knuckles she had given him earlier, it pleased him to be awkward.

'The snow, Father,' she clucked, 'the snow in July. It'll be gone in a flash. It never sticks and never lasts above a minute or two. It's not uncommon but it is rare. I worry about it.'

'About the snow?'

'It unsettles the girls. They talk about it, I know. I don't listen but I know they talk. And if it stops tomorrow they'll be convinced it means something. I'll have a word with them afterwards.'

One of the nuns came to the door, the cow-eyed one called Gertie he'd met last night. She was pretending unsuccessfully that he did not exist or, if he did, that he was no more than dirt on the church step.

'We're waiting to start, Mother Tess.'

'Yes, yes, Sister. My, you're impatient to get her buried.'

The nun's plump face seemed to cave in at such an accusation. 'Oh, don't say that, please, oh, don't!'

'It's all right, don't upset yourself. We'll be in in a tick. Go and sit down, Sister.'

Sister Gertie turned to go but Devlin called her back. She looked up at him boldly, a child's drawing of a brave face, but she edged back into the chapel at the same time.

'I wanted to apologise, Sister, to make amends for last night and the things I said. It was late and I was tired. I never intended to upset.'

That was a lie. He had intended to upset. The apology was not quite sincere but Sister Gertie took it as it sounded. She smiled at him, a smile brimming with instant forgiveness.

He had learned that such smiles came easy here. It explained why Ursula had settled amongst these nuns, why she had finally grown happy; what criminal would not be, with forgiveness there for the asking of it? Wasn't that what she had wanted, what she had always wanted, searched for, expected as a right, a privilege that was owing to her and of which she had unjustly been deprived? And to find it at last, here, her old home turned now into a warm, accommodating hotel with forgiveness, like hot water, on tap.

'Tell Father Dunn we're coming in, Sister Gertie.'

Sister Gertie stepped back into the candle-lit darkness of the chapel. Devlin allowed himself a quiet snort of contempt.

Mother Tess, mind-reader, fixed him with a look that was cold and unassailable. 'You're a prig, Father Devlin. Young priests often are. Perhaps that's why you never got on with Ursula. Ursula liked a laugh. She was one of the girls.' She entered the chapel.

Devlin, as he could do nothing else, followed her. They walked down the narrow aisle, genuflected and took their places in the front pew, the coffin of Ursula Trench, gleaming in the honeyed light of the many candles, an arm's length away.

Mother Tess tapped her nose as a signal for the service to begin and Father Dunn seemed to wake and sit up in his chair by the coffin with the jerk of a puppet whose strings had been twitched. He moved behind the small trestle-table covered in blue cloth that was the little chapel's altar. He wormed his head through the greasy opening of his stole and, arranging the scanty strips of hair that fell across his skull, nodded vaguely at the nuns who then struck up the first hymn, some insipid limping tune praising the Virgin sung with a shrill gentility except for the deep and gravelly bass of Sister Gertie who lagged two beats behind, but who was loud in her sincerity.

'I like to think', whispered Mother Tess who did not sing, 'that the dead are with us both in body and in spirit at this time.'

Devlin nodded appreciatively at what he thought a banal comment. He looked at the coffin, pondered the woman it contained and considered the July snow. He imagined the corpse in that coffin, imagined it awake, lying in its dark cot and listening still, lapping up all this praise and grief and interest, imagined its mind still active, still turning, still working on the world, and on him, in its own malevolent and insidious way.

To watch Father Dunn stumbling through the mass, hands quivering with senility and voice fogged by more than one drop of communion wine, was unbearable. Devlin himself gave a good mass, a proud mass like a performance, everyone said so – but, then, Devlin had been practising since he was seven.

At the age of seven, an Irish aunty had given him a comic book of the mass, step-by-step cartoon illustrations and all the words and prayers the priest said, even the quiet ones when he broke the bread and crumbled it into the wine, the ones the congregation could not hear. Every Saturday the little Devlin would practise the mass after his mother had brought him breakfast in bed. He'd nibble his toast into a circle and use it for a host, a cup of tea would be his chalice, the bedspread pulled up around his shoulders his vestments. Using the window-sill as an altar, he'd say the mass from his comic book, speak the responses and sing the hymns. Sometimes he would catch his mother sitting on the landing listening in through the closed bedroom door.

There was never a time when he had been brought to God, when he had discovered some priest-shaped mark on his soul; he had always been with God, the mark had been there from before birth or so it seemed: God had sent his soul to earth clearly addressed.

He was odd and effeminate and slow to mature. In a school where boys tattooed themselves with biros and bowie knives, sported bumfluff with pride, swore and spat, and girls talked about sex and swore and scrapped, he was picked on. Two girls regularly flirted with him, made him say swearwords in his squeaky and unbroken voice, obscene words as oddly shaped in his mouth as threepenny bits. They made him walk them home, bring them money and toffee, made him put his hands down his trousers and tell them how big his willie was. They called him Millimetre Devlin.

But, then, girls were never fun for Devlin, and his body clock ticked on five years later than other boys'.

He left school at sixteen for a seminary in Leatherhead and he had his first erection when a boy with whom he shared his room taught him to masturbate. So began one more problem, for Devlin fell in love with the boy and then another and another; silent, secretive loves, some of them reciprocated. The other problems fell away or diminished in importance as puberty accelerated. His body grew hair and he found he was indeed a priest and not play-acting at one or explaining his oddness by being one. As for that one problem, it was controllable; strange men in public toilets, at irregular

18

and well-spaced times, in towns or places where he was not known, helped alleviate but not solve it.

Father Dunn mumbled on, raising the host with trembling hands as if it were a weight he could hardly bear and sipping from the chalice with an audible slurp.

Devlin daydreamed about an Ursula different from the one he had known. He tried to imagine her as these nuns said she was, a dear, a pet, a laugh and one of the girls. He imagined meeting such an Ursula, chatting with her, at ease, but his own idea of Ursula was too vivid for another to be superimposed upon it and, surely, his idea of Ursula was the true one. His Ursula led more logically to the final Ursula, the Ursula who had died in the street, Ursula Riot Saint Trench.

Riot Saint! She would have loved that. She had always thought herself misunderstood, neither mad nor murderous but a saint, some Holy Joanna touched by God's own finger, but all the while she was sick and sinfully proud.

What had she been doing that night? Had she wandered there clueless or had she come on like Gandhi to quell a riot? Had she been making a public expiation of her sins (where better to do it than in Brackley Street with a ready-made crowd)? Whatever, if she had survived, she would have claimed to have been wafted there on God's breath. God, she would have said, had wanted to make a martyr of her.

Although the Ursula he had known had talked constantly in terms of sacrifices and holy purposes, Devlin could not allow himself to call it a martyr's death. Martyrs die for a cause. Ursula, he was sure, had turned up in Brackley Street for attention's sake. She could not have planned on a burning.

Yet burned she had been and Devlin could not dispute the aptness of her death, the place, the crowd, the fire. They set up a series of echoes, echoes that resounded down the dark tunnel that had been Ursula Trench's life, echoes that called out and argued for some organising principle. Death by fire, fire which burned and consumed itself with a noisy roar. Ursula could not have chosen a more appropriate way out.

Father Dunn blessed the coffin, sprinkling it with holy water, splashes of which hit the candle flames and spat and fizzled in the air. Behind him, Devlin could hear the soft, occasional sob

19

of one of the nuns and the deep, untunely moaning of another, probably Sister Gertie.

The mass over, the congregation rose. Six of the nuns took up the coffin and led the procession out of the tiny chapel. Devlin winced as he heard the soft slide and thud of the body shifting from side to side as it was carried out on the nuns' shoulders.

The snow had stopped, as Mother Tess had said it would. The drizzle, however, continued, chilling the air, greying the light and shrouding the garden in a pale mist which seemed instantly to catch the mourners' dark habits, the damp furring every strand of wool, turning them almost white.

The procession made its slow, faintly marching way across the lawn down to the far end where there was a fence of slender spruce trees, their wet trunks black as licorice, and beyond that another, longer lawn bordered with blood-red fuchsia and orange blossoms so shadowy white it seemed as if the mist had made them.

From his place at the back of the procession Devlin considered the swaying bulks of the ample nuns who bore the coffin, their habits swishing rhythmically on the wet grass. Only Sister Gertie lost the funerary beat, stumbling slightly and threatening to go off at a tangent until Mother Tess took her by the arm and brought her back in line.

Because their guests were often people of power and import, the nuns had learned something of the world they had vowed to renounce. They knew how to deal with it with cunning and assiduousness. But they were true nuns when the occasion arose and the death of Ursula was such an occasion. The funeral, their prayers, the stately procession to a grave they had dug themselves, the tender way in which they lowered the glistening coffin into it, attested to their nunly integrity and their deep love for Ursula Trench.

Deep love indeed, for they were burying Ursula Trench as one of their own in the small cemetery that was intended solely for nuns who had lived and worked in the Cenacle. This was the spot they called the Pasture, where each nun would retire when the work had been drained out of her. The sisters were paying Ursula this compliment because they had come to regard her as an honorary nun: as one of the girls, she had a right to be there.

Devlin doubted whether the old bitch deserved such regard.

There were other reasons to be uneasy about burying Ursula Trench in that exact spot, reasons which explained the need for a dummy funeral. If the press discovered that Ursula Trench was to be laid to rest in the grounds of the Cenacle, what might not be made of it? Ursula Trench, buried in the garden of the house that had once belonged to her own blood-spattered family? The house where she had fornicated shamelessly with the man she later murdered so savagely? Now to be buried in the garden of that house where, as a girl of seventeen, she had killed her young brother, cut his throat with a cheesewire and stabbed him repeatedly with a bread-knife?

The nuns must have felt that her claims to honorary sisterhood were strong indeed to fly so recklessly in the face of decency. What level of ignorance, Devlin wondered, must they have achieved to carry this business off? What whim made them choose to ignore how the house, and garden, no matter how changed and enlarged, remained a black museum to the terrible things done there?

The prayers for the dead over, the party stood back and gazed into the open grave, pools of water forming on the black coffin-lid, the sides soiled with mud. On each of the sister's faces was an expression of love and regret, each sorry to leave their friend down there in the dirt.

Devlin sighed, disappointment causing his lips to pout and his chin to sink, becoming the little boy in a fret once more. He had expected release at the sight of Ursula in her grave, for the doors in his soul to breeze open and light to flood in; instead he found that nothing had changed within him, all was still, cold. His trip, the lies he had told to get here, had been wasted.

By his side, Sister Gertie grunted and trembled with grief, mouth open as if to catch the tears that dribbled down her face. She slowly lifted up the hem of her habit until it reached her knees, held it out and gave a little shake. From it dropped a bunch of red roses she had concealed despite the general wish that there be no flowers. They lay scattered in the mud at her feet. Devlin noted the thick black hairs on her legs.

21

'Pick them up, for heaven's sake, Gertie,' snapped Mother Tess.

Sister Gertie gathered up the muddy roses and let them fall in a shower into the grave. They hit the coffin with a series of wet thumps, scarlet on the glossy black lid.

'Sorry, Mother,' Sister Gertie muttered.

No one noticed Ernie Mather behind his bush. He had watched them closely and had waited for so long before taking a photograph not out of respect but because Mother Tess had blocked two of the other nuns from view. Now she stepped back and his view was clear. He could see all eight nuns, both priests and the grave. A classic snap.

FLASH!

It was a rude awakening for them all, and for Sister Gertie an embarrassing one. Believing the flash of the camera to be a flash of lightning and the flash of lightning to be a sign from God, she had fallen to her knees and then on her stomach and was waiting for God's voice to thunder forth. She heard instead Mother Tess's sharp command: 'Gertie, pick yourself up.'

FLASH!

Another picture, another flash – and for Gertie another flash of fire from God's own fingertip. She raised her face heavenwards and cried aloud: 'O God, I hear you! We've buried a saint, Mother Tess, a saint!'

FLASH!

'Thank you, Sister love,' said Mather to Gertie.

His monkey face was suddenly before her and Sister Gertie was not a little confused. Surely this was not the face of God?

'That was lovely, Sister, really lovely.' He patted her on the back and she collapsed yet again but this time from shame, not from ecstasy. The others looked on, helpless, horrified.

Ernie Mather began to prance gleefully around the grave and the mortified mourners, camera clicking and flashing. The mourners were so still they seemed to be posing, until surprised by visions of the next day's newspapers, the nuns lifted their skirts and chased the prancing Mather around the garden, slipping and sliding on the wet grass and making vain grabs at his coat. Mather was better-skilled at this game of tiggy-it than the bulky nuns. He skipped merrily away from them, turning frequently to take a picture whenever nun

22

crashed with nun. Finally, perched astride the garden wall, he took one last snap of the chaos he had caused: a garden of muddy nuns and two priests rigid with embarrassment by an open grave. He blew a kiss and dropped behind the wall.

'Do you think, Father Devlin, that we'll be in the papers now?' asked Father Dunn as together they struggled to carry a weeping Sister Gertie back to the house.

'I feel such a fool,' Sister Gertie whined as they bumped her along between them. 'Such a fool,' she repeated at short intervals between sobs and snuffles.

'Would you just look at us!' said Sister Biddy, displaying her muddy habit. 'And this new on this morning. Don't we look like a rugby team leaving the pitch after a hard match?'

'And just when it was going so well,' said Mother Tess. 'Sister Grace, Sister Meg, fill in the grave. The Bishop will not be pleased. Oh, look!'

Up above, through the clearing mist, the sun, a white disc like a new moon, was clearly visible.

'We have our heatwave back,' said Father Dunn to Father Devlin.

V

The Door in the Wall

Mother Tess was at her desk, deeply involved in that morning's edition of the *Daily Star*: 'I SHARED CELL WITH RIOT SAINT . . . Gloria, 32, said, "She wasn't that holy and she give me the creeps." ' Mother Tess wondered if thirty-two wasn't a little old for a sex kitten but supposed there wasn't a set retirement age.

The door to her parlour was ajar. Devlin knocked and pushed it further open. 'You said you wanted a word.' Devlin had meant to say it politely but, as ever, it came out sullenly.

Mother Tess folded the newspaper into a tube and rubbed the lower of her chins with it as she considered what word in particular she had wanted with him. 'Yes, come in, Father. The funeral's not for another half-hour yet so we've time for a talk.'

Her desk was scattered over with ripped-open envelopes, letters and cuttings from a week of newspapers. She scooped up a handful of papers and shuffled them into some kind of order. 'Fan mail, Father, or most of it. Ursula's. There is the odd unpleasant one, very odd some of them, but never mind. You slept well?'

'I was very comfortable, thank you.' Devlin's voice was stilted and he himself uneasy, not knowing quite what the woman wanted but knowing that somewhere there'd be a telling-off in it for him.

'Comfortable. That's good. It's our job, you know?'

'Yes, I appreciate that.'

'You do? Good. Sister Biddy, who fried your bacon this morning, calls us a spiritual bed-and-breakfast. I've never felt a hard bed and cold porridge made for a cosier relationship with God.'

24

'They don't follow, no.'

'I've never been one for the hair shirt and I wonder if He can really be doing with all this killjoy palaver. No, it was Ursula who put it so well. She said that living a good life had something to do with living it well.'

'Ursula said that?'

'Yes, though she wasn't one for pronouncements, as you probably know. Not one of life's thinkers, Ursula, poor lamb. As I said, we have our guests. They come for a day, a weekend, seldom more than a week. We discourage the long-term visitor. Over-pious. But we do have our regulars. We have special priests who visit, missions, and Father Dunn has a very high turnover in confessions. As for us, well, we do what we can in the way of good food, a homely touch. That is what we do.'

'I'm sure you do it well.'

'I think we do. Sit down, Father, and we can talk. I think we need to talk, don't you?'

She pointed to the chair facing her desk. Devlin sat down, the naughty boy in front of the kindly but severe headmistress. He looked about the office. Ornaments and holy statues stood to attention on every surface, books were crammed into shelves, *The Dogs of War* on top of *Princess Daisy*, paper was strewn across the floor, falling in drifts from the desk. He noticed, too, the profusion of flowers, fresh-cut from the garden, freesias, carnations and gladioli, exploding colourfully from fussy vases in the shape of swans, castles and Spanish ladies. On the window-sill was a row of clean milk-bottles, each holding a single rose.

Mother Tess walked to the window, her back to Devlin. His poor attempt at civility and her well-trained cheerfulness were not enough to smother the air of tension in the room. She leaned forward slightly and placed her face an inch away from the bottles of flame-coloured roses as if to warm herself against them. Her face caught their colour. Turning, she asked: 'Did you enjoy your breakfast?'

'Yes, the food was very good even if the company was a little strained.'

Mother Tess sat down opposite him. 'We can speak freely?'

Devlin nodded and prepared himself with a tension-easing cough.

25

'You said the company was a little. . . .'

'At breakfast? Yes, a little. . . .'

'Strained. Surprised?'

'Well, yes, a little . . . well no, not entirely.' Devlin floundered and, with a shrug, gave up. 'I should have expected it.'

'After last night you should have expected it, most definitely you should have expected it. You invited it, or as good as.'

'Sister Gertrude. . . .'

'Sister Gertie, yes. I told Sister Gertie to wait up for you. My fault. Not a bright idea. I should have chosen someone else. Gertie was only to feed you, show you to your room, not engage you in conversation. I told her not to bother you with talk as you would be tired from your flight and she is a deeply tiresome woman.'

'Then, it was my fault. I asked her to tell me about Ursula.'

'She would have needed no prompting. Sister Gertie was close to Ursula, very close. She is a silly woman but a good nun and she cared greatly for Ursula, greatly. She asked to wait up for you. I thought seeing an old friend of Ursula's would do her good. But that was it, wasn't it, Father? You weren't a friend of Ursula's at all, were you?'

'No.'

'No, not at all. The opposite, it seems.'

'Perhaps.'

'Then, why are you here?'

Devlin said nothing, although her pause gave him ample time to reply. His silence was wilful and the way he shifted in his seat told her as much.

'You know of our plans for today. You know we have made exhaustive efforts to keep this funeral select. Our plans have had the Bishop's full OK and there's not many as get that. We invited you because you were, we thought, a friend from her past. Your call implied just that. You seemed to want to come so badly.'

'None of her old mates from prison?' asked Devlin, mock-innocent.

'Smart remarks like that are probably what upset Sister Gertie but you'll find me a tougher nut to crack, Father Devlin.'

'I am sorry.' Devlin's apology was smoothly insincere. Devlin was not a child to be scolded.

Mother Tess changed tack and softened in a second. 'Sister Gertie woke me early this morning with some tale of what you'd said. She is not a woman to keep quiet. By the time the toast was under the grill your opinion of Ursula was known by all. Hence your frosty reception at breakfast, for which I apologise. They showed you the body?'

'Yes, just now, before I came in.'

'Satisfied with it?'

'*Satisfied* is not the word I'd use.'

'Then, why did you come?'

'To see her buried and to find out how she'd been with you.'

'Ursula lived with us for over four years. During that time you never once visited her, never once wrote to her or to us, and, certainly, she never mentioned you.'

This last shocked him, wounded vanity drawing a deep dent between his eyebrows.

'She never once mentioned you. She never once referred to the time in which you knew her and, from what I know of it, I'm not surprised. Prison had been kinder to her. So why did you come?'

'To find out how she died,' Devlin said limply.

At that Mother Tess's hands fished through the sea of paper that washed over her desk, splashing about in it with quick, angry, searching gestures until she pulled up from it a copy of the *Daily Star*. She folded it and flung it at him.

'There! That's how she died. In a street at the hands of thugs.'

He shook the paper like a wet and dirty rag and dropped it on the floor. 'I know this.' Contained rage made him speak with great deliberation. 'I want to know why. I want to know why and how and I want to know who and what she was.' He spoke as if such knowledge was rightfully his, as if it were something consciously and unjustly denied him. 'I want to know these things and I want to know them for certain.'

'You want the dirt?'

'If dirt there is, then, yes.'

'Well, you can't have it.'

'Why not?'

'Because there isn't any.'

27

Both knew they had gone too far. Each settled back with a sigh that was meant to calm the other.

'We'll start again, shall we?'

'Yes,' Devlin agreed.

'Did you have any trouble getting here?'

'No, not at all. A straight flight from Dublin.'

'I meant leaving your parish. It is in Dublin?'

'Yes, it is, and no, no problem.'

'With Ursula not a relative, I thought there might be. I used to know Dublin well. Where is your parish exactly?'

'On the outskirts. Not really Dublin at all. A postal district of it.'

She nodded. 'And what did you hope to find here?' Her voice was cool and smooth as milk, its tone suggesting a sympathy that would be as sweet as balm to his wounded soul if he would just accept it. 'You can talk to me, you know that?'

Devlin knew it. It seemed of a sudden as if he would cry and that Mother Tess had created this pause to let him. He looked over at her, the round face a pleasant symbol of tolerance, the smile of one who was eager to comfort him. This is how she looked to Ursula, he thought. 'You can talk to me, Ursula, you know that?' he could hear her saying and Ursula, like him, melting. That was the trick of these nuns and this house that they had rebuilt anew, for just as the house knew no austerity, only soft pillows, warm sheets and filling food, so its nuns were strangers to severity and had no sharp corners in their hearts.

'I thought I'd find the Ursula I knew.'

'Not a nice Ursula, the Ursula you knew.'

'No, not nice at all.'

'So why?'

'I came here thinking it was the same Ursula. I came here to crow over her grave.' He searched the nun's face for outrage. There was not a trace. 'And also to forgive and bless and ask God for mercy.'

'For her or for you?'

'For us both. For me because I treated her badly and for failing her. I find her easy to hate but it's not easy hating her. Hating isn't easy if you've no outlet for it. It turns on itself. I

28

hoped coming here and seeing her dead would be an outlet. It wasn't. She stole something from me, something I cared about, ruined me in a way. When I came here last night I expected . . . so much. I felt, I feel cheated. The Ursula I knew was mad. She was sick and twisted and stoked up with this horrific pride, someone not to be trusted, someone soaked in a lifetime's blood. I came here to bless that Ursula. She seemed in need of a blessing. But your Sister Gertie, she spoiled all that.'

'Because our Ursula was not your Ursula?'

'They couldn't be more different. Your Ursula was a sweet old lady.'

'That's how she was with us. There was no badness in her. I think, considering her past, you might have read evil in her. We didn't. She was one of us. She was at home.'

'And she never talked about me?'

'No.'

'Or her time at The Wounds?'

'No.'

'Denbigh? Prison?'

'Never. We never asked.'

'Andreas? The child? This house? When I knew her she talked of nothing else.'

'The past no longer worried her. Somewhere between you and here she must have made peace with it.'

'Isn't that strange?'

'It was fortunate. Necessary. You can only live for the dead for so long. I doubt the dead care. Too much living is done for them. Perhaps Ursula realised it.'

'To come back to this house and never once mention or refer in any way to what happened here?'

Mother Tess hesitated and then said: 'She'd changed. Doesn't her death say as much?'

'No, the opposite!' Devlin jumped up and down in his seat like a child catching an adult out in a lie. 'My Ursula, my mad, sick, proud Ursula would die like that. Yours wouldn't.'

'But she did.' Mother Tess was matter-of-fact. 'I can't begin to understand the impulse which drove her there. Her life had been so ugly. She'd known such violence. She tried to prevent it when she saw it spilling out into the street.'

Devlin wasn't convinced. 'It was a performance. Another performance. She couldn't do a thing without thinking of its effect on others. She always had one eye on the audience. She was evil and part of that evil was the way she passed it off as some kind of gift from God.'

'And you came here to forgive?' Her face had an expression that was pure regret.

'I did, truly.'

'I am so sorry for you.'

'So I came here for the wrong reasons and I have been disappointed and found out. Now you know. I'll give the funeral a miss. Attending would be a morbid exercise and I can't say I approve of where you're dumping her. It wouldn't be right, my staying. You all loved her. She was your friend, one of you. She wasn't like that to me. I wouldn't let her be. Perhaps if I had. . . . I'll go now.'

'I won't hear of it. You'll stay. You ve come too far. Give me your hand.'

He gave her his hand without thinking and, when he realised, when he saw his bony white hand in her podgy grip, it felt too comfortable there to withdraw it.

'You said Ursula was bitter and twisted?'

'She was, she was,' he insisted in a voice that was hardly above a moan.

'And aren't you more so?'

'Yes, I am, I am. She made me so.'

Mother Tess shook her head. 'You're very young.'

'I've been younger. I was younger when I met her, fresh from the seminary almost. Afterwards I was sent to Liverpool, the university. I was good. I did good there. Young people, their problems, boyfriends, girlfriends, drugs, problems of faith. Such bright people, the type who terrified me when I was their age, and I found I could help them.'

'You were young, too. It helped.'

'Yes. She sought me out, you know. Ursula chose me. I won't forgive her for that. She must have known I'd fail her. She ran me ragged.'

Mother Tess squeezed his hand and then released it. 'Poor boy.'

'Some nights I wake up sweating from a dream of her.'

'I think that you're not long for the priesthood.'

'You think right. I'll be going over the wall soon enough.'

'I don't think you'll need to climb over any wall. I think you'll find there's a door in that wall, a door that's well open.'

Devlin could see that she thought he would be no great loss and that hurt him because his one consolation was that he would be.

'The funeral service will start soon. You know where the chapel is?'

'Yes, I went there this morning.'

She rose from her chair and moved towards the window. The light there was greyed by the snowy drizzle outside yet the roses in their milk-bottles still blazed bright in the gloom.

'Not the best weather for a funeral but I expect we'll manage. Poor Ursula, she'll be at rest soon. You did say you'd seen the body?'

'Yes, before I came in.'

He rose to go but Mother Tess, during the time she held his hand, had created such an intimacy between them that he wanted to linger awhile.

'Tell me,' he began and then paused.

'Tell you what?' asked Mother Tess, patience itself.

'Does it all make sense to you? Ursula, how she lived, how she died, what she was, what she did? Do you *understand* her?'

Mother Tess looked blank, raised her hands palms upwards, then laughed. 'Me? Understand? I don't even try. I mean, why bother? Who understands anybody else? I doubt even Ursula knew what she was about. No one knows the full truth about a person, only God, and He keeps it to Himself.'

VI

Viewing the Body

In a kitchen full of them, he was served breakfast by nuns in pink pinnies who would not speak to him. The food was hot and the company was cold. One of the nuns, the Irish one, sat in the corner by the microwave and read out to the others from *Woman's Weekly* the secrets of successful pie-making: adding cornflour to stewed apples soaked up the juices and so kept the pastry light and dry.

'Apple pies made with Bramleys come particularly soggy,' the one making the toast observed. There was a general murmur of agreement.

He could not see the one he'd met the night before, the one called Gertie, the fat one he might have said but he saw now that they were all as large as each other. Planted at the pine table, Devlin felt like a willow among oaks.

The one called Gertie wasn't there but she had been. He could tell that she had spoken with them, told them what had happened the night before. It explained their refusal to speak to him, the huffiness they had about them because he was there. He finished his tea and wondered if he could decently leave not just the kitchen but the house. He had no right to be there and he no longer had any wish to be there.

'Mother Tess wants a word with you,' said one of them. Her face was a perfect circle and as flat as a door but for a knob of a nose on which sat a pair of tiny square spectacles.

'Liz,' said another and pointed up at the ceiling.

Liz understood and tapped the side of her knob of a nose to show she had got the message. 'Do you want to see the body?' She made it sound like a dare, so Devlin had to say yes.

She took him upstairs to a first-floor bedroom.

'She's in there,' she said, as if Ursula was sitting up waiting for him.

The curtains were not drawn and there was netting on the window which softened what grey light strained through it. Sister Liz explained that they had kept it light because a darkened room would have made it obvious the body was there and not in the Mallet Chapel of Rest. The room was bare, the walls white and the carpets mauve. The open coffin rested on two trestles in the centre of the room. Beside it, slumped on a hard-backed chair, sat Sister Gertie. Her heavy lump of a body bridled when she saw him.

Sister Liz led him to the open coffin. 'There she is,' she said pointlessly. 'At peace. The lid's in the airing-cupboard. We'll have to nail it on soon.'

'You screw it on,' said Gertie, still keeping her back to them. 'The screws are in the biscuit-barrel.'

Devlin looked down, face to face with Ursula for the first time in four years. For a moment she seemed so unfamiliar he doubted it was her. The face was glazed with a deep yellow wax and then powdered a violent pink. The eyes were closed and the lids painted a glossy blue, the lips inked in the red of a cheap biro. Her face looked like an inexpertly drawn mask, as if a child had coloured it in. The hair, a wig, was blue-rinsed, thick lacquer collecting in globules on its strands like dew on dry grass. She was dressed in a two-piece suit the blue of her eye-paint, with white bobble buttons, a suit more suitable for a bride's mother than a burial. Carrot-coloured stockings and white gloves almost hid the charred flesh they were meant to cover. Most weirdly, she'd been given a handbag, blue again but not quite the blue of her suit, with a white bobble clasp. The handle was laced through her gloved fingers. He wondered about the need for it and wondered, too, what it might contain. Was it full, packed with items for her journey into the next world – compact, address-book, tissues, matches, a bread-knife?'

She did not look well but he'd imagined worse. It wasn't Ursula, this corpse, but a badly made effigy, a guy for the bonfire, a life-size voodoo doll. He felt cheated and a little afraid. If this was not the real Ursula, then she was somewhere else, still active, watching maybe.

He leaned forward, aware that Sister Liz was studying him and Sister Gertie was clutching the other side of the coffin, with podgy fists ready to defend the corpse should he try to attack it.

'Hours of work went into rebuilding her,' Sister Liz told him, 'and an awful lot of cotton-wool and hot plastic.' She sounded indifferent but not callous, as if she, too, thought that Ursula was elsewhere and the corpse a dummy just for show. 'They proposed having her eyes open, as is the fashion now, but we said no. She lost one. A stone hit it, pushed it right in, so they got rid of it. They said they'd put a glass eye in for the one she lost. They showed it us. A perfect match it was. They said they could even make it swivel from side to side.'

Sister Gertie turned from the coffin, shoulders chugging up and down. She made strange spluttering noises as she choked back tears the size of gobstoppers. For her the soulless corpse was as real as the living Ursula and everything about her was precious, sacred even.

Devlin looked out of the window. Through the veil of the net curtain he could see the garden. It was bigger than he'd imagined and more innocent, its wet lawns lime-green in the early light. Shavings of snow were mixed in the soft drizzle of rain.

'Weather's bad again,' Sister Liz said and she shared a smile with the tearful Gertie that was both sly and triumphant. The weather was proof of something to them, something of which the stuck-up priest did not approve and in which he could not believe.

'Silly little priestlet,' muttered Sister Gertie as Devlin left to have a word with Mother Tess.

VII

Midnight with Gertie

When he arrived it had been close to midnight. His hair had been sleeked back and his black cord jacket and soutane silvery damp with rain. He had been expected before ten and the house was dark enough to make him think they had not waited up for him.

The placard in the garden told him that it was the Cenacle of the Lancashire Martyrs – the words were written in a lacy medieval script and the placard was shaped like a scroll – but he knew it better as the House of Content, for so it had once been called. 'I lived in a house called the House of Content,' he heard her say again and he shivered as a raindrop which had wormed its way down his collar now snaked down his spine.

A wide, plump nun opened the door to him. The hall light had come on the instant he rang the bell, and the bolts drawn back, as if she'd been sitting in the dark waiting only a yard away.

She beamed and whispered welcome, tutted over the rain and the silly weather they'd had of late, explained that everyone else was asleep and Mother Tess would see him first thing come morning. She told him she was Sister Gertie who was to give him supper should he need it and show him to his room.

Chatting quickly, but just above a whisper, she wrestled the sodden jacket off him and handed him thick yellow towels to dry his hair and mop himself down. This done, she fell into reverent silence until Devlin said he was as dry as he could be.

'A nice place you have here,' he said, not meaning it.

The hall in which they stood was a thing of gold and red wallpaper, embossed patterns of pagodas and fleeing geishas.

There was a mirror, butterfly-shaped and fleeced with lace, the carpet a thick green that looked as if it needed mowing.

With a giggle in her voice, Sister Gertie told him to follow her into the kitchen. Before moving off he caught sight of himself in the butterfly mirror. His colour was high and he half-patted, half-stroked his burning cheeks with pale, rain-cooled hands. He studied his reflection with pleasure and a little relief. A priest's face, he thought, and for the first time in over a year was pleased that this was so. With such a face as evidence, who would question his identity? He had had no reason to fear these nuns.

The kitchen was a brightly lit cave of warm air and rich smells. Whatever wasn't painted orange was blue Formica and the floor was a wet-look draughtboard of yellow and green. He sat at the long table and Gertie poured him tea in a rose china cup.

'It's fresh made,' she told him. 'I've been brewing up off and on to pass the time.' Sister Gertie, now that she spoke above a whisper, had an accent he knew to be local and said so.

'Mallet-born and Mallet-mannered,' she told him. 'But I've spent time in Basildon.'

Devlin explained that his plane had been delayed and apologised for coming late and keeping her up. Nuns, he knew, kept strict hours and he had disturbed them. She told him it didn't matter and, truly, to her it didn't. She said she was happy frying up at any time, and for him . . . well, it was a treat. She shifted curling bacon, ballooning sausages and globed tomatoes in a bucket-sized frying-pan with a spatula, which could have powered a fair-sized canoe, and a dexterity born of love and long experience. A syrupy smile on her wide white plate of a face, Sister Gertie might have been entertaining an angel. She stirred and poked the food and stole reverent glances at him but whenever he looked back at her she turned quickly away, as if frightened of catching his eye or as if looking at him too closely and for too long might use him up.

Devlin, sipping hot tea in the bright kitchen, was too much in the daze of the traveller to take much account of the adoring Sister Gertie. Not six hours ago he had been in Dublin, leaving his narrow bedsit and a note for the nurse with whom he now lived: 'I decided to go. They said I could and so I am.' The nurse, if he'd bothered to look, would notice Devlin's 'party frock' had also gone, the collar and black garb he was no longer supposed to wear.

There was indeed a door in the wall. Devlin had left by it some eighteen months before.

He was here now, a priest again. He was in the House of Content at last. He was here to be pacified and praised after being exiled and dispossessed. He was in the house of his enemy now that his enemy had fled.

Years ago his father had brought him to this place, had held his reluctant hand as they stood looking up at a ruined house.

'This is it,' his father had told him, 'the House of Content. This is where she lived.'

He had not been interested, had stamped his feet and looked away. Who was she and what was she to him but a name his father was forever mentioning? There had been a park opposite, Radcliffe Park, and the boy Devlin had tugged hard at his father's hand and demanded to be taken there instead. The park had been swings and flowers and ducks on a pond. His father had ignored him and had carried on looking up at the house, ugly, empty, broken, as if it was a question to which he was trying to find an answer.

Devlin had heard the ducks in the park tonight. After the taxi-driver had dropped him by the gates of the Cenacle he had stood just as his father had stood but then he had turned, run, clambered through the bushes and into the darkened and padlocked park. He'd strolled along its wide and curving paths, the tarmac silver in the moonlight, calming himself, convincing himself that he could once more play the priest and convince the nuns, guaranteeing himself, if he carried off the charade, he'd have the pleasure, the relief, of seeing Ursula Trench in her grave. A young man in a white vest and shiny shorts had followed him for a while and then had gone into the bushes where Devlin followed him. The young man said his name was Howard and he'd never been sucked off by a vicar before but he'd had a policeman coming off duty during one of the riot nights, the night the old bird had been burned. Then it had rained and Devlin, renewed, had gone back to the Cenacle.

The kitchen where they sat looked out on to the garden but the black night meant that the window-pane reflected the bright kitchen, Gertie and himself with the accuracy of a mirror. There were bushes just outside, the top leaves of which scuffed softly against the window. He would see the garden come daylight. He had promised himself a long walk around that garden. The nuns would take him. They would lead him down its paths, across its two lawns, to the wall at its bottom over which, tip-toed, one could see the milky canal that knifed its way through Radcliffe Park and up under Brackley Street.

'She must have gone by the canal that night,' the nuns would tell him. They would cluster about him at the bottom of the garden. They would point at a spot by the wall and tell him: 'This is it. It was here that she did it all those years ago.' He'd shiver, they'd all shiver. He would nod wisely and say: 'Yes, it was here, right here. She told me so herself. I know it for a fact.' The nuns would look admiringly. To carry the weight of such a confession, how remarkable a priest he must be. The nuns would shake their heads and say how they prayed she was not in Hell but that, at the last moment, she had found forgiveness, that the flames had melted her resistance to true repentance, that God had understood.

'What else has He to do?' he'd ask them and they and he would nod wisely. They'd bury her without fuss, some corner of an urban cemetery, in Mallet maybe, and then they would return. They would make him tea and in the lounge they would quietly talk of how she had been with them: 'Difficult, Father, so very difficult, and the lies she told us, the race she ran us to control her.'

'I know,' he would say, 'I know all about it,' and he would tell them how she had been with him and they would listen, nod and say: 'Exactly so, exactly as she was with us.'

'But maybe', one of them would add, 'not quite as bad.'

'No,' he'd agree, 'not quite as bad.'

Sister Gertie interrupted this hopeful reverie of how his visit would pass when she placed in front of him a plate piled high and dripping with food and said: 'I'm so pleased you could come, Father. We all are. It's so good to meet a friend of Ursula's, someone who knew her well, loved her as we did. We loved sweet Ursula, we really did.' The words came out in a gush that ended in a sob for the memory of sweet Ursula.

'Yes,' he said limply. 'Yes.'

He no longer wanted food but ate what there was in a deliberate silence that he hoped would help him think but which didn't. Sister Gertie wiped her tears on a blue check tea-towel and looked on appreciatively with red-rimmed eyes.

'More, Father?'

'No, I've plenty and I really can't manage it.'

'Tea, then, to wash it all down? Another cup before bed? You can't say no to more tea.' She poured him a cup so full that a mere touch of its handle caused it to brim over and spill into the saucer.

'I get the idea you'd like me to stay,' he said, considering the cup. He no longer relished the thought of listening to this nun.

'If it's no trouble, Father. Mother Tess said not to bother you. It would be really lovely to talk about her. She deserves talking of. I miss her so.'

Devlin grunted and then asked: 'Mother Tess, does she know of her nickname?'

'Oh, it's no nickname, Father, we call it her to her face. It's how we are here. We've all been shortened. I'm a Gertie and there's a Biddy, a Kath, a Liz. That's how it is, all girls together, as Mother Tess puts it. We have a laugh.' Sister Gertie gave a giggle that turned into a honk. Sister Gertie was beginning to relax in Father Devlin's company, Father Devlin the reverse in hers.

'Did Ursula have a nickname?'

'You know,' said Sister Gertie, rather surprised to say so, 'she never did. When she first came here it was "Miss Trench", very much mind-your-manners-and-tread-carefully kind of thing. She was a bit remote.'

'So she was never one of the girls, then?'

'Oh, she was and no mistake. I said "remote", but only at first. After a bit she said to us: "Oi, you can stop this 'Miss Trench' business. It's 'Ursula' to my face and what you will behind me back." She was that much of a laugh but genteel, never crude, which is surprising in view of the life she'd had to lead. All that – it never seemed to touch her. She was one of the girls.'

Devlin grunted once again.

'I can't quite see Ursula Trench as one of the girls.'

'Oh, yes. Why, we're burying her in the garden as if she was.'

Devlin did not understand.

'All the nuns are buried there . . . well, two of us so far.'

'That garden?'

Sister Gertie looked as if to say 'What other garden could it be?' She saw only one objection he might have and proceeded to rid him of it. 'It is hallowed ground. We had the Bishop hallow it when we first came. We call it the Pasture.'

'I am amazed,' he told her and was. She, feeling complimented, said thank you. Unbidden, she told him of the plans for the dummy funeral. She told him of it with a pride that would have been comic to anyone but Devlin. To him, the whole business was tasteless and beyond comprehension. He listened, blank-faced, saying nothing. Gertie took his silence for approval.

There was nothing for it but to say: 'Tell me about her.' As he said that, he heard within himself the echo of his own voice from years before: 'Tell me, Ursula, tell me all about it,' and Ursula had.

'Tell me, Sister, tell me all there is to tell.'

There was nothing that Sister Gertie wanted to do more. She topped up Devlin's cup.

'She was remote at first, Father, when she first came but that was to be expected. She'd not been well, after all. We'd heard of how she'd been at that place you knew her in and, of course, she came to us fresh out of hospital. We took her on willingly and not blind or deaf to what she'd done. We've always taken an interest in her, followed her life, you know, like fans we were almost but not quite. You see, we have reason to be grateful to her. When she first left prison we hoped it would be to come here but she didn't. She'd have been better off here. Not wishing to be rude, Father, but am I right or am I right?'

'You're right,' he said quietly but with conviction, and added silently: 'And I'd have been better off, too.'

'Did you ever hear of what she did in prison? You must have. The special things she did there? Miracles?'

He could have said a thing or two about the special things she did but he just nodded that, yes, he'd heard. He wanted Gertie to speak on.

40

'Of course, coming from round here myself, I've always known about her. I was but a girl when they put her in prison. I remember my dad taking us to Blackpool one Bank Holiday, Madame Tussaud's, to see her statue.'

'I saw it, too,' Devlin admitted. 'I was a boy. My father took me.'

There had not just been a statue but two tableaux, one of Ursula, eighteen or so, mousy and malicious, and another of Ursula in her thirties, a bleached blonde in tart's make-up: two Ursulas, one with the child, one with Andreas. The Girl Ursula had been darkly lit and had stood by a shrub. She'd worn a nightie, white, pink-frilled, its hem touching the mock-grass floor. She had held the dead child by its legs like a plucked chicken. The child's head had been partly severed and, ingeniously, blood had been made to drip regularly from its neck and drip, too, from the knife the Girl Ursula held in her other hand. The Woman Ursula also wore a nightie or maybe it was a slip, shiny, pink and short enough to show her knees. It was a bedroom scene. Andreas's effigy lay on the bed; Ursula, looking sluttish, a little like a glum Diana Dors, stood murderously over him. His arms had been flung over his face, disappointingly because it was said he'd been a good-looking lad, but the rest of him was well on show, dressed only in underpants and a long-sleeved vest. It was a lovely body and it was a pity that its true-life model was no longer walking the earth. The many black hairs that had been sewed along the insides of his muscular wax thighs and the boulder they must have hidden in the crotch of his underpants were the inspiration for the Boy Devlin's first truly erotic memory.

'Were you a boy then?' asked Sister Gertie. 'Yes, I suppose we are of an age. Are you from round here?'

'Nearby. But you were saying.'

'I was saying that when we heard she was in that hospital Mother Tess called us all together in her parlour-cum-office. She's ever so democratic in her decision-making, although no one would dare argue against her when her mind's firm. She says to us, she says, "It's either us or a home and we know what's meant by *home*. Well, this is her home," she says, "this house, and it's we who should take her in." You did know that this was once her home?'

41

Devlin said he did. He could have added that, considering where they planned to bury her, it was they who had chosen to forget what had been done there. True, the house seemed no longer the Gothic wreck that he had gazed up at with his father years before. It was too bright, too full with cosy looks, nuns and good intentions. He had never been inside before but he had imagined it, imagined how it had been when Ursula had lived there. In his head he had carried an image of it so dark it seemed like a negative, a house where thick dust silted the corners and shrouded every surface, noisy with ghosts, and shadowy with bad faith. That house, the House of Content, must still exist, must lie under the cosy palace in which he sat now – black bones under plump pink fields of flesh.

'She gave it to the Bishop, who gave it to us. She was in prison and had found God. An aunty had been living here alone, a Miss Matchett, sad case, a suicide, hanged herself with her own tights in the garage here. The house was a ruin. Mould, it was everywhere and not your common or garden kind but red it was, great clumps of it as big as your fist. So, anyway, Mother Tess, she said to us, she said: "Our home was once hers. She gave us a place. Can we deny her one?" Well, we didn't need a speech although Mother Tess gives a lovely oration when she's a mind, and so we all said hear, hear, and yes, of course, she must come. We'd asked for her before but it had always been refused. On grounds of taste.'

Sister Gertie shook her head, unable to see how, when charity was being offered as a solution, there could ever be a problem of taste.

'I remember the day she came, or night I should say. It was late and it was raining just like now. She wasn't by herself. There was a nun with her.'

'Sister Michael.'

'It may well have been. Skinny woman with a face too long for her neck. A bit of a misery although I never got chatting to her. She was away out of the door the minute her business was done, which is no manners for a nun in my book but who am I to judge, so I'll say nothing. As for Ursula, well! We'd all waited up for her. We had tea and a bit of food laid on but she was tired, she said, and I was shocked by how she looked, I was, really.'

'How did she look?' There was no need for him to ask. Gertie was happy to tell all.

'Well, I thought she'd look as she'd done in Madame Tussaud's but more mature obviously, but she looked that old. She was, what, sixty and she looked seventy or more even. Thin as six o'clock she was and as frail as a wafer. The draught from under the door could have wafted her six inches off the floor and I'm not kidding because she was so feeble-looking. I'll tell you, she was so drawn and pale and her hair was that long, past her shoulders, and not a curl in it and lank. It hadn't seen a comb all day and it hadn't seen soap for a month. Well, I thought, they could have at least washed it for her before she came. My heart went right out for her there and then and I don't mind who knows it. She saw right past us. She was looking about her as though she knew the place, which of course she did although it must have been twenty years or more since she'd last stood in that hall. We didn't let her hang about and get morbid, so I was told to take her up to bed. It was my job to look after her. That had been decided.'

'So you were her nurse?'

'Not nurse, Father, friend. Ursula had no need of nursing, not then, not ever.' Gertie was fierce on this point. 'She was never sick, not ever. They'd no need to put her in that hospital and I don't care what's said.'

Devlin said nothing but wore the smile of one who knows better.

'So, anyway, I took her upstairs and, as I did, I heard that nun, what was her name?'

'Sister Michael. A good, a caring woman.' Sister Michael was his only kindly memory of The Wounds.

'Well, that's as maybe. She said to the others: "You will find her very difficult. You cannot rely on a thing she might do or say. She is never to be trusted. You will learn this eventually." She said it like it was this big warning and I heard plain as day and I know Ursula did although she didn't let on. She hung on to my arm quite tight but her face was a closed book, you could read nothing in it. I took her to her room. Second floor, small rooms, we all sleep up there. The other rooms are larger

43

and are for guests. I stayed with her and helped her undress, talking all the while because that's me, isn't it, natter, natter. She didn't talk much but she didn't mind me being there. She seemed to need another person, anyone really, and I'd do fine. She was that bewildered, poor lamb. I helped her into bed, legs like pipe-cleaners. I said, "Shall I stay?" and she said no, and then she said thank you and closed her eyes and I knew we were friends because if you can fall asleep in another's company you must be, mustn't you? I dithered about a bit, folding her things and making tidy but really to watch over her and then I left her snoring happily, bless her.

'Well, she was remote, you know, for a good few weeks, settling in, no bother, not once. She kept to her room or wherever it was quiet and avoided the guests. Mother Tess said give her time and we did and, slowly, without our really noticing it, she came over. She'd help make a bed or lay the odd table. She put on weight, which isn't hard in this house. She filled out quite nicely. Then she asked Mother Tess if she could have her hair done and Mother Tess said she'd no need to ask permission. So she had a perm and a rinse and looked dead nice. I went with her and afterwards we went to the mini-supermart in Brackley Street which is not where we do our bigger shopping but they're very big on Continental vegetables and she said how she'd like to have some new clothes. After that she was great, did more than her bit about the place, fitted in well, one of us in a flash. She kept aloof from most guests. There were some who recognised the name and there's not many who don't know the history of this house. For a while there'd be the odd guest who came here for nothing but to gawp at her but we soon spotted them. Not many. We don't have a morbid clientele.'

'Did she ever talk about prison or about the past, any of it?'

'No, not really,' said Gertie, as if to say, 'Why should she?'

'Did she ever talk about the convent, The Wounds, Andreas or . . . anything?' Or me, he wanted to say, or me.

'No, never, but I'll tell you this for nothing: she couldn't have been as bad as they made out. They put her in an asylum, may God forgive them. To think of our Ursula there . . . well, it breaks the heart, it does really. You knew her then. You were there. What was she like?'

Wasn't that his question? 'She was . . . difficult.' It was the least he could say. He was no longer certain. Maybe Ursula had never been mad, never known evil, never done wrong? Maybe it had been a game, a test for them both or a cry for help that had been louder and more sustained than intended? Maybe it was him, him with a grudge? He remembered a drawing she had done of him and thought: No, his Ursula was the real one, a figure worth hating and never forgiving.

'More tea?'

Gertie did not wait for an answer but made a fresh pot. It was past one o'clock and the desire for sleep was stinging his eyes. Gertie was wide awake, talking seeming to supply her with the energy that listening sapped from him.

The disappointment he felt made fatigue no easier to bear. He had come to hear bad, to hear only bad, to exchange grievances. However, it was clear that if Sister Gertie was representative of them these nuns had none to air, and he knew they would not stand in the draught of his without complaint.

What had he hoped to achieve? If these nuns had agreed with him, if they had drawn for him the same portrait of Ursula as he carried in his head, he would have felt vindicated in some way. He would not be just a failed priest with a grudge but a victim of an evil woman. Being a victim made it easier to feel blameless; he would not be responsible for his own downfall. He wanted a scapegoat. He wanted proof that he had not fallen from grace, he had been pushed.

The steam from the boiling kettle formed a cloudy map of Africa on the kitchen window. The rain outside had stopped but the bush outside the window was still glossy with it.

'Tell me more.' He meant to sound encouraging but in his voice there was something sharp and jagged that even the unsubtle Gertie could discern. 'Tell me about the night she died.'

Gertie was sadder but no less eager to tell. She stirred the pot and poured the tea. 'These cups are only a mouthful. If you're anything like the priests we have here you'd prefer it in a pint pot.'

'What made her do it? How came she to be out at night? Didn't anyone watch her?'

'No one watched Ursula, Father. She wasn't an invalid to be watched over or a prisoner to be locked up. She was often by herself. When she wasn't with us, we didn't worry.'

'If you had she'd not be dead.'

'Oh, Father, don't say that!'

'It's true.'

'No, don't say that. Ursula and me were so close. She was one of us. I couldn't bear to think you blame us for what happened.'

'What did happen? I don't want what's in the paper.'

'Well. You know the riots?'

'Who doesn't?'

'It was the second night she died. The first night we knew nothing about them. We heard sirens but thought maybe a factory further up Brackley Street had caught fire. In the morning it was in the papers and on the radio there was more.'

'You heard nothing that first night?'

'Nothing but the sirens, and Sister Liz heard what she thought were some drunks screaming in the park. This is Park End, the quieter part of Radcliffe Park. Once it was the posh part, less so now perhaps. This is a grand house but there are others just as grand, although many have been turned into bedsits and one of them is now a mosque run by some very nice people.'

None of this was new to Devlin. Sister Gertie seemed to forget that he had admitted to being local and he did not remind her. It was always possible she might have heard that there was a priest from Mallet, one just a little younger than her, someone who was a priest no longer.

'The troubles have been mainly up on Brackley Street and round about where the shops are. They say there's been children not yet six throwing bricks at policemen, but of course the problem is national. Down in London it's as bad and in Liverpool it was worse. Mother Tess said we were not to go out. Luckily we had no guests. We spent the day pottering about, because in a house this big there's always something that needs doing. We were never far from that wireless, though.'

Gertie pointed up at the battered red transistor on the blue

Formica dresser, as if it had acquired a morbid significance in the light of what it had broadcast.

'There were reports on the local radio all the time. They had a van out there. It was frightening to know it was all so close and only the radio to prove it. Ursula said she could see smoke from her window. She said Brackley Street was on fire and we all went up and looked and it was true. The sky was all orange with it. There were interviews from hospital beds on the wireless. A policeman shoved through a plate-glass shop-window and almost cut in half at the waist. It didn't say what shop but he was very cheery, no bad feelings, but thanked God for letting him live which I thought was nice, policemen not being noticeably devout. We gave up all pretence of pottering about and were sitting round this table drinking tea by the gallon and losing count of I don't know how many rosaries.'

'When did she go missing?'

'I couldn't say precisely. I remember her getting up to go about eight o'clock but I thought nothing of it. We'd drunk that much tea that one or other of us was always popping up to go, begging your pardon, Father. But when we did notice she was missing it was me who noticed first.'

'When was that?'

'When it was too late, Father. There we were in this kitchen around this table, the radio on. They were playing a record. I don't know which one because I've never been one for music although I like a good sing, but they stopped it halfway through and said they were going over to the van. I could have turned the wireless off right then and said what happened, don't ask me how but I could. It was awful. I never hope to hear something as bad as that again. As the man said how she kneeled and prayed, prayed for an end to violence and blood and flames – and who better to pray for such an end than her with a life spoiled by too much of them? – I could hear the fire crackling and people jeering and screaming and I thought that it was Hell.'

Sister Gertie could not go on. Tears dripped down smooth curved cheeks and her shoulders chugged up and down as if there were a little motor revving up in the middle of her back. She gave out a series of outsized sobs that the handkerchief

47

clutched over her nose and mouth did little to muffle.

Comfort her, he told himself. This is what a priest should do and that is what you continue to call yourself. But he was a priest no more and his pity was all for himself.

Gertie ripped off a few sheets of kitchen towel and wiped her face. For all that it was reddened and swollen with tears, her face was beatific.

'It's snowed each morning since.' She said it as if it were a boast.

Devlin had heard of the snow. The papers had made much of it. 'A few flakes,' he said grudgingly.

'But in July, Father, snow in July.'

'You don't believe this Riot Saint business. You can't. You knew her. How can you?'

'It's snowed each morning since.'

'You can't believe it.'

Sister Gertie bowed her head and her silence was affirmative and proud.

'She was no saint. Consider her past. Think of what she'd done.'

'I do.'

'She was a murderer. She murdered once definitely, twice probably, and that a child. I know all this. I know it for certain. I know it from her own lips, her own lips.'

'Great sinners can become great saints. They are all the greater for having been sinners. And God forgives.'

'Well, I don't and He doesn't. He can't. I won't let Him. Saint Ursula Trench! That's a joke, a sick joke. She died from a burning and she deserved no better fate. She'll carry on burning. White hot she'll be, white hot in Hell, and as for snow, any snow that lands on her will sizzle, it'll sizzle and steam away.'

II

The Wounds

I

No Handle on the Door

The drivers had been told to drive out to the convent at Gwytherin to pick up some nun who'd flipped her lid twice over. When the ambulance set out from Denbigh it was a wintry but bright afternoon and the market was just beginning to close. There was only a promise of snow in the air. By the time the ambulance had reached Gwytherin it had been dark hours past, the snow was thick enough to be called deep, and the woman they collected there was not a nun but someone half-dressed like one. A real nun and a young priest came along to look after her. They said her name was Ursula and the driver could tell that no one was sorry to see her go.

At best the road between Gwytherin and Denbigh was narrow and twisted, never meant for anything wider than a cart or faster than a donkey, and in parts it was little better than a dirt track. Now the road was varnished with ice and dusted thick with snow. It was pure guesswork to keep to it, as it merged with the fields and the fields with the mountains, becoming one vast region of icy white, blank acre upon blank acre of snow.

Such was winter in that slice of Wales between Denbigh and the sea at Gwytherin where the mountains outnumbered the people and the sheep outnumbered the mountains. Snow fell here whenever the Lord was tired of holding it back and the Lord was easily tired. Not that it was too frequent a problem for ambulancemen: the only thing in Gwytherin was the convent and the convent seldom had need of ambulances in the thick of winter or any other season.

The ambulance made slow progress through the winter landscape. A cold wind blew clouds of soft snow against the windscreen and across the dazzling fields, snow stained a watery blue by the navy sky.

'Snow falls an inch thick soon as look at it round here,' said the driver to his mate.

'Twelve inches if you don't,' replied the mate.

'Still, safe enough, aren't we?'

'Should be.'

'With a priest and two nuns at the back of us, we should be.'

'Not two nuns. One of them's no nun.'

'Well, one and a half nuns, then.'

Their conversation was nothing above a mumble to their passengers or to two of them, Ursula being asleep. A red blanket lay at her feet where she'd kicked it. Her dress, a nun's habit in coarse black wool, had risen up past her knees. Her legs, thin sticks, paddled and scuffed the sheets as she slept, battling with unhealthy dreams. Yet from the waist up she slept like a child with an old woman's face, thumb near to her mouth, peaceful, happy, still. Devlin, sitting opposite her, envied her seeming calm, could have spat at her for it.

With him sat Sister Michael, a small, anxious body with no shoulders to speak of but a face with so broad a nose and so generous a pair of nostrils they would have sat happily on a horse's neck. The tiny face that had to carry this load and the black veil that framed it seemed cruelly designed to make her seem all nose, but she was a good nun, one of the few who still had time for Ursula and the only one who had helped Devlin get through the last few days. Father Devlin was grateful to her and she, as all the nuns did, loved Father Devlin with a girlish passion more suitable for a pop star than for a priest.

'She's sleeping at last,' said Sister Michael. 'That must be the first time in days.'

Devlin nodded slowly and said beneath his breath: 'Peace.' He watched the sleeping Ursula as if she were filled to the brim with nitroglycerine and, at one bump of the ambulance, might burst and explode.

'It'll not be long now, Father. When she's well again, she'll thank you for what you've done.'

'She'll never be well again. She never has been and she'll never thank me. I've no need of her thanks. She's done enough for me.'

Tiredness makes him bitter, thinks Sister Michael. She understood. The things that Ursula had said to him, about him, done to him, no priest should hear and easily forgive. Sister Michael could not think her hero base, could not believe he lacked charity, but knew that if Father Devlin hated Ursula, then he had cause and right to do so. It was easy to hate Ursula Trench. Think of her history, of what she had done to that child and to that man, and look at her, lying there, snoring, smelly, unwashed. Yes, it was easy to hate her. She frightened you so.

The ambulance fought on through snow that fell ever thicker and driving through it was like pushing through walls of white linen.

Ursula continued to sleep, occasionally to moan, to turn, and at each swerve and dip of the road almost to wake. At such moments the priest would bite his bottom lip and look heavenwards and the nun would grip a bead of her rosary so much more tightly the ends of her finger and thumb would whiten and the bead between them seem about to crumble to dust under the pressure.

The unhealthy dreams that had made Ursula's feet so restless now disturbed the features of her face. A grunt would cause her nose to wrinkle in a snort and her thin lips trembled when she moaned. It was an old woman's face, a hag's, but how old was she? Not old enough to have a face so lined and creased, so cragged and shadowed that dust could find a home in its folds. Her grey pallor suggested dust or ashes maybe. The withered face was not of time's making but something else, some fearful thing that could be read in the line of a mouth that seemed to cower and fall in on itself.

Sister Michael was still considering how right it was to hate Ursula Trench and decided that it was not right at all. Then she pondered how little one had to love her.

'What will happen to her now?'

'They'll look after her in Denbigh. They know how to better than we.'

'Will she ever come back to us?'

'No, I don't expect so. I don't think there would be much point. Would you want her back?'

Sister Michael lowered her head and did not reply. This was how much we could love Ursula Trench: we can wish her well but not wish her with us.

'If there's nowhere else, Father, she'll have to stay with us.'

'Perhaps she'll stay in Denbigh. Or those nuns in Radcliffe Park. They keep on asking for her.'

'That's good of them.'

'Returning a favour, I suppose. You know that Ursula gave them a house when an aunt of hers died. She was buying grace for herself. I doubt they know what she's like. It's a gesture. They'll change their tune if they ever see her.'

'No, I'm sure not.'

'Are you? From what I hear they run the house like some religious motel. The Needle Eye Inn. I doubt they'll want Ursula scuttling about their cenacle like a tarantula, frightening off their clients. Besides, how can she go back there after what happened? God knows what she'd be like.'

They spoke in whispers. Up front, the driver and his mate were laughing at some joke. The priest and the nun winced, fearful that the sound would awaken Ursula.

'Don't wake,' Devlin prayed silently. 'Don't wake and then we can dump you in Denbigh and forget about you.'

Out of idleness, he asked Sister Michael how long a journey it was from Gwytherin to Denbigh. She did not know and with the snow it was hard to guess, so she said she would ask the driver. She rose and moved gently past Ursula, as if her shadow were a heavy thing that could wake the sleeping woman, to the half-open door that separated them from the driver and his mate.

'When do we reach . . . the place?' She could not bring herself to mention the exact place for fear of Ursula hearing it.

'Denbigh? Half an hour more, miss.'

'Thank you.'

' 'S all right. The asylum's just after Denbigh.'

Sister Michael thanked him again and withdrew.

'They said half an hour more, Father. Sleep a little, Father, why don't you? I'll wake you.'

'No, I'll sleep once we've delivered her. When she's off our hands I'll sleep for a week.'

Devlin sighed.

Sister Michael sighed for company's sake.

The driver swore at the snow and his mate laughed out loud.

Ursula grunted and drilled her face deeper into the pillow, the spittle she had dribbled leaving a fine line of silver like the first skein of a spider's web.

'I was just remembering the first time I saw her.'

'At the convent?'

'No, in Radcliffe Park, a place called Brackley Street.'

'Not the day she killed that man?'

'Yes, that day.'

'You must have been a child then.'

'I was. I couldn't help her then, either.'

Sister Michael looked away and nodded sadly. If Father Devlin could not help Ursula, then, truly, she was beyond helping.

'I saw her again a year later. Well, not her obviously, she was in prison. It was at Madame Tussaud's I saw her. There were two of her, one as a young girl and one of her killing Andreas. She was quite a star then. Now here she is in front of me. The three ages of Ursula Trench.'

'It's so dark outside. I can't see out of these shaded windows.'

'Nothing to see but snow.'

'I've never been in an ambulance before.'

'Nor me. We've Ursula to thank for that. It's nice to be able to thank her for something.'

'Yes, a new experience for us both.'

'Look at her.'

Sister Michael looked.

Ursula's repose seemed made to mock the haggard pair who watched over her, whose conversation rang to the dull, desultory rhythms of those deprived of sleep and who are now long past it.

The ambulance reached Denbigh and made its way up the main street, shops darkened, pubs closed, everywhere deserted, as if the town had been warned of the coming of Ursula Trench.

She woke with a start, with a violence which suggested that someone had screamed her name aloud. She sat up and glared about her, mouth warped by a sneer and her eyes puffy but bright with malice.

'Did you have a nice sleep, Ursula?' Sister Michael cooed.

'You look the better for it,' lied Devlin.

Ursula said nothing, only glared the more, a wild animal resentful at being trapped, ready to snap at any friendly hand that reached through the bars to soothe her.

'There's nothing nicer than a nice sleep, is there, Father?'

'A nice sleep is what she needed, isn't it, Ursula?'

'Piss off talking to me like I was a kid.' She spoke out of the side of her mouth – she often did, a prison habit – with a voice foggy with phlegm. 'It's a loony-bin you're taking me to, not a fucking nursery.'

'Yes, Ursula,' said Devlin coolly. 'You're right. I apologise.'

Ursula settled back but kept her eye on them both as if they were the dangerous ones, not she. Her face, awake, lost its fragility, became hard-set, a bruiser's face. She'd have done them a violence if she'd wanted to enough. A fist in the face of the nun first off, easy, no bother. And him, Devlin, what wouldn't she do to him? Give her a knife and she'd make lacework of his guts, wouldn't she, wouldn't she just? But when the driver stopped the ambulance and hollered that they'd arrived, the tough little face, the bully's face crumbled like the plaster-cast mask it was, and she was once again a frail child, a child cowering from an adult's blow, hoping an imploring look would be enough to fend it off.

Devlin saw the change in her. Instinctively, with a care he had long thought she had exhausted in him, he took her by the arm and held her close. It was all right, he told her, it was all right, everything was all right and all was for the best, the best for her, of course it was, what else could it be, hush now, hush.

The driver opened the back door and the cold air rushed in, chilling them in an instant. Ursula held on to Devlin more tightly and the driver helped Sister Michael down, then Ursula and Devlin.

The asylum was a grand mansion and stood black and Gothic against the white mountains and the navy sky. Its roofs were white with snow, and snow, too, lined the fussily crenellated balconies and capped the squat turrets that cornered the building. Its dark rectangles of window spoke of a place uninhabited and eerie.

'Lord Something-or-other lived here,' the mate told them as they trudged through thick clean snow, careful not to slip. 'We go in by here.'

They had reached the far side of the building and stood now in front of an oak door at the foot of a tower that ended in one of the turrets. The turret, a wretched half-deflated balloon of a thing, sat oddly on the tower, a tower which belonged to a fairy-tale, Rapunzel's tower, a narrow, windowless prison. But it was the door that Devlin noticed, the door that seemed familiar to him, an oak door pock-marked with mould. The dry and blackened stems of old roses, leprous and gnarled, traced and knotted their way around the door-frame and crept up and along the dark brick walls like so many skeletal fingers before curling out and away in beckoning twirls, reaching out to implore or to infect. It was 'The Light of the World'; a sad-faced Christ in a dark wood, lantern held high in one hand, knocking with the other at just such a door: a painting by Holman Hunt. It had been on the wall of his primary school.

'See, class,' the teacher had said, 'how sorry Jesus looks. That is because there is no handle on the door. He can't open it. Jesus can knock on the door but it must be opened from within.'

'There's no handle on the door,' said Devlin.

'No, it's opened from within. One of the nurses will be down with the key. I've rung the bell, see.' The driver pointed to the bell.

'Ring again,' Devlin told him. 'It's cold here.'

The driver did so but still they waited. Their feet damp and numb, they shuffled and stamped to keep warm and Devlin pondered on the treachery of doors. Doors could be opened from within but other people could slam them shut if they wished. Here he was, ministering to his enemy, helping the woman who, out of nothing grander than spite, had barred his way to God, denied him the rôle of Christ's servant for which he had trained all his life. As for the door that faced him now, this real door, why was there no handle? Surely it was the point to keep the mad in, not keep those bringing the mad out.

'They take their time, don't they?' said the mate.

'I've come all this way to the madhouse and they won't let me in,' complained Ursula.

It was meant as a joke and so they laughed, but uneasily; the mad were not supposed to make jokes. And who could be easy standing in the grounds of an asylum, when it was dark with the snow seeping through your shoes and a madwoman for company?

Finally, they heard a key turn in the lock and the door opened. A pin-headed nurse with an itchy backside beckoned them inside. 'Come on, it's straight up,' she barked at them. She led them up a narrow, winding staircase of whitewashed stone steps, humming 'La Cucaracha' as she did so, and then shimmying to it as she waited for them to catch up.

'Go through that door.'

Through that door they went.

'Stay here.'

They stayed and she left them and the driver and his mate went with her.

The priest, the nun and the madwoman were left in a room the size of a great hall, lit by fluorescent strips that flickered and burred high over their heads. The walls were yellow, a stale dusty custard, and there was not a window to be seen. Single beds with pine wardrobes and bedside tables attached on either side filled the room. They were not placed in neat rows. They were not placed in any order but haphazardly, at all manner of angles about the room like slabs of crazy pavement. It looked like the aftermath of an explosion of bedrooms, a fallout of furniture. It was curiously disturbing, this chaos; it spoke of encouraging madness, not of regulating it. The wreckage stretched ahead into some dark area; beyond that could well be infinity. Only a few of the beds were occupied. Bulky shapes under yellow candlewick bedspreads stirred occasionally. From a bed nearby a pale arm, thin, knotted through with hard blue veins, rose up, stretched and curled itself like a snake writhing up from an urn, then wove its way down and back under the blankets. Ursula had not once let go of Devlin's arm and now she held it more tightly. Her other hand searched for Sister Michael's. Thus linked, priest, nun and madwoman stared at the weird dormitory until the nurse returned.

'Ursula Trench,' she called, ticking off the name on a clipboard with the Snoopy ballpoint she kept on a thong round her neck.

Ursula gave no final parting look to either Devlin or Sister Michael. Devlin wondered later why that hurt him. Was it just more proof that he was unimportant to her, a toy of which she'd tired, a noisome fly she could not be bothered to swat? It was callous the way she left them without a word or a look. She glided from them and sailed over to the nurse, a biddable child, happy to please.

The nurse took her away and Devlin and Sister Michael were left alone in the dormitory.

II

That Morning

'I'm innocent, as God's my witness I am, and I'll have no one say I'm not, you hear? You hear me?'

Devlin nodded and said he'd heard. 'Come down now, Ursula, come down. It's all over. It's best to come down.'

She shook her head and her veil worked free. The wind caught it and it fluttered and fell in swoops down the cliff-face to be caught by the nuns on the rocks below.

'I'm not coming down. Not with you. Not with anybody.'

She was threatening to jump but, then, she was always threatening something. She'd do anything for attention, this much he had learned. He wanted to say, 'Then, jump, Ursula, go on, jump,' because it would have given him pleasure and, besides, he knew she wouldn't. That said, it would be like her to jump. She'd do it out of spite. She'd do anything out of spite. He had learned that, too.

It should not have come to this. She should not have been left alone. He and Sister Michael had stayed with her all through the night, a vigil broken only when morning came and he had gone for a bath and Sister Michael for food. When they returned they found that the nun who had taken over from them had fled and Ursula had escaped. The convent had been searched, the gardens, the fields, the roads and the beach.

He had known that she would be found. He had known that he would be the one to find her or, rather, that she would let him find her. He could even have guessed where he'd find her. Where else? he had thought when he had looked up from the beach to see her standing above him at the very edge of the cliff, her habit ballooning round her knees, standing straight as a nail in spite of the heavy wind. She had been looking down on him all the while. She had been waiting for him.

He faced her now. They stood together at the cliff-edge a yard or so apart like a pair of tightrope walkers, she the balanced professional, he the wavering amateur. Below them, at the cliff's foot, white-habited nuns gathered and flapped together like anxious seagulls.

'Don't be foolish, Ursula. Come away from the edge.' He tried to sound caring but failed. If it were not for the audience of nuns, he thought, I would let her jump, I might push her even. 'Come on, Ursula, come down.'

'With you!' She spat the words out and stepped even closer – although that seemed impossible – to the edge of the cliff.

Drama at the top of the cliff, consternation down below and beyond a grey sea with an aluminium sheen that slurped and aahed as if it, too, were in suspense, interested in the outcome. Attention, such attention, it was all she'd ever wanted: I will remember this, she thought, I will treasure it as a happy moment.

'Don't,' he said softly and held out his hand slowly, as if she were a wild bird he wanted to have perch on it.

Close up she seemed less fierce, less the monster of reputation. A pathetic creature in the shabby black habit she had stolen, stained and grimy, a dark sliver silvered over with dust, vulnerable in the way a slug looked vulnerable under the shadow of a heel.

Out of the tired sea rolled a strong, foam-headed wave, a sign of the changing tide. It coasted the beach, dispersing the seagull nuns, and slapped against the foot of the cliff.

Ursula, habit billowing in the wind, rising up her bare white legs, shivered and considered his outstretched hand.

'I don't want to go away.' She sounded sulky, no longer hysterical. 'Not to Denbigh. Why should I? I'm not ill. I was pretending. I thought you'd gone and left me.'

'I hadn't gone and left you. See, I came back.'

She waved away his answer.

'I'm not going back to Radcliffe Park. Or them nuns. I've had my fill of nuns. And I couldn't go back there, not to that house, could I?'

Devlin, glad for once to be sincere, agreed. 'No, that'd not be right.'

'If I went back there no one'd have it. No one would

61

stomach it. My presence . . . well, it would offend, wouldn't it? Even after all these years they'd not have forgotten. It'd not be history yet and they'd not put up with it. They'd come for me. They'd come looking for me and they'd find me and drag me out into the street. They'd take me out and burn me in the street if I went back to Radcliffe Park.' She sounded so proud of herself for that. 'See, I'm not mad. I can see it all plain.'

'Radcliffe Park is not an issue. It can wait.' He was happier now she was talking to him and no longer staring mutely at the rocks below. 'The nuns there asked for you, that's all. It was just something for you to think about.'

'And what about Denbigh?' Denbigh was what scared her. Denbigh was indeed the issue. It wasn't something for her to think about. It was real. It was what came next.

'Denbigh's for the best.'

'I'll take no drugs. I'll not have straps on my bed. I'll not be put in a cage.'

'It's not like that.'

'I know what things are like. I've been there. Have you?'

'That was years ago and another place. Things change. They have different methods, a different attitude. . . .'

She was not convinced. 'Look at them down there.'

Devlin looked down. The nuns looked up.

'Sister Michael down there?'

'I suppose so.'

'Got the hots for you, has Sister Mick. All of a quiver for you. Got it bad, dead bad.'

'Come down with me.'

'Watch her, you see if I'm right. Follow her eyes. I have. Always has her eye on your bum.'

'Come back down with me.'

'Nice bum.'

'You're cold.'

'I suppose you know it, though. I suppose folk have said to you. "Nice bum, that," they might have said.'

'If you're not cold, then I am. Come down or I'll leave you here.'

'Folks'd say that as didn't know you for a priest. Still, for a priest you wear them trousers very tight. Very tempting, very

62

provoking in this house of women to see trousers at all really and trousers as tight as that . . . well?'

'I want you to come down now!'

'Is that you being masterful? Yes, them trousers, very tempting, very frustrating, you being forbidden fruit, you being . . . well, what you are.'

'You're cold. You're tired. You're not well.'

She shrugged and seemed of an instant to grow smaller, frailer. It was a trick she had, a way of melting.

His hand was still outstretched but more for balance now than for her. She looked at it, studied it.

I could take that hand, she thought, I could take it and when he was off guard I could tug it, swing it. He would lose his balance and I could push him over. I could watch him fall or I could fall with him. I could do that easy. It would take no strength at all.

She took his hand.

'Thank you. You're a good girl really. Let's go down now.'

He smiled at her and she smiled back.

'No way, priestlet,' she answered brightly and threw herself over the edge.

The sea hissed and the nuns screamed out as they saw the two inky cones they had been watching suddenly collapse and tumble earthwards. Devlin also screamed as he was forced to his knees. His arm felt as if it were being ripped from its socket. He pulled back but the weight of the dangling Ursula, a dead weight, dragged him forward. He dug in with his knees and toes and prayed that God, gravity and his own dubious strength would hold him steady. Ursula swung below him, twirling and slapping against the cliff-face, happy and laughing.

'You mad bitch! I could let you go now! I could let you go now and not feel a thing.'

'Then, do it, priestlet! Do that much for me! You've done bugger all else.'

He could not let go of her although that was what he most wanted to do. A dead Ursula would not have been an ungrateful one but his conscience had been wakened and, besides, the nuns were now hurrying up the cliff-path towards them.

'If you wanted yourself dead you should have done it yourself, not involved me.'

He pulled her up. She did not resist. They lay on their backs, panting, the sky spinning.

'That was fun, Devlin.'

He rolled away from her, sat up and nursed his arm. 'Cow,' he muttered.

'I heard that. Oh, don't sulk, Devlin. It's all over now. I give in.'

He got up, pulled her to her feet and held her tightly. Sister Michael appeared at the head of the nuns, her horse face red from galloping up the path, her breath steaming in powerful jets from her outsized nostrils. She cantered towards them.

Ursula broke free of Devlin and waltzed drunkenly into Sister Michael's embrace. She hung her arms around the nun's neck, nuzzled her shoulder and became at once a tearful child.

'I've been bad,' she kept repeating between thick gulps and fresh tears. 'I've been bad but I'll get better.' The promise was being made to Sister Michael but her eyes kept looking over at Devlin. He had turned away and was walking back across the fields to the convent. She had lost him. She had lost him well and good.

Swooping and circling like seabirds, nuns gathered about her, anxious to comfort and curious to see poor Ursula finally turned mad.

Snow began to fall. It dotted the grass, settled on habits black and white, and did not melt.

III

I Thought You'd Gone and Left Me

Mother Lawrence had a voice that was smooth, chill and severe; if a steel bar could speak it would speak with such a voice, a voice that made the merest suggestion the most inflexible command.

Mother Lawrence had suggested he go away for a while. He did not help the situation but exacerbated it. He had failed to solve the problem of Ursula Trench; instead, he had become a part of that problem. His presence excited and disturbed her: if he were to go away for a time she would grow calm again.

'When you return Ursula will be gone,' Mother Lawrence had promised. 'While you are away wheels will be set in motion.' Her bony hands had traced two perfect circles in the air.

He had been grateful for such a promise. He had risen from his chair by her desk and thanked her for her kindness, her understanding. He had felt such relief. She had given him time away from The Wounds; when he returned there would be no more Ursula. He could ask for no more. Life was suddenly right again.

As he reached the door he had turned to thank her yet again, gratitude making him gush, but he caught sight of the low table by the door, caught sight of what lay there, and looked back at the razor-faced Mother Lawrence and saw in her expression not benevolence but contempt.

Like Ursula's, his time at The Wounds was about to end. His time as a priest was also about to end. The wheels that were to be set in motion belonged to a vehicle that would not only ferry Ursula away; it would also ferry him.

*

He took a fortnight and spent the first few days with his mother in Mallet. She made him wear his collar to impress the neighbours, who were eager to see him again. They wanted to know how true were the rumours, spread by his mother, that he was now an intimate of Ursula Trench.

'It is *the* Ursula Trench we're talking about?'

Devlin had not wanted to talk about any Ursula Trench. He said yes wearily but little else. The neighbours needed little else.

'And is she not in prison still?'

'Should be.'

'Should be too right.'

'I think we're too soft on women like her.'

'Woman? She's no woman, her, not even human.'

'We are, though, aren't we, soft? There was a woman in the paper last week. Put her dog in the oven when it was still alive. All she got was fined. Little corgi it was.'

'And how is she in herself?'

'Hard, I bet. Her type are.'

'Or holy holy if she's in a convent.'

'Oh, I'm never convinced when women like that get all holy from being in prison.'

'I think they turn to religion for something to do. For recreation.'

'Or they do it to say: "God's forgiven me. Why haven't you?"'

'Well, if she's waiting for me to forgive her she'll have a long wait. God may not be fussy but I am.'

'Oh, I'm sure God couldn't be doing with her sort, not if He's really God.'

'Well, is she, our Ayomon?'

'Is she what?'

'Is she hard or is she holy holy?'

'Bit of both,' he'd say.

'Still, the coincidence of it, Ayomon love,' said his mother, when he asked her not to bring the subject up in front of others, 'seeing as how it was your dad as found her in the canal that day and risked his life saving her although she was better off dead by that time. Does she remember your father? Does she remember that day?'

'I don't know. I've never asked her.'

'I'm sure she'd remember the day if not your father.'

'I can't talk about any of this easily. This whole thing, it puts me in a position.'

'Is it the confessional?' she asked and he said it was, to keep her quiet.

From then on whenever anyone looked poised to mention Ursula Trench his mother would tell them, 'Our Ayomon cannot talk about that,' and then she would mouth the word 'confessional' and give them a look that was a promise to tell them all about it after. The curious would then sit back, disappointment weighing down the lines of their mouths, pause and then change the subject to rug-making, lagging, lawnmowers and why you could never find Barmouth biscuits in the shops these days.

What else was there to talk about to a man you'd known when he was three foot tall and in short pants and who had now given up women for God? Mind you, a funny family, the Devlins, the father, Irish and dead, known only for fishing Ursula Trench out of the canal that day and forever going on about how he did it, and the mother, soft . . . well, had to be, what kind of mother was she to have had but one child and him a priest?

'This confessional,' his mother persisted, 'surely God wouldn't mind a boy telling his mother.'

He thought of going to Radcliffe Park, of going to that house, Ursula's house, the House of Content. He would see it differently now. He would see it through Ursula's eyes. It might explain her to him. He could visit the nuns who now lived there and warn them about Ursula.

His mother told him that the house was now quite changed, all dolled up and twice the size it had been what with the extensions and the renovations. There was even a tiny chapel and a cemetery for the nuns.

He did not go to Radcliffe Park but to Brighton. He knew not a soul there, which is why he went. The black jacket, trousers, sensible shoes and dog-collar were kept at the bottom of his suitcase, hidden. He wore red cotton polo-shirts, a blue cambric jacket, red shoes with white laces and denim jeans.

He sat in bars and clubs where he could sit and eye men who sat eyeing him and if it wasn't a man a night it was near enough, and more than one man, more than five, the day he spent in Pinky's Sauna Palace where men passed from partner to partner like a parcel in a party game and bodies were sticky with more than sweat. David and Jonathan at the Apollo Hotel didn't mind who their guests brought back and that was nice because satisfaction and fun could be had between clean sheets and in privacy and not in the corners of public lavatories, one eye on the entrance, one ear on the street outside.

Each encounter he memorised as if it were a holy text. His lips moved over men's bodies as devoutly as if they had been prayers; the blond plumber whose torso had been covered in a golden fuzz, the married policeman on an Awayday trip who just wanted to be watched as he wanked into one of Devlin's socks. The idea was to forget himself in others; to rub against a man's body with a passion and a force that would erase his own; press his face so hard against another's that he thought sometimes he might leave an imprint as Christ had on Veronica's veil.

There was no one to guess he was a priest. When asked, he was Ralph from up North and he worked in a bank or a rent office, some dull job about which no one would question him. Thinking up jobs for himself was difficult; all he had ever been was a priest, all he'd ever wanted to be was a priest. It was hard for him to imagine being anything else, even if it was a prospect with which he might well be faced.

When he returned Mother Lawrence would have arranged for him to see the Bishop. He would confess all and the Bishop would listen, speak softly and forgive. Forgiveness would come easily. It would flow without constriction. There would be no damning words, no verdicts to interrupt the flow of mercy. He had committed no crime but would be found guilty of having a criminal nature. This condition would be thought neither grave nor unusual, simply, at first, a nuisance. There were ways of dealing with such as him and those ways would be followed. He would be sent on retreat and then to a quiet parish or a cathedral post maybe, until he fell and was found out again, as he knew he would be. Another retreat, another quiet post, another fall from grace, and so it would go on until the circle of those who knew of his nature grew too wide for secrecy.

The Church would not give up on him but slowly withdraw its love.

It was not a future he could contemplate happily but at least it was predictable, visible. The alternative was to give up, go over the wall and be . . . what? Do . . . what?

Then, again, it didn't matter, nothing mattered. Whichever side of the wall he chose to live on he would always be a priest. The priest-shaped mark on his soul could not be shifted and the hands that ached to curve round another man's body would always hold the memory of hands able to change wine into blood. He would never hold anyone as reverently and as pleasurably as, in celebration, he held up Christ in the shape of the host. But to be a priest no longer was to become a man without meaning or purpose. It was to fall down to zero, a fall as heavy as gravity and just as relentless.

He did not blame himself for this fall but Ursula. Ursula had done this to him. She had ruined his future because he had been unable to free her from her past. He hated her for what she had done. He hated her with such a vengeance he could hear the blood bubbling in his brain at the very thought of her.

Driving back he comforted himself with the thought that she would no longer be there. Time away had given him sufficient strength to face Mother Lawrence again, the Bishop even, but to see Ursula would cause him either to buckle inwardly or to erupt with rage.

The sea came into view, a grey sea, flat and oily-smooth but underneath a cat's cradle of devious and forceful currents. The sea licked and sucked at a grey beach, a narrow strand of dappled sand that knew no sun, shaded as it was by a tall sandstone cliff. The cliff, sheer-faced and a murky tangerine, was topped by a level mile of browning grasslands that gave way abruptly to a sudden sweep of mountain.

This was Gwytherin although it was a place hardly worth naming and was given one only on the most detailed of maps. There was no town, no village, no house, no signpost even. At Gwytherin there was only the small shadowy bay scalloped out of the beach and the sandstone cliff by a placid sea and, rising up out of the brown fields, the Convent of the Sweet Wounds of Mother Mary.

An odd building: two vast and perfect half-bubbles of white granite standing either side of a squat obelisk that ended in a blunt crucifix. Inappropriately reminiscent of male genitalia scrawled on a toilet wall, it was an architect's idle doodle made granite flesh. It did not belong to the landscape although it matched the colour of the sheep that grazed about it. At any moment its globed walls threatened to begin humming, the tower would rotate; it would glow brightly and then blast off; it would return to Mars where it was best suited and from where it looked as if it had been stolen.

Self-evidently it was not an ancient building but, then, the Sisters of the Sweet Wounds were not an ancient order. Both building and order were barely a decade old. Thirteen years before, a newspaper-proprietor-cum-telecommunications-millionaire on a walking tour of Wales had been stopped at Gwytherin by Mary, the Mother of God. It had been a brief but successful visit. She had beamed down from Heaven and landed at Gwytherin expressly to see him. 'Build me a convent,' the Virgin had demanded and, spiritually awakened, he had returned home, initiated plans for a convent, diverted funds for its upkeep, laid aside for it in his will a significant proportion of his estate and was killed in a car crash on the way to its opening. The second mass to be said in its white-walled chapel had been his requiem.

The Convent of the Sweet Wounds of Mother Mary was to be a place of contemplation and physical work. It would encourage a mild form of mysticism in its nuns. It would seek out privacy and privation but it would also handle the business empire of no small size that was its founder's legacy. The Mother Superior had not only to guide her charges as they followed the Way of Perfection; she also had to deal with the more complex ways of the Stock Exchange. She had to be as alive to market forces as to the will of God. Religious orders have had stranger histories. The Convent of the Sweet Wounds of Mother Mary was proud of its short past and its novel duties. COSWOMM was doing rather well out of the newly arrived Recession.

This running together of God and Mammon found expression in the very buildings in which the order was housed. For all that its exterior looked as if it belonged to some comic-book vision of the future, the interior looked back to a more pious and remote age. Long wide corridors curved and gently snaked and gave no echoes; walls, floors and arching ceilings glowed eggshell white; graceful cloisters fenced in lawns tidy to the last blade of grass. At the very heart there was a chapel of angular, stark and surpassing beauty. Here the air of prayer was so thick and rich one could float on it. Not a detail could have dated it beyond the Renaissance except the radiators and the light-switches.

He rang the bell and wondered why he had to wait. The convent had few visitors but there was always a nun on door duty. He rang again a little impatiently. The door, a circular hatch of red-painted timber, remained unopened. He kicked at it gently, impatient for it to be opened. There was no handle, no other way of entering the convent, and so he had to wait.

As he waited, increasingly impatient and so increasingly anxious, he read the legend that ran round the frame of the door in a medieval script of gold lettering: 'And a sword shall pierce your own soul also.'

The Virgin in the founder's vision had appeared to him with a sword pierced through her neck (a novel place for the soul to be situated), the handle of the sword lodged just below her left ear like an outsized earring. This sword was the cause of the wounds that gave the convent its name; the words were spoken by Simeon to Mary as he blessed her and the child Jesus. The wounds were sweet because they partook of Christ's suffering but they were also thought to stress the human quality of Mary, our intercessor in Heaven; they suggested the pain she must have felt as a mother to see her son killed in so ignominious a way. More darkly, it suggested doubt, the doubt she must have felt when, seeing him hanging on the cross like a common criminal, she might have wondered if she had not imagined the visitation of the Angel Gabriel. Had it been her imagination or had it been madness in her to believe that she was God's chosen one? Devlin had made a sermon of it. So had most of the priests who had visited the convent.

He rang again and wondered what it was that made his heart beat fast, his breath short and his chest tight with dread.

71

A sister came at last. 'Father,' she said, half-shocked, half-grateful, 'it's Ursula. . . . '

He pushed past her then, did not wait to hear what the nun had to say. He dropped his suitcase and ran off down the long curving corridor and towards the main staircase.

He tried the chapel first. It was empty and in darkness but for the light of the red candle on the altar. There was a heavy smell of wax and smoke and he could feel cold puddles of candlewax beneath his feet as he walked down the aisle, could make out splashes of wax on the ends of the pews. The altar rails were covered with it, too.

He ran back up the aisle, out and up the main staircase to the dormitory wing, a honeycomb of cave-like cells. He ran to the end, to Ursula's cell, slowly pushed the door open, expecting to find her there, dead on the bed maybe, but the cell was empty and the smell of wax and smoke heavier than in the chapel but mixed here with aged sweat. The chair and the bedside table were overturned, the bed unmade, the sheets ripped and the blanket pinned over the window to keep out the light. He pulled back the blanket, light fell unimpeded, the room brightened and Devlin saw what had been done to the walls.

There was not a patch of clear space, everywhere covered with words, holy words, swearwords, her name, his name and pictures, crudely drawn, of hearts entwined, hearts pierced by arrows, couples rutting, men with men, and large-breasted women with vaginas like tunnels. Pride of place, on the back of the cell door, was a naked man, bent over, prick dangling, a crucifix stuck in his anus and above it the name DEVLIN and arrows, many of them, pointing from his name to the naked man and to the words below: CHRIST FUCKING DEVLIN SOME HOPE. Weaving jaggedly through the obscene words and pictures a zig-zag line of red crayon: Ursula's attempt at Hell-flames.

The walls horrified him. They seemed to grow in on him as he stared at them. He blushed and yet felt faint, was sick with disgust, shocked and ashamed. He could not stop staring at the drawing on the back of the door. He knew it was meant as an insult, an attack, knew, too, that it was meant to excite him, which it did. This room was for him. She had made it so for him. The room was Ursula. He felt he had entered her and had met with disease. This child's drawing of Hell was what she was like inside. The obscene words, the rutting couples, the hearts entwined were Ursula's idea of love, love turned loathsome, turned acid, turned mad. The walls were also a reproach. He had gone away and left her. He had left her to go sinning and she, hundreds of miles away, had been watching him and had recorded his sins on these walls.

He heard someone in the corridor outside. He rushed out but he saw no one. Why was the place deserted? Then, from a window, he saw a nun scurrying along the path towards the cloisters. He ran down the stairs, across the lawn towards the cloisters' granite arches.

'Sister,' he called out. The nun turned and stopped. She waited for him to catch his breath, composing her sharp bony face into expressions of resentment and impatience. 'Ursula?' he gasped at last.

'You've seen the cell, I suppose,' she snapped at him.

'Yes, just now.'

'Well, I'm not cleaning it. If you're looking for Ursula, then she's in the refectory.'

'Refectory?'

'It is time for meals, Father. At least she was there a minute ago. I think she was trying to drink the soup through her nostrils. I left because I didn't give up the world to watch someone do that.'

'Is she still there?'

'She might be, it's hard to say. By now she may well be scaling the bell-tower or burying herself alive in the potato-patch.'

Devlin pushed past her.

'It's my belief, Father,' she called after him, 'that your Miss Trench has finally shown herself up in her true colours and I've said as much to others. She's mad, mad as a hatter, and should be locked up for good.'

But Devlin had gone and the nun was alone in the cloisters with only the echo of her voice for company. She coughed and crossed herself. She should not have raised her voice. It was a sin, a step away from inward silence. 'Well,' she whispered, 'it was all true.'

Devlin pelted his way along airily lit corridors towards

the large hall with white walls and blackened oak benches and trestle-tables where, in silence, the Sisters of the Sweet Wounds of Mother Mary took their meals. It was a place of great quiet but when he arrived, skidding through the swing-doors, the place was already in some kind of commotion. The nuns were gathered in the far corner, a crowd of them like a rugby scrum. They seemed to be engaged in lifting some heavy object off the ground. The heavy object was Ursula Trench.

He made his way through the scrum of nuns who parted instantly and smoothly when they saw it was him. Ursula lay, as if dead, on the grey stone floor. Her eyes were closed, her mouth open, gormless, her hair, stringy, greasy, striping her face. She was wearing – half-wearing – a black habit grimy with dust, frayed and dotted with scorch marks. The skirt was raised to her thighs and the collar and bodice ripped open. Her legs were like spindles and half her breasts were on show, mottled flesh, sagging and creased, a sickening sight. He was reminded of the dirt daubed on her wall.

'But I am a priest still,' said the voice in his head. He held out his hand to her and, magically it seemed, for she had not opened her eyes to see him there, her hand reached out and met it.

He pulled her to her feet and she, previously inert, a dead weight, was as light as a breeze. She rose and fell against him murmuring: 'Thank God, thank God, thank God!' She smelt of unwashed sweat, candlewax and smoke.

'Get a doctor,' he whispered out of the side of his mouth. The nuns seemed not to be listening but were watching the two of them, as enthralled at the sight of Ursula on the arms of the young priest as if they had witnessed a miracle.

'Get a doctor!' he said again more urgently.

One of the nuns, Sister Michael, began to flap her hands and shake her head. The other nuns did likewise. Ursula ignored them all and pushed herself deeper into his embrace, rubbing her face against his and whispering: 'Take me back, take me back to my room.'

He picked her up and carried her out, while the nuns, a snowy *corps de ballet*, acted out a dumbshow of gratitude and concern.

He carried her back to her cell, a flotilla of nuns following in his wake. He dropped her gently on the unmade bed and Sister Michael pinned the blanket back over the window. Nuns and priest tried hard to ignore the walls. Devlin pulled the habit down Ursula's skeletal legs and turned to go but Ursula caught his arm and began tugging at it, pulling him closer. He tried to break free but she was insistent. Her hand was fastened tight around his wrist. He tried to prise her fingers one by one but her grip was unrelenting. He would have liked to hit out at her – that would have made her leave go – but the nuns were crowding round the door and Sister Michael was standing not a yard away. Ursula then reached up, put her arms around his neck and pulled him down towards her. He could not get away so he sat on the very edge of the bed and held her as she began to shake. Her body shuddered and rippled and her eyes stared out at him, those fishy eyes staring into his.

'I love you,' she whimpered. 'Don't leave me.'

He hushed her like a child and she curled up against him, wrapped herself round him like a lover, like ivy round a tree, like a snake through the letter 'h' on an illuminated manuscript. She sighed pleasurably while he almost retched at the smell of her, at the feel of her around him, at the sound of her whining and the long blob of spittle that hung from her mouth like a pear. She covered the back of his neck with her stale breath and slobbering kisses and he could feel the burning-hot triangle of her crotch against his spine as she coiled about him. A bitch in heat, her sex was on fire for him. He could feel it even through his jacket.

The nuns continued to marvel quietly at the calming of Ursula by Father Devlin. Sister Michael exchanged with the other nuns a look that praised God for sending such a Saint to ease the frantic mind, to cast out from it the devils which haunted the sorry Ursula. He must be a Saint to calm her so, thought the nun. How God must love him.

Ursula caught sight of the nuns by the door, stiffened, her thin-lipped mouth clamping shut. She uncoiled herself from Devlin, turned her face to the wall and wept.

The nuns beckoned to Devlin. He followed them out of the room and down to the cloisters, where they sat him on a bench.

'Why wouldn't you go for a doctor when I asked you to?'

They all wanted to answer. Early mornings and afternoons were times of strict silence. In the hours of daylight no words above the most urgent and necessary were to be spoken. The sun had not yet set but the light had a smudged charcoal look to it and they let it pass for dark so that they could talk freely to the young priest.

Sister Michael spoke first and most. Sister Michael was senior nun after Mother Lawrence. She had taken the veil in 1933, had been in Kenya and the Belgian Congo. Parkinson's disease had yet to be diagnosed in her. It had not yet touched her equine features but was sometimes to be seen in her hands which, in times of stress or impatience, grew claw-like and quivered as she spoke so that she looked as if she were accompanying herself on an invisible piano.

'We couldn't get a doctor. She isn't registered. A doctor won't come unless a patient's registered with him. If she was physically ill he'd come but she's not *physically* ill. She never registered with a doctor. I think she knew how things like this go.'

'That's ridiculous.'

'It's how things go. The doctor said he couldn't help her unless she asked. It's the law. She has to go to a hospital and commit herself. She won't. We asked her and she laughed at us.'

'Can't we commit her?'

'No, Father. How can we?'

'Isn't Mother Lawrence responsible for her? Isn't she *in loco parentis*? She can commit her.'

'She can't. She's not. She isn't *in loco parentis*. Ursula's not a nun. We have no claim on her. She's a guest here. She has always been a guest here.'

'Where is Mother Lawrence?'

'She isn't here. She's away. She went to see the Bishop. She's been gone three days.'

'Did she leave before or after Ursula became this bad?'

'After,' said Sister Michael and bit her lip. The other nuns looked away, ashamed of Mother Lawrence's flight from responsibility. Devlin smiled. So getting rid of Ursula was not as easy as she had thought: Devlin could have told her that.

'We're so glad you came back, Father. We've been on our

own and not known what to do. You can handle her. You've just done so. You've no idea how she's been.'

'How has she been? Tell me.'

They told him, each nun adding her own bit to the telling.

She had damaged the statue of Our Lady that stood at the base of the bell-tower. She had tried to saw off its head with a cheesewire. 'And we know where she got that habit from.'

She had walked naked along the beach – 'A woman her age' – after diving into the waves fully clothed.

She had stolen communion wine and had challenged Sister Michael with a broken bottle.

She had stolen seven boxes of candles – a hundred to a box – and had lit them all in the chapel and some in her cell. 'All along the altar rails, down the aisles, along the pews. The chapel was brilliant with them.'

She hadn't slept for a week. 'We could hear her in her room shifting her bed.'

She had stolen a habit, not a white one but a black one, the ones used whenever a nun went outside the convent which was rarely: 'And you saw the state it was in just now, dirty and ripped, and indecently ripped at that.'

She had taken to fainting. She waited for a person to walk by and then she fainted on top of them, bringing them down to the ground.

She screamed for minutes on end for no reason, and idly, as if passing the time by it.

She smelt. She had not washed for days.

She had vandalised her room. She was on her third mattress that week, the other two soaking still. 'And you've seen the walls?'

She walked about looking wicked, deliberately wicked.

She had been told that she was leaving the convent to be looked after by nuns in Radcliffe Park. 'That's what started it, that and you leaving.'

'She kept saying she'd throw herself off the cliff.'

'She kept asking why you'd left.'

'I hadn't left exactly. I was given time off.'

'The Mother said you'd left, that you'd not be coming back. She told Ursula that you'd run away.'

Why had Mother Lawrence lied like that – or had it been a

lie? Was there perhaps at his mother's house in Mallet a letter telling him not to return?

'I didn't run away. Mother Lawrence told me to go away for a while. She said it would be best after what had happened the last time I'd said mass.'

Each nun remembered what had happened the last time he'd said mass. Each nun bowed her head and crossed herself.

'What do we do now, Father?'

'We must persuade her to commit herself.'

'Yes, Father.'

'I will talk with her.'

The nuns could not guess how much this took for him to say but were happy to marvel at him none the less.

'Continue with your routine. I will keep Ursula to her room. I will try to persuade her.'

'God will help you, Father.'

'We will pray for you.'

'And for Ursula so that she may know peace.'

'We will start a vigil in the chapel, Father, and pray for your success.'

'Thank you, all of you. Just one thing. I don't want to be alone with her. I would like one of you to stay close by in case she turns. . . . '

'Nasty, Father?'

'Yes, nasty. Would one of you?'

All of them offered but Sister Michael first.

'Thank you, Sister Michael.'

Sister Michael needed no thanks. She went with him to Ursula's room and the other nuns headed for the chapel to pray for Devlin's success.

They cradled her in their arms in turn and together they held her down when she became violent or aggressive, turning on them like a cat with her teeth and claws. Sometimes they could hear the Sisters singing for them and that gave them strength. Often Ursula lay calm and unmoving, her body wrapped around Devlin's, that hot triangle of her sex burning his spine as she pushed against him, but even when her eyes were closed she did not sleep, she was alive to every one of their movements, so that Devlin and Sister Michael could never rest easy or shorten the long hours with harmless talk.

How ugly madness was, how completely dull and without poetry or wisdom, Devlin had never realised.

In the morning her eyes were closed, her breathing deep and regular. Finally, it appeared, she was sleeping. Sister Michael's stomach growled for want of food and Devlin longed for a bath to cleanse his mind as much as his body. He told Sister Michael to find them all some breakfast and perhaps someone to watch over Ursula so that he could bathe and change.

Sister Michael left and he was alone with Ursula. They were no nearer persuading her to commit herself but at least she was quieter now. He sat in the chair opposite her and studied the walls. He had been looking at them throughout the night but covertly. Now he had the time to look at them without guilt or haste. There was the picture at the back of the door. For all its crudeness she had caught his likeness and the dangling prick was a compliment of sorts. Unconsciously his hands rested on his crotch as he gazed at the drawing, lost in contemplation of it until he heard her giggle.

She was awake and watching him.

'I thought you'd gone and left me.' She looked fixedly at him with dull eyes; not a single muscle moved in her face. 'I wanted you back. I knew that if I was bad they'd not be able to cope, not if I was really bad, and so I've been bad and they sent for you again. I knew they'd send for you. I can be normal again now.'

'No,' he said sadly.

'Yes, I can. It was all a game, a trick to bring you back and they brought you back. They'll have to keep you here now. It's worked out all right. I knew it would.'

'They're sending you away. They're sending you to Radcliffe Park. I'm going away, too.'

'With me? To Radcliffe Park?'

'No, I'm going . . . over the wall.'

A nun came in to take his place. Ursula turned away as Devlin left. The nun sat down. She was afraid of the walls, of Ursula more than anything. When Ursula suddenly sat up and smiled at her – an evil smile, the nun claimed – the nun ran off and hid in the linen-room.

Alone now, Ursula rose from her bed, smoothed out her wrinkled habit with the palms of her hands, unpinned the blanket from the window and then left the cell, making her way to the beach and the cliff-edge where she would sit down and wait for Devlin to find her again.

IV

What Would Be Best

He knocked on Mother Lawrence's door and waited for her to say 'Enter' before doing so.

'Are you free?' he asked her.

'Of course,' she told him but the words had frost on them and her smiling face could have been carved out of an icicle. Mother Lawrence claimed always to be available. Should anyone wish to talk to her, she said, her door was always open. Her words were inviting but her voice was not.

It was in the woman's character to be aloof. Although she was ultimately responsible for it, she did not take part in the general life of the nuns. Occasionally she would eat with them and, less occasionally, pray with them, but as a rule she studied them from afar. She commented on their progress or behaviour sparingly and usually cryptically. She seldom conversed with them but would listen coldly to a particular grudge or private misery. Like God she kept her distance yet, like God's, her presence in the convent was surprisingly omniscient.

She lived apart from them in a building separate from the main body of the convent. The building was of the same pearly granite as the rest of the convent and as perfectly spherical as the two domes, but smaller and glass-roofed.

The idea of the glass roof was that the Mother could sit at her desk, look up and contemplate Heaven. Mother Lawrence thought the astrodome silly, an architectural affectation. She never looked up. Heaven lay inwards and it was there that one's gaze was best directed. Besides, seagulls flew over and shat on the roof. Hosing down the astrodome was one of the convent's little jobs; in summer, a hot sun baked the stuff and the nuns had to climb up and scrape it off.

At night the astrodome would glow greenly and passengers

in ships miles out at sea would take it for the dim lights of a UFO, but the glow came from a bank of telescreens housed in Mother Lawrence's office; her gaze was also directed at them, concentrated on the control and development of their founder's empire, his legacy.

This legacy further isolated her. She had duties which the nuns in her charge were unable to share, indeed had vowed to spurn on taking the veil. Mother Lawrence's day was not taken up with prayer but with rates of interest and exchange. Commodities not Compline occupied her evenings. Elected as Mother not for her pastoral skills or spiritual qualities but for her family background in banking and, from pre-nun days, a degree in economics from Strathclyde, she controlled a wealth that was there not to be fretted away in charities and good works but to be re-invested, to accumulate.

The Founder's legacy was Mother Lawrence's cross. Its weight distracted her from things divine but it was a cross and so had gladly to be borne. She carried it soberly and with consummate success.

Devlin sat down opposite her. He, she and the neat, functional office furniture, its surfaces smooth, uncluttered, its lines angular and severe, were all drenched in the green light of the telescreens. Mother Lawrence found the green light restful. It mellowed the room and made her content. It made Devlin bilious but he said nothing. It was best not to offend her: he needed her on his side and so he nodded and listened intently as she told him of the Green Ray. Had he heard of it? He had not.

'It is an atmospheric phenomenom,' she explained in that drilling monotone that made even her lightest statements oppressive. 'An effect of the light on summer evenings. One is supposed to stare into the setting sun and for a chosen few the sun will emit a green ray. To see this ray – a rare occurrence – is to have bestowed upon one the power to understand one's own heart and those of other people. A legend, of course.'

'A pity, I could do with such a gift as that.'

Devlin had meant it as a joke – or half-meant it – but jokes, even half-jokes, were lost on Mother Lawrence.

In the green light her eyes appeared quite grape-like, round and dullish, and her complexion olive-stained. Her face had a sculpted look to it, as though the flesh had been smoothly chiselled back to the bone, and the high curving forehead underneath the turreting wimple and ample veil suggested pure undecorated skull.

She stretched out a bony arm to the keyboard behind her and with skinny fingers tapped out the rhythm of a favourite hymn. She did this without looking, out of idleness and to fill the pause she knew Devlin would take before talking of why he had come. She stared at him as her hand busied itself at the keyboard, the fingers rap-tapping and figures, graphs and isometric charts zipping and spinning across the monitor screens, fracturing and scattering the light so that the room seemed in the grip of a green snowstorm.

Devlin, dazed by the light-show, wondered at the purpose of it. Was it to hypnotise him or just to unsettle him? He was already unsettled. He always was in her presence. There was something about her that repelled intimacy, confession, gossip or tale-telling and he had come for all four.

She stopped her tapping abruptly. The monitors returned to a green blankness and the light became whole again. She brought her hands together, cupped them as in prayer and laid them in her lap. She leaned forward and gave him a look that was meant to be kind.

'I think it would be best if you went away for a while.' She hesitated. 'A short while. I think that would be best.'

Devlin hung his head low and agreed without enthusiasm. The thought of going away, of leaving Ursula behind, was a sweet one but to go away was to admit failure. His face was drawn, haggard. Inky-black circles were stamped about his eyes.

'I've failed, haven't I?'

Mother Lawrence tut-tutted.

'No, no, Father.'

'I have, though. God was testing me. Ursula was my test and I failed it.'

'You are too hard on yourself.' She reached out for his arm and squeezed it. A comforting gesture, out of keeping with her character and clumsily done, it moved him all the more. 'Ayomon,' she said – she had never called him by name before – 'don't judge yourself too harshly or you will fall into self-pity.'

'When I saw Ursula I thought that here was a soul lost in evil, and wouldn't it be great to fight with it and save it for the Lord.' There had been more than priestly pride involved. He had tried to best his dead father. His father had once saved Ursula's life and Devlin had tried to save Ursula's soul. 'It was a challenge. There was a bit of glamour in a challenge like that, I thought, but there's been no glamour in it. It's been a slog and a nuisance and an embarrassment and a putting up with lies. I'm worn through with it.'

'Yes, I see. You talk of Ursula's soul – as you should – but the problem is Ursula's mind. We must act on that.'

He wanted to tell her how much he hated Ursula, how much she sickened him, but instead he said feebly: 'I've failed her. And God. And you.'

'Don't give me a thought. I have not been blameless in this matter. I have watched you. I have watched Ursula. I have not helped either of you. I have let you be tested. I thought it would be good for you. A priest here has little enough to do. Ursula was to be your hobby. I was wrong. I think you should go away now. Your presence does not help any more. It excites Ursula. It disturbs her. She will be quieter if you go away.'

'What will you do with her?'

'Get rid of her. There is a group of nuns who have asked for her. They wish to take care of her. They have asked before. They have asked frequently. They are welcome to her.'

'If they have asked before why were they refused?'

'They run a cenacle in Radcliffe Park in the house where Ursula once lived.'

'Where the child was killed?'

'That is the house, yes.'

'And him . . . the man Andreas, where they used to. . . . '

'Meet? Yes.'

'I know the house. I saw it as a boy. She can't go back there. It would be wrong. She might. . . . '

'Kill again? I do doubt that. I have never studied the case – I find the woman repellent enough without delving into her past – but I doubt if she murdered the child. There were other suspects. Her father. The child's own mother, even?'

'But she died the same day?'

'The verdict was of accidental death but it could be seen as suicide.' Mother Lawrence knew the case better than she had admitted.

'No. She was killed, too. By Ursula.'

'Ursula told you that?'

'Ursula has told me many things.'

'But mostly lies, I imagine. That is the way with women of her sort. They have morbid minds that distort the truth. She probably lies to make herself interesting.'

'She did kill Andreas.'

'Yes, of that we can be sure, she did kill him. But women have killed men before and usually for love. A sordid affair. If it had happened today she'd be given a suspended sentence and a social worker. Unlike you, I do not see Ursula as a monster. I find her pathetic. I find her a nuisance. I dislike her. I want her out of my convent. Radcliffe Park, a special home, a hospital for the mentally ill, a bus-shelter in Birmingham, her fate does not concern me. I have never wanted her here. She was thrust upon us. I knew she would break. The life here is much too hard. I have waited for her to break. When you first came and I saw her with you I knew that I would not have long to wait. Now you say you cannot cope with her and now I can say: "Take her away, we have done our best, we have done our duty, take her away." '

He could have objected, argued that Mother Lawrence was disposing of Ursula too coolly, that she minimised the evil that Ursula had done in the past and was being deliberately blind to the evil she might yet do, but he did not argue, he did not object. He could not blame her for wanting rid of Ursula Trench: it was what he most wanted, too.

'You will go away for a while and when you return she will no longer be here. I shall arrange that wheels be set in motion. If she refuses to go to Radcliffe Park, then there is the asylum in Denbigh. Given the choice, I'm sure she will see sense. This madness of hers is an act put on to impress you, to interest you in her. It is a rather desperate feminine ploy.'

She leaned back in her chair and began to pick at her fingernails with a paper-clip – a gesture which signalled that their talk had come to an end.

Devlin muttered his thanks and rose from his chair. The

ordeal was over. He could relax. Ursula was to be spirited away and he was to be given time off. He would go away somewhere quiet and he would pray. When he returned it would be to a quiet convent, a quiet life. He would take the time to study, to become a better priest, a wiser, purer man.

He reached the door and turned to thank Mother Lawrence. 'Life will be so peaceful without her, won't it?'

Mother Lawrence looked doubtful. 'Problems have a way of recurring. One goes, another comes. Don't expect too quiet a life.'

Dark tones shaded her voice. There was a warning in it but Devlin was deaf to it until he glanced down at the small table by the door. A dog-eared collection of magazines lay scattered there.

'These magazines' – she waved a bony hand in their direction – 'they are yours?'

All he could do was say yes and hang his head like a schoolboy.

'You don't need to ask who found them and brought them to me?'

He did not.

A cooler mind than his at that moment might have appreciated the situation's irony: while he had been pleading for her ejection, Ursula had engineered his.

Mother Lawrence pinned him with a steely eye. 'I have no experience of dealing with priests with your particular sickness. I have informed the Bishop. We will wait and hear what he has to say. Until then I think you go away for a short while. Leave before breakfast. It is best that Ursula not see you again. You will go to Brighton? You often go there. I imagine you have friends there.'

She turned her back to him in her swivel chair and began to tap out a message on her word processor. The monitors flickered and came alive once more.

Devlin, no longer happy, the reverse, boiling hot with anger and frothy with resentment, trudged back to his room. If he had met Ursula he would have hit her, pushed her over and kicked her until she cried out for him to stop, but he passed by her unawares.

Ursula was hiding in the shadow of an alcove. There were

few shadows in the convent – the white walls did not allow for them – but she could always be trusted to find the dark places. She watched him pass and considered calling out his name. She imagined him turning round and glaring, the sound of her voice striking him like a stone on his neck. How angry he would be. Already she regretted what she had done.

I will think of some way to get him back, she thought.

Dressed as she usually was in a dusty black overall that clung to her withered figure, hair ash-grey, she looked like a burned thing, an ember from a dying fire. An idea blew through her mind, a mad idea to get him back, and her eyes were suddenly aglow with it.

V

Dear Priestlet

Everything was white: the walls, the statues, the altar rails, bone white, like a soul that knows no sin. The bands of frosted glass that spanned the domed roof bleached the light, softening it and giving pearly haloes to the white-habited nuns. Their voices, high and pure, so filled the chapel that from where he stood it seemed the very walls were singing. He, in purple Lenten vestments, arms outstretched towards his snowy congregation, was the silent, the colourful and commanding centre – and he loved it.

The mass was ending, the performance near-complete. This was the best of times, the time when he was most what he wished to be: a priest with a priest's power. He brought his hands together to make the sign of the cross. The nuns knelt to receive it, their going down on their knees a dull, unanimous shuffle and thud. All knelt except one and she no nun but Ursula in dusty black overalls standing proud and screaming.

'Bastard!'

The word went through the silence like a hammer through sheet glass. Devlin froze in mid-blessing.

'Bastard! Fake! Fake! Fake!' Her voice was still loud but no longer a scream. The chanting controlled it and her expression, eyes glittering, giving out skittering glances, showed that she knew exactly what effect she was producing. Then she seemed to glide into a fifth gear, into blood-red anger, hand slapping the pew in time with the chant of 'Fake! Fake! Fake!', spit coming in sprays.

The nuns nearest to her made moves to pull her down, calm her. Ursula swatted them away. Other nuns turned to help or to watch, moving out of their pews to get closer.

Only Mother Lawrence at the front of the chapel remained still and glassy-faced, her eyes burning holes into the frozen priest before her. She raised her hand as if to say 'Leave her'. Slowly and reluctantly, the Sisters returned to their seats and faced the altar once again. Those who had held Ursula let her go and stood straight to receive the blessing she had interrupted. Ursula, no longer supported, attention denied her, fell to her knees and began to cry. She was sorry, she sobbed, so sorry, so very sorry.

'Go in peace. The mass is ended,' said Devlin and waved a limp sign of the cross at them. The nuns cleared the chapel in single file, Sister Michael taking Ursula with her, hurrying her gently to her room. Mother Lawrence remained until last, still staring at the priest but without anger, her face a blank. The last nun gone, she rose, walked up the aisle and left. Devlin relaxed, sighed and leaned forward, elbows on the altar, face in his hands.

Ursula had gone public. She had been worse. She had said worse but never so loudly and always just with him, in the confessional, her cell, the cloister-walk or the cliff-edge. She had made a habit of interrupting his life but never the life of the convent. She had called out in chapel. She had broken his blessing. She had spoiled a mass, his mass. His dignity had been attacked. It occurred to him how essential dignity was, not just to him but to any priest, and how a mass could not be said without it.

Back in his room he sat on his bed and tried to calm himself. He thought of whisky but had none and so thought of sex. He lay back on the bed and rubbed his groin but his groin was not deeply interested. He thought of Glenn. Glenn was slim and blond with a patch of dry skin in the shape of a map of Africa down the back of his thigh, but Glenn had a wonky eye and buckled mouth and so he thought of Scott who was also slim and blond, a motor mechanic and physically flawless. Scott lay next to Glenn who lay next to Sailor Hans who berthed next to Sporty Malcolm and Massive Martin who all lay under his mattress in magazines called *Him*, *Size* and *Cock and Bullworker*.

He got off the bed to lift the mattress but was interrupted by the sound of footsteps outside his door – familiar footsteps.

Keep her away, he prayed, and his prayer was answered. An envelope was slipped under his door and the footsteps scurried away.

He picked it up. Wearily he opened it.

Dear priestlet
I am sorry about just now but you havent helped me and you said you would but you never. A rat sits in my head and he chews and he chews and you never caught him like you said you would so I'm going to get you back for that, get you back good. You are a miserable wimp of a priestlet and your days are up, a fucking queer with your tongue up an altar boy's juicy bum if you had altar boys here so you use Mother Larry instead and you stick it so far up it comes out of her head and she must love you for it for you're not much use otherwise are you priestlet? I loved you. I love you now. I always will. I plan my days around you and sit thinking of you hoping you think of me and I'll sit in your head and be as close as close can be. Like Andreas was. I thought you were him, you are like him. I loved him dead bad but he had to go and so do you. I always seem close to tears and my throat hurts from choking it all back.

Later he would think about the note and why it was that which made him give in. He had had other notes, worse some of them, more threatening, more bitter, less coherent, and others more sickly, more loving. His decision to surrender came in an instant.

'I do not need this,' he said slowly, distinctly and aloud. 'I do not want this. I can do without it.' He repeated it. He would go to see Mother Lawrence. Ursula would have to go. Either Ursula or him. He could not cope and no one should have expected it of him.

He zipped up his flies and left the room but not Mechanic Scott and Sailor Hans who were lying in wait for him on a table in Mother Lawrence's observatory.

VI

Face through a Veil

She loved him and sought him out at least once a day to tell him so. She was seldom far from him and always knew where he was even when he took to hiding from her. She was such a nuisance but seemed not to care. She followed him like a dog and whenever he was away she would pine like one; she would sit by his door and quietly whine. Down corridors his footsteps would be echoed by hers. At midday, in summer, when he sat in the cloisters with a newspaper or a Len Deighton, she would be close by in the shadows watching him, reading him as intently as he read his paper or book. She envied the sun for touching his face when she could not, envied the breeze for the freedom it had to caress him. When she was certain he wasn't there she'd visit his room. She would breathe in the air, run her hands over the furniture, sit in his chair, open his wardrobe, put his jackets and underwear against her face and her feet in his shoes. One day he caught her. She'd pulled off the blanket from his bed and was smelling his sheets, drinking the scent of him in, burrowing her face into the mattress, filling her mouth with the corner of his pillow. He had sent her out with a kick and a curse. She had drifted in bliss for a week after.

'If Ursula needs help, then give it to her,' Mother Lawrence had told him after this incident. 'Ursula is not in my charge. She is not a nun but a fellow-traveller of sorts. We no longer chide her when she strays from the path which we have set ourselves.'

'She needs help,' Devlin had repeated helplessly.

'Then, it is your help she will get. Your life here affords you no other duties. You say mass – a little melodramatically. You hear confession. You work – indifferently and irregularly – in the gardens and you once fixed the spin-drier. You lead an enviably peaceful life for a young priest, a life that has made you flabby and cowardly if you cannot cope with the one problem with which you are asked to deal. What would you do if they sent you to a parish in Liverpool or Glasgow or Belfast, even? Come running to me? There are women like Ursula Trench all over – men, too – worse, some of them, people who see God as one giant ear and themselves one long cry for attention. How would you deal with them?'

Devlin knew guiltily that his life was made all the simpler for being attached to the convent. In the convent it was easier to die to the world because the world seemed not to impinge upon it except for the green glow of Mother Lawrence's astrodome and the low burr of the telex machine in the main hallway. He knew his strengths and weaknesses and so did his superiors who had sent him there. On this he could not defend himself and Mother Lawrence knew it. She had a knack of finding the Achilles' heel; she could not successfully address a person without knowing it.

When he first began to find Ursula a problem and had come to her for advice he had been surprised by her off-handedness. She told him to make a hobby of Ursula. He had not understood.

'Find out about her past. Did she really kill the child? Who did? How was it done? If it was her, how did she get away with it? It's a famous case. You could write a book on it. Solve the mystery.'

'I'm not clever enough for that.'

Mother Lawrence silently agreed. Most priests were stupid, she had found. Only the dullest or the most hearty survived the training; the clever ones kept meeting up with doubts and difficulties they were too vain to ignore and too weak to overcome. A clever priest would have been company for her but a clever priest might have solved the problem of Ursula. She was not interested in solving Ursula, only in removing her, and she needed a dull priest for that.

Again he would come to her.

'Won't you speak to her?'

'I have spoken to her. I have asked her to behave many times.'

'And she does, she does. She listens to you.'

'Yes, she does seem contrite whenever I speak to her. Very well.'

Mother Lawrence had located Ursula's Achilles' heel. She simply withdrew her love. She would look down on Ursula with a cold face and her voice would be icily sharp.

'I cannot know what passes between you and Father Devlin in the confessional and I do not wish to know but you must not worry him with your fears and your stories.'

Ursula would lower her eyes and mumble: 'Yes, Mother, sorry, Mother.'

'If you do not behave like a good girl, Ursula, I will send you away. I do not want bad girls here. Do you want to be sent away?'

Spoken to as a child, Ursula would answer like one. She'd tug at her hair, swivel her body, pout and say that she was so sorry, she was not a bad girl but a good girl.

'You like this place, don't you, Ursula?'

Ursula nodded.

'It is a good place. The outside is ugly, so modern. A futuristic tower and two granite bubbles: architecture à la page. But inside, Ursula, ah, inside! Look around you. These walls. These windows. Outside we have today. Inside we have the past. What we are is determined by what we were. Our order is new, barely a decade old, but everything we do, our rituals and traditions, go back to the Middle Ages to which the interior of this building hearkens. Even my work on the founder's legacy has its roots there. History helps us. It explains us. It clears away detritus and shows up the clear lines of the soul. Don't you find this so?'

Ursula did not. Mother Lawrence could not have cared less either way and had spoken on this theme out of boredom and to confuse Ursula – something that was easy to do and so hard to resist – but Ursula had been asked a question and to please the Mother she tried to think of an answer.

History must come in somewhere but neither she nor it seemed to know the cue. Andreas had died on Coronation Day and Coronation Day had been history even if Andreas's death had not. On that day, too, a man had climbed Everest and Ursula had plumbed the depths. Perhaps there was meaning in that. Her father had talked of war and country. War had meant something to him. He had known two of them. Anna Matchett had also spoken of war and had done her bit in the second one. She had said it was a time for women. Anna had said that it was right to keep an eye on the world's doings and had told Ursula off for not doing likewise. Well, Andreas was dead, Father was dead and Anna Matchett had hanged herself with her own tights and perhaps that had a meaning, too, but it was all beyond Ursula. It had always been beyond her. Maybe there were clear lines to be drawn between what happens to a person and what happens in the times in which they live but it was all too much of a cat's cradle for her to unravel. She understood history no more than a pebble understands how it is smoothed by the river's flow or a fish understands the stream in which it swims.

These thoughts or half-thoughts never broke the surface but bubbled, gasped and drowned deep inside her. Mother Lawrence's idle question was left unanswered. Mother Lawrence had gone back to her original point.

'So you don't want to be sent away from here?'

'No, Mother, not for the world.'

'And you won't be if you are a good girl. Do you promise to be a good girl?'

Ursula promised and Mother Lawrence patted her on the head and, with a smile, seemed to return all the love she had never given in the first place. Ursula blushed and grew girlish and behaved well for as long as a week sometimes until the pull of Devlin's presence was just too strong and the desire to speak with him itched in her mind like a sore and she would seek him out once more.

She was persistent in the attentions she paid him. She never spoke to him unless they were alone. Although he tried hard not to let this happen, Ursula had always one last recourse: the confessional. He could not refuse to see her then.

It was not always of sinning that she spoke. For Ursula confession was not a sacrament but a chance to be in his presence and to woo him, maybe. Divided from him by only a veil of dark gauze that made his face look as if it were composed of smoke, she talked not only of murder, of dead fathers, babies and lovers but also of life in prison. She would tell him how a typical prison day would pass – 'pretty much like here, Father, but more, you know, restricted' – and of the famous visitors she had received – 'I had a reputation and you don't want for company if you've one of them'. She told him of the miracles she had performed inside, 'very minor ones, very small beer. Impressive enough at the time, mind, but I've lost the knack for them now.' Occasionally she would tell of people she had known there, like Sonny, her best, her only friend, or Beryl, a warden – 'Beryl and I were dead close. I used to flirt with her for fags' – and a lady governor who'd later killed herself – 'Went to bed with nothing on but a fur coat and a plastic bag over her head. I saw it coming. God loved me then and I had a sixth sense but it's gone now like the miracles. It was a lovely fur coat. She wore it on her rounds sometimes. She'd let us stroke it if our hands were clean.'

Devlin had heard all this before and often, although sometimes details changed: Sonny was not her best friend but Lucy was or Celeste, Beryl the warden had been a cow and the lady governor had been put away for molesting her charges. That was the way with Ursula's stories: they changed all the time. Even in mid-telling a story could have its characters renamed. There were details and themes that never varied, things that might have been true simply because they remained unchanged, but the only constant in Ursula's prison-time tales was her claim to have performed miracles.

He felt it his duty to pray for her but did so without conviction or success. A hollow man, his prayers fell as far from the ear of God as a paper plane aimed at the moon. She seldom left his mind and her face was always in his thoughts; a grey-lined face, the texture of faded parchment, the beaked nose, the square chin and wide cheeks, the web of hair, the thin-lipped mouth, the fishy eyes, glistening black pupils swimming in milky puddles.

She was mad, he was convinced of it: twenty-odd years in prison and now a convent, a stranger to the ways of the world, she had forgotten what was normal. Prison would have been hard on her. A child-killer was the lowest of the low in there and no mercy was ever shown to them. She would have known no rest, no solace. And then she had come here to live among women who had rejected the world. I will know some peace here, she would have thought, I will know if not forgiveness then people kind enough to forget. But the nuns were all for God, mere conduits for prayer and grace, no attention for themselves or others. Ursula, bored, restless, a little insulted that her reputation was considered so lightly, would then rebel to gain attention, disrupt their quiet lives.

But no, it hadn't quite worked like that. Ursula had been a good girl. She had lived amongst the nuns quietly until he had arrived. It was his attention she wanted, his quiet life she wanted to disturb.

I am the first man she has had to deal with for how many years and only the third who has meant anything in her life. There had been her father, then Andreas, now him. Look what had happened to Andreas. Look what happened to the father. When Devlin slept he sometimes saw the wax tableau at Madame Tussaud's, Andreas sleeping on the bed, a pretty man with fine legs, Ursula standing over him poised to kill. In his dream he became Andreas and the dummy Ursula grew grey and old.

He would wake from such dreams anxiously patting his chest, his arms, his legs, struggling for breath.

'The woman is driving me mad.'

She had chosen to love him. She had told him that. At first he had been amused – 'Yes, yes, Ursula, and I like you, too' – then slowly he became appalled as she became ever more insistent and her passion ever more obvious. He looked like Andreas, she had said, the spit of him. He knew that was a lie.

Devlin would look at his face in the mirror over the washbasin. The light was weak and the greasy surface of the mirror distorted his reflection but he knew it well enough – too round to be good-looking, a boy's face with a sulky droop of thick lips, not one to break a heart.

She loved his face. She never tired of telling him so and she would trace the shadow of his profile on the gauze veil of the confessional.

'Another of your stories, Ursula. You said your father died in his bed of cancer. Yesterday he was a suicide and last week you said you'd smothered him with a pillow.'

'You don't believe me, then.'

'If I believed what you told me today, I'd have to forget what you'd said the day before. These stories of yours change all the time.'

'I'm sorry, Father.'

'One day you plead guilty for innumerable crimes. You did this, you say, you did that and then you cry and ask for forgiveness. The next time you deny it all. You change the story round and round. Is it any wonder you're not believed?'

There was no response to this but he could see the imprint of her hand against the veil and hear the soft and regular hiss as she stroked that part of the veil where his shadow fell.

'If you could find one version of your tale and stick to it, call that the truth, then perhaps you – and I – can find peace.'

'I do keep to the truth as I see it but it changes so in my mind.'

They would both sigh and there would be a pause as Devlin hoped that she would leave the tiny booth and Ursula desperately searched for some new sin, some new lie, any excuse to stay.

'I killed my step-brother.'

'You said.'

'I did?'

'You told me.'

'Did I say I strangled him?'

'No, you smothered him.'

'Did I?'

'So you told me last time.'

'Did I say I used a bread-knife, too?'

'No, you said you didn't stab him.'

'I didn't but he was stabbed. He was stabbed bad, loads of times, loads.'

'You said Gabriel stabbed the child.'

'Gabriel? Who's Gabriel?'

'See, you're changing the story again.'

'Am I?'

'Yes, again. You said he stabbed the child. See how you lie and lie and get lost in the lies. There are so many of them and you never mention Andreas. Never. He was the one we know for certain. He was the one you can't lie about and so you play round with the truth about others. You tell me this. You tell me that. You lie and lie and fantasise, sick fantasies, but never about him. You never mention him.'

'Andreas? You want to know about him?'

'Yes, Andreas.'

'He was a shit. Who's Gabriel?'

VII

Tell All

She had sought him out but hadn't he sought her out, too? Hadn't he, in fact, been the first to go looking?

When he had first come to the convent he had noticed her. He had asked Sister Michael about the woman in the black overall, the rather decayed-looking woman. Sister Michael had told him that the woman had once been in prison and had asked to come here when released. She had followed the life of a nun but had not become one. Sister Michael had said that long ago the woman had done a terrible thing. There was talk of other terrible things, things she'd done and had got away with, evil things, but that she was sorry now. She kept quiet, she kept busy, tried not to be noticed and was harmless. Devlin, only mildly interested, had asked her name and when told his mouth had fallen open and he had gasped, half-thrilled and half-amazed.

'I know her', he said, 'or, rather, I know of her.'

Sister Michael had not been surprised. Ursula Trench had been famous in her day . . . well, not famous, notorious.

'My father met her once. I saw her, too.' He remembered the times when neighbours or relatives called, the coffee-table scattered over with tea-cups and plates of the best biscuits, the air blue with cigarette smoke. His father would be asked to tell about the time he'd met with Ursula Trench. It had been an important day in his father's life but the son had guessed even then that to Ursula the meeting, if remembered at all, would have meant nothing. She would have had other things to think about that day in Brackley Street.

Still, the coincidence of it appealed to him. There was also the chance to best his dead father. His father had met Ursula but now the son was going to live under the same roof as her, see her daily, even give her Communion and hear her confession. That night he had written all about her to his mother and his mother had replied, saying how proud his dad would have been to know that their Ayomon was maintaining the family link. Perhaps what his father had done for Ursula twenty-odd years ago he would also do – in a different way, of course.

Once settled in the convent and pleasantly aware how light his duties were to be, he took almost to courting Ursula. Mother Lawrence, he noticed, encouraged his interest in her. Whenever he met Ursula in the corridor or the refectory he would smile with studied kindness and his eyes would express a desire for her attention that would have shamed him in later years had he not chosen to forget it.

Despite his feeble courting, Ursula was ignorant of him, polite but cold. Although he sometimes waited especially for her in the confessional, long after the nuns had gone, she never came. At mass she was a regular attender but she seldom came to the altar rails to receive Communion. When she did, she kept her eyes lowered as she raised her head to accept the host. He had felt frustrated by her coolness, even insulted. He asked Sister Michael why Ursula, who did not seem very pious, was allowed to reside in the convent.

'That goes back to the founder. She wrote to him once. She told him how her own conversion to God's way coincided with his almost to the hour. He visited her once. She had lots of visitors after her conversion and there was talk of her being holy. The founder remembered her, mentioned her in his will, said that should she ever want a home this convent would welcome her. She wanted to be a nun. She wanted to take the veil and go to the Congo. She said that was where all good nuns go and she wanted to do good upon the earth. Of course, it wasn't to be. How could it, at her age and with her history? And mental illness had occurred at one point, I believe. She came here, though, as a postulant. The first year she was fine, tried very hard, but she hadn't the call. She was very brave. She said to me: "Sister Michael, I can cheat myself but not God. I am not a nun nor ever will be but I love Him not one bit less. He's been good to me and I'll be good for Him." And she has. She misses mass now and then but there's not the same pressure on her as there is on us and she works hard, no trouble. I've a soft spot for her. If bygones can't be called bygones what can they be called? Love and forgiveness, Father, these are gifts given by God that we must give to others.'

It was deep into Lent and Ursula had not done her Easter duty. Devlin was now sure she was avoiding him.

'She never comes to confession.'

'That surprises me, Father, and, then, again, it doesn't. Perhaps she's shy. Perhaps she needs an invitation.'

'You're so wise, Sister Michael,' said Devlin and had watched with interest as Sister Michael squirmed and blushed. It was easy to flirt with a nun: there was no threat in it.

'But have a word with her, Father. Go to the beach or the cliff. Catch her there. It's where she goes when she wants quiet. It's out of bounds to us unless we go in pairs.'

He found her the next day walking along the beach. It was dull but warm, the sun intermittently shining. The tide was out and the strand was smooth and wet, marked only by Ursula's footprints and now his as he ran to catch up with her.

'Can I walk with you?' he asked and she smiled graciously. She was smarter then but her face was heavily lined although she could not yet be in her fifties. It was a tough face, mean and pinched except for the eyes, large and black but without warmth. The hair was still more dark than grey. The wind from the sea mussed the severe page-boy bob into which it had been cut. Walking beside her he was surprised by how small she was, how narrow. He had thought her taller, broader, stronger: it was what her reputation led one to expect.

They walked together for a while in an easy, unembarrassed silence. He slowed down to her pace which was really more of a trudge, each step small and wearily made, more of a shuffle than a walk, a prison shuffle.

Although the silence was a comfortable one it surprised him. He had come to talk, so this was *her* silence. She had imposed it on him. Later he was to realise how much else she imposed on him; the silence was just one imposition, as was the cliff-top where she said would be nice to sit and rest.

The cliff itself was almost sheer and some thirty feet above the sea but there were enough folds and dips to make a stairway for them.

'It's easier to go up than go down,' she told him as they

climbed, 'but the convent's just across the fields so we won't have to come down.'

When they reached the top they were breathless and laughing as though the exertion of climbing had broken a barrier between them.

'I always come up here,' she said. 'See, it's very comfortable.'

She pointed to a series of rocks only a few feet from the edge that one could sit on and yet be sheltered from the wind. Around and between the rocks grew wild bushes of fuchsia. Ursula held one of the dangling red blossoms between her thumb and forefinger.

'Do you know what these are called?' she asked him. He noticed that she talked out of the side of her mouth and her eyes glanced from side to side as she did so. A prison habit, he thought. He noticed, too, how delicate her movements could be, how gently and even reverently she held the blossom. 'They grow around Easter-time. Sister Michael said. Christ's Blood, they were called. Lovely, aren't they? I like Easter. I like coming out of Lent. The purple cowls coming off the statues and the flowers back on the altar.'

She was staring at him. For so long she had been only stealing glances, she had not looked him full in the face.

He was surprised to see that she was wearing make-up: lipstick, a little rouge, pink on her eyelids, crudely and inexpertly applied. Her face was so drawn and bloodless that the make-up stood out like a mask, a child's drawing of a face superimposed on her own. It occurred to him, but with no real force, that she was wearing it for him.

He sat down beside her on the rock but a little behind so that he saw her face in profile, her hooked nose prominent, but their true view was of the sea.

The tide was still way out but beginning to turn. Feeble, sand-foamed waves clawed up the beach, a fraction further each time. The sound of the sea was little above a hiss, indistinguishable from the ruffle of the wind across the fields behind them. He turned and saw the convent a mile away, the two white globes and tower impressive and odd against the green and purple fields and the grey-sweeping-up-to-black mass of mountains that made up the horizon.

'You said you liked Easter. What about Lent?'

101

She laughed, snorted really, and he laughed with her for company's sake and to gain her confidence.

'What have you given up for Lent?'

'God,' she said, and laughed. This time he laughed less readily.

'Is that why you don't come to confession?'

'Maybe.' She turned towards him. 'You know who I am? What I've done?'

'I know a little.' Should he tell her that his father had met her once in Brackley Street and he'd been with him? He said nothing. Let her speak, he thought, let her talk. That is why I am here.

'To know a little about me is to know more than enough. None of it's nice to know. I'm shy of people, ashamed really, especially priests. I suppose I was waiting for you to say come on. I was waiting for an invitation.'

'That's what Sister Michael said.'

'It's what I told her to say.'

'You've talked to her?'

'I asked her to talk to you. Didn't you guess that? Sister Michael was glad to do it. Any excuse to talk to you.' She was smiling. It was not a shy smile but a bold, teasing one as if she knew a joke against him. 'Thinks you're wonderful. All the nuns do. Quite a fan club you've got there. Because you're young, I expect.'

'She told me to come here. Did you tell her where you'd be?'

'I wanted to be alone with you with no interruptions. I wanted to make confession, I suppose. To tell you about myself, what I am, what I did. You remind me of someone I used to know. Someone I used to know well. Someone I used to . . . trust. He was called Andreas. He wasn't foreign, just had a foreign name. He was the man I was put in prison for, the one I killed.' She paused, laughed sadly, a little embarrassed. 'One of the ones I've killed.' She laughed again, a dry short laugh with no humour in it. Devlin felt a chill between his shoulderblades.

Ahead the sea grew closer, the tide a little stronger, a little faster. Curve-bellied waves, grey-bearded, broke on the smooth beach in quick succession so that it seemed that there was only one wave, paralysed in mid-roll, caught as in a painting. Above, the sky was turning from grey to almost-lilac. Rain-clouds hung like thick bolts of gauze ready to fall.

'Tell me,' he said. He was aware that such a command might not be wise, that he might regret it. The command once given would not be retracted. Ursula, like the Ancient Mariner, would hold him with her skinny hand, fix him with her glittering eye until her tale was done.

'If I tell you, then you'll hear it all.' She made it sound like a threat.

'Tell me,' he repeated, thinking as coolly as he could that he was a priest and this is what a priest would say, but knowing that it was no longer as simple as that. She had chosen the time, the place, the subject. She had chosen him. She had chosen everything. 'Tell all,' he said.

'There's an awful lot of all to tell.'

She turned from him, her face once again in profile, sure of his attention. She sat, hands in lap, back poker-straight, a child ready to say her over-rehearsed piece at a Sunday-school concert. She said she wasn't sure how to begin but she sounded so assured that this must have been a lie. As she told him he was aware of how rehearsed it sounded and yet he believed her when she said that she had never spoken of such things before.

'One of the problems I have with my life, in judging what I've done, is how much I am responsible for it. If there's a God – and there is, for me there is, there must be – why has He let me go on living? Why has He let me do what I've done?

'Oh, I know we've all got free will. I've heard that before. I don't mean none of that. I mean that whatever I've done I've done with His knowing, with His blessing almost you could say. I've felt a kind of approval. All my life I've had a feeling of being under His gaze and of sharing something of His power. He has lent me something of His power at certain times and not when I wanted it but when He wanted to give it to me.'

As she warmed to her tale her voice was no longer soft and tentative but flatter, flippant. She seemed almost to be gossiping and the rocks on which they sat a garden wall, a washing-line and she a nosy neighbour telling another all she knew about So-and-so. Not that she took notice of Devlin. She seemed as indifferent to him as she did to the wind, keener now, forcing him to bring up his knees and hold the lapels of his jacket together for warmth. She was lost to him, her head full of her own words, her own noise.

'I lived in a house called the House of Content. A lovely house, close to the city but facing a park and in grounds of its own. There were bigger houses nearby but somehow the House of Content overshadowed them. You noticed it more. It was right next to the park so people remembered. My grandfather had it built. He was a chemist, a pharmacist. He started from nothing, got one shop and then another and built up a chain of them around the North before diversifying into property. He owned whole streets in Radcliffe Park. He ended up a wealthy man but he only had one child, a daughter, name of Miriam, and Miriam was my mother. Miriam was a problem to her father. He'd come from nowhere and now he had all that the North could give him: position, money, a little respect. The only person he had to hand it on to was her. My mother was not a well woman. She'd never been well. Born sickly and the death of her own mother. She'd had polio as a child and had been forever weakened by it. She was paralysed, her left leg. She wore a calliper. Illness was a continual state with her. She was bed-ridden by the end of her life and that was a short one. Well and whole, she'd have had any man with her being so wealthy.

'She could have had the best but who amongst the best wants a cripple for a wife, even a rich one. Being Catholic made it worse. Few amongst the best were Catholic in that city and at that time. Now, Grandfather was a caring man. He felt his heart each day, examined his lungs often. He was a medical man after all. He knew he was badly. He didn't want his poor Miriam left alone. He'd have raffled her in the Exchange if he could but he'd no need. My father came along. How he'd heard of her, how he'd introduced himself, I don't know. I supposed he battened on to her like all the other viruses that she was prey to. He wasn't rich but he had looks, he had charm, he was willing and he was there. So Grandfather said: "Here you are, have her, love her, look after her, marry her." I suppose some bargain was struck between them, some price agreed, and poor Miriam none the wiser, just not believing her

104

luck that a man with my father's looks and airs was happy to be with her. Grandfather died and left everything to my father. I suppose that was the price.

'Mother was happy. She bloomed for a while, she said. And who knows, he might have loved her then or at least been kind, attentive: they had me, after all. I was the only child to come to full term and still living. There were miscarriages before and after me. Each miscarriage brought her down and every illness going the rounds dropped by on her. I suppose with all that she didn't welcome his advances but he still kept plugging away at her. I suppose the doctor might have warned him off, said it could be dangerous, but he was a very sensual man was my father. If there was a hole in a wall he'd put his prick in it. You don't mind my language, do you?'

Devlin shook his head and said he didn't mind.

'That's good. There's more to come and worse things I've yet to say. If you want me to stop, then I'll stop. Shall I stop?'

'No, don't stop.' What else could he have said? But he could have said it less eagerly. Later she would accuse him of having made her talk and he would feel that listening to her story had made him an accomplice, vaguely responsible for what she'd done.

'It's not easy to tell your life-story. Bits of it you miss out or skim over. Sometimes you change it to fit some point you're making but what I'm saying happened.'

'How do you know so much about your mother, about things before you were born?'

'From her. We were that close. She loved me. She did what she thought best, which included telling me things no little girl should have to hear from her mother. She was genteel, properly brought up, but sometimes pain made her blunt. I suppose she knew that she'd die soon and maybe I'd forget her, so she told me these things so as to make an impression. Or maybe she knew she'd not be here to help and advise me. She hadn't much to give me, so she gave me wisdom. She wanted me to know that for some of us life was all suffering and all sacrifice but that was good because that way brought you God, which was the whole point of living. "But listen," she'd say, "life's hard because it has to be. You

105

have to lie back, Ursula, you have to let happen what happens and God'll reward you. Promise me you'll do that, promise me." So I promised. Imagine having to promise such a thing, but she was my mother. She had no one else but me and I loved her. I had no reason to doubt her and every reason to believe her. Suffer, sit back and suffer and God'll come shining through. That was her advice. The times after she died I repeated those words over and over to myself, those same bloody words. Sit tight. Suffer. God'll come shining through.'

A tear travelled down her cheek. There was no other sign of grief: no sob or shake of shoulders, not even a tremor in her voice. It was not a public display but a private act. If I was not looking at her, he thought, I would never guess she was crying. It was like a secret.

'Poor woman. Things were like that then. For women especially. If things went wrong you didn't moan. You kept your gob shut and thought of higher things. She said to me, she said, "When I'm gone you'll have so much to bear and you'll have to bear it with dignity and for the Lord Our God." She was right there. I had much to bear, much to put up with, so much she couldn't have guessed how much. Or maybe she did. Maybe she was warning me, preparing me for what was to come, telling me to keep quiet so as to protect him. She knew him after all, knew his appetites. Like I said, anything with a hole in it.'

Devlin looked dim – what was she trying to say? – and then he brightened only to darken again. 'Do you mean that your father did . . . that . . . '

'Yes,' she snapped at him, 'I do mean that he did *that* to me. He did *that* to me more than once. He did it often. I was fourteen.'

She glared at him and then sat back sulkily. He looked away, embarrassed by this revelation yet guiltily excited by it. He imagined a child Ursula, a pretty young thing, lying bare-limbed and vulnerable on a bed, a randy father standing over her ready for villainy. The thought was erotic but eerily familiar and then he remembered the Tussaud tableau: the child Ursula, the dead child in her arms, white nightie spattered with blood, raised to reveal equally white and blood-spattered thighs, and the other tableau with Ursula by the bed of the near-naked and, to Devlin, achingly handsome Andreas.

Incest. He should not have been too surprised. The case of Ursula Trench was as redolent with the aroma of sleazy sex as it was stained red with blood but the thrill was to hear it from her own lips.

'Go on,' he told her, trying to keep his voice calm, and uninterested.

She said nothing. She looked out to the sea, dusty green now, at full tide almost, lapping at the foot of the cliff. Grey clouds thickened and gathered overhead. Darkness grained the lilac sky. The wind blew her hair and the fragile light made the outline of her face smoky, as if seen through a veil.

'This is me,' she said finally. 'Me as I am today, after a life not even my mother in her darkest moments could have envisaged for me. When I think of him I feel such hate as would burn him off the face of the earth if he still walked on it. At the time I thought he was God. He could do no wrong in my eyes. He was tall, slim, a beautiful body, no fat on him anywhere, not an ounce. And he was pale, all over, a bluey-white but not a soft body, hard, muscly. He'd have made a lovely crucifix. He had brown hair, coppery. It caught the light and he had a beard that tickled me when he ran his face down my body.'

She lifted her right hand as she spoke, traced the contours of his body in the air and then moved it slowly, absent-mindedly, across her breasts, her belly and down along her thighs and up back to her lap where the left hand met and cupped it again.

'He said he missed my mother. Perhaps he did. I was very like her in my looks. He never went all the way. He petted me mostly or made me sit on his lap and rubbed his thing against me. Too big for a little girl, he said to me, though if I'd said yes he'd have done it. He used to rub it between my legs. I knew it was wrong but I loved to be held. It was his wanting it to be private that worried me. "Tell no one," he'd whisper. I had no one to tell. That's it, that's the thing about it. If your parents abuse you, beat you or treat you as he treated me, who do you go to? Your world gets so small. There's no one on your side and nowhere you can go and somehow, although you've not welcomed it, it seems more your sin than his so you think even God has turned away from you. So what do you do? You suffer. You sit tight. You hope God'll come shining through.'

'Your mother's advice is not bad advice.' Devlin felt that the priest in him should defend God's rôle in all this. 'In certain circumstances, in many, it is a way of dealing with a problem and of attaining grace. But perhaps not this one. Was there no one you could tell?'

'No one. I felt the criminal because I let it happen. I let him do it. I liked being held. I did like that. The rest was the price I paid for being held. He'd not have held me otherwise. He wasn't a holding man. He could have been worse. I've heard of worse cases than mine. I've met with, lived with, shared cells with women who could tell you of worse. I've heard of such cruelty that I've looked back and I've thanked him in my mind for being as nice about it as he was. He was gentle about it. And you have to consider the time. If sex is dirty now it was dirtier then and nice girls could always say "no" and once that word was said no man would go further. If a man didn't listen, if a girl said "no" and he still went on, it was because she didn't really mean it in her heart. There were no rapes then, no preying on innocence or weakness, only girls who didn't say "no".'

'So you were the one who felt guilty?'

She nodded. 'You understand, don't you? I was right to choose you. All my life people have said, "Tell me, tell me," and some of them were good and wanted to help but most wanted to hear what dirt there was so as to fling it back at me. I've chosen right in you, Father, and it feels right to tell you.'

Devlin, flattered, glowed.

'Yes, I felt guilty but you grow used to it. Every night for two years there was just him and me in that house. There was a cook who came in the day and a girl who cleaned, a man for the garden, but at night there was just him and me. We never shared a bed. He visited me and I waited for him until it was a habit, like brushing your hair or going to the toilet before you go to bed. In the day there was nothing. You'd not have guessed. Then one night he didn't come. And the next and the next after that until it seemed he was never going to come again and, of course, because we'd never talked about it, to ask him why was something I just could not do. The truth is I had come to desire him and to feel such a desire as that is the cruellest thing I've ever had to bear and I've borne so much. He had no right to make me feel like that. That was his crime, his biggest one. I'll not forgive him for that.

'And so I waited and the thought that he had stopped was a relief but an agony, too. And when he didn't come to me I went to him . . . I went to his room, thick with the smell of cigars it was. He was awake and in his pyjamas and I said, do it. I said, do it all the way and he did and there was nothing that he didn't do, not a part of me not kissed, not stroked and petted and licked. The works. There was no pain but there was a lot of blood, more than you'd think possible, and we'd done so much moving and twisting it had smeared all the sheets like a raspberry ripple.'

'You say it with' – Devlin searched for a diplomatic adjective that would describe the glow on her face and the warmth in her voice as she spoke – 'pride,' he said limply at last.

'And why not?' she turned on him. 'It was one of the few pleasant things that ever happened to me.'

'Incest? How could you possibly find that pleasant?'

'I thought you understood. I thought you'd not judge.'

'Well, yes, I know but . . . I'm sorry. I'll try not to.'

'Anyway, I cleaned the sheets myself, sponged down the mattress and hung the wet sheets to dry in the garden. We had a girl come in to do our laundry but we couldn't have let her see this particular dirty linen now, could we? Funny, there I was, washing away bloodstains and moving about the garden in the still of the night – all to cover up a crime – and not long after I'd be doing the same again. But that's all to come. I went back to my own room, not happy or content, just numb in a glad kind of way. I sat at my mirror and I just stared. Come morning, breakfast, things were as ever they had been but different. He ate, I ate, he read the paper and I sat there saying nothing. He finished eating and folded the paper and then he said dead casual: "I'm getting married. What do you think to that?" I didn't let on what I thought. I just said, "To who?" and he said, "To Norah," and I said, "Norah who?" and he said, "Norah Matchett," and I said, "Oh," and went on eating my toast.'

'Norah? She was your mother's nurse.'

'Norah was never a nurse, never a proper nurse, a glorified skivvy more like. If puffing up the odd pillow and buffing up your nail-varnish while you sit by a sick-bed like a vulture sharpening its claws is being a nurse, then Norah was a nurse but I'd have different names for what she was and none of them nice. She'd left the house when my mother died. I'd not thought of her since and I'd had no occasion to. Now here was her name again and he was going to bring her back, he was going to marry her, just like that. But it wasn't just like that. Things never are. At first I thought it was noble of him. I thought he was thinking of me. We'd gone too far together, been too close and marriage was an escape for him and a way of protecting me. It was a sacrifice, or so I thought.

'I thought wrong but not for long. The moment I saw them together, not a few days later, I knew there was nothing rushed about it. It'd all been planned. You could tell by their eyes and the way they stood together. Thinking back, I realised they'd always been lovers. Norah had left only so as to put a respectable gap between the death of one wife and the taking of another and for him all I'd been was a stopgap, a hole to plug while she was away. He was an evil man. Of course she hated me. Perhaps she knew what had happened between my father and me, perhaps she guessed. She was the jealous sort and the kind who look for the dirt in others because they're so full of it themselves. She soon settled into my mother's place. She was more comfortable there than my poor mother ever was. She became pregnant soon after. An ugly child she had, made uglier by her spoiling him. She made him pampered and snotty and foul and even the way she spoiled him was an attack on me. She never let up attacking me or pushing me out into the cold. She never wasted an opportunity to disparage me or my mother's memory and he was so disloyal, sided with her, withdrew his love from me absolutely. That was the worst. Worse than Norah's sniping ways was him deserting me. It was like one moment I was drowning in too much love, waves of it going over my head and me going under, floundering and desperate, and the next moment nothing. I was standing in a desert, alone and with nothing. What was I to do? Sit tight? Suffer? Well, I tried for as long as I could. I did, really.

'Norah became pregnant again. She'd dropped her first

110

child like a stone but she was having a hard time with the next. She screamed and moaned from the moment of conception onwards and she had her jealousy to contend with. Her sister. She came to visit and stayed to keep Norah company and help out. Anna was more a hindrance than a help. My father started in on Anna and Norah knew it but couldn't prove a thing. My father was a weak man, easily trapped by what's between a woman's legs, but it took a clever woman to keep him there. My mother had been rich but she'd not been clever. Norah was a bitch but she wasn't clever, not really. Anna was. She must have been. How, I never saw or understood. Sex? Maybe she had a gift for it. Whenever she was in a room with a person she could signal it with her eyes and her conversation was like a secret code. Norah hated to be touched and so he turned to the sister – or tried to. Norah was too sharp-eyed. The three of them played a game of watch and wait. I was forgotten and I formed my plan.'

The tide had reached the rocks below. A seabird cried.

'What is it?' Devlin asked.

She shivered.

'Are you cold? Should we go in?'

'Don't you want to hear?'

'Yes. I just thought you were cold.'

'I stopped because I didn't know if you were ready to hear what I've to say.'

'I'm ready.'

'Are you ready to believe?'

'If it's the truth, then of course I'll believe you.'

'You'll not think bad of me either way, will you? You'll remember that I trusted you enough to tell you, whether you believe me or not?'

'I'll remember.'

'And you'll not think bad of me?'

'I'll not think bad.'

The sun was lost in a grey swath of cloud and there appeared, hazily visible, a thin slice of leprous moon.

'I was in the garden when I formed my plan. I had the child in my arms. It was morning and sunny. I was thinking of my mother and of Norah. Out of nothing but spite, I pinched the child. On the thigh I pinched him hard, dead hard, as hard as I could. He started to cry, to screech, and I yelled at him to shut up. I yelled: "I wish you were dead, you little bastard." I must have yelled so hard that it shocked him out of crying and he just whimpered instead. I'd wished him dead and I just suddenly thought: Why not? It seemed simple enough to get rid of him and it would give me such pleasure. I deserved a bit of pleasure. I had it coming to me; I was owed. He slept in Anna's room. Norah said she kept him awake. For a baby he was a light sleeper and Norah had taken to moaning in her sleep and crying out whenever the baby inside kicked her.

'That night I felt like a sleepwalker, I was awake, though, aware of just what I was doing. It was no fit of madness. I've never had one of those. I've always known just exactly what I was doing. I got out of bed. I crept out of my room. I slept at the top of the house, looking over the garden. Father, Norah, Anna and the child slept on the floor below. I went down the stairs. The floorboards creaked. I can hear them still. So loud, so very loud. But I wasn't afraid. I was calm, dead calm. Noise wasn't really a problem. Only the child slept lightly. No matter if he wakes, he'll sleep again soon enough and deeply this time. I crept into Anna's room. There she was, snoring away, a common woman, with a hair-net over her lovely hair to keep it in place. I thought: Sleep on, sleep on. You'll get the blame for this if anyone does and I was right in that. They were to point the finger at her more than at the rest of us because the child had been in her room. It wasn't until I killed Andreas years later that her name was fully cleared. I had no particular grudge against her. She died not long since. Poor Anna. Anna never heard me that night, her breathing never altered once.

'I went over to the cot. He slept in a cot although he was too big for it. I lowered the sides. He woke and was silent for a moment then he began to whine. I shushed him. I was so gentle. He looked up and smiled. He liked me, you see. Why, God knows. He called me "Silla", couldn't say "Ursula". Drove Norah mad the way he fawned on me for no real reason.

'I lifted him up. He was all warm from the sheets. I carried him down the stairs, shushing him all the time and gurgling, loving it all, rubbing his face against the crook of my arm. "Silla, Silla," I could hear him saying. I went to the dining-room. I couldn't go through the back door or the front door. They had big heavy bolts and made too much noise. The dining-room had sash windows. They opened easily once the catch was off. I placed the child on a chair and opened the window, took him up again and climbed out of the window and into the garden. No moon – or if there was it was hidden behind a cloud. A large garden we had, very green. There were trees galore and a long lawn, very wide, which ended in a line of shrubs and smaller trees and then another, smaller lawn. At the bottom there was an old toilet, an outside privy. There was a compost-heap nearby.

'Then the moon I thought wasn't there suddenly appeared. It shone down so bright, like daylight it was. The child screwed up its face, made half-struggling movements in my arms. I found the cheesewire I'd hidden that afternoon under a brick by the wheelbarrow. See how planned all this was, how I'd thought of everything? Then I wrapped the cheesewire round its neck, quickly, tightly. It didn't struggle much. It seemed stunned. Only a trickle of blood, a neat red band round its neck like a ribbon. I had expected more blood.'

The sea, at its full height, slapped relentlessly against the face of cliff with a dullish roar and a shower of fine spray. The sun had gone for good and the light of the black-spotted moon silvered the dark. Devlin shifted uneasily in his seat. Ursula moved not at all.

'Strange. You said there wasn't much blood. I'd have thought otherwise.'

'Expert, are you? Know all about it, do you? Anyway, there's stranger yet. When the child was found next morning it had been stabbed seventeen times. I had cut its throat with a cheesewire and left it lying on the grass like a sacrifice. They found it in the privy in age-old piss and shit. Seventeen stab wounds. Seventeen.'

'But how?'

'I know how but you'd not believe.'

'I would.'

'Would you? Maybe you would. I killed the child just as I said. I wrapped the cheesewire round its neck and I pulled. Perhaps I snapped his neckbone. Perhaps there was a snap. I didn't hear. I left the child neatly on the grass. I walked away. I had a lot to do. There was blood on my sleeve and the cheesewire to clean.

I turned and looked back and what do you think I saw, Father, who do you think I saw? Guess, Father, go on, you have a guess who I saw.'

'Who?'

'It was God, Father, it was God. I turned and saw His angel, Gabriel. I heard the voice of Gabriel as sweet as a bell and as loud. He said unto me, he said: "You do this for your God." His voice was smooth yet it shook the ground on which I stood. "You do this for your God," he said and he held in his right hand a sword of sharp light and he plunged that sword into the child's body as it lay on the grass before him. Right in it sank, deep into its chest. The child screamed and its limbs trembled and curled around the blade. You see, the child was living yet. I had only left it for dead but there was Gabriel and his sword. He plunged it in again and again until the child was like a tattered and bloody bag.

'And then before me all was transfigured. Gabriel was a pillar of blazing white, a pure dagger of light, arms outstretched like a cross that spans the space between heaven and earth. In his right hand he held the sword and in his left he held the child, no longer child but pure soul, a white shadow, and together they ascended into Heaven. I have seen Heaven, Father, and I am amongst God's chosen. I have sat, I have suffered, I have seen God come shining through.'

She was ecstatic, so enthused by her own tale she almost glowed in the dark, for the moon had disappeared and darkness had fallen. The two of them had become no more than vague shapes, dark outlines to each other.

'No,' Devlin said at last. 'I don't believe you.'

There was a pause in which the smile on Ursula's face slowly died and then in a shocked voice she asked: 'Why don't you believe me, why?'

'God couldn't do that.'

'God couldn't do what? God can do anything. He's God. He can do what he likes.'

'But why that? Why should he kill a child?'

'Babies die all the time.'

'Not killed.'

'Some get killed. Quite a few.'

'They don't get killed by Him and He doesn't send down

one of his heavies to do the job, either. Even you can't believe that. You've made all this up.'

'I said you wouldn't believe me. You said you would. You promised.'

'Well, I don't. How could I? How could anyone? God doesn't stab babies.'

'He did this time.'

'Why? Why should he do that? Tell me why?'

'Because. . . . '

'Yes?'

'Because. . . . '

'Go on.'

'Because. . . . '

She had begun confidently, sure that she could answer him, but words deserted her. They were all in her head, a flood of them, surging and heaving like the sea beneath her, but they evaporated on her tongue, all of them except 'because'. She could find no explanation for God's conduct and, consequently, less and less justification for her own. She was sorry she had spoken. She should have kept her vision to herself where she could cherish it for the truth it enshrined and ignore the lie it really was. It had been a comfort to her, her last comfort. It had served her well. It had kept her going through prison, out of prison and here. It had brought her to this rock, to this young priest, to one last attempt at human union. Everything went in the end. All comforts. Father. Andreas. God. Gone, all gone. Why would God kill for her? It was the one question she had never thought to ask.

'Because,' she said again to no one, not to Devlin, not to God, not even to herself, but to no one, to the air, the wind, the sea.

Mad, she was quite mad. He had known the word and now he knew the condition, could put her name to it, her voice, her words. She was sick. Her lies would make a leper of her in God's eyes as her deed had made her an outcast from society. She had tried to put the blame on God for her actions and had failed. Sick woman, poor soul, he thought.

He held out his hand. 'Come, it's cold and it's dark. They'll be wondering where we are.'

She took his hand, a cold hand. 'Cold hands, warm heart',

a northern saying. Had he a warm heart? She had chosen him believing so. But then he'd turned on her, ruined her tale and left her with nothing. But such a nice face. Perhaps she'd not been left with nothing after all. Perhaps he would give her himself. Perhaps he would save her. Her tale had been wrong; she had misremembered. Memory is weak, it trips and lies, and imagination fills up the gaps so convincingly. He would help her. He would sort out the truth of it all. He would know it. He knows everything. He has God's bright halo about his head. He is a holy man.

They walked back along the fields, the white globed walls and the green glow of the astrodome the only relief in the darkness. Devlin led the way. Ursula, her hand in his, followed silently. There did seem to be something familiar about this walk through the dark, over grass, towards something white, something green, but she could not pierce through the fog the colours made in her head. All she could remember was Gabriel and the sound of wings beating against the air.

III

Prison Saint

I

The Last-Stop Motel

Ursula loved her room. They were rooms, not cells, although there were large white locks and peepholes on the outside of each door. Prisoners were allowed to decorate them as they liked and the bedspreads and sheets were bright and floral. Each room even had its own radiator but it was July and they were off now.

The walls were painted a soft beige. Ursula would have preferred white. White walls were best and a room with no clutter was what she liked. No pictures except a small one of the Sacred Heart in 3-D with glass eyes that followed you round the room and glowed in the dark. There was also a crucifix over her bed which she had made herself in Woodwork out of balsa. Thick circles of brown glue rimmed each joint. By her bed she kept a fish-shaped vase filled with dusty holy water from Lourdes with which she blessed herself when making the sign of the cross.

The sun poured in golden as nicotine. The beige walls glowed in the rich morning light but the shadows made by the rusted bars on the window striped them black. The rooms on the east side caught the early sun. Some mornings it was pleasant, sun in your face, cheery, made you love the Lord; other times you just rolled over and wished yourself out, away or dead. Mornings were like that. Today it was pleasant.

It was not yet half-seven but she was up, her bed made, her room neat, already swept. She sat at the trestle-table in her pink nightie, her bucket by her feet, soap, flannel, face-towel and comb in her lap. She was usually up before the wardens came at seven-thirty. Prisons are never quiet, even this one, and sleep for her had always been a fitful thing.

A missal lay on the trestle-table. Mornings usually found

her deep in the service for that day but she was too excited to concentrate on prayers and, anyway, in her present mood of nervous joy, every breath she took praised God.

Down long corridors, wallpapered with a green and zig-zag pattern, two wardens came banging thick clusters of keys against panelled doors and stopped to watch through peepholes as each prisoner moaned, turned over or sat upright. A prisoner had to make a sign that she was awake. Prisoners who did not do so could expect their doors to burst open and the wardens to rush in and shake them to see if they were dead. Sometimes they were but not often, not in this particular place.

It was less a prison than a secure hall of residence. The atmosphere was easy, open, for all the locks. This was the Last-Stop Motel. You topped yourself here only if you were frightened of leaving it. For some the outside world was a horrific prospect. You dreamed of entering it and panicked when the dream looked like coming true. Still, the outside world was not a prospect for Ursula. She was not going to be released into it. She could view it with equanimity.

At the sound of the key against the lock she looked up.

' 'Morning, Mary,' she said to the door.

' 'Morning, Ursula,' came a voice, 'and it's not Mary, it's Rhona.'

'Oh! 'Morning, Rhona. Where's Mary?'

'Next door on. Mary! Ursula says 'morning.'

Further off, muffled by the walls, the jangle of keys and the clack of leather soles on tiled floors, dulled by the groans of the waking prisoners, came the voice of Mary. Ursula's face shone to hear it.

' 'Morning, Ursula.'

' 'Morning, Mary.'

'Your big day, Ursula.'

'My big day, Mary.'

Ursula relaxed back into her chair smiling but a little sad about the eyes. 'Nice Mary,' she said to herself.

Rhona and Mary, still buttoning up their tunics, met up at the end of the corridor to walk down and repeat the door-banging and peeping.

'Ursula was up and dressed this morning,' said Rhona.

120

'Aw, bless her, was she, the pet? Wouldn't you be, though, if you were her? Today of all days.'

'I know. Bless her. Oh, listen to them all groan. Come on, Alice, wakey-wakey, the sun has got his hat on, rise and shine.'

'I've never got used to the noise in this job. I'm sure chicken farmers have quieter mornings. Come on, girls, up and at 'em.'

'I know. Well, I live on a main road as you well know. We've them juggernauts up and down all day and her next door uses her washing machine at some very odd hours but it's peace compared to this, it is really. It's seven-thirty! Face the world! Up you get!'

'The end of a shift my head's splitting that much it's only my hair as keeps it together. Get up, Gwen. Do you hear me? I said, get up. Lazy sow.'

'Well, Mary, you always have been a martyr to your ears. Hallo again, Ursula.'

'Well, the doctor has said he's not met up with more sensitive drums. Hallo again, Ursula. He wondered if I had a vitamin deficiency but I'm a great one for carrots so that can't be it.'

Back at the top of the corridor they stood guard as the prisoners emerged out of their rooms to form a sleepy crocodile and file lazily past them to the washroom.

' 'Morning, Linda, Tracee. Oh, cheer up, Tracee, face like a wet week, I'm not kidding. 'Morning, Kris, Nicky, Gwen. You did manage to get up then, Gwen? Marvellous what you can do with a bit of effort. Hiya, Carol, Lillian, Pamela. 'Morning, Urs, up bright and early, we noticed; but, then, it's your big day, isn't it? Come on, girls, hurry on down.'

She did not think as she washed her face and hands, combed out the knots in her hair, rejoined the crocodile to the dining-area, picked up her fried breakfast and Krispies, said Grace and chatted with her friends: This is the last time I will do *this* and *this* in *this* way and in *this* place. She tried to bear in mind that her future within the convent would not be a departure from prison life but a joyful continuation of it. Life in prison was a perfect preparation for life in a convent. There were so many similarities, not least in the way both divided up

121

the day and made each one the same as the last. She liked to see time disciplined. Both nun and prisoner led sequestered lives. The quality of a prisoner's life was determined by favours and penalties, the nun's in terms of grace and falls from grace. Both lives involved renunciation: society renounced the prisoner and the nun renounced society. She liked to look for similarities. It made her happy when it seemed as if her past life and her future seemed set to rhyme or even half-rhyme. She loved the way it fell together in her head; the outside world had made her a murderess and prison had made her a nun. Would the convent make of her a saint?

Pride! Pride and Vanity! Kick that thought down.

Prison had not made a nun of her. She wasn't one yet. Remember that, Ursula. She had much to do, much to prove, but she would do it. She would exchange these prison walls for the walls of the convent – white walls they had there, she had seen a photograph – and she would prove herself worthy of joining them. She would impress God with her piety, her obedience and fidelity, and the nuns would marvel at her and make her a missionary, send her to the Congo where the real nuns go. Little black children would cluster round her, old women, too, and mothers would hold up their babies for her to bless them. Her sins would not be reflected in their dark faces and after her death she would let fall a shower of roses, white roses. They would fall from Heaven on to a mustard-yellow veld and a turquoise Congo.

Pride! Pride and Vanity! Kick that thought down.

Oh well, the Lord would forgive her this once. It was the excitement. The Lord was good and understood the giddy antics of a soul so deep in love with Him.

The love showed in her face, bright with a smile as she bent over her bowl and spooned the Krispies into her mouth. She looked up at Warden Mary and Warden Rhona over by the hatch. A smile for everyone had Ursula Trench, a smile that suggested a calm few prisoners at any time possessed. But, then, Ursula was always pleasant, never a problem and deserved release no matter what she'd done so long ago and who cared, who remembered?

Quite a few remembered.

CHILD MURDERESS BECOMES NUN
Slayer Takes Veil

She wasn't in prison for child murder, she said, when a prisoner had shown her the papers.

'Only because they didn't get you the first time. You're not denying you killed that baby.'

'I'm denying nothing.'

Although she did not deny the dead, she tried hard not to think of them. When she did, she liked to imagine them in other than human form. She had read how bodies rot, deliquesce, sink into the soil. The bodies of her parents, of Norah and the child, Andreas, even Anna Matchett's, had long ago disintegrated into the earth. They had become leaves, flowers, fruit, no, they had become roses, white roses. Maybe they all grew on the same bush. That would be nice for them. It did her good to think of them in this way, pretending that she had taken their ruined lives – ruined by her – and given them back to nature, done them a service almost. It made living after them easier for her. It helped disperse guilt. She had enough of that, more would not be fruitful to her development. She had found peace, and finding peace always involves a little dishonesty. She could live with that.

At nine Rhona tapped her on the shoulder. It was time to say goodbye to everyone. ' 'Bye bye, girls,' she shouted and there were tears to see her go from some of them but one or two stood aloof. Even now some people found it hard to forgive and forget. She smiled at the back of a woman who had turned away. The smile said that God was good because He forgives and Ursula could not expect anyone to be as good as God in that respect.

She was told that the Governor wanted a word. All departing prisoners had a word from her, nice woman. They were all nice at the Last-Stop Motel.

The Governor sat up when Ursula was brought before her, leaning across the desk to shake hands with her. Sad-looking woman, thought Ursula. Drab, elongated face she had, with drooping features, as if you were seeing it on the back of a teaspoon. She introduced Ursula to a horsy-looking nun.

123

Sister Michael, she said, had gone to great trouble to get here. As Ursula should well know, nuns of Sister Michael's order were not great ones for consorting with the world but she had done so nevertheless in order to accompany Ursula to her new home.

'The convent will be your new home now, Ursula. It was what you wished?'

Ursula said it was, truly, and praised God for letting it be so. The Governor shook her hand again and, nice touch, asked Ursula to say the odd prayer for her. Ursula said that there would be prayers a-plenty for her and for her wardens and for all the poor souls in their charge.

'I was one of them for long enough, after all.'

As she turned to go, she saw the Governor's coat hanging from the back of the door, a cocoa-coloured mink. She reached out automatically, then froze, but the Governor nodded her permission and Ursula stroked the rich pile of fur so warm and smooth it almost purred.

II

Prison Saint

She had restored the statue of Saint Beatrice in the prison chapel after a violent prisoner had chiselled its nipple off. 'Poor Beattie,' Ursula had said and had passed her hand over the saint's scarred and naked breast. The next day the nipple had magically re-formed.

This was not the first nor was it to be the last of her miracles. She cured a cellmate's athlete's foot simply by kissing it and then confused everyone further still by attacking the same girl in the dinner-queue a month or so later. She had grabbed the girl by the ear and thrown a bowl of minestrone in her face. The attack seemed motiveless and out of character: the girl had been a friend and Ursula had long lost her reputation for violence. She was dragged off for two days' solitary. She had not protested but had said that she would use the time alone to get to know God a little better. ('Rather God than me,' someone had muttered.) The girl, on washing the soup from her hair, then announced that she had been suddenly freed from the migraine she had suffered constantly all that week. To prove it, the girl shook her head like a frisky horse and asked to be lifted up to the ceiling so that she could look without wincing directly into the fluorescent lighting.

A circle of the more religious prisoners petitioned for Ursula's release from solitary but the request was denied. The same circle refused to eat their evening meal and clanged their cutlery against their empty plates until the plates and cutlery were removed from them, after which they mumbled prayers instead.

There were other, smaller miracles or, rather, gracious coincidences: letters long expected suddenly arrived, a warden's mother received a remission from cancer of the neck,

125

a prisoner with an allergy to fish ate ten fishfingers in one evening without getting a single rash, and a white rose was found growing in a dark corner of the prison courtyard.

The miracles took place in Stockton Quays. It was not an open prison exactly, more slightly ajar. Its governor was a Miss MacGregor, a lady who believed that women were intended to be ornaments of the earth and who now found herself in charge of a prisonful of Toby-jugs.

Fastidious, cold-hearted and naturally bald, she wore a heavy bouffant wig, nylon-coated and rinsed a blue so bright it touched azure. The wig sat awkwardly on her head like an outsized cap and wobbled when she spoke.

Miss MacGregor disliked her job and disliked her prison, walking its cold corridors only occasionally and in the company of two wardens. She kept to her office which was always subtropically warm from the constant heat of a two-bar electric fire in front of which sat a shivering terrier by the name of Muff.

Muff was Miss MacGregor's one bright love, the breath of her nostrils, her mavourneen. It was the supposed perk of only the most trusted prisoners to take little Muff for 'wetties'. 'Wetties' meant holding the dog over the toilet-bowl until it decided to piss in it. A prisoner was not allowed to flush the toilet until Miss MacGregor had first inspected its contents and thereby judged the state of little Muff's health. Miss MacGregor's heart and mind were all for Muff so there was little left over for those in her charge. The wardens she treated as servants. For the prisoners she felt the same mix of distaste and fear she felt for the worms for which she so scrupulously studied little Muff's stools.

She kept to her office, a treasured sanctum where she could relax, unpeel her hair and play Friends with little Muff, but her control of the prison was unassailable. She knew everything that happened. She relied upon her wardens who, in turn, relied upon a band of prisoners who snitched for favours. She created a 'bribery' allowance that was substantial enough to keep the wardens and their narks sweet and herself almost omnisciently informed. Word never failed to reach Miss MacGregor of Ursula's miracles but, while her informants were divided on the subject, Miss MacGregor viewed Ursula as the English must once have viewed Joan of Arc.

'A prisoner who is able to gather around herself a coterie of admirers is a potential cause for chaos. Idolatry is always harmful. It disrupts.'

'It's the miracles are doing it, Ma'am.'

Miss MacGregor was unconvinced. 'Miracles? A scabby foot and a phantom headache?'

'There was the statue, Ma'am. It did grow a tit, begging your pardon, Ma'am.'

Miss MacGregor's pardon was not to be begged. She abhorred such words. If reference needed to be made to such parts the word 'bosom' would suffice but added that she herself always preferred to call it 'the unpressed bone'.

The miracles divided the prisoners but division was to be expected: miracles excite suspicion more than faith. Ursula's crimes as well as her personal manner had made her unpopular. The miracles helped to change that. There had now grown about her a small but vocal clique – a fan club almost – who began to credit every beneficent happening to her saintly influence.

She cultivated the fan club, learned to widen its circle. Admiration was something she felt she deserved, something she had earned. She had sinned, she had been punished, she had done her penance and now she expected to be forgiven. The widening circle of devotees suggested to her that, at last, the icy and unrelenting grudge the world had held against her was finally thawing. When asked, she would lead them in prayer or intercede between them and God, sighing a little or tutting and saying, 'You don't think God'll listen to *me*, do you?' She knew the answer but she liked to hear them say it.

'You're getting quite a reputation as prison saint, Ursula love,' said Vera, a warden and special friend. When Vera was on lates she'd open up Ursula's cell and spend some time there. 'It doesn't impress me one bit, as you well know. It's nice to see you so popular but I've known you too long and too well to be taken in by it. I've known you since you came out of C1. Right mess you were in then. I knew you in Bromsworth when that girl died. Remember?'

'I remember.' Ursula laughed and carried on brushing Vera's hair.

'In fact I was with you the night all this holy business started. Am I right or am I right?'

'You're right, Vera, dead right. You always are.'

'Not that it's not done you good because it has but if it's parole you're after you don't need none of this Holy Joanna stuff.'

'I know I'll get parole. I'm long due it.'

'I'll miss you when you finally go, Ursula love.'

'And I'll miss you, Vera pet.'

'And what'll you do? What *can* you do, let's face it?'

'I shall be a nun, Vera pet. I shall take the veil.'

'You'll take the bloody biscuit. They'll not have that. Who'd have you?'

'I have set things in motion, Vera pet, and I have faith. I have faith like nobody's business.' Ursula lay down the brush and kissed her on the cheek. 'You look lovely now, all sleek, like a cat.'

'They tell me, Trench,' said Miss MacGregor in an insane and unctuous croon sung less to Ursula than to soothe little Muff shivering in front of the two-bar fire, 'that you want to join an order of some kind.'

'The Convent of the Sweet Wounds of Mother Mary.' Ursula said it with pride and pleasure, the name honey in her mouth. 'I once corresponded with its founder.'

'The newspaper millionaire who met up with the Mother of God, yes. Your conversion was as sudden as his, if less flamboyant.'

'I am not a convert,' Ursula explained slowly as if to an idiot child. 'I have always been with God. I lost Him for a while but He never lost me.'

'So, if not a conversion, what shall I call this sudden change of heart?'

'My Vision,' Ursula said simply.

'Mm, oh dear, Vision. Well, previous to this mystical event, your record was a poor one. Recalcitrant. Withdrawn. Unruly. Aggressive.' She summarised the contents of a well-packed and dusty manila folder. 'At Holloway it was worse. All that time in solitary and a little matter of a warden's death.'

'That was an accident!' Ursula snapped and instantly regretted it. Be calm, calm. Nuns speak calmly. They do not raise their voices. 'It was an accident,' she said again, her voice as smooth and slow as sand running through an hour-glass.

'Did I say otherwise?' asked Miss MacGregor, glad to see Ursula's composure finally, if only momentarily, unsettled. The prisoner's angelic complacency seemed to her quite grotesque. 'There is, too, the time spent in C1.'

'Does that count against me?'

'Let's say it doesn't count in your favour. Still, you are overdue parole. That, of course, is nobody's fault but your own. We haven't kept you here either for decoration or for the love of it. And since your *conversion*. . . . ' Miss MacGregor savoured the word, using it deliberately to rile, even pausing so that Ursula could protest. Ursula said nothing and kept her gaze steady. 'Since then, you've made every effort to please. Quite a contrast. Compliment follows compliment in every report. You would blush to read it, Trench, truly. And look, what's this? O-level Latin, grade C. What a clever girl! O-level Greek, grade F. Oh dear.'

'I'm resitting that one.'

'Very wise. O-level Scripture, grade B. Well done. And the A-level Scripture?'

'It's a bit harder but with God's help I shall get through it.'

'I wouldn't worry. It's not one of life's essential qualifications. Well, parole's a certainty, you know that. As for this becoming-a-nun business. . . . '

'Father Ashbery is helping me there. He's my link with the Convent of the Sweet Wounds of Mother Mary. I have a place there. The founder mentioned me in his will.'

'How nice for you. Let's hope that you spend the remaining time well.'

I shall spend my time doing good upon the earth, thought Ursula, and after my death I shall let fall a shower of roses.

'By "well" ' Miss MacGregor added, 'I mean that I want you to spend the time quietly. You understand what I mean by that?'

Ursula nodded. There would be no more miracles. Ah well,

never mind. She could live off her reputation for a while and soon she would be moved to another prison. The miracles had served their purpose. She would ask God to go easy on them. She moved in her seat, just about to cross her legs, but stopped herself in time. Nuns do not sit cross-legged.

Little Muff had moved from the two-bar fire and had begun to paw the carpet at Ursula's feet. Miss MacGregor looked down fondly and then, narrowing her eyes, over at Ursula. She wondered if Trench could be trusted and then decided that if Trench had ideas about sainthood she wasn't likely to do little Muff any harm.

'Trench, would you take little Muff for "wetties"?'

III

Amongst the Lost Things

She'd been for the rope and deserved to hang if anyone did but somehow the noose never found its way round the neck of Ursula Trench. When the sentence of death was repealed and one of life imprisonment given instead, no one was happy. Newspapers let out howls of disgust on their readers' behalf, a question was asked in the House, the Home Secretary was booed and later that week, while he was visiting a Northern town to open an extension to a railway yard, eggs were thrown at him and at his car. In Brackley Street a bonfire was built and an effigy of Ursula Trench was burned on it to the delight of the people of Radcliffe Park.

Ursula judged herself no less harshly than the judge, the jury and the people of Radcliffe Park: she should have hanged. Hanging would have been a kindness.

From the time of Andreas's murder and throughout the trial, her life had acquired a meaning precisely because she could see an end to it. There had been in her head a vision of a road that ran straight and true to a gallows and a noose. From the moment of reprieve, the gallows disappeared and the road that had run straight and true grew narrow and twisted. She saw it peter away from her, dissolve into a desert, some flat, blank and uneventful place where she would be condemned to wander, clueless.

To be denied the noose did not seem like clemency but its opposite, for she had developed her own mathematics of mercy. She had killed Andreas in order to hang and, in dying so, she had hoped to pay in kind for the death of her father, mother, of Norah and the child. She had worked it all out and to be allowed to live upset the careful equation she had made.

If she was hungry for punishment she need not have worried. She would receive her fill of it in prison.

She went straight to solitary which was her right as a prisoner. She made no contact with any of the prisoners but heard them often. When she was walked along corridors, a warden on either side of her, she heard them calling her from behind their locked cell doors. When she was exercised in the yard by herself, she'd hear them and see their hands grasping the bars of their windows. At night she would also hear them, way, way into the early hours of morning, always audible, distinct, no matter how great the wind, the rain, the number and the thickness of the walls.

'. . . Oi, Fishface . . .

    . . . fucking whore . . .

    . . . murdering bitch of a cow . . .

. . . wait till we get you . . .

    . . . we're gonna get you . . .

. . . I've got kids of me own . . . somewhere . . .

    . . . you ain't safe . . . enjoy each breath . . .

. . . it might be your last . . .

    . . . her brother it was . . .

    . . . her own pissing, bleeding brother . . .

    . . . poor bleeding baby . . .

    . . . a baby . . . killer . . .

. . . killerkillerkillerkiller . . .

    . . . die, die, die, you bitch, die . . .

. . . If you wake up one morning . . .

    . . . bitch . . .

. . . and you find your throat cut . . .

. . . killer . . .

. . . well, it were me what did it.'

Her wardens were no more sympathetic than the prisoners, but did their best to persuade her. They could not force her out of solitary. For Ursula to be so constantly alone was a strain on prison resources. It wasn't good for her health, either. So what if she was frightened? Hiding only postponed the problem. She'd have to face people some time. It was no good putting it off. What was she going to do? Stay in solitary for life? They cajoled and threatened her until, finally, on the first anniversary of her sentence, she consented to come out.

A woman attacked her with a broom and she was shunned by every prisoner. She ate alone, took her bath alone, had her own cell for safety's sake. Her hands shook. She could hardly swallow her food for fear and didn't know where to look because every eye she met telegraphed small, precise messages of hate. She walked with her back to the wall and heard 'slut', 'child-killer', 'murdering bitch' whispered softly close by. The first weeks were not so bad, though, not as bad as she'd imagined. She was still alive.

Then, at dinner, six women joined her at her table. She flinched but they ignored her. They ate and chatted amongst themselves. Finishing, they rose to go and one of them, a thin girl with ringlets, a large jaw and a vacant look, said to her, 'Fancy a game of cards, Ursula?' and smiled at her. The others walked off and seemed not to mind. The girl took her hand and said: 'It *is* Ursula, isn't it? My name's Claudette, after the film star Claudette Colbert. Are you named after anybody?'

Ursula said she didn't know. The whole hall was silent as if curious about her reply and everyone, prisoners and wardens alike, watched as Claudette and Ursula walked across to the card-table swinging hands.

'You sit down right here, Ursula.' Claudette patted the chair next to her. 'We'll play Happy Families.'

Ursula looked at her suspiciously. Was she making a joke, getting a dig in? Ursula couldn't be sure. The girl seemed sincere enough. She remembered how lonely she was and hoped the girl could be trusted.

'All right,' said Ursula.

'Now, are you sure? I can always find someone else to play if you don't want. I just thought you'd like some company.'

'I'm sure . . . Claudette.'

'Now, that's more like it.'

'It's a lovely name.'

'Why, thank you very much. I think Ursula's a *reely* pretty name. Memorable, you know what I mean?'

Claudette smiled and Ursula smiled back, two real smiles, and Ursula fell in love. Love bubbled up and her smile felt like it would stick there for ever and she would be ever joyful in this sweet girl's company. They would be friends. Ursula had never had a friend. To think that she would find one here and so easily.

When Claudette stretched out her hand Ursula held hers up to meet it but the girl knocked it away and flew for her throat. Ursula fell back on to the floor, her chair breaking under the fall, with Claudette on top of her, digging her nails deep into her neck, and she was not alone, the other women had joined her. Screams and a riot broke out as everybody rushed to join in.

Wardens came with sticks to beat away the pack to the tune of sirens. Ursula was dragged free, dress ripped, bite marks on arms, legs, belly and breast, bruises, too, her face a pulp of blood and battered flesh.

Putting Ursula back among the prisoners had been like putting the cat among the pigeons except it was the cat who came off worst. After a stay in hospital, Ursula retreated to solitary once again.

Time, loneliness and her own incessant company chipped at her sanity, but time and loneliness were neither strange nor fearsome to her, and sanity had never been her strongest quality. She survived solitary well, almost had a gift for it. The years spent alone in the House of Content she now saw had been a period of apprenticeship just as, later, she was to see the time spent in prison as a preparation for a life as a nun.

Not that she thought of convents or, indeed, of God. God

had gone the way of her father, her mother, of Norah, the child and Andreas. In her head He was as dead as they: she had killed Him as surely as she had caused the death of those whose names she mumbled to herself as if she were stocktaking. They had all gone from her. They were beyond calling, beyond help or understanding, beyond everything but regret. She was in a dark place, amongst the lost, the forgotten things and she had earned her passage there.

Amongst the lost things, it was easy to forget the real world, the outside world of cold wars, election battles, marriages and sports results. For her they took place elsewhere, in some other universe, even if they could still impinge on her. They were all part of the same river, a river down which she drifted but whose contours and currents she had never understood. She read the papers, heard wardens speak of families, sicknesses, and buses that ran late, but it grew to mean less and less to her: keeping up with the world and its doings once she had been effectively excluded from it was like learning a language she would never speak or the geography of a country that she would never see.

In the early years of her imprisonment she heard that Andreas's mother wished to see her (wished to see her dead). Denied a meeting, Mrs Andreas sent her letters, exhaustive litanies of hate without grammar or full stops to constrict or dam the flood of rage and grief. Ursula read them like love-letters. They proved to her that she did indeed have a past, that once she had moved about the world, had lived and loved, even if she'd never been loved. She couldn't care less about Andreas's mother but was flattered that anyone could hate her that much. She had always wanted to inspire passion.

Anyway, the Andreas his mother remembered and her Andreas were unrelated: they shared a certain deep and fatal handsomeness but that was all. She remembered Andreas well and for longer than she remembered the others. When parents, Norah and the child had dwindled to ghosthood, Andreas stayed vivid. She remembered his face, his body; even his voice stayed true in her mind, and she would finger herself to the memory of him. Eventually images of him would fade and mingle with dimmer, lewder visions of her father, or of the old priest who came each week and whom she always turned away. She imagined all three in turn and then brought together as one, lying on top of her, grinding away between her legs, punishing her as much as pleasuring her. In the vacuum of solitary, however, desire suffocated and masturbation became hard labour. Andreas's face became cloudy as if seen through a veil of smoke. The letters from his mother came to a sudden stop.

Anna Matchett sometimes wrote, said that she'd visit, you know, whenever, but she never did.

What other prisoners would have taken as punishment, Ursula took as refuge, but even solitary had a way of turning treacherous. Without warning the air in her cell would vanish and she would begin to choke for want of it. The blood in her head would beat a deafening tattoo and induce in her a pain so searing it was as if her eye-roots were being slowly cauterised. She'd beg for silence, for air, for an end to it all. The walls would buckle inwards or belly outwards and she would cower under the mattress until they were steady once more. Most often they pressed in on her. She would run to each wall in turn, pushing it back, back, back, a frenzied rush, until she collapsed or screamed out to be released.

'Let me out! Let me out! Let me join the others, please! I can't stand it no more, please!'

The wardens would come. She'd see their eyes through the slot in the door, hear them mumble to each other. She'd tell them what was wrong and they'd say, was that all? If she wanted out she had only to ask.

There was more to it than asking but not much: permission to be had, a paper to sign, no more. Sometimes she'd persist in her demand, convince herself that was what she wanted. She would find herself being marched down long corridors that twisted and had door after door, each with a lock or two or three. As they came nearer, she'd think she could hear the other prisoners, hear them whining, howling, imagined them a mob hungry for her blood, and she would beg to be taken back. She would grow hysterical and the wardens would sigh and turn round. It was a regular occurrence. They called it Ursula's trip.

'You're pissing us off, girl,' one of them warned her. 'One

day we're not going to listen. We're just going to throw you in and walk away. You see if we don't.'

After such trips, solitary became a palace again, a playroom, but never for long. Life would settle. There was nothing to do, nothing she wanted to do. Time stopped, became stone, and so did she, became part of the walls and then grew separate again, grew small and threatened then panic! panic! panic! the walls would press in, the air suddenly vanish, and it would begin again.

She was told that she would be considered for parole in two years' time. She had little chance of getting it, still less if she stayed in solitary, so she came out.

She looked about for Claudette but she wasn't there. Something in her felt disappointment. She was told she was to share a cell. She said she had shared nothing with nobody for years and she was told: 'Tough! You'll have to get used to it.'

Her cellmate was a girl called Esther but everyone called her Sonny. She was a wide woman, still young. She had a mean red face that looked as if it had been boiled and a smirk in the line of her mouth that suggested that the boiling had been fun.

Sonny had said 'Hiya', all friendly like, which was nice of her because she preferred to show her bad side first. Ursula had not replied and had just stared at her defensively, glumly. She was remembering Claudette. She had vowed not to be fooled by apparent friendliness again. So Sonny said, 'Suit yourself, bitch,' and got on doing time.

At night they never spoke and during the day each moved about the cell as if the other did not exist. Ursula was well practised at being invisible, at being thought of no account: the years alone with her father in the House of Content had taught her to do that. Sonny ignored her in exactly the way her father had done but this time Ursula was grateful to be ignored. She had an idea that Sonny's attention could be a terrible thing. Sonny could have trodden her brains into the floor with ease and just to pass the time. It was evident in her manner, her deadened eyes, the muscles on her arms and the way the other prisoners stood aside to let her by.

The tougher prisoners bullied Ursula but only in small ways, such as tripping her up when she was carrying her food on a tray or stealing her cigarettes in front of her face. Other prisoners shunned her or whispered words but really it was all bearable, all quite mild, thanks to Sonny and a misunderstanding. Ursula was protected by Sonny because it was commonly thought that she was Sonny's wife. Sonny had let it be known that she quite fancied 'the little killer', as she called Ursula with something like respect. Ursula had been the last to know.

Closeness between the two of them grew overnight. It was dark and she heard Sonny crying in the bunk above. At first she pretended not to hear. Sonny sobbed on, tiny hiccups of tears, daintier than Ursula would have thought the hefty Sonny capable of. The sobs became more frequent and louder until Ursula could no longer ignore them. It was obvious that Sonny intended her to hear.

'You all right?' she asked, trying to sound casual, but her voice came over all cracked, odd to her own ears. It was the first time she'd spoken to anyone in the dark since she'd been in prison. It seemed so intimate an act that it embarrassed her.

'You got a fag?' Sonny asked her.

Ursula passed a cigarette up.

'You have one, too. Have one with me, why don't you? I got the miseries. I do sometimes. It helps to have company.'

Like an actress being given a new stage direction of which she was unsure, Ursula pushed away her blankets and climbed up to join Sonny.

'It's nice this smoking in the dark, isn't it?' said Sonny, and as the smoke plumed about them, rose up and was lost in the dark of the ceiling, Sonny's head came to rest on Ursula's arm and their hands met in her lap. They passed the night just so; Sonny snoozing softly, happily, and Ursula, brightly awake yet calm, unmoving but her soul fizzing, sweetly aware of Sonny's weight leaning heavily against her.

'Dear Sonny, I could stay this way for ever.'

The years in prison had changed her. Her hair, which she kept long like a girl's, was peppered grey, dry and tough, her face was pitted with shadows and her gait had grown hunched, a walking cower. She was sorry she was not pretty, sorry she was old. She would have liked to have been nice for Sonny but Sonny never minded.

'You're my tart, Urs, and I love you as you are. Sure, I could get some young fluff, some cherry, if I wanted, but I don't.'

'I've never been young,' Ursula complained. She could admit stuff like that to Sonny. 'I'd have liked to have a child.'

'Not many as'd trust you with a kid.'

'I know that, but it would have made amends somehow. I'd have had one but I'd not have kept it. I'd have sacrificed it, given it away to someone else, someone who'd have needed it and loved it. It'd have made up for what wrong I've done, the lives I've lost for folk.'

'I can't see a judge handing out a sentence like that – "Ursula Trench, I sentence you to nine months' pregnancy." You're a silly cunt, Ursula.'

Ursula laughed. You could tell Sonny anything and she made a joke of it. She had the right attitude. She was tough and made light of what was dark.

'Do you not miss having kids?' she asked Sonny, who said no, she wasn't maternal, and a good job, too, one of life's few kindnesses.

Sonny, as a teenager, had had sex with her dad – or he'd had sex with her. He said that, seeing as how she was fat and walked like a fella, she ought to be glad of a bit of dick from her dad because she'd not get it from any other man. Sonny had told on him to a teacher and the dad promised not to do it again and he and Sonny had shook hands in front of a social worker to show everything was all right. It was her mam who'd made her shake hands. She said it was a sin for a daughter to get rid of a dad by telling on him. Men had dicks and they put them wherever. Women had to learn to make do with it. Sonny had made do until her dad came to her with an asbestos glove, the forefinger dipped in battery acid. He said it was revenge for telling on him and that the burning would be like a brand on her, making her his and spoiling her for other men. Sonny had screamed and screamed and her mam had come upstairs to close the bedroom door. If they were going to make such a racket, she said, they could at least turn the wireless up. Aged

139

sixteen, Sonny left home. From then on life had been a matter of thieving and being caught.

'I'm a big girl, so I don't get no bother.'

At night Ursula would explore Sonny's ruined genitals with her tongue. Sonny was neither ungrateful nor unmoved.

'Thank you, Ursula love. The feeling's mostly gone but the need's still there.'

'He burned your clit but not your heart, eh?'

'Almost, though, the bastard, almost.'

'No, the heart, it doesn't burn.'

'Don't it?'

'No. Joan of Arc's didn't burn.'

Sonny lay back, contented. 'She was a saint, though. And so are you, Ursula my love. Do it again.'

They swore to love each other for ever or until Sonny's time was up and, once it was known for sure that Ursula and Sonny were lovers, even the muttering and the name-calling stopped. No one wanted to upset Sonny, no one dared. Sonny was all muscle and her red hair was cropped to a quarter-inch from her skull. Ursula thought her handsome.

She made Sonny's bed, carried her food, cleaned her Doc Martens, cut and filed her nails and soaped her back in the showers. She'd have done anything for Sonny and Sonny had Ursula's name tattooed on the back of her neck. Ursula wanted one, too, on her arm, the name 'Sonny' wreathed about with roses, red roses, but Sonny said that no tart of hers was getting a tattoo.

When Sonny's time was up – thirty-six months for mugging a woman in a council-block lift – they wept. Ursula clung to Sonny's thick shoulders and begged her to come back soon. Sonny said that, knowing her luck, she would, but that she'd visit whenever.

Lips bruised from Sonny's final kisses, she was left alone in the cell. She stood adrift in it. Everything in it was Sonny's. The very bricks smelt of her. Without Sonny she didn't want to go on living. What would become of her without Sonny's love and protection? She could not contemplate it. A desolation she had not known in all her time in prison fell down on her like gravity.

A warden came with another prisoner, a soft-looking drip of a girl.

'You're sharing with her,' the warden said, pointing at Ursula. 'Her name's Trench. Trench, you're sharing with Gloria.'

Ursula turned on the warden. 'No, I'm not! I'm not fucking sharing with any bugger.'

'Trench, you mind your mouth and do as you're told.'

'You mind your own, arsehole. Get out and take that fucking drip with you.'

'Hey! We'll have less of that, Trench, a lot less, do you hear?'

'I hear fuck all. Now get out. Out! Out! Out!'

Ursula set up a chant and with each repetition of the word 'Out!' she turned nastier. Her face was red, puckered and streaked with crying, her lips curled into a sneer and her eyes narrowed into slits. What would Sonny do now? she was thinking. She bent down and ran at the warden, butting her in the stomach and out on to the corridor.

The warden fell back against the railing, face all of a sudden pale blue, arms clutching at her stomach then grabbing at her chest. She teetered against the railing and seemed to be begging for breath. Ursula was, as ever, unmerciful. Her head filled with the beating of wings. She stepped calmly forward. By now prisoners were running to see the fun and the wardens were pushing through to stop it. Gloria was standing behind Ursula giggling nervously. Ursula, fluid and fast as in a dream, pushed the warden again, pushed her hard, very hard. The warden flipped over the railing and fell on to the safety-mesh where she bounced and bounced to the cheers of the prisoners. Her skirt above her waist, she flapped chunky legs and flailed about with her arms, her mouth biting bits out of the air but unable to swallow them. Then she stopped dead and only moved with the bounce of the wire mesh.

'Heart,' whispered someone.

Ursula stayed as she was, arms outstretched. She gazed at her arms like a gunfighter admiring his two favourite pistols. My aim is true, she told herself – half in wonder, half in congratulations – my push is fatal. She brought one of her hands to her face, marvelling at it, then she licked the index finger, made three strokes in the air and then another stroke right through them. She was taken off to solitary looking pleased.

'Does this mean I get the cell all to myself?' asked Gloria.

In solitary Ursula whooped and skipped. She was back home. If she couldn't be with Sonny she would rather be alone.

The little matter of the warden's death meant nothing to her nor could she be blamed for it officially. No malice aforethought could be discerned. The cause of death had been heart-failure. Ursula could not therefore be held strictly responsible but because of it, she was told, she would not be seriously considered for parole even though she had now served ten years of her sentence.

'You couldn't try again, not for another three years,' a warden had told her, 'and if we have anything to do with it you'll not get it then, either.'

'So? I'm happy as I am.'

'Happy, are you? We'll see how happy you are, don't worry.'

One night – morning? – the bulb went in her cell. She banged against the door. A warden came eventually, pulled back the slot in the door and asked what she wanted. Ursula saw a head silhouetted against the wall of the brightly lit corridor.

'My bulb's gone.'

'Has it?'

'It's dark in here.'

'Tough.'

Sod the bitch, she thought. Be like Sonny. Sonny wouldn't have shown she minded. Sonny was tough. Sonny would say, 'Sod the bitch,' and mean it.

What she took for a day passed and, when the warden came again, Ursula reminded her politely that the bulb had gone.

'Has it?' said the warden sweetly.

'I'm all in darkness.'

'Well, that's where you belong,' the warden answered and pulled back the slot.

'Cow!' yelled Ursula, impersonating Sonny.

Who needed light? She knew each crack in the walls, knew where the mattress was, the iron sink-cum-toilet in the floor, the exact centre of the room; knew, too, how the dust formed in swirls on the floor. She passed what she thought was another day – or was it two or was it only half? – playing with the dust, making piles with it, sifting it with her fingers, gathering it in her fist and pouring it down her cheeks, her neck, her chest and belly in imitation of a caress, imagining Sonny's touch, but the dust caught in her throat and choking seemed worse in the dark and she feared for her life. Her eyes stung from lack of light.

'Give me a bulb, you cow!'

'But you tried to eat the last one,' the warden explained sympathetically.

'Lying cow! It went. It just went out.'

' 'S what I put in my report. You've had four bulbs this week. Three you smashed and the fourth you'd have ate if I hadn't stopped you. No more bulbie-wulbies for you till you behave.'

'I never did. What you doing? Why you lying like this? I'll report you.'

'Who to? Our word against yours anyway, Ursie-wursie.'

'Why you doing this?'

'She was a friend of mine, of all of us. We look after our own.'

'Who was?'

'Who do you think, you murdering bitch, or have you lost count?'

'That was an accident.'

'Accident? Was it an acci-wacci-dent, then? Like it was an acci-wacci-dent when you killed that fella and an acci-wacci-dent when you killed that kid? We are careless, aren't we, Ursie-wursie?'

'You can't do this to me.'

'But, Ursie, we *are* doing it. You enjoy your meal?'

'What meal? You've not fed me since — '

'Prisoner enjoyed meal. That's what we'll say if anyone asks, which they won't. You're forgotten here, like lost property gone unclaimed. Byesy-wysey, Ursie-wursie.'

Darkness was all. Darkness was it. Even when her eyes were closed and she was looking inside her head the light was dim. Sometimes it faded altogether.

The dead came. They traipsed through her cell without so much as a glance at her. Norah came and stood awhile with the child in her arms. Her body was swollen with pregnancy and browny-blue with rigor mortis. Her nostrils were shrivelled and her hair hung from her head like an old cloth. The child was a fresher blue, however, and was sleeping happily. He looked sweeter than he had done in life. Blue suited him. Her father passed, too. He also ignored her. Some things, they never change. Only Andreas came close. He came red as a tilestone and freckled black and he held her with hands like paws by the throat. He covered her all over so that he was as close as breathing. He smelt of filth and smoke and wouldn't let her go though she screamed and screamed. She yelled for help but who was to hear? She was in the dark, among the lost things.

How long she was left unattended and in darkness she never found out. A prisoner who'd witnessed her being brought out said that she was black with dirt and stinking, and her hair was matted so bad with blood from the banging of her head they'd had to shave it off.

She remembered only voices and wardens laughing. One of them came towards her with the light behind her so that she looked like a shadow. Ursula, crouched in a corner, cringed as she gazed up and the shadow retreated, the door closed and darkness came like a lover and covered her.

The door opened again but this time there was no light in the corridor, only the sound of the door opening, steps coming towards her. It was the warden, the bad one. She could not see but sensed it was her. Then knew.

'How are you, Ursie-wursie?'

A rattling sound. A match was struck. It flared before her face. After only blackness, unrelieved and without blemish, here was a festival of colour so vivid it seemed to burn her vision clean away, bleaching it totally until there was no blackness, only white.

When she woke she found that she was in a cage, a white wire-meshed cage in a long room with other similar cages, each with a white-sheeted bed. The walls of the long room were also white as were the bars on the frosted-glass windows. It looked as if a snowstorm had settled there. She thought for a moment she was somewhere pure. Heaven? she thought. But

144

would Heaven have cages? When she tried to move she found that she had been bound by the wrists and ankles to the bed-frame. She was in a mental ward, she realised. Good. I can relax now, she thought, and slept deeply.

'Hallo, my name is Theresa.'

A woman in a red smock was sitting on her bed. She was little more than a dwarf, had grey hair that frizzed around a smooth flat face and a mouth that boasted only one tooth, perfectly brown. She had a child's voice and was most genteel. Ursula knew her for a simpleton.

'We've got a big garden and in our house, which is ever so big, we have blue curtains. They are real velvet so you're not to touch them or they'll spoil.'

Ursula slept.

Two women in the cages on either side of her woke her sometimes. They seemed like sisters. They wore the same red smocks and vacant expressions. When she was awake, Ursula followed their conversation like a spectator watching a tennis match, turning her head from side to side as they spoke across her.

Sometimes they spoke to her.

Their voices were flat and their words sounded stilted and over-rehearsed.

'We're your neighbours.'

'I sleep here.'

'And I sleep here.'

'I'd be careful if I were you.'

'Are you telling her to be careful?'

'I'm telling her to be careful.'

'Because things drop from that ceiling.'

'I was telling her.'

'Well, tell her, then.'

'Things drop from that ceiling.'

'I know because I used to sleep in that bed.'

'She used to sleep there.'

'But they moved me.'

'They moved her.'

'Things dropped on me while I was in that bed.'

'Like water.'

'Big drops of it on my head.'

145

'And other things dropped, too.'

'Like . . . bricks.'

'Not a good bed to lie in, is that bed.'

'But it is nice in here, isn't it?'

'Yes,' said Ursula, 'it is,' and slept.

When she woke again the weird sisters had gone. The bed in the cage to her right was empty and in the one on her left was a young girl with clean hair and an intent look. She was as upright as the binds would allow and had both her hands clenched round an imaginary steering-wheel. She made car noises and swerved this way and that, eyes ahead on what seemed a treacherous road and then glancing round behind her to see if she was being chased.

When Ursula woke again in front of her stood a woman in a veil.

'Are you a nun?'

'No, a nurse.'

The nurse was withdrawing a needle from Ursula's arm. Ursula could not see the girl in the next cage but could hear her spluttering into fourth gear.

'Where she going?'

'Who? Celeste? Celeste is going nowhere. She's just out for a quick spin, aren't you, dear?' The nurse swabbed Ursula's arm. 'There, you'll sleep now.'

'But I've already slept.'

'Then, sleep again. You're not missing much.'

Whenever Ursula woke there was always a second or so when the whiteness of the ward suggested she was in Heaven. When she realised she wasn't, the disappointment was only slight because it was enough like Heaven to do.

'Oi, you!'

Ursula woke. The dwarf lady, Theresa, was poking her in the ribs.

'How did you get in here?' Ursula asked.

'They don't lock the cage doors,' answered Celeste. She was sitting up, still, presumably parked. 'They don't need to.' She raised up her arms to show the binds. 'They let Theresa wander about. Been in years, Theresa. Part of the walls, aren't you? Fuck off, you soft bitch, or I'll run you over. Vroom! Vroom!'

Theresa screamed and waddled away at full pelt.

'Your name's Ursula.'

'And your name's Celeste.'

'Well, what a lot we both know.'

'Do you want to be my friend?'

'Will I be one of many?'

'No.'

'All right, then, but I'm not fussed either way.'

Eventually Ursula slept without medication. She asked the nurse if she was mad and was told no, she was just tired. They let her read magazines and she asked for ones about cars so that she had something to talk to Celeste about. They took off her binds and she was able to move about from cage to cage. She stayed mostly with Celeste.

'If you're dead bad, then they send you to C2,' Celeste told her. 'If you're not too bad, then you come here. This is C1. And if you're OK you go back to the other prisoners. It's best to be not too bad.'

C2 was the pits, according to Celeste. 'You don't want to go there. No radiator because you bang your head on it. Only a mattress because you'd do the same if there was a bedstead. No sheets, either, in case you wrap them round your neck. They got it all worked out so you can't hurt yourself but you can be clever. See this.' Celeste showed Ursula a red-rimmed neck. 'I used my cardigan. They took it off me, though. It was a good one, too. From Primark. A green one.'

Celeste seemed to Ursula unlike anyone she had ever met in prison. She was completely uninterested in Ursula. She didn't want to know what she'd done, didn't even want her company but didn't mind it, either. It was the first relationship Ursula had had where she did not expect to gain or lose anything. It was refreshing. Celeste was open, friendly and liked a laugh. When she wasn't driving her bed, she was bright and softly spoken. Ursula could have loved her, felt at times that she did but not like she'd loved Sonny. There was something brittle about the girl, something tense and about to snap. It made Ursula feel protective.

'If I had a daughter,' Ursula told her, 'I'd have liked it if it was you.'

'I've got a mam, thanks.'

Celeste wasn't one for slobber. She liked it best when they

acted just friends, girls together, giggling and chatting in the dark about nothing at all really.

They were friends only a short time. They didn't even get to say goodbye. Celeste began accelerating more and more, foot down so hard on the pedal that she ripped the sheet. She drove on and on, never pulling over, never parking. Ursula tried to talk to her but Celeste was oblivious to all but the road ahead. She seemed to speed off leaving Ursula on the pavement trying in vain to flag her down.

'One day you're going to crash!' Ursula yelled.

'Do you think so?' Celeste had yelled back, hope in her voice.

Celeste drove her way back into C2.

'You're off out,' the nurse told Ursula. Now that Ursula was passing from her care she had turned abrupt and distant. Every word she spoke seemed to be snapped out of the air.

'Oh, good.' She supposed that it was. 'Am I better?'

It was only when they took her out of the caged ward to the prison wings that she realised that she had been moved from her old prison to another.

'Where is this place?'

'This is Shreve, Cumbria.'

She tested the words in her mouth. They tasted strange but harmless. Shreve in Cumbria. It sounded nice.

Built as a poorhouse in another century, Shreve was a grim palace of blackened red brick surrounded by high walls of breezeblock decked with barbed wire. At Shreve, the prisoners outnumbered the wardens by two hundred to fifteen and the wardens were nervy, snappy women. The prison day on paper was a round of classes, physical training, occupational therapy and raffia mat-making but there weren't enough wardens to supervise it, so most days were spent banged up.

But Shreve could be fun. One Christmas seventy-two inmates broke out through the fire-escapes and ran riot around the grounds for two hours. Some made it to the purple moors and filled their pockets with heather. One even made it to Shreve New Town where she had a Wimpy burger and a Cola before she came back. They all came back of their own accord. It had shown the wardens that they were outnumbered and how little authority they really had. It was meant to make them nervous. It was called Turning the Screws.

The women of Shreve had their own ideas on justice, their own laws, fines and kangaroo courts. Riots and fights came about out of boredom as well as out of frustration. One summer they set fire to the mattresses on the top floor of both wings. They did it to see the fire engines and ogle the firemen. While they stood in the yard and giggled, imitating the siren and calling out to the firemen, Ursula watched the flames lick and dance along the rooftops.

Ursula was one of the better prisoners. She mopped and polished the under-used recreation room every morning and had a reputation for being useful at small, messy jobs. She was easier with the other prisoners. It had taken her this long to realise that prison was not the place where one was punished but was itself the punishment. She no longer acted the martyr. She was no different from anyone else and didn't treat herself as though she was. Sonny had taught her that; Celeste, too. It was all girls together, that was how to be, not the monster, not the victim, either, just one of the girls. Apart from anything else there were prisoners in Shreve whose crimes were more lurid, more numerous and more recent than hers. The days of her fame were fading. She had become an old lag.

A quieter woman had emerged from C1, her mind an empty pocket waiting to be filled. Thoughts of Sonny could not fill it, although she thought of Sonny more than she could bear, imagined her swaggering into her cell and saying: 'Hiya, tart of my heart, I'm back.' She thought of Celeste, too, often, but never with any pain. She smiled and wondered what had become of her. She had never expected to find out but over-heard a conversation one morning about a girl who sounded just like her.

'Did you say a girl called Celeste?'

'What if I did?'

'Is it the same Celeste as I knew?'

'How would I know that, you dozy mare, and how many Celestes are there in this world anyway? This one was a right daft bint. She thought she was a motor car.'

'That's her. Did you know her?'

'Know her? She ran me over twice. She was here for about a

month and then they took her off to C1. Vroom-vrooming all bleeding night. When they took her off to C1 she wouldn't go at first. Said her engine had stalled. So the wardens got clever, threw a belt round her neck and gave her a tow.'

'It's the same one. What about her?'

'What about her? It's in the paper. She's dead. Here, have a look.'

The article was about Celeste Hutton, brunette. She had worked as a nanny in London after leaving her Rushholme comprehensive. She took her work too seriously and began to worry. Pretty Celeste's anxiety drove her to take an overdose. Back in Rushholme she became so depressed that she attempted suicide once again and became a patient at a day centre. She moved to a Levenshulme flat with another girl. They rowed and Celeste left. She was always screwy, said flame-haired hygienist Joleen, nineteen. A passing taxi-driver picked her up, assaulted her and stole her things. She developed a fascination for cars and a hatred for all taxi-drivers. She was arrested several times for shoplifting headlamps and tyre gauges. For the last of these offences she was sentenced to thirty-six weeks' imprisonment, most of which was spent in a psychiatric ward. Nine months after her release she climbed on to the roof of a multi-storey carpark in Dugdale Street, Greater Manchester. She waited for the taxi-drivers' handicapped trip to Blackpool to go by before throwing herself down. Her body had been quickly cleared away and the majority of the handicapped children had not been disturbed by the incident. Celeste Hutton's stomach was found to be bloated with the petrol she had siphoned from an Audi Quatro minutes before her fall. She was aged twenty-one. There was a fuzzy picture of her in a bikini in Ibiza taken in happier days. The headline was 'CAR NUT'S SUICIDE PLUMMET ON CHARITY RIDE' and its subheading was 'Girl Rains on Taxi-Drivers' Parade'.

'Have you read all?'

'Yes, I have.'

'I'll have my paper back, then.'

'Can I have the picture?'

'For two fags you can.'

'She was a friend of mine, a daughter almost.'

'It'll still cost you two fags.' The price paid, she ripped

out the picture and handed it to Ursula. 'I don't know. If you've got to go, you've got to go, and if you want to go I don't think you should be stopped, but . . . well, there are more subtle ways of leaving this world, aren't there?'

'She died with an audience. She didn't go unnoticed. She won't be forgotten.'

'Are you all right?'

'I once tried to do the same. A long time ago. In Brackley Street.'

Ursula walked away and back to her cell, the photograph of Celeste in happier days held to her chest. She sat down on her bunk, shoulders slumped. Her face was blank but underneath its crêpey complexion tiny muscles around her mouth and eyes began to tremble and jitter like corn about to pop in a pan. 'Celeste!' she managed to say, the name odd and heavy in her mouth. She gagged on it. The name acted like a detonator. Her mask shattered and tears burst forth.

She cried for the dead girl whose history she had never known till now, whose surname she had learned for the first time that day.

Tears were nothing new for Ursula. She had cried before. She had cried as a child. She had cried as a woman. She had cried in the darkness and isolation of solitary and in Sonny's wide embrace but tears like that were coins she had spent only on herself. For the dead child, for Norah Matchett, for her father, Andreas, the warden dead of a heart-attack, she had never cried. Why, then, did she cry for Celeste? Because here was a death which moved her, one she envied and had once tried to achieve herself. Here was a death for which she could not be held responsible, the death of a girl she had loved for the sake of it and not for gain, her one unselfish love. These were the reasons she offered up her very first tears for the dead.

Still crying, she rose from her bunk and walked back out into the corridor. Prisoners parted for her. They could see that something was up. She held her head steady as if her face were a shallow bowl brimful of precious liquid she was fearful of spilling.

'What is it?' said one of the wardens who thought she must be sick or mad again.

'Vera?' She had never called a warden by her Christian name before, although it was a common enough thing to do. She would make a point of doing so from then on. 'Have you a mirror?' She muttered the words through clenched teeth as if she thought too much facial movement would shake away the tears.

The warden kept a compact in her breast pocket. Puzzled, she gave it to Ursula who opened it and brought it to her face. A circle of prisoners drew round. She seemed not to notice anyone, intent on studying the reflection of her crumpled face in the tiny mirror, a reflection dusted over with a fine veil of pink powder.

'See these?' she asked the warden, pointing to her face. 'They're tears. They make me beautiful.' The women about her laughed but the warden said, 'Yes, dear, you look lovely. Can I have my compact back?'

Ursula returned to her cell and sat awhile wondering why, if she was crying, she felt so happy. Vera came by and asked if she was OK.

'Me? I'm fine. Can I borrow a pen, a red one?'

'My, we are on the cadge this morning. I'll see what I can do.'

When she had first arrived in prison she had been asked her religion. She had shaken her head. She had no religion. A white card indicating this had been placed on her cell door and on every other cell she had inhabited. Given a pen, she took down the white card and, with great care, shaded it red to show that she was a Roman Catholic again.

When Father Ingram came on his rounds he saw the changed card.

'I've long hoped to see that card change colour,' he told her.

'I want a mass said,' she told him, 'for Celeste Hutton, aged twenty-one.'

She attended the mass but did not take Communion. She cried again when Celeste's name was mentioned in the prayers along with a warden's dog called Benson, dead of the mange. Ursula wiped her face with a handkerchief she'd borrowed from Vera.

It wasn't a conversion, just a return to old ways. She'd go to mass on Sundays and on Holy Days of Obligation. She sat in one of the middle pews but did not take the sacraments.

She said she wasn't ready for them, her soul was too unclean. Father Ingram did not push her further than she wished to go. He'd just say, 'Confession on Fridays?' and then wink. Ursula told him she might come but he'd best not hold his breath.

Vera suggested a new look to go with the new Ursula.

'I think a perm would suit you lovely. I can get Brenda to do it for you on the next shift. I'll have a word.'

'It's never Ursula, is it?' asked Father Ingram. 'My, such a beauty. You're enough to make me give up my vows.'

Ursula giggled like a schoolgirl, patted the mustard-coloured fluff into which her hair had been turned by Brenda the coiffeuse, and sat in the front pew.

The mass ended and, as Ingram had promised them the week before, there was to be a speaker. A treat this, he told them, Shreve was not one of the glamour spots like Holloway or Styal and visiting speakers were rare. He hoped, no, he was sure, that his ladies would give their guest a warm Shreve welcome. There were not many in the congregation, six or seven, and they managed only a meagre but sincere spattering of applause.

Ursula had already spotted the man far back in the dimmest corner of the chapel. She had tried to sneak a few glances but he had been sitting too far back for her to make him out clearly, though she could see his feet which had stuck out from the shadows. They were sockless and bony, sandal-clad. He tapped and shuffled them restlessly throughout the service.

'This is Aled Gwyn Maradoc,' Ingram told them as he beckoned the man from out of the shadows. Maradoc emerged from the darkness like a crane rising up out of a black lake, gangly in shape but elegant in motion, a tall, stooped man in white priest's garb and with a stiff plume of silvery hair that shimmered in the evening's dying light. 'Mr Maradoc has come to speak — '

Maradoc interrupted him with a gently raised hand. 'No, I've not come to speak but to talk. Ladies, would you, please, each of you, take up one of the folding chairs at the back of the chapel and form a circle about me? Circles, I have found, are more conducive to conversation. That's it. Lovely.'

They gathered around him in a circle. Ursula's heart was beating fast – it was as if some long-winged bird was trapped inside her flapping to get out – and there was a drumming in her ears. She knew it was Maradoc who made her feel this way but could see nothing about him to explain why she should feel so uneasy and, yes, so expectant.

He asked them to pray a while silently. All hands joined dutifully together in laps and eyes were downcast in a mimic of prayer, all except Ursula's, who studied the man. His hair was white but his face was not old although it was narrow and well-lined, the skin tightly stretched so that the muscles stood out, giving him a haggard look. He was tanned, golden but without health, and dry-seeming like old parchment. His fingers were lemon-coloured with nicotine.

He brought the silent prayer to an end by asking Ingram if it was all right if he smoked. Ingram hummed a little but did not object. When Maradoc lit up so did the ladies and Ingram had to look about for an ashtray. They used the chrome tray on which the cruets of wine and water for the Eucharist were carried. Ingram said he didn't think that God would mind.

Maradoc's edgy presence seemed to unsettle them. When he began to speak Ursula noticed the way his hands fluttered and played about his face like yellow moths but noticed, too, for all his jerky ways, how smooth his voice was, how certain and fluent was his expression.

Maradoc told them that he was Welsh but they would have guessed that. Born in the Rhondda, he would have been for the mines but for a quick mind, an ambitious father and a scholarship. He had gone to Cambridge and had made his parents proud but himself unhappy. One vacation, he had gone with his parents and neighbours to Clevelys, part of a miners' holiday club. 'It was all gossip, beer, dirty jokes and loud singing. It sounds fun now but at the time I was miserable . . . well, more than miserable, despairing. It wasn't that I was a snob – or perhaps I was. You see, by educating me out of my class, my parents had made me a stranger to them and to the people amongst whom I had been raised. My ambitions and interests were not theirs. Prig that I was, I was ashamed of them. And remember that in England when one moves out of one's class one doesn't necessarily become accepted by another. I had become an outsider. I found my family and neighbours vulgar and the new people I had met at college I thought affected, cold but elegant and eloquent in a way I'd never be with my clumsy ways and my accent. And there was no one to whom I could turn, no one who would've understood. That's how I was that summer in Clevelys, full of self-pity and very alone.'

His voice had a lilt that entranced her, rich and low as if it were coming from a church organ softly pedalled yet delicate, too. And he never looks straight at you, she thought, but you feel his eyes on you all the same.

He is a man and he comes from the outside like a messenger from another country. Listen to him, listen.

'One night I stole down to the beach. It had been so hot that summer. We're talking about before the war when summers were summers, 1938.'

'Yes, it was hot that summer, so hot.'

She hadn't meant to speak but had become involved in his story, and then for him to mention *that* summer, one she had cause to remember and to remember well. He looked at her strangely, they all did. She blushed and mumbled about how it had been a lovely summer and then clenched her lips together as a sign that she would not interrupt again, promise.

'Yes, you're right, it was. You and I would know that. We're of an age, I'd say. You others, you're too young to remember, but it was sweltering. That's why I went down to the beach. I wanted cool air or better say that was the excuse I gave so I could leave their loud company. I had other reasons for going there. The beach at Clevelys is a stranger to sand. It is a rocky, stony beach. You do not walk along it, you stumble. I was so alone, you see. If there had been anyone to talk to, anyone who understood, I would not have done what I did. I filled the pockets of my jacket and the pockets of my trousers with as many pebbles as I could and I went down to meet the waves. Lovely waves they were, curve-bellied, thick delicious lashes of them, foam-headed. So very inviting. "Come to me," they seemed to say. The swish of them on the shore was such a soothing sound. I wanted to lose myself in them, lose all my worries in their cold embrace. There seemed no better place for me than to be deep in the thick of them, lost to everything.'

Rain had begun to fall outside and the church was so quiet one could hear it mumbling on the roof. Even the warden on duty by the door, previously lounging back in her chair indifferently counting her keys, leaned forward to catch his words.

'And then', Maradoc said finally, 'I saw God. A vision was granted me. It was emblazoned above me, diamond-bright against the black sky. Two intersecting bands of white. A cross. *The* cross, all brilliant white. It spanned the sky. It touched the sea's horizon and reached as high as Heaven and was wide enough to catch the world in its arms. I felt myself leave my heavy body, the body I had made even heavier with pebbles and had wished to disown, to melt into the sea. I was lifted up and I felt myself become pure soul, a white shadow risen up and part of that cross. It was such bliss I cannot tell you.'

His face, uplifted, broke into a smile, a private one, and then he hung his head. Ursula watched as she had listened, fascinated. He raised his head again and continued, his voice still calm but sadder, a tone of deep, long-held regret thickening it.

'I was back on the beach, my shoes and socks soaked through. The vision had gone. I was still alive. I could not believe that I could experience such joy and not die of it. Then it was over, gone, all gone. How long had it lasted? A minute? A second? For too short a time but long enough to change my life. Why had it occurred just then? Why to me? Why there? God on Clevelys beach and all for a miner's boy. I wasn't a pious boy nor was I wild and atheistic. I was a blank. Was I an empty vessel waiting to be filled? I don't know. Did it really happen or was it an illusion? Questions, questions, I have them in abundance and not the ghost of an answer to any of them. What I experienced in that vision was something short, ambiguous, intensely real, but anything I say to explain it becomes like a fable which fails to illustrate the moral. I don't claim to understand. To contemplate it puts me amongst the lost things but it puts me among the found, too. I explain it so badly.'

He hung his head again and paused. The church had grown dark. The warden by the door reached up to the light-switch but Ingram shook his head, got up and lit a

156

candle from the altar. He carried it to the centre of the circle where it threw its wan light on to their faces and made giant shadows on the walls. Smoke hung in graceful folds from the ceiling, and the window-panes, like black ponds reflected back the room's hunched figures.

Ursula's eyes glistened in the candlelight and, when he raised his head, so did Maradoc's.

'And the meaning of it all? Another question, but one that needs an answer, deserves one. There I was on the beach in Clevelys and the sky that had contained my vision was black and star-filled, pretty enough but just a sky. I mentioned the waves, didn't I? I mentioned the sound of the waves as they slid up the shore. I listened to that. I listened to the swish . . . swish . . . swish of the sea on the shore and in that swish . . . swish . . . swish, the soft hiss of it, there was the suggestion of a word and the word was sacrifice . . . sacrifice . . . sacrifice.'

The sibilance chilled the room and the word chilled Ursula's soul. This vision occurred one night in September. She knew it. She did not need to ask. Oh God.

'There was the meaning of it all. All the meaning I was left with. It was the only clue, the one remaining piece of evidence. Sacrifice, a word as short, as ambiguous and as intensely real as the vision had been. A tainted and abused word but a necessary one. Sacrifices are always necessary. The sea on the shore gave me that word – sacrifice – and my life has been lived in honour of it, so much so that I have never wanted a life of my own but want always to live for others. That is what God wants. That is what God praises. That is what He wants all of us to do. I know that. I am certain of it.'

He looked about the circle, studied each face quickly and expertly to see if he had been understood or, better still, believed, even if only imperfectly. It was important for him to be believed. He looked about him and saw faces that were interested, serious, puzzled or just polite. He saw only one who looked as though she believed.

As he had spoken, the rhythm of his words and the tune of his voice a rich soundtrack, she had played his story in her head like a cinema but she was the one who starred in it. She saw herself in his place, standing on a beach witnessing God.

She had never seen the sea for herself. Forty-nine years old and she had never seen the sea. Her father had never taken her, though they'd been rich enough for holidays. She could have gone with Andreas one bank holiday maybe but he'd always been too ashamed to be seen with her. She promised herself that she would one day see the sea. She would sit there for hours and wait for God.

I have never seen the sea, she thought, but I have seen God. I must have once. I must have seen Him once . . . I must have.

Maradoc told them how he had returned to Cambridge a committed Christian and had gone to India as a missionary.

'But I couldn't stay. I grew sick and they sent me home. Stomach trouble,' he said and then, as if to prove it, he gave a belch as big as a tennis-ball which made everyone laugh.

'I have been back there since and I have been in Africa, too. Squalor, starvation, atrocities, I will not upset you with the details. I have worked here in this country, too. There is no need to be complacent. I have seen here things unforgivable. Poverty that is not supposed to exist, violence and wretchedness and an ignorance that is so great it can only be burned away. It will be burned away, too, and I fear that fire. I fear the world burning and exploding with its rottenness and know of only sacrifice to beat out the flames. To sit back, to do nothing, will make you worthless. You will be fuel to the flames. That sweet hiss of the waves that murmured to me on Clevelys beach will turn to the hiss of the flames.'

Ursula sat further forward in her seat at the mention of fire but the others had given up. Maradoc had gone on too long, had become too obscure and boring. Ingram noticed the unrest.

'I'm afraid our time is up,' he said as breezily as he could.

Only Ursula was disappointed. She had understood about the flames, understood why he was so impassioned and why he had lost all fluency. He was like a leaf trying to understand the tree on which he grew. She had tried to do that herself. She knew how difficult that was.

Maradoc was sitting with his head bowed again and the ladies, prompted by Ingram, applauded him only a little more vigorously than they had applauded his entrance. The warden came forward to chivvy them back to their cells. Ingram apologised to her, knowing it was late.

Ursula wanted to stay so badly. She wished she were a slab of concrete, that she might never move again, but when the warden came and touched her elbow she followed like a child. She stole one long last look at the white-haired preacher who was sitting back in his chair smiling politely as she left the church.

'Well done, Aled,' Ingram complimented him. 'I've heard you tell that story twice before and it always works. I love it. And every time you say, "Gather round and we'll have a conversation," and for the next hour the only voice to be heard is yours.'

'Yes, it went well enough, a little over the top towards the end. It's so difficult to know where to pitch it and hard to know how intelligent women like that are. Do you think I had an effect?'

'Oh, yes, did you not see Ursula?'

'Which one was that, the one with the blonde wig and the caved-in face?'

'Oh, unkind. It wasn't a wig but a new hairdo and a great improvement. You're only saying that because she dared to interrupt you. Interesting that you should end up talking about fire. That was *the* Ursula Trench.'

I will never see that man again, thought Ursula. She sat in her cell in the dark. Her cellmates were sleeping but she knew she wouldn't sleep and didn't want to. She wanted to remember everything, his face, his hands, his words. Strange how here in the dark as she ran them over in her mind they no longer seemed his words but her own. She had the feeling she had known them always and was simply recalling them and then they became all muddled in her head. Never mind, they were still beautiful. Even jumbled up they made music for her. She would remember his voice, she'd not forget that. It sounded in her head like a bell, distant but clear, a bell summoning her to church, to the sacraments and to God. She would remember, too, his face in the candlelight wreathed round with cigarette smoke, veiling his features.

IV

Found Out for Sure

I

The Blonde in the Dock

Silence.

The blonde in the dock was standing to receive sentence. She was not a natural blonde nor even a convincing one: her hair shone like metal wire and had the look and texture of it, too. An attempt had been made at glamour, but the perm was too tight, the face too heavily and pinkly powdered, the lipstick too thickly and imprecisely placed. The perm had been done grudgingly by a warden at the remand centre who had not wanted to touch the murdering bitch with a bargepole, let alone a comb and a tube of Permotint. There had been no mirror in the cell below the court where she had applied the make-up hurriedly before being brought up to the dock. She was happy enough with her appearance. She thought she looked smart.

The judge leaned forward. He spoke solemnly and just above a whisper. 'I must repeat to you that you are charged with having wilfully, intentionally and with malice, killed Michael Samuel Andreas. Are you Guilty or Not Guilty?'

'Guilty!' she replied far too loudly, so that it sounded like an exclamation of joy.

Then Burchill, her man, stood up and stated to the court that the prisoner wished to inform the court that she alone was guilty of the murder, that she wished that guilt to be made known and to atone for her crimes. He spoke in the weary professional manner he had used throughout the trial but he should have watched his words more carefully. The court had picked up on that last word. There was a murmur of 'Crimes, he said, not *crime*'. For Burchill it had been an unfortunate slip but he could not correct it without drawing even more attention to it.

163

The clerk then read out: 'Ursula Miriam Trench, you have confessed yourself guilty of the murder of Michael Samuel Andreas; have you anything to say why sentence of death should not be passed upon you?'

It looked as if she were about to speak but she was interrupted by two balloon-shaped women who stood up at the front of the court. They had spent the trial knotted in each other's arms, sobbing intermittently and in tandem. They rose up now as if further inflated. One of them, a Mrs Rimmer, had been a witness, and the other was Mrs Andreas, mother to the dead man.

'I hope you burn in Hell, in Hell I hope you burn!' the mother cried repeatedly while Mrs Rimmer, in a voice as smooth as a nail dragged across a brick wall, reminded Ursula Trench of a baby she'd killed and how everyone knew it. She'd hang for the baby, too, no matter how long ago it was. The mother's screeches were the more passionate but a few bangs of the judge's gavel quietened her. Mrs Rimmer went on a little longer about a dog that was also killed and that there'd been no mention of that, either. Ursula Trench would die for the dog an' all, Mrs Rimmer shouted and then together the two women sank slowly to their seats as if suddenly deflated.

What Ursula Trench might have said had she not been interrupted can only be guessed at. When the clerk repeated his question she just shrugged her shoulders.

Throughout the outburst, indeed throughout the trial, Anna Matchett sat at the back of the court hiding behind a black veil hanging from a wide-brimmed hat. She picked at the fingers of her glove, pretending to be invisible.

It was time for the judge to speak. He reached for the black cap. Ursula's varnish began to crack a little about the eyes and the corners of the mouth but by the time the black square was on the judge's head it was once again the gaudy and unmoving mask it had been throughout her time in the dock.

'I can entertain no doubt, after reading and hearing the evidence put before us together with your confession, that you are guilty of the murder of Michael Samuel Andreas.

'His murder was one committed under circumstances of great deliberation and cruelty as well as one of moral sordidness. Jealousy, anger and the fears of an ageing and

164

spurned woman worked in your breast until they assumed over you the power of the Evil One.

'A reputation for murder precedes you. Evil hangs around you like cheap scent. You corrupted a young man from the paths of moral righteousness and you debased both him and yourself in a seedy affair, the fruits of which were obsession and savagery on your part, dishonour and death on his.

'Whether Her Majesty, with whom the prerogative of mercy rests, may be advised to consider the fact of your sex, and that you were convicted in no small part upon your own confession, is a question I am happy in knowing it is not for me to answer. The jury has decided on their verdict. I pass the only sentence allowed, adding that it well behoves you to live what is left of your life as one who is about to die and to seek a more enduring mercy than one this court or country can ever supply and to rely upon the only true redemption and satisfaction for all the sins of this world.'

Ursula listened to these words with no sign of interest. I do not need their judgement, she thought. I am my own executioner. I am fire. Fire burns itself, punishes itself. The image warmed her mind and she took comfort from it.

The judge continued speaking but now with the forced passion of an actor at the end of a long run who must say lines made stale by repetition freshly, and with conviction.

'It only remains for me to discharge the duty which the law imposes upon the court without alternative, and that is to pass upon you the sentence which the law adjudges for wilful murder: that you be taken from this place where you now stand to the place from whence you came and that you be hanged by the neck until your body be dead; that when your body be dead it be buried within the precincts of the gaol in which you were last confined. And may God have mercy on your soul.'

Ursula remained calm and still throughout the sentencing, moving only when she heard the phrase 'hanged by the neck', her hand darting to the orange beads about her throat. When the sentencing was over she sat down rather stiffly and searched about for her handbag. She brought it to her lap, opened it and brought out a tube of Polo mints. She unwrapped the silver foil and offered a mint to the policewoman who stood behind her.

'Have one,' she said. 'They cool you down wonderfully. They're good for heartburn, too.'

The makers of Polo mints did not relish the endorsement. Sales slumped that year.

II

The Fire on Brackley Street

In 1938, the year in which Ursula Trench first gained her reputation for murder, the sky over Radcliffe Park was the brown of an onion soup. The chimneys of three tyre factories fired out endless ribbons of tobacco-coloured smoke and had done so since before the turn of the last century. These chimneys competed with others in the area to create a smog so deep that in winter street-lamps were lit the whole day through, and people had skins bronzed and lungs blackened by it. When a child was born in Radcliffe Park it was said to emerge from its mother not screaming but coughing.

Golden flesh, tar-lined lungs and washing that never came clean on the lines that were strung between the backs of houses: these were part of the price for living where what jobs there were lay close to doorsteps whitened weekly with donkey stone from the rag-and-bone man. The more dirt there was in the air, the more jobs were likely to be going. The world ran on tyres made in Radcliffe Park. It was only a pity that the people who so helped to move the motor of the world had to live with their mouths wrapped around its exhaust pipe.

Glass, paint, cotton, hair tonic, shampoo, Bronco Buck toilet paper and Albery Carpets For That Elegant Home were also made in Radcliffe Park. Anything that made the twentieth century brighter, cleaner, smarter could be found nascent or in production somewhere there; it made the place duller, dirtier and shabbier, true, but that was the twentieth century for you.

The park which gave the area its name was, in comparison, a thin slice of the Garden of Eden. Twelve acres of manicured green, full shrubs, graceful trees and a boating-pond, it was a bright spotlight aimed on to an otherwise dark stage. The shadows cast by its trees, bushes, pavilion and conveniences had a touch of green in them; rhododendrons flamed deep red and daffodils shone electric yellow; if the boating-pond was mud-coloured it was only because it reflected the sky above.

Leading away from the park was a street called Park End. Park End was where you dreamed of having a house if the Pools came up and you were foolish enough to want to stay in the area and not move out to Chisum Moss where the real snobs lived. There wasn't a house in Park End that didn't sleep at least six and with no thought of sharing a bed. They all had gardens – front *and* back – but the house with the biggest garden was the one just by the park gates.

It was called the House of Content and was built by a man called Hewitt who had started with one shop and by the end of his life had owned property all over the city. It was called Content because he had originally planned the house for the almost-child bride he had married in late middle age. Content was what he had hoped she would fill it with. As it happened the only thing the almost-child bride did fill was a grave one year and one daughter later.

He had had most of the house built in the final decade of the last century but he gave up after the death of his wife. The child she had borne him was a sickly thing, often ill in hospital or abroad somewhere, recuperating. The house had remained unfinished and unoccupied until the year the First World War ended, when Hewitt and his daughter finally moved in. He kept the name Content in the hope that his daughter would find for herself all that death had cheated him of.

By the 1950s the house was a battered thing. The bricks were a blackened red; the roof, once egg-custard yellow, was now speckled brown as if the sky had grown flaky and scattered its crumbs on it. The fancy decorations on the gutterings and drainpipes, faces of devils, angels and snarling dogs, had grown into rusty blobs. The wide windows were fogged over with a decade or more of grime and the once famous orange paintwork was leprous and peeling; the gardens were tall with weeds.

Park End led on to Brackley Street which began as an impoverished but genteel impersonation, a few semis and bungalows with names like Bovium and San Simeon, then cut through a belt of factories and became lined with shops and hoardings for PRESTON'S SENSATIONAL RINGS, CLEVELAND BISCOL: ALCOHOL FOR ENGINE POWER or DON'T SAY WHITE, SAY OXYDOL. The street grew progressively seedier as it snaked its way onwards and upwards until it lost itself in the heart of the city.

Parallel to it ran a canal, milky white with effluent. Thick with the smell of burned cabbage, banked off by high walls, it was a place of rats and flies. It ran alongside Brackley Street until it crossed it almost exactly midway, forcing Brackley Street to arch its back and form a bridge.

By 1953, when Ursula's reputation was assured by the slaying of Michael Samuel Andreas, the sky over Radcliffe Park was still brown but it had started to lighten. These were times of relative prosperity but already things were running down. One of the tyre factories closed down. It seemed they did such things cheaper in Malaya.

In 1953 there were fires in Brackley Street, the sound of a crowd shouting and singing, glasses being broken. A queen was being crowned that day and there was a street-party with a bonfire to celebrate the occasion.

There was another fire in Brackley Street that day but at first no one noticed the mink-coloured plumes of smoke that rose out of the back of Ma Rimmer's newsagent's. Ursula Trench had gone unnoticed, too. She was underneath the bridge and there was blood on her dress. She was kneeling on the canal bank, bringing up cupped handfuls of milky water to her mouth and drinking deep.

III

From Content to Brackley Street Bridge

In the autumn of 1938 a hearse crossed over the bridge in Brackley Street before turning left down Odsall Lane for the cemetery. The hearse carried the black oak coffin of Norah Trench. On top of Norah's coffin lay another, much smaller coffin containing Edmund Trench, her child.

The hearse moved slowly and with great state, as hearses should, but a wreath fell from its roof as it joggled over the tramlines turning into Odsall Lane. A dog snapped it up and carried it away like a bone.

The human bystanders looked more considerate. Brackley Street was packed with people that day. They'd come special. They stood still as it passed. Men took off their caps and women threw shawls over their heads out of respect for the unfortunate dead, but it was on the black Rolls-Royce following the hearse that their eyes fastened. The car carried the husband of the dead woman, his daughter and the dead woman's sister. The windows were smoked and the two women heavily veiled; it was hard to see how they were taking their bereavement. Very lightly, it was supposed.

Sleet gathered and thickened into snow as the hearse turned into the cemetery. A crowd had gathered in wait. Policemen stood at the gates to prevent disturbances.

Three gravediggers in brown overalls and cord leggings shared a cigarette behind the canvas set up to hide the mud and clay brought up from the grave. A fourth gravedigger directed the bearers to the muddy hole in which the coffins were to be buried.

Behind the cemetery fence the crowd was watching with ghoulish interest. As first the coffin of Norah Trench was lowered into the ground and then the child's fell with a clump on top of it, they wondered which of the three mourners would finally break down. They were too far away to see Trench's pale face, bleached by grief. The faces of the two women, their expressions, could only be guessed at through the dark veils. One of the gravediggers said he thought he saw a bit of a glitter around where Ursula's eyes should have been. The glitter of a tear, perhaps? And, if so, a tear of grief, remorse or joy?

'Not many tears at this funeral,' someone said.

'They'd be crocodile tears if there were,' said another.

'Poor woman.'

'Poor child.'

'Somebody'd do something like that to a child, they'd not have tears in them, no, nor pity.'

'Which one do you think did it?'

This had been the question for weeks. Repetition had not staled it and the inquest had failed to provide an answer.

'I bet it was him.'

'His own son?'

'I bet if he didn't kill the son he killed the wife.'

'When a wife dies it's usually the husband what's done it.'

'That's marriage for you.'

'I think it was her what killed the baby.'

'Which "her" do you mean?'

'The daughter?'

'Or the sister?'

'Well, it was one of them.'

'Or both of them?'

'Or all of them? Who knows but them? They'll never say.'

'They ought to hang, if not for doing it, for letting it happen.'

'Hanging's too good for them. Too quick. Burn them, is what I say.'

The mourners returned to their car. As they passed through the gates the crowd, no longer silenced or restrained by thought for the coffins, gathered about the car, slowing its passage, kicking at its sides, pressing up against the windows and yelling obscene threats at the people within. The vehicle sped off down Odsall Lane and lost the crowd by the time it reached Brackley Street.

Brackley Street was still full but this time heads were no longer bared of caps or covered by shawls. No respect was shown for the mourners, only curiosity and contempt. People shook their fists and names were called. A small boy, spurred on by his mam, threw a bottle of red ink and it splattered the door in the shape of a giant blood-red rose. Inside the car someone screamed. It accelerated and the little boy ran off, a proud mother's praises ringing in his dirty earholes.

Anna had been going to stop for the weekend but the crowd and the bang the ink-bottle had made as it hit the car unnerved her. She was getting out of Radcliffe Park as soon as she could. The funeral was done. She'd be off in the morning. Trench didn't argue. It was wise of Anna to go, he could see that.

'And where'll you go, Anna?'

'I've not thought. I've not thought proper, anyway, but away somewhere would be best.'

'You'll keep in touch, though.' Trench sucked at his moustache to still his quivering lips.

'Oh, yes, I'll keep in touch and let you know how things are, of course.'

'I'm sure things will go fine for you eventually. I'll write, too. I'd like that. You remind me so of Norah.'

'Yes, you write, Freddie.'

'Freddie? She used to call me that.'

'I know. That's why I said it. She's worth being reminded of, the best sister a woman ever had.'

'And the best wife, Anna, the best wife.'

They cried together in each other's arms. Death had brought them closer. Anna wiped away his tears with the back of her glove.

'Freddie, if you do write, you're not to call me Anna Matchett.'

'I'll call you Sister, Dearest Sister, because that's what you are, that's what you've become.'

'No, I don't mean that, Freddie.' She broke away from him, smoothed out her black silk dress and studied her reflection in the mirror above the mantelpiece. Of her red hair, bunched into a generous loop at the back, not a wisp was out of place. Her make-up needed a bit of doing about the eyes but that was crying for you. Well, it didn't do to look too perfect after a funeral.

'You're to call me Anna Farrell. Farrell was my mother's name and that's what I'll call myself from now on. A name like Matchett gets remembered and I want to be forgot.'

'I'll not forget you, Anna. You remind me so of Norah.'

'Don't take on again, Freddie, please. Whatever's holding me up through all this won't hold me up much longer if you start taking on again.'

'It's just that I'll miss you. Who else have I left to care about?'

'I'll miss you, too, Anna,' said Ursula. They had forgotten she was there. She was still in her black coat and veil and had sat in the darkest corner of the room so as not to be noticed. 'For what it's worth, I'll miss you, too.' Anna, at a loss, looked away. Ursula hung her head. She should not have spoken.

Anna did right to move away. Suspicion, at the time, had fallen heaviest on her. The child should have been in her room that night and there had been rumours of rows between her and her sister. Moving away, she took her name with her. Whenever the story was told she became the Sister or the Aunty, an imprecise detail.

In Radcliffe Park and elsewhere the name Trench was associated with blood – and unavenged blood at that. If Trench hadn't killed his wife and child that night, then he hadn't protected them, either.

Like Anna, Trench should have moved. He had the money to start a new life elsewhere but he stayed. He stayed in the House of Content because that was the place in which his wife and child had died. Their ghosts moved about the place, in the dark corridors, the unused rooms and the shadows of the garden. He could hear them, he claimed, in the creak of the floorboards and the cracks and rumbles of the house as it settled in the night. He felt their breath cold on his cheek whenever he woke from thin dreams of them. Their company was his only solace and his most constant pain.

He would never leave Content, nor would Ursula. She would stay with him, live with him in an unloving silence, as if it were a penance she had to pay.

Whether this penance was deserved only father and daughter knew, but it benefited neither her soul nor her reputation. The way she hid herself from the world seemed proof of a guilty conscience whereas, curiously, Trench's solitary ways seemed to absolve him in some way. He lived, it became known, like a Mr Havisham in a palace of cobwebs, not a wedding but the funeral of his wife and child the still point around which his mind played and his life turned. In the slowly decaying prison that the House of Content became he no longer looked like Ursula's cellmate but like her warden.

The following year war came and Ursula was glad; it diverted people's attention away from her. War meant that there were other deaths than Norah Trench's and her infant child's to occupy their minds. While the world fought with itself it would leave her in peace.

At first Trench ignored the war as he ignored everything that happened outside the House of Content. During the day he kept to the parlour. He said he was reading through the encyclopaedia but he never picked up a volume beyond *Ant – Bul*. In the evenings he would go early to bed. If sleep evaded him, as it often did, he would sit by the window and stare out into the garden with deadened eyes. His lips traced words he dared not speak and he had light by him throughout the night. He had grown afraid of the dark. Even the gloom of a winter's afternoon was enough to make him yell for a candle or get Ursula to turn up the gas. The dead were not dead for Mr Trench. He knew them well.

As the war went on, however, his attitude to it changed. He came to see it as a mirror in which his own life was reflected large. For him, the war meant that other families, other fathers would know a grief comparable to his. It was as if the war was the world's weak attempt to keep him company: it, too, was experiencing a devastation similar to his own. It made him feel less lonely. A wireless replaced the encyclopaedia. He followed the war on it, keeping detailed records of Allied casualties in the back of his old account-books.

Whenever bombs fell on Radcliffe Park, Trench and Ursula took refuge in the cellar, but they fell rarely. The city was too far inland and its docks were on the other side to Radcliffe Park. One bomb landed on the paint factory and made the sky browner than ever. A black greasy dust settled everywhere. The people of Radcliffe Park called it God's blackout.

On the worst night of bombing a mill, two shops, a whole street and the boating-pond in the park were hit. Ursula crept up to the top-landing window to see the show. Down in the cellar her father had called out for her, a weird croaking call, but she'd ignored him. Let him call, she thought, and pulled up the blackout blind. She stood in the dark, shivering in her nightgown, and watched Radcliffe Park burn. Enemy airplanes swelled the air above and searchlights threw hot yellow beams against the sky. She wished she was out there. She wished she could see the walls crumbling and the people running and screaming, the flames licking away at homes and shops, factories falling in on themselves, the air loud with cries and sirens and breaking glass. Come on, she urged the planes, come on, bomb all of Radcliffe Park, this house and me, too. What wouldn't she give for such a death!

A bomb fell by the park gates but did not explode. Another fifty yards to the left, there would have been no House of Content and Ursula would have had part of her wish granted. Content quivered as the bomb fell and its walls were made brittle by the reverberation. Two gables now hung awry and three of the shutters had come loose from the wall. Inside, plaster dropped in clumps from the ceilings or sugared rooms already heavily powdered with dust.

Neither Trench nor Ursula did anything to repair the damage. Like its inhabitants, the house endured decay, even welcomed it. It was as if it, too, were being punished. Fungus grew along the skirting-boards and up through the damp carpets. In autumn the rooms were awash with dead leaves blown in through broken windows and the gardens had grown into a high sea of weeds and waving grass.

It was to this crumbling mansion that Anna Matchett returned one day when the war was halfway done. She was in the WAAF and drove a jeep for someone in Intelligence. More than most she noticed how far not only the house but also its inhabitants had fallen into ruin. The knocker, stiff with rust, brought a pale ghost to answer the door. It was Ursula, hair unwashed, loose and lank about her dingy face, squinting out at the daylight. She recognised at once the goddess in khaki who'd come to call and threw her arms about her. Anna stepped back.

'No, I'm sorry, dear, but you smell bad.'

Ursula's enthusiasm could not be dimmed. 'Anna, Anna, you've come back. Father! Father! It's Anna come back.'

She dragged a reluctant Anna through the dark hallway and into the parlour where Trench, bent and grey, scuttled towards her like a hungry spider.

'Anna, I'd never have known you.' His voice was a squeak and his eyes were brimful with tears.

Moss grew on the curtains which Ursula pulled back when Trench ordered more light by which to see his sister-in-law. The sun caught on the waves of Anna's red hair and the buttons of her uniform. She had never looked better.

'How like Norah you are. She'd have been that proud.' The tears that had brimmed his eyes now dribbled down his white-bristled face. 'Ursula, make tea.'

Ursula left them but stopped to listen through the closed door. She could hear Anna's voice, quick and deep and always bubbling up with laughter. She could also hear the rusty cackle that she supposed was her father's chuckle: it wasn't a sound she heard much.

When she returned with a tray of tea things she had boiled and scrubbed to get rid of the germs, the talk, animated and low, between Anna and her father stopped. She put the tray down in front of Anna and withdrew to the corner of the room where she sat on a hard-backed chair. Anna sat on the sofa, a handkerchief under her seat to keep her uniform free from the dust. She poured the tea and chatted. In Intelligence she was, yes, her, Anna.

'I don't do none of the secret stuff but I drive them about as do. I love it. When this war ends I'm going to get me a big car, you see if I don't.'

It could not be doubted that Anna would get whatever she wanted. Anna was made to be happy, made to get by. She lit up the dark parlour. Who would have thought that in years to come this light of hers would dim and that she herself would smother its flame with her own tights? Neither Ursula nor

Trench could stop looking at her as she chatted on, waving her arms and laughing about the funny things that happened. She seemed to the dark pair who watched her like a sunburst chandelier spangling the gloom.

'And do they never bother you?' asked Ursula.

There was no need to ask what they could bother about. Trench scowled at his daughter. It was as if she had caused a cloud to pass over the sun. Anna, however, was not to be overcast for long. She looked away for a second or two, tapped the ash of her cigarette on to the carpet, stretched out her arms, the generous chest straining the jacket, and, yawning, said: 'No, they never bother me and they never bother me because they don't know.'

'Do you think she goes around telling everybody?' Trench snarled. 'Anna's a right to a new life.'

'And I've got one. I changed my name, as I said I would. Deed poll. It's quite legal and quite cheap, too. I don't know why more folk don't try it. Anna Farrell's what I'm known as and Anna Farrell's what I am.'

'I'm pleased for you, Anna. You deserve it.'

'But you, Freddie, you deserve more, too. Why do you live as you do? You weren't to blame, yet you live as if you were. Look at this house; our Norah was so proud of it. She tried to make it nice for you and look at it now.'

'That's Ursula's fault.' It was all Ursula's fault, he seemed to say. Silently Anna and Ursula agreed that it probably was.

Would Anna be stopping the night? (In this dump, thought Anna to herself, when I've got a date with my man from Intelligence at the Mansfield Hotel? Am I hell as like.) She said she couldn't stop. She had to be off.

'I came back to see how you were and I'm not happy with what I see. I'll say that straight 'cos you know me, Freddie, I speak as I find.'

'Anna, I'll tell you straight, I'm waiting to stop living.'

'Freddie Trench, that's dead morbid, that is! You were never morbid. This house was, though. I never liked it. Our Norah, she tried to make it bright for you. You were a bright man, Freddie, you deserved a bright wife, a bright house.'

'I had one.'

'Happen. This house, though. Calling it the House of

Content was asking for trouble. House of Misery, more like.'

'Calling it Content was the old man's idea. He wanted to wish everything well, the house, the people in it.'

'He'd be disappointed if he saw it now, wouldn't he? Mind you, I like his spirit. Oh, live, why don't you, live proper! This war won't go on for ever and when it's done there'll be some living to do then. There'll be days of honey coming to all of us. They're here now for some and I count myself among them. Ursula, you should join up like me. This war's been good for women. You'll do things like you never thought. I mean, I know one woman who drives a tractor. Come to think of it, I know a lot of women who drive tractors. You're still young, girl. Your country's crying out and you sit in this dust-pile. It's criminal. You live, too, Ursula, live, why don't you?'

Throughout the afternoon Ursula had just looked on. She had looked on in awe at the bright flame Anna had become and in envy, too, of the easy, intimate way she had with her father. To be suddenly included in the warm circle of Anna's good wishes made her feel weak. She ran to Anna and wept, rubbing her face against the delicious roughness of her uniform, the brass buttons cold on her cheek. Anna tried not to mind the smell this time and patted and shushed her until she was calm. Trench looked on in disgust.

'Ursula's done harm enough,' came his cold words, 'without her harming her country, too. She's best here. She belongs in this house and she's not safe out of it.'

'Now, hang on, Freddie, there's a war on and duties to be done.'

'Happen there is. As for duties, Ursula's duty is to be by me.'

'Well, I don't approve of that at all. And what happens if there's conscription for women? My man in Intelligence says it's a certainty.'

'I've taken care of that. Doctor Sartori can be called on to help out there.'

'Is that old fish still practising?'

'He'll always be sober enough to sign a sick-note. Ursula'll stay by me.'

Sentence had been passed. The women stiffened and withdrew from their embrace. Ursula trudged back to her corner and pressed her face against the wall. She felt like a prisoner who had been handed the keys to her cell only to have them snatched away.

'You're too hard on that girl, Freddie,' Anna said as she was leaving but she didn't labour the point. She didn't care enough for Ursula to fight her battles and she didn't really have the time.

That evening, Ursula and Trench, alone again, discussed the day. It wasn't something they did often, mainly because days were lived to be forgotten, but Anna's visit had made this one special. To talk of how she looked and of what she'd said allowed them to savour again its deliciousness.

'She looked well in her uniform, didn't she, Father?'

'Yes, she looked fine.'

'She looked so' – Ursula searched hard for the right word – 'soldierly.'

'And yet womanly, too. Anna and Norah were always that. They knew how to be women.'

'And with her hair the way it is now, all short and wavy, she looked like . . . like Joan of Arc, do you not think, Father?'

Yes, like Joan of Arc, thought Ursula. Who could look finer than that? Images of Anna Matchett as Joan of Arc played in her head, soft, pastel pictures like the covers on the *People's Friend*. And, if Anna could do it, why not she? She saw herself in armour on a white horse and holding a white standard, head up, eyes heavenwards.

'Do you not think, Father, as how I could do what Anna's doing? Wouldn't you be proud of me again?'

'I was never proud of you. Have you not learned that yet?'

She had. She had learned that well. It was just sometimes she forgot and sometimes she hoped that he'd forgotten, too.

'But isn't it wrong for us to live like this? Criminal is what Anna called it. I could be fighting for my country.'

'Criminal?' He savoured the word. 'Fight for your country? I've fought for my country. In 1914.'

'Ay, you've said.'

'Have I ever said how?'

'Often.'

179

'Have I told you about the trenches?'

'Yes. Don't go on. I'm sorry I spoke.'

'In the mornings, if it was quiet, we had to sort out the dead.'

'I'm not listening. See, I've got my fingers in my ears. I'm not listening.'

'There was a procedure. Step by step. First, you had to – you listening? – first, you had to retrieve any equipment. Guns. Bullets. You waded through the mud and if the body wasn't too badly mutilated, then you searched them for equipment. If it was hard to get, then you had to hack at the body. Sometimes it was a friend or someone you shared a smoke with the night before. It made no odds. You hacked away at them.'

'Why will you never let me be?'

'Perhaps you should join up after all. You'd be good at hacking a body up. You've got experience. Tell them that when you go. They might make you a general, give you a whole army like Joan of Arc.'

'Why do you do this to me, Father, when all I've ever done is love you and all I've ever wanted was for you to love me back?'

'You killed my wife and you savaged my son like a butcher. Love? Vomit!'

It had not been like that at all. She could never explain it to him and he would never listen, never even try to forgive. She pretended not to care but she did, she did. She turned to him and said as coolly as she could: 'I'll be glad when you're dead, you old bastard. I'll spit in your face and I'll laugh.'

'I wouldn't expect you to do owt else,' he said with a sweetly artificial smile. 'So you do that, Ursula, and see if I care. I'll be dead. What'll it be to me what you do?'

Such scenes of open hostility were rare and even then there was much that was left unspoken between them. Neither of them felt the need to lay their cards on the table: both believed they knew the deck too well to have to deal it out.

The war ended in Europe, as did the war with Japan, in cities of ashes and debris.

Radcliffe Park had been burned but, like the nation they supplied with tyres, paint and cotton, they had come victorious through the flames. Fire steeled them for the future, a future they welcomed and celebrated that VE-Day with a party in Brackley Street.

Trestle-tables laden with meagre rations blocked off the streets and flags fluttered along the gutterings. It was a time for being with family and neighbours and for thinking of those soon to return and those never to return. Songs were sung – 'Can-Can', 'Knees Up, Mother Brown' – and beer was drunk by the barrelful. Evening fell, a bonfire was lit and more barrels were split. By midnight children had grown sleepy and the grown-ups maudlin. Ma Rimmer, who ran the newsagent's, sang 'My Dreams Are Getting Better All the Time' as well as a deeply gloomy 'Lili Marlene', to which she gave a tramping funereal beat by kicking her club foot in its elevator shoe against the kerb. Ma Rimmer's torch songs warmed nobody. To lighten the mood a mother pushed her young son up before the bonfire and told everyone that her Micky wanted to sing. Her Micky wanted to do anything but and glared at his mother for embarrassing him so.

'Sing summat happy,' someone cried, and the boy obliged because it was the quickest way of getting the ordeal over with. A plump little lad with skinny legs, the backs of them hot and shiny from the heat of the bonfire, he was fair and pretty enough to catch the eye and attention of all the partymakers on Brackley Street. In a voice that was as yet unbroken but which didn't have long to wait, he sang:

> You are my sunshine,
> My double Woodbine,
> My box of matches,
> My Craven A.

'Who was that lad?' someone by the beer-barrels asked.

'He's from up Mallet way. His mother's Ma Rimmer's sister.'

'Well, it's well for him he doesn't take after his aunty in the face. Good-looking lad, that.'

'Your Micky sings proper nice, Mrs A.,' said a neighbour and Mrs Andreas glowed.

*

The boy had been sulky the whole week. The war had ended without his permission or approval. He'd wanted to fight in it but you had to be eighteen and he was nowhere near. Why couldn't the war have gone on four more years? He couldn't celebrate what for him was a lost opportunity but he had, despite himself, enjoyed standing by the fire and singing. Everyone had looked at him and he could tell they were saying he was a fine lad, a good-looking lad. That had been good, had that.

That evening Ursula lit a fire in the parlour – a poor cousin to the one that raged in celebration up in Brackley Street – and Trench poured out two glasses of sherry from the bottle he usually kept for himself. It was an awkward moment when they both raised their glasses. Living as they did in a heavy-hearted silence, coming together for a toast embarrassed them. They had lost the gift of celebrating.

Trench proposed the toast but could not think to what. To the future? suggested Ursula. What future? they both thought and then Trench said: 'To Anna's future.'

'To Anna's future?' repeated Ursula, clinking her glass against his, putting it to her mouth but only pretending to drink.

'Why not *my* future?'

'Have you one?'

'Everyone has, haven't they?' As she said this she became unsure.

'I've not got one. I had one. With Norah. You denied me that.'

'If Norah had lived, there'd have been no future.'

'That I've never believed. Remember how well I know you, what you are, what you've done. I've watched you. Since you were a child I've watched you.'

'Ay, you've watched me, Father.'

'And you know what I've seen? Child? You were never no child. You've never felt like no daughter. You've felt like some spirit of ill-will haunting this house, haunting me. Why, I'm not quite convinced you're even human. Evil is how I see you.'

'No, not evil,' Ursula moaned.

'Yes, evil.'

'No, it was love I wanted, love. Evil's what came out of it but it was love as started it.'

It was always to the voice of love that she had listened even when its sound had been tinny and discordant in her head. It was always her heart which she had followed, though it beat so loudly, so quickly sometimes that it was as if a great bird was trapped inside her, flapping to get out. Even now, although it had grown cold and twisted, it was love that kept her by him, love that made her submit to his idea of justice, a love he had never given or had for her, a phantom thing, a thing of her own devising.

'Are you not drinking that sherry?' he asked her.

'No, you have it.'

She had wanted to say something that would hurt him because he had toasted Anna and not her but there was nothing she could have said. He was, like Norah, like the child, beyond being hurt.

As Britain, and with it Radcliffe Park, struggled to renew itself, the House of Content persisted in its decline. The garden was overgrown and yellow with decay; the grass high, waving, but spindly and dry. The once shapely bushes had grown so rampant and wild they had exhausted themselves. The trees, gnarled and skeletal, were hunchbacked and heavy with rotting fruit, and ivy spread over the walls of the house like a skin disease. Inside the dark house damp furred the cushions and dust from the carpets rose up in clouds whenever a draught rifled through the rooms. Fist-sized mushrooms of red fungus grew out of the skirting-boards, birds broke in and made nests in the unused bedrooms and small plants appeared between the joins of the parquet tiles.

Ursula sat at the kitchen table tracing patterns in the wood or reading tales of capable wives and responsible daughters in old copies of the *People's Friend*. Trench, meanwhile, had taken to his bed claiming his heart was wasting. Ursula nursed him dutifully but coldly.

One evening she came upstairs with a bowl of soup and a barmcake to find her father dead. He was sitting up, arms folded, mouth and eyes wide open, his face cross and disappointed, as if he'd been waiting for a bus and death had come instead. She put down the tray and did what she had once promised to do: she spat in his face and watched with interest and some satisfaction as the spittle lurched down his face.

'Now I am free. Now', she said, remembering the words of Anna Matchett, 'I can live.'

The funeral was a quiet one – only Ursula, Anna, a priest to say the office and four professional bearers for the coffin. There was as little fuss and ceremony in slotting him in his grave as in posting a letter.

The two women walked away from the grave. Anna said: 'This is how he'd have liked it done.'

'Yes, cheaply.'

'Well, he's with Norah now and little Eddie. He's found peace.'

'I doubt he'd find peace with them two. I doubt anyone could.'

Anna had grown a little thicker about the waist and fuller about the face but black, as ever, suited her. She looked well and was back in the North again now that the war and two failed affairs were over. She'd changed her name once more, this time to Turner, and had set up a taxi firm in Levenshulme. It was she who had arranged the funeral. Ursula had been all for putting the old sod in a bag and burying him in the garden.

'It'd make a good cemetery, would this garden.'

'You've always been morbid, you, and with no more taste as to what's decent as next door's cat.'

Trench had left a will which made it plain he had no money to leave. What money there was – and there was a good deal – was Ursula's and had been all along. Trench had acted as if the money was his even though he'd only been entrusted with it until Ursula had married or reached the age of twenty-five.

'The times I've asked for money for bread and such and him begrudging it when it was mine all along,' she murmured when she heard the will. She almost respected him for his secrecy. Her father had had a talent for deceit; it was from him she had inherited it.

184

Ursula found that she owned property in Petergate, Humsey, two whole streets in Mallet and half the shops in Brackley Street. She also discovered that Trench, in her name, had been giving Anna Matchett a substantial allowance.

'Very substantial for a woman with no ties.'

'He could spare it.'

'Don't you mean *I* could?'

'I'd not have taken it if I'd known it was yours. He just wanted to see me settled.'

'Off his conscience, more like.'

'*I* wasn't the one on his conscience.'

'It was to keep you quiet, to keep you sweet.'

'I didn't need no money to keep me quiet. Oh, Ursula, leave me be, leave it all be. The past is the past.'

'Is it?'

As if to prove that the past is never the past but eternally present, the news of Trench's death and burial was reported on the front pages of the *Mallet Observer*, the *Humsey Gazette*, the *Manchester Guardian* and the *Daily Star*. Anna had said that, seeing it was such a piddling little funeral, she was surprised there was the fuss. The next day there was more of it. Each of the papers had an article on what they called the Content Killings, reminding people of what had happened. The articles called Ursula 'a recluse living guiltily among the shadows' and also disclosed that the sister-in-law was now calling herself Turner and was running a successful fleet of taxis in Levenshulme.

'It's never a fleet. I've only the two cabs on the go.'

'It'll not be successful, neither, not now anyway. Looks like you'll need that allowance more than ever.'

'I've always needed it. I'd not have taken it otherwise. I've had to make my own way in this world and it hasn't been cheap and it hasn't been easy, what with folk pointing accusing fingers at me and saying such awful lies.'

'Well, you've no need to worry. I'll carry on paying it. It's yours, and this house'll be yours and the money with it when I'm dead. I've no one else to give it to.'

'You're a young woman yet.'

'I'm past thirty.'

'That's no age at all. Time enough yet to marry, have kids.'

185

'And you're forty and you're not married and won't be.'

'Ay, if I'm not wed it's not for the want of being asked.'

'No, it's because you've always been found out.'

'You're worse than them papers, forever dragging it all up. Put it behind you, like I've done.'

'You haven't, though. You've always made such a flap about getting on with life. The way you left this house, moved about all over, the Army, your taxis. Have you not noticed it's made no difference?'

'But I'm trying, aren't I? They'll not get me for not trying.'

'Do you remember that day you came during the war and you said to me: "Live, Ursula"? I loved you for that saying that.'

'I remember what your dad said.'

'Do you think I don't?'

'I've always thought he was wrong to treat you as he did. I never said owt because it was none of my business what happened between you and him. He should have forgiven you. I forgave you. Well, *forgive* is the wrong word. I understood, I suppose. I understood about Norah, about how you felt and why you did what you did, but not the child. Norah was my sister but even so I understood. But not the child, I never understood that. But he was your father and he should have tried. He's dead now and let's hope he's happy. He's gone and now it's your chance to live.'

'Happen it is, but how, Anna, how?'

She had spat in his face and declared her wish to be free but it was not as simple as that. Her father's death had not liberated her. How could it? Her father had only appeared to be her warden. She had been a prisoner of her own accord. Although the life she lived with him had been neither comfortable nor enviable it had been easy because an encloistered life, a prison life, is always simpler to lead: the choices are made for you. The other life, the free life that she fancied Anna lived and to which she now aspired, was one where you had to make your own decisions. It was the difference between sailing down a river and swimming it. The prison life meant that there was someone else to navigate and row the boat: you could sit back and take the direction for granted. The free life meant discovering and coping with the currents on your own and as best you could.

Although she did not grieve for him, she missed him in that panic-stricken way any passenger would miss a pilot who had fallen overboard taking the rudder with him. On a day-to-day level he had given a pattern to her life. She had had to rise each morning to make his breakfast and to see if he was still alive. Meals had been like markers, distinctive events in a day that, otherwise, would have passed her blandly by. Without the regimen his existence had imposed, time grew shapeless and hung about her like a baggy sweater.

His death also instantly aged her. She was no longer a daughter, no longer young. She had become a terminus, the last of her line. It was this feeling of age that finally acted upon her. The realisation that she was truly alone hit her like a bottle flung at the side of a boat that had stayed too long in the dock. She moved creakily and in far from ship-shape fashion out on to what was for her an uncharted sea.

There was some trick to life, some knack to it she could not master. Her visits to the Humsey Palais convinced her of that.

The Wishing Well was a dance-hall in Humsey, a large basement in fact. Its reputation was not good but it was where you went on a Friday night if you were young or single or both. Inside, men deserted their partners for the bar and each other's company while women in ballooning taffeta frocks sat around little tables on which were glued standard lamps with crêpe-paper shades. Serious dancers came together and never left the dance-floor. They wore dancing-pumps and carried their ordinary shoes in carrier-bags which they either hid under tables or carried about even when they were dancing. Except for the serious dancers the dance-floor would be empty for most of the evening but shortly before the end it would suddenly be swirling with couples who had magically come together. Men would leave the bar and girls rise from the tables, meet and pair off with only a word said or a look given.

There was something monotonous and routine about the way the people at the Wishing Well enjoyed themselves: they came every week because there was nowhere else as cheap and because it had become a habit. It made Ursula feel more than ever excluded from the world's doing.

As she sat in the corner, watching them, she became convinced there was some unknown password to this world of music and soft drinks and lights that changed dreamily from red to blue to gold. During the slower numbers the lights were dimmed and a chandelier descended from the ceiling. As it spun, it spangled the walls, the tablecloths, the faces of the dancers, the watchers, the wallflowers, the men at the bar. It picked out the glitter of the girls' sequined frocks and the shine on the men's oiled-back hair.

She felt old watching them, sweaty and plain in a dress that was too full, too bright and too young for her, but she was asked to dance twice.

The men who had asked her were neither attractive nor persistent. They were easy to turn down, which is what she did although part of her regretted doing so. One had been fat, nearer fifty than forty, and his belly had wobbled as he walked over to her. The other had asked, without a please or a thank-you, if she wanted to have a spin round the old dance-floor with the best dancer seen in Humsey since Fred Astaire had been on at the Palace Cinema. When he'd smiled he'd clicked his dentures forward.

'No, ta,' she said.

'What do you mean, "no, ta"?' he asked her, breath thick with Steradent fumes. 'I can't see an old hen like you getting many offers. I thought you'd be glad of me. I only asked you out of pity.'

She saw only one man who met her ideal – and after waiting so long she wanted nothing less than the ideal. She saw him the second time she went. He was fair-haired and tall but he'd been too far away for her to get a good look at his face. She supposed that it was perfect, an angel's face. She called him Gabriel in her head and spent the evening looking at him. He never looked at her but she thought that if she came again, came often, one night he might recognise her. She did not, however, go again to the Wishing Well in Humsey.

Towards the end of that second evening she went to the ladies'. It was crowded and she had to wait for a cubicle. Just as one came free, a girl who had been re-applying eye-liner and talking about which liquorice allsort she liked best saw Ursula's reflection in the mirror. She stopped in mid-flow, trying to place the woman, and then, remembering, screamed: 'It's Ursula Trench!' The way she screamed it was as if it had been King Kong or Frankenstein's Monster she had seen, not a near-to-middle-aged woman with an over-made-up face and a droopy dress. Ursula, wisely, fled.

After that she spent some evenings at the Mansfield Hotel. Anna had said that there was a nice class of man to be met there: rugby-players, accountants, men with their own cars. The Mansfield was a powdery-gold building, not quite the biggest hotel in the city but nearly. It had no millionaires among its guests but there were enough men who travelled without wives but with money to make it a profitable hunting-ground for a single woman. The place was used to single women and only barred them if they made their business too obvious.

Ursula was too innocent to be obvious. Besides, she wasn't looking for profit but for love. She was looking for one man, someone like the Angel at the Wishing Well or a man like the men on the knitting patterns in the *People's Friend*, handsome, kind, as unlike her father as possible and worth surrendering everything for.

It might have been better for her if she had been like the other single women at the Mansfield Hotel. A little promiscuity might not have harmed her. Certainly it would not have damaged her as much as her pursuit of the romantic ideal eventually did. But whenever a hand touched her knee or a key to a hotel room was casually swung around a gentleman's finger after the port and lemon he had bought her had been downed, she would turn prim and tell them that she was not that sort of a girl.

This brought a variety of responses, mostly surprised ones. If she wasn't like that, what was she doing in the bar of the Mansfield Hotel? Some men thought she must be playing hard to get and brought her another drink. Any woman was expected to be a little coy and to say no at least once; that was how the game was played.

These men she found difficult to fend off, but when they became persistent she would ask herself, 'How would Anna cope with this?' and she usually found a way to get rid of them. Usually the man would be quite relieved. They seemed almost glad to have a strange woman's company for an evening without having the obligation either to pay or to perform at the end of it. One or two became angry but were much too embarrassed or discreet to make much of a scene. Only one man asked for the money back on the port and lemon he'd bought her.

She was doing her best. She looked quite handsome some evenings. She could afford to dress well and did so as far as she could. Her ideas on fashion and make-up came mostly from the 1930s magazines that had belonged to Norah, which she had spent the war reading and rereading. When she went into Lewis's or Madame Modes she looked at what the dummies in the window were wearing and bought that.

The inevitable happened just as it had at the Wishing Well in Humsey: one of the women recognised her and told the other women. It was always women who recognised her. It was as if they were the ones who kept the flame for all that was bad, tragic and never to be forgotten. The next time she turned up she was stopped at the door. The doorman told her to go away and keep away. Her sort were not wanted at the Mansfield Hotel.

It felt like everyone knew who she was and what she had done, but fewer people remembered her than she thought. Fewer still could have linked the middle-aged woman with the fish-eyed girl of the pre-war newspapers, but it had now happened twice. It unnerved her.

On subsequent outings to the pictures or a café did people really stare at her? Was it because she was a woman alone in a public place – had she no man? no girlfriend? no morals? – or because they recognised her as Ursula Trench, who had killed a kid and its mam and had got away with it? A guilty conscience and an uncertain social sense made her feel there was no place she could go unrecognised. She found herself on the rim of a nightmare world where she could expect people to turn on her in a moment. She withdrew once again to the House of Content.

To live like a prisoner, a nun, seemed to be her fate, yet the more inescapable a fate the more urgent, even crazed, became the need to transcend it.

She became a blonde. It was not the answer to life's problems but at least it did not add to them. The hairdresser had said she looked like a Diana Dors or a Marilyn Monroe: what she didn't look like was Ursula Trench.

She thought of returning to the Wishing Well in Humsey or the bar of the Mansfield Hotel, but her nerve failed her. Instead she sat in the dusty parlour of the House of Content. The house was still a near-ruin but she herself would be immaculately painted, polished and bleached. She drank and smoked more than was good for her but she had money enough to support any vice to which her loneliness led her. She peered out through the net curtains stained nicotine yellow. She hoped to see angels floating down Park End and up the drive to her house but none came.

Nothing changes, she decided. Ten minutes later, Andreas passed by and everything had.

She saw a handsome man, a boy really – the Angel Gabriel or so she thought – entering the park. She got up, left the house without a coat and headed after him. She acted on instinct just as she had all those years before, the night the child had died, just as she would years later when she met her death in Brackley Street. The sound of wings filled her head, flapping and suffocating all thought.

She walked behind him for a while, studying him like the scene of a crime. He was twenty, maybe, but it was hard to say because he kept his back to her.

This is him, she thought, this is the one. He was tall, his shoulders broad but not overly so, enough to give his body a tapered look. He wore a blue suit of cheap cloth, shiny at the elbows, a concertina of wrinkles at the back of the knees. He tries to look smart but he hasn't the money for it, poor lamb, poor pet. She would help him out. His hair was longer than was fashionable or even proper for the time but it was blond not the ash-white blond of the Angel at the Wishing Well but yellow, yellower than even her own unnaturally coloured hair. He was not the Angel Gabriel from the Wishing Well in Humsey but, no matter, she was committed to him all the same. She had fallen and he had caught her, even if he didn't know it yet.

191

He walked at an easy pace around the park, unaware of being followed and heading nowhere. He sat on a bench by the boating-pond, stretched out his legs and yawned.

The day was too cold for most people to go strolling in the park. There was no one else about but the two of them. God had been kind. He had arranged the park just for them.

She sat next to him on the bench.

'It is free, this bench?' she asked him after she had sat down.

'Yes, 'course.' He looked at her oddly. There were five or six other benches around the pond and the park was full of places to sit. He smiled to himself after a bit.

She was as pleased with his face as if she had designed it herself. True, such was her lop-sided state of mind, she saw only its virtues, the watery-blue eyes, the pale skin, the fair hair that fell straight and shiny over his eyebrows until he flicked it back with a toss of his head. Such graceful eyebrows, too, almost semi-circles, half-hoops that gave his face a look of puzzled innocence.

Here, she decided, was her one bright love, the breath of her nostrils, her mavourneen. Ursula believed in love at first sight. She believed in many dangerous things and understood none of them.

'It's cold, isn't it?'

'Yes, isn't it?' Nerves made her voice high-pitched. She sounded prim but did not feel it. She forgot that, with her hair and painted nails, prim was the last thing she looked. She tried to put a tone of inviting warmth to her voice when she added: 'For November it is cold, yes.'

He spoke. I sat down and asked him if the seat were free but he spoke first, really.

He spoke again. 'You've no coat on,' he said. It wasn't the most perceptive observation. It was November and she was shivering in a skirt and cotton print blouse, green with magyar sleeves.

He's not just speaking, he is conversing. We are having a conversation. Panic! Panic! What to say? Following him round the park she had been drowning in words, questions, witty things to say and to impress him with, but the words had evaporated in her head and her mouth was as dry as a desert.

'No, I came out without one.'

She had answered him. Words came just like that.

'Why did you come out without a coat?'

She couldn't say why. He'd think her mad or daft and she didn't want that, so she said: 'It's not far, my house. It's by the gates. Would you like to see it? It's called Content.' She bit her lip but he seemed not to know it. He was laughing and smoothing his hair down, embarrassed.

'I could make some tea.' This was bold of her. It was not how the game was played; the man should take the lead. She'd learned that much at the Mansfield Hotel. They didn't like it if you rushed them but she could think of no other way and he wasn't turning her down, either. Well, not quite. He was laughing still but quietly, not at her, just shyly.

'It's cold here. You said so yourself. A cup of tea . . . well, it'll warm you up.'

'All right,' he said. 'What can I lose?'

She wasn't sure whether it was because he was a quick walker or whether she was just too eager but they seemed to hurry out of the park.

'I come here at weekends, on Sundays anyway,' he told her. 'I come when I can. I like parks.'

'Yes, they're very likeable.'

'I like the peace. Not all the time, mind.'

'Yes, I know what you mean.' Words threatened to desert her again. Make yourself interesting to your man. Show him you have things in common. 'I like peace, too, now and then. And parks.'

'Is this where you live?' he asked as they walked up the drive. 'I thought this place was empty.'

She saw Content through his eyes and was ashamed. What must he think of her to live in a place like that?

'I'm having it done up,' she said, and instantly resolved to do it. 'Top to bottom, the works.'

'It'll cost you.'

'I can afford it.'

His lips made a small 'o' and he whistled. He was impressed, as she'd hoped he would be. If he likes me for my money, that'll do for a start. She wasn't proud.

'Are you not from round here?' she asked as she opened the door and they went inside.

He did not answer. The house's dilapidated exterior was nothing to the decay inside. He put his hand over his nose and mouth and began to back away. She could tell he was trying to leave, but she took him by the arm into the parlour.

'As I said, I'm having it all done up, top to bottom, inside and out.'

'It needs it.'

'Don't be put off by how it looks. When I was a girl this was a lovely house. People said. Are you from round here?'

He shook his head.

'I thought not.' He hadn't recognised the house, he hadn't recognised her, so he wasn't from Radcliffe Park.

'I'm from Mallet.'

'No parks in Mallet.'

'Not like this one. Must be nice to be so close by.'

She would have offered him tea but she would have had to leave him to make it and she wasn't sure he would stay if he was left alone. There was the sherry she'd been drinking from dawn onwards and she offered him that. She directed his attention to the mantelpiece – 'Proper marble, is that' – while she used the curtains to wipe the glasses. She gave him the sherry and sat down on the sofa next to him.

'What do you do?'

'I work in a shop. A paper shop in Brackley Street. It's my aunty's. Ma Rimmer's. Do you know it?'

'I more than know it.'

'I've not been there long. I don't like it but I got laid off from Bradbury's. I was in dyes. I wanted to go in the Army but I got consumption when I was a kid so they don't let you in. I'm all right now. I don't cough or nothing.'

'You know, here you are, telling me all this, and I don't know your name.'

'Me mam calls me Michael, but I'm Micky really. Micky Andreas.'

'Andreas? You don't look foreign with that hair.'

'Me dad was foreign but he didn't live long. I hate Ma Rimmer's but I got plans.'

'I'm sure you have. You'll get on. You've a look about you.'

'Oh ay! I've a look, have I?'

'Oh yes, you've a definite look. How old are you, then?'

'I'm old enough.' He sounded grouchy, as if being thought young was no advantage in life. 'Do we do it down here or have you a bed?'

'I've a bed.'

'Well,' he said, getting up and putting his sherry on the mantelpiece, 'we'll leave the sherry down here. It's piss-awful. I hope your bed's better than that sofa. Smells like a dog died on it.'

She led him by the hand through the hall and up the stairs to her room. They moved slowly but easily as if through water. The great dark house was indeed like a sea-filled cavern, the light dark green, the air soupy with must.

'Ay, you know what? You know my name but I don't know yours.' He sounded peeved as if she had deprived him of some treat when he had been generous enough to give her one.

She hesitated. Should she spoil it all? He'd not recognised the house but he might the name. 'Anna,' she said. 'Call me Anna.'

Micky Andreas was not an angel, nor was he especially good-looking. It was true he was blond, strikingly so, and being blond in a place as dark as Radcliffe Park assured him of favourable glances, but his mouth was full of yellowing teeth and he had a wall-eyed look that made him seem a little simple.

It was not his first time but he was neither practised nor sensitive enough to realise it was hers. For Ursula it was not quite the foamy bath of bliss she had hoped but she acted as though it was – for his sake. She wanted it to be worthwhile for him. He rapped out commands, 'Lie back', 'Open your legs', 'Scratch my back, go on, scratch it' like a sergeant on drill duty. He entered her smoothly but there was still pain and some blood, only a little, not enough for him to notice. The pleasure for her lay in the fact that it was happening at all. Her hands met behind his back and she hugged him and, sweet, he hugged her back.

As Andreas, lean and sweaty, grunted away, his whole

195

weight on her, she pantomimed delight and gratitude in order to please him, make him stay, make him come back for more. So intense was the performance, she convinced herself that what she was feeling was the result not of her own intense desire but of his expertise and kindness as a lover. The general ache for love and attention had narrowed itself into a precise and painful desire for him, just him, no one else.

He stayed until evening came and the brown sky outside darkened to black. Then he said he had to go. He lived with his mam in Mallet. She'd be wondering where he was. He had work in the mornings. He had to get up early for the bus from Mallet and have the papers sorted before Ma Rimmer arrived.

'She comes later than ever now she's got me and swans off early an' all.'

'Doesn't she live over the shop? I know there's room to.'

He wondered how she knew a thing like that. 'She used to live up top but she got herself this bungalow in Roston. She's done well out of that shop to buy one of them up there. It's a good earner, is that shop, and it's going to be mine.'

'You said you had plans.'

'I have. Ma Rimmer, she likes me, likes me a lot. I'm her nephew. She says she's got her eye on me. Trusts me, she does. Look.'

It was meant to be his turn to impress her. He pulled out a huge clump of keys from his jacket pocket.

'Keys to the shop, these are.'

Ursula shook her head. Was there no end to this boy's many talents and charms? The keys to his aunty's shop! Without irony she told him: 'That's really good, is that.'

He was getting dressed now. Reluctantly she picked his trousers off the floor and handed them to him. 'You need a new suit. It's all shiny. We'll have to see what we can do.'

It hurt her to see him getting dressed. Clothes made him distant, unobtainable.

'You'll come again?'

He didn't answer for a long time. Ursula went through agony until she realised that he was grinning at her and his hands were slowly, very slowly doing up his flies. He'd been teasing.

'Yeah, I'll come again. I'll come next Sunday. You've got the taste for me, haven't you?'

There was something cruel and superior in the way he said that and in the way he was standing over her. It was as if her appetite for him and her lack of restraint lowered her in his eyes.

'I'll build a fire in the parlour. I'll tidy up, buy new sheets and that, and you'll want feeding, too.'

She went downstairs with him and they kissed by the door. He broke the kiss first but before he moved away entirely he pressed his crotch against her because that was what he thought she most wanted about him.

He waved goodbye at the gate and walked off up Park End. She watched him go and prayed that he'd turn round and wave again.

Monday morning she set about cleaning the House of Content. She went up Brackley Street to buy a new mop, brush, bucket and cartons of liquid detergent. She stood awhile by the bridge and saw him come out of the shop to wipe the window down. He did not see her and she had not had the nerve to go up and speak to him.

What would he think, she wondered, when she told him that the building that housed the shop was hers as well as other shops along that street? Even the house in Mallet where he lived with his mother might belong to her. She had an empire whose wealth she had never exploited. She had lived off it but had never governed it. She would do so now. She would discover its full extent and he would reign over it with her. The House of Content would be their palace; at last it would live up to its name. She made enquiries about builders and decorators.

'Yes, the whole house, top to bottom, and the garden, too. I'll have it bright with flowers.'

She had money. She would spend it. Wasn't this what Anna would call living?

Sunday came. She sat in the still dingy but now spick parlour by a full fire or by the window hung with fresh velvet curtains, blue and cold to the touch. In her anxiety that all should be well, she would scurry up the stairs to inspect the bedroom, as if five minutes could make the clean sheets dirty again, the air grow stale once more and the dust settle thicker than ever.

The long day lengthened and grew dark. He had not come. Then she saw him by the gate, saw him stand there, hesitate, and turn away.

She blamed the house. She had the painters come to do the doors and window-sills bright yellow.

'There's other work more pressing to be done on this house,' she was told. 'Some of this wood's rotten right through.' They showed her the thick flakes of wood that had come off in their brushes. She told them, never mind. The rest of the house would be attended to in time. The paintwork was only to cheer up the house just as make-up had wakened her own tired face.

The garden, too, was fixed. She paid some Scouts five whole pounds and they tore up the dried and skeletal bushes, mowed and clipped the yellowing grass and turned the soil after dragging out armfuls of knotted weeds. When they had finished, the garden had a bald, shaved look to it, stark and unattractive, as if the tidying had been a violence done to it. She brought them biscuits and Tizer on a tray. The boys nibbled at the biscuits nervously and mimed polite sips at the Tizer. Only the verdant and uncreased pound-notes gave them comfort. They held them up to the light and considered how much they would give to the Scouts' charity and how much they would keep for themselves.

She built a bonfire with the litter and deadwood they had harvested. Its chocolate smoke rose up in rich folds and melted into the sky. The fragrance of fire and autumn leaves, the spit and crackle of the flames as they licked at the black twigs reminded her of murder and of roses.

The house looked half-normal in the half-light of the November evening when he came again. He had dithered by the gate but this time he made it to the door. She was too grateful to ask him what had kept him.

'I didn't know who you were,' he said finally.

'And who am I?'

'You're not called Anna. You're called Ursula Trench and you killed a kid and its mam – or so they say.' Strangely, although he looked sullen and his voice was slow and heavy with a grudge against her for fooling him, he sounded almost respectful, even admiring: she had done all that and got away with it. He couldn't quite believe that the woman he had heard about was the one standing before him now but he felt safe from her. He knew about her; it made him feel clever and invulnerable. She'd not fool him twice.

And she was thinking: This is what will always happen. Life will pass us by, men will, for what was done in this house and never mind that it was done for love.

'This house,' he said, waving his hand, not noticing how she had transformed it for him, 'this house, it gives me the creeps.'

She found pride, held her head straight and looked at him levelly: 'And do I give you the creeps?'

He thought about it for a while. 'No, you give me the hots.'

God has given women wiles and men on whom to use them. Ursula, thinking it wily, lay down and let him cover her.

This was the time she would best remember, the night he came of his own accord, knowing full well who she was and what it was she was supposed to have done. Him, lying on her in front of the fire, his skin red as a tilestone in the light of the burning coals and speckled black from the flakes of soot that floated down from the unswept chimney, his mouth on hers, his hands on her thighs, her breasts, her throat. She held his cock, hard and slippery with a pearly gloss, his juice forming a pool in her cupped hands. This memory of him would stay when all others became unfixed. She would use that night as evidence of his love when nothing else remained to prove it.

While he was thinking how what you got easily you held cheaply. He didn't believe in love, at least not with the likes of her, but if a thing was going free you didn't turn it down. He kissed her and all that, but he kept his eyes open, so it didn't count.

'I've seen what you've done with the garden and that,' he said, 'but this house, it's still creepy. Is it haunted?'

'Only by me.'

Anna Matchett would have recognised a rare joke, Andreas did not.

'I've seen what you've done with the garden and that,' he said, 'but this house, it's still creepy. Is it haunted?'

'Only by me.'

Anna Matchett would have recognised a rare joke, Andreas did not.

'There's a room on top of Ma Rimmer's. I asked her about it and she said it wasn't up to her.'

'If you wan them rooms, they're yours,' she told him. She had wanted to surprise him but it was obvious that he already knew. It was no longer a gift but something he could take for granted.

'The thing is how do you give them me without her knowing, you know, how I got them?'

> Fish gotta swim
> Birds gotta fly
> I gotta love one man till I die
> Can't help loving that man of mine.

Ma Rimmer had a voice as flat as a squashed bucket and about as soft. It gave no one pleasure but herself. She had a wireless in her shop on a shelf above the Woodbines. She twiddled its dial throughout the working day in search of songs and singers who could accompany her.

'News again! I can't be doing with all this talk on a wireless. Now, how about Anne Shelton or Lee Whitely? Lovely voice, Lee Whitely, although she's been blind from birth.' Ma Rimmer had a particular empathy with disabled singers because of her own club foot. 'And there's Jane Froman. No legs, poor woman, but lovely shoulders.'

> With a song in my heart
> I behold your adorable face
> Just a song at the start
> But it soon is a hymn to your grace

And when the music swelled the shop counter would scatter, the backdrop of shelves and faded *News Illustrated* would be replaced by a canvas sky hanging over a garden of muslin trees among which Ma Rimmer would find herself trilling in a lamé gown with a full orchestral backing to the left of the stacked cans of Ideal Milk.

To the less musically-inclined, the shop was a dark hole, light from outside being blocked by pyramids of sweet-jars, yellowing copies of *Reveille* and *Woman's Own*, tin-plated adverts for Cadbury's cocoa and Brooke Bond Dividend tea. Inside, the smell of stale newsprint, Ma Rimmer's sweat and burned cabbage was thick enough to slice.

She was broad in the bone, she liked to say, toothless, too, but for one long brown one that she liked to wiggle with her tongue when in a pensive mood or when the music was particularly sad and she didn't know the words. She had a habit of rustling when she walked; underneath her woolly cardigans and thick skirts, she wrapped layer upon layer of newspapers around herself for warmth. She moved noisily and slowly because of her club foot. Her elevator shoe was a magnificent black altarpiece so heavy that, at a trot, it could have cracked a paving flag.

God had not been generous to her but had had the kindness not to let her realise it. Ma Rimmer loved life as she loved her music: with great passion but no real gift. She was the centre of her universe, the star the earth travelled round for light and wisdom, and she scared Ursula Trench to bits.

'You've no objection to tenants above your shop, Mrs Rimmer? I dislike the waste of space,' said Ursula in her best Anna Matchett Levenshulme businesswoman's voice. Andreas was kneeling down with his back to her, pretending not to know who she was.

'Well, this place isn't mine. I just pay the rent and keep the profits as your father used to put it – a good man in his day, although there are some who say he had blood on his hands and murder on his conscience. But I'm not one of them. No, it's not my place to object to anything you want, Miss Trench. Not that we know what you want, you not being much about. And who can blame you when folk say what they say about you?' Ma Rimmer smiled charitably on the murdering bitch.

'So you'll not object to folk above the shop?'

'Me? No, the more the merrier, and a bit more money for you, I dare say. I wouldn't know what to do with money like yours, I wouldn't really. No, tell a lie, I'd have me own band

and I'd be a singist.' Ma Rimmer's small eyes glazed over in a vision of herself squeezed into a tight frock and in front of a microphone, lips shaped to croon and horribly red.

'She's a dead good voice, has Ma Rimmer,' Andreas simpered, the flirt.

Ma Rimmer simpered back: 'Isn't he a pet? I could eat him.' Her leer was wide and unworried by incest. 'Yes, if I had the money, I'd go on the road with our Stock. He knows a few tricks, does our Stock.'

Stock was her dog. A distant cousin to a terrier, he had the head of a frayed and balding mop but his body was a mystery, only his head above the butterfly clasp of Ma Rimmer's handbag was ever visible. The handbag, an old brown leather case, the sides streaked grey with dribble, was the dog's permanent home.

Stock was her poppet, her pet, her lamb, she told Ursula – she told everyone – as she pressed her face against his matted mouth in search of his pink tongue and an affectionate lick.

'And do you know of any likely tenants?' Ursula asked, trying not to look at Andreas. 'It'd have to be someone you'd be happy with.'

This was Andreas's cue. 'If you don't mind, Miss Trench,' he muttered stagily, 'I'd like it if I were considered.'

'What, Micky!' Ma Rimmer said. 'And leave your mam in Mallet?'

'It's a long way from Mallet each morning, Aunty Joyce.' He called her that only when appealing for something directly. 'It'd help in the mornings with the papers and you could get here as late as you like and find them done. And you'd feel better at night if you knew it were me keeping an eye over things.'

'Oh, he's quick,' giggled Ma Rimmer. 'He's after taking over this shop and no mistake. I doubt he'd be as quick in my grave. Mind you, quickness is a virtue in a man and won't he be a terror with the ladies when he's on his own? Can we trust him, do you think, Miss Trench? Will he be as pure in his deeds as he is in the face?'

She knows, thought Ursula.

'What'll you do for furniture, Micky, because it's a right mess up there, Miss Trench. There's not a stick. And what there was is mine and in my Roston bungalow.'

'Furniture is not a problem, Mrs Rimmer,' Ursula explained. 'I've more than I need or use. The accommodation will be furnished. I'll expect you to move in promptly.'

'Oh, look at that, our Stock.' Ma Rimmer snuggled up against her dog. 'Furniture, too. That's special treatment. I hope you'll not be giving him your best bits, Miss Trench. Men don't appreciate them. And let's face it, all this young fella needs is a good bed.' She gave Ursula a knowing look, her most regular expression even when in deepest ignorance. 'Love, oh love, oh careless love,' she sang with the wireless, swinging her hips and rustling. 'Aren't them wireless men clever, the way they put on the song you're feeling just when you're feeling it. Marvellous, they are really.'

Whereas she had once dreamed of turning the House of Content into a passion palace for both of them, not even her own excessive love could have made of the rooms above Ma Rimmer's shop a mansion sufficiently buttressed against the world's animosity or sufficiently decorative to keep its tenant happily imprisoned there.

There was a kitchen without a stove or shelves but Andreas had said he'd not want either; he'd eat at the café at the top of Brackley Street or go home to his mam in Mallet. There was a bathroom without a bath but there was a tiny sink and a toilet which he thought was dead posh, being used to the outside type only. She offered to have his bedroom decorated and properly furnished but Ma Rimmer was right: he wanted only a decent bed, somewhere to hang his clothes and a mirror maybe. He did not care for décor, it not being a manly concern. He preferred the fading wallpaper with its pattern of rosebuds and orange milkmaids to the thought of having decorators in and folk finding out who was paying them and what Andreas was doing to deserve the attention.

The first month she saw him nearly every night. She had nothing else to do but dance moth-like about his flame. She was always available, leaving her life empty in the hope that he would fill it. He was young and full of it and wanted to prove it, turned on by the novelty of a woman in his bed and him not wed to her. In time, however, their meetings levelled off to every other night, and then two nights, three nights, a whole week could go by – and often did – without her seeing him.

It was such a dull affair, hardly worthy of its violent climax and undeserving of the passion she invested in it.

Its secrecy impelled them to observe certain rituals and take precautions against being found out. For him but not for her these soon lost their criminal appeal and became dull and routine.

She would wait until dark then travel up Brackley Street, hang round the streets thereabouts in a mac and scarf, hoping not to be recognised, before taking up her post under the bridge. She called it that, her post. It made her feel like a soldier, someone with a purpose, on guard against passers-by and watching out for the signal to advance. The back light would come on. This meant that Ma Rimmer had gone home and the shop was locked up. It meant that Andreas was now alone and she could sneak in through the back door which he'd left on the latch and go up the dark stairs to his room.

In the early days of their affair he would be in bed and daringly naked but for his socks which he kept on because his circulation was not of the best. As the affair went on she would more likely find him not in bed but dressed and sitting at the dressing-table that had once belonged to her step-mother. He would be resting his feet against the side of the paraffin heater, picking at the blisters counting newspapers had given him, or cutting off the tops of dead matches with a bread-knife for the model battleships he liked to make.

She would undress and get into bed, keeping her cardie on for warmth while he looked about for anything he could do to stave off the moment when they would have to lie down together and do it: he insensitive and quick, she moist and too giving.

They did talk but not much. He had nothing to say to her except how his day had gone – 'Same as usual' – and she had too much to say, so much that she was unable to say anything. They could, of course, speak, as all lovers can, through their bodies but even this was less an erotic discourse than a dreary gossip. Their bodies spoke different languages and each misunderstood the other. She would take his grunts and groans as being expressive of tenderness and desire because that was what she most wanted, needed, to hear. He took her loving sighs as the sounds of a woman begging for a bit of dick, any dick although his was best.

'You're a right slag, you,' he would say, smiling so that it looked as if it were a playful insult. 'Can't get enough of me.'

Yes, yes, she was anything he wanted; anything he made her.

'Only you,' she would whimper in his ear, 'only you,' and he would think that was what all women like her said when you had them in a bed.

They might, of course, have talked of childhoods and the past, but Ursula's past was best left unmentioned and he kept quiet about his own.

Giving a woman information, he believed, was like giving her a bit of your soul and you'd not get it back easily, either.

Anyway, he had long ago decided that Ursula was not for talking to. There was another girl on his mind, not one he had necessarily met as yet. This girl was not a woman without shame, not a woman who waited in the dark and gave up her sex without a struggle. This girl was younger than he was, a nice girl who would say no, a girl he could wed and not worry about.

The humping over and done with for the night, they would fall asleep. He always suggested, the bed being so narrow, him having to get up so early and the chance that Ma Rimmer might catch them one morning, that she go home. She'd just have to nip out the back, down the canal path in the dark, it wouldn't take long. Sometimes she did go, leaving in a huff, hurt and hoping to hurt him back.

Unless he insisted otherwise, she would stay. She would not even sleep, only share his bed. It was best that way: there was no danger of oversleeping or meeting Ma Rimmer as she went out. Also she could watch him.

She preferred looking at him to almost anything else. Looking made her feel that he was hers. He had skin like china, she told herself, bone white with perhaps a faint blue patina from veins palely visible. When he was peaceful and snoring she would lift up the blankets and look down his long body and would become so lost in contemplation of it that it became no longer a body but a gallery of precious sights and objects down which she could wander, a warm museum of flesh.

And every month she would pray. She would whisper God's name as fervently as she whispered his in the hope that a prayer would be answered and a child would be granted her. A child would take the place of one lost. A child would make up for so many things – for the past and for an ignoble present. A child would be recompense and consolation for a life spent loving one man and now two without reward or gratification. She dearly hoped for an Angel to visit her with glad tidings but each month the opportunity for an Annunciation passed.

She was not quite stupid. She was alive to the fact that he did not love her as much as she did him but she hoped that he loved her enough to make it last. So what if, at times, he was lukewarm? So what if, at times, he turned her away with a feeble excuse, was brusque and unaffectionate, even ashamed of her? There were other times when he would relent, times when he could be loving, times when he himself believed that theirs was a grand romance, one with a purpose and a future. (To those who have lived on crumbs a whole biscuit would be a banquet. Ursula could be grimly happy with very little.)

When he refused to see her some nights she would send him notes through the mail, pink envelopes heavily scented that Ma Rimmer would pick up and sniff but never directly mention.

'I love you,' she would write.

I plan my days about you and sit here thinking of you and hoping you think of me. I think of you all the time and sometimes I think of you so hard that it's like as if you are sitting in my head and we are as close as close can be. I love you dead bad and must see you soon because otherwise God help me I don't know what I'll do. Last time you didn't say when we'd see each other again but I must see you. I always seem close to tears and my throat is all sore from choking it all back but I will not cry or make demands next time we meet. Promise. Promise. Promise. Thursday I'll come round. Be in. Love, Ursula.

Andreas would burn these notes and covertly sprinkle the ashes into the milky canal.

Poor Andreas. How had all this come about and how would it end? He could not tell. He had never liked her and she no longer excited him. She disturbed him. It wasn't just her need for him, this appetite for him that was large enough to swallow him whole; he sensed, too, that there was something dangerous about her. The past, which they had agreed to leave unmentioned, began to worry him. He wondered if she had chosen him not only as her lover but also as her torturer and victim, too. She was leading him into a moral shadowland and he was scared of the dark.

The time when she had sucked his dick, her own spontaneous idea and a thing that had shocked him as much as it had pleasured him, he had come in her face. It was not intentionally done and he had apologised sincerely. She had not minded at all. She had even wiped it round her cheeks and rubbed it in as if it were face cream. Disgusted, he had told her to wipe it off. Didn't she know what germs it might have in it? She had searched about the room for a cloth of some sorts and had come across his undershorts, greying cotton and mustard-coloured at the crotch. She had pressed them against her face.

'Hey!' he had shouted, snatching them from her. 'I've got to wear them tomorrow.'

This had pleased her. She said she hoped she had left an impression on his shorts as Christ had done on Veronica's veil. All her passion and her suffering would leave their mark on his underpants. She thought she had said and done a beautiful thing. He thought she was filthy and a nuisance. It had been a Wednesday and he changed his underwear on Sundays. He cursed her for mucking them up but he promised to wear them. She liked the idea of her face resting against his body in this way. He had not much choice, his other pair being at his mam's in Mallet and in the wash.

He flew through her mind like a shuttle through a loom. He was woven into the white fabric of her days in blood-red check. Love occupied her totally and even on the hardest days she was not bored as he was.

Then she found there were fewer and fewer nights when

he was available and the time spent waiting for him under the bridge at Brackley Street lengthened. Long after the thunderous clump of Ma Rimmer's elevator shoe had been heard overhead, Ursula would be standing in the cold, the wind, the rain, waiting for the back light to come on. Some nights he said he just clean forgot to turn it on – 'I was up here waiting for you. I wondered where'd you got to' – and some nights, when she had given up being patient, she hammered at the back door and there was no reply.

He said he had been at his mam's in Mallet. His mam did his washing and liked to feed him when she could and a boy had to see his mother, after all. Ursula could not argue with that.

She couldn't argue with anything, even after she found in his jacket pocket a book of matches from the Wishing Well in Humsey.

'So what?' he had asked when challenged. Ursula had no answer.

On that final morning, she took her time leaving. She moved dully about his room and dressed slowly to antagonise him. He sat on the edge of the bed shoving her clothes into her hands, hurrying her none too gently along.

Dressed finally and leaving without so much as a kiss from him, she paused at the bedroom door and looked at him a while. The early-morning sun greased his bare shoulders but pitted his face with shadows. He turned away embarrassed by her stare and covered himself in the blankets.

'When will I see you again?'

He didn't answer and she did not press him. If she had, the answer he gave might have been the one she feared most. She could not have borne that.

She closed the door behind her and stood on the dingy landing. She liked to dawdle there because it dragged out the time she spent with him, cut down the time spent waiting alone in the House of Content with only its ghosts and a growing number of sherry-bottles for company. As she stood there envisaging the lonely hours ahead, there came from downstairs the click and shuffle of the back door being opened.

It was Coronation Day and Ma Rimmer had come early. The young queen was having to rise sooner than was her custom in order to prepare herself for the big day and what was good enough for a Windsor would do just as nicely for a Rimmer.

She wasn't quite surprised to see Ursula on the stairs. She had seen the back of her disappearing down the canal path quite a few mornings but had said nothing to the boy because she realised that, whatever it was he was playing at, he was having the sense to keep it quiet.

'Well, Miss Trench!' she cooed in mock-astonishment and Stock in her handbag yapped just as brightly. 'What a keen landlady you are. Half-five in the morning, the dark hardly lifting, but here you are keeping a watchful eye on your tenant.'

Ursula had pride enough left not to want to suffer Ma Rimmer's innuendo. Subterfuge had been for the boy's sake and there was no point in it now. If they had been more open from the start, things would have gone better for them. She was half-glad that Ma Rimmer had caught her.

Love needs a witness and now she had one.

'You always knew about us, didn't you?'

'Well, if I didn't, I do now. Quiet, Stock, the lady's leaving.'

Ursula did not move. She stood at the top of the landing and looked down at Ma Rimmer and her dog. The dog yapped on. Across the landing she heard Andreas stir in his room and saw his shadow flit across the foot of the door. No doubt he was listening but was too much a coward to come out and face his aunty. She would give him courage.

'I love him.' She said it simply but clearly, and in the hope that he would hear, take heart, and join her, hand in hand, on the landing.

'If you want a conversation with me, Miss Trench, which I hope you don't, you'll kindly come down off your perch. You're giving me a crick in the neck looking up at you.'

Ursula slowly walked down the stairs, aiming at majesty and missing. She would have walked on past Ma Rimmer but didn't. Something made her stop and repeat again, 'I love him,' but she whispered it this time like the dirty secret it was.

'You? You just love trouble.' Face to face with Ursula, Ma Rimmer had also decided to have the pleasure of uttering words long kept back. 'You make a decent woman's flesh creep and I'm surprised a lovely lad like that one upstairs has owt to do with you. Yes, trouble's what you love, so you leave that lad alone.'

'I love him.'

'So you've said, but does he love you? Listen here, while I tell you something.'

'Tell me what? I'm not listening to anything you've got to say.'

'Oh, you'll listen, landlady or not. I've not been deaf or blind and I've never been stupid. I can see what's gone on. See it? I've smelt it. But I haven't said owt. I've had no need. Oh, I could have put the mockers on it right away and no mistake. I'd have just had to say, "No more, our Micky, all right, no more," and he'd have dropped you there and then. I only had to say, "I'll tell your mam on you, our Micky," because a boy always wants his mam to think well of him. I only had to say, "Folk are talking, our Micky," and that'd have been the end of that. But I didn't, I said nothing, and why? Out of kindness to you? No. I know him, you see. He's a pretty boy but simple, not simple-minded but simple in his needs. He wants my business, this shop. If I get my way, he'll have it, too.'

'I think I have something to say about who has this shop.'

'So you do, but if you want to put the mockers on it, it'll make no odds. There's other shops and I've quite a bit put by. I've told Micky this but I've also said he'll have to get a wife to run it with him. A shop needs a woman. It can do without a man – look at me – but it can't do without a woman, no shop can. You see, there's this girl in Mallet his mother has her eye on. Met his mother, have you? My sister. Lovely woman, hard life: foreign husband . . . well, it didn't help. She'd not think much of you but, then, you'll never meet. You're not the sort of girl a boy brings home to his mother.'

Things had to run their course, Ursula told herself. What had to be . . . well, it had to be, and there was no arguing about it. She had to stand and listen. She had to hear it all.

Andreas came out on to the landing in vest and pants.

'Are you still here?' he moaned and then saw Ma Rimmer. He

gave her a look that his aunty rightly interpreted: 'Deal with it for me, Aunty Joyce.' Aunty Joyce nodded up at him to say she was doing just that. Relieved and ashamed, he scuttled back to his room and closed the door.

'Good morning, Mrs Rimmer,' Ursula said with excessive politeness and walked over to the door, determined to leave, if not with hope, at least with a little dignity.

'Anyway, this girl,' Ma Rimmer went on as if she had never been interrupted. 'Iris is her name. Her dad has a shop in Mallet, a greengrocer's, and her mam was on the meat-counter at Lewis's Food Hall, so selling is in her blood. She's been around for tea at his mam's three times to my knowledge which round here is as good as wearing a ring and putting it in the papers. You see, Miss Trench, there's girls as men wed, like Iris, and there's girls . . . well, you're no girl, are you? Not been a girl this long while, have you?'

Ursula's hand was on the door-handle. She turned it back and forth, making the lock go *click, click, click.*

Ma Rimmer stepped back and studied her for a moment, taking her in with a dismissive flick of her lizard eyelids.

'Iris will keep him in line. She's that sort. She's like me. She loves life, knows how to live it, but knows how to live it sensible. Our Micky'll not know what hit him when he weds her. And he will wed her. There's nothing been said as yet but it's all decided more or less. Then they'll come here to this shop and take over from me. I've my bungalow in Roston, nice area, nice bungalow. I've worked hard for it and the mornings are getting to me. The foot slows me down more than it did and I've a right to some peace and quiet, an easy time after all these years of counting newspapers and being nice to customers you'd not spit on if they were burning, if truth be known. Micky's mam'll come live with me. There's a nice wool-shop near by, so she'll not want for something to do. We'll all be set up, all happy. It's what life intends. It's how things would have been without you poking your nose in. It's how things will be despite your nose having been put in. You'll not make much difference to anyone's life, you won't. You've done your damage long since. You've none left to harm decent folk like me and that lad upstairs. You're done here, Miss Trench.'

Ursula seemed not to be listening any more. She turned the handle back and forth again and again. The *click*, *click*, *click* sounded strangely comforting, like the click of a gun when the trigger's been pulled and all the bullets have been fired and there's nothing left but the *click*, *click*, *click*, though why that should be comforting she could not think.

Ma Rimmer almost felt sorry for her standing there dead pathetic and nearly said so.

'I'd go now, if I were you. You're finished here.'

'I'm not finished. I'm not. I'm not,' the finished woman mumbled and hardly noticed how the words coincided with the *click*, *click*, *click* of the lock. Then she seemed to wake and shake her head as if she had risen up through water. She said, very coolly, almost with ice on her breath: 'I'd watch out if I were you, Ma Rimmer, with your knowing ways and whatever right it is you've got to meddle in my business. I've a reputation, I have, and I've not got it for nothing.'

'Oh! Watch out, should I? Or you'll do what? Send me the way of Norah Trench and her little kiddie? They get in your way, too?'

'Yes, they did actually, Mrs Rimmer.'

Why not say it out loud at last? Why not be honest? And proud.

Ma Rimmer was not to be frightened. She was an expert on the world and its doings. Didn't half of it traipse up Brackley Street and into her shop every day, and hadn't she been there every day for the past thirty years to meet them with a song and a smile and an ever ready ear for their troubles and opinions? And wasn't the world and its doings, as reported in the papers, spread out before her on her counter and her purveyor of it all?

'Reputation, you? I wouldn't refer to reputation if I were you, no, dear me, no. A woman with your history and done up like a doll. My, you're an evil bitch and a body feels filthy just talking to you but you're done here.'

The final word was to be Ma Rimmer's. Ursula was never allowed the final word.

'Leave the door open as you go,' Ma Rimmer told her. 'Our Stock likes to have a wee in the yard of a morning.'

She clumped off to the front of the shop. Ursula could hear the tinkle of the bell as the door opened and Ma Rimmer called out: 'Micky, come and drag these papers in!'

He appeared at the top of the stairs, unwashed but dressed. He hesitated only a second before walking down and passing her without a word.

She watched him disappear into the dark of the shop, heard Ma Rimmer turn on the wireless and sing 'Zing went the strings of my heart', and Andreas, a tuneless baritone, join her.

Ursula left by the back of the shop but did not return to the House of Content. Instead she stood awhile under the bridge in Brackley Street which, after so many months, seemed more like home.

She wasn't crying, no, they'd not get her for crying. She was as dry as a stick ready for kindling.

Overhead she could hear Radcliffe Park coming alive, people passing over the bridge to a world of work and school and families, of buses and cars, of things to do and people to do them for.

There was a world and it all fitted together quite well without her. She wasn't some missing piece that could be slotted into a gap in the pattern, she had never belonged.

Nor had Andreas ever belonged to her. In this world from which she had been barred as if by a door, a door with no handle, he had been the one who had opened it from within.

He had been the key to her prison cell, only borrowed to be taken away. He was lost to her now, of course, but he was too precious to lose. Even now his words rolled like dice in her head; images of him flapped and tumbled about her like so many paper kites in an angry wind.

She reran each encounter she had had with him, from the afternoon in the park to that morning on the stairs. She replayed them endlessly until one became superimposed on another, became blurred and cacophonous, fog and thunder, and she could take no more of it. She pulled her coat over her head and wept. She kneeled down under the bridge and wept until all tears had been wrung from her, and her face was as dry and red-raw as she felt inside.

A factory siren howled and she came up the steps to Brackley Street. All tears gone, there was nothing that showed what was in her head except her murderous grip on the handrail.

She saw Andreas putting up the hoardings for that day's newspapers: 'Coronation Special' and 'Everest Climbed'. She walked right past him but his back was towards her and he did not notice.

The past months she had been happy but that happiness had been like a glass floor over which she had had to tread carefully when she had really wanted to dance. It had been perilous and fragile and now it was shattered. Perhaps that was why she walked down to Callick's hardware shop to buy herself a hammer.

Back at the newsagent's, Andreas was leaning over the counter feeding Stock marshmallows and Ma Rimmer was shimmying to Glenn Miller on the Light Programme.

'Lovely man,' she said, the newspapers under her overalls crackling as she swung her hips from side to side. 'Sound of the war, that man was. Pity he died, though there's some say he didn't. Man came in here last week and bought a *Titbits*. Spit of Glenn Miller he was, so you never know.'

Ursula stood in the doorway, hammer in her handbag. It was Stock who noticed her first. He spat out a marshmallow to yap at her. Even the dog hates me, she thought wryly.

'I want to see you,' she said. She didn't sound as if she were begging.

Andreas looked to Ma Rimmer for support. Ma Rimmer gave it.

'Well, he doesn't want to see you, so hop it.'

'Can't he speak for himself?' Ursula answered, brassy as anything now with the woman who had struck her half-dumb not hours before.

'Well, she's right,' answered Andreas, equally brassy now that he knew Ma Rimmer's skirts were his for the hiding in. 'I'm done with you.'

'That's right, our Micky. Tell her about Iris.'

'Ay, Iris,' he said without conviction, not knowing what he had to tell about Iris who was next-door neighbour to his mam, sixty years old and had just had her ovaries removed. 'I'm done with you,' he said again because the words summed up his sentiments and he couldn't think what else to say.

'Oh, no, you're not done with me, not yet.' She shook her

head sadly but firmly. 'We'll have one last word together, you and me. I'm owed that.'

A man came in for a packet of Woodbines and to pass the time of day. He was a regular and Ma Rimmer wasn't having her regulars upset by her nephew's doings, so she said under her breath: 'Well, you'll not see him now. He's on my time. Shop closes midday. You can see him then.'

'But the street-party's on then,' Andreas whined.

Ma Rimmer shushed him and turned to her customer. 'It's just the Woodbines, is it, Mr Sweeny? And how's Mrs Sweeny getting on now that she just has the one lung?'

'It won't take long what I have to do,' Ursula told Andreas and left smartly.

She did not wear a watch – time was always a foreign country around which she wandered without compass or clue – but she knew when midday came because sirens brayed out across Radcliffe Park. It was Coronation Day. Work stopped. Trestle-tables began to line Brackley Street and men on ladders strung necklaces of tiny Union Jacks from lamp-post to lamp-post.

She had been under the bridge for three hours, three hours since she had walked into Callick's hardware shop and bought herself a hammer. She could not and would not claim to be in the grip of passion. She had the time to know her own mind yet, truth to tell, she had not planned what she was about to do. The hammer in her handbag had been an impulse buy. She had no thought of how she was to use it, only that use it she would.

At five past twelve she was in Andreas's room. Stock was in his mistress's handbag on the shop counter and Ma Rimmer was somewhere in Brackley Street putting a trifle on a trestle-table.

Andreas had left the back door open and was sitting with his back towards her. He was changing his shirt for the street-party. He did not turn; it was as if she did not exist.

Finally, he looked at her and asked: 'So what is it you want?'

'This,' she said.

She had the hammer ready. It hit him fair on the forehead and he received it like a blessing. She followed it with twelve more blows; two hit his shoulders but the others were true.

His head seemed to melt and lose shape, and petals of blood splashed the walls so that it looked, too, as if his head were an enormous rose bursting into bloom.

The beatings over, he fell back on to the bed. She dropped the hammer but she could see he was not dead. He was twitching and wriggling on the spattered sheets like a squashed insect that refuses to die. So she set fire to him.

There was a paraffin heater in his room. They had sat by it naked often enough. She had seen his body in its orange glow. She took off the back of the paraffin heater, detached the bottle, flipped off its cap and sprinkled its contents on the boy.

Perhaps it was because his face was a mess and she had loved him for it once or because the wriggling frightened her into thinking that, no matter how many blows with a hammer she struck, he would not die.

Her handbag hung open. She dug deep inside for matches, stood well back, lit one and threw it at the bed. The bed and its occupant whooshed into flames.

She felt the heat immediately, a thick wave of it rushing over her. Black smoke rose up and made a second ceiling just above her head. Andreas flapped long slow arms and tried to rise from the bed. He was a black shadow encased and caressed by flames, and then lost in them.

She left, coughing madly, stumbling down the stairs and out the back door. She returned to her post under the bridge, the smoke following her like an accusing finger.

She looked down at her blood-sprayed dress and hands and a memory came of Norah Trench lying crumpled at the foot of the stairs, blood running from between her legs as if from a bowl. She remembered also the dead child on the kitchen table, waxy and wrinkled and quite, quite still. Now she could add to her gallery the thought of Andreas boxing with the flames that covered him.

Norah, the child, Andreas: she had made a trinity and felt something like accomplishment.

The Coronation party was interrupted by the sight of smoke pouring like a muddy waterfall over the roof of Ma Rimmer's newsagent's. Ma Rimmer was at the Flag and Knot sharing a sherry with the pianist before launching into 'It's Only a

Paper Moon' when a lad rushed in to tell her that her shop was on fire.

The fire brigade reached the shop before she did. She was all for charging into the burning building but was restrained by firemen. She tried to tell them that her Stock was in there.

'Your stock's insured, I should hope, love,' a fireman said to cheer her up and calm her down and when she cried out, no, no, *her* Stock was in her handbag, he asked for someone to sit her down away somewhere. 'Confused, poor cow.'

Ma Rimmer, horror skewering the very marrow from her bones, was lost for words.

A large crowd of street-partygoers formed on either side of the burning shop or sat across the road from it. No one gave a thought to Andreas. He was a young man and could look after himself. No one thought he would be stuck inside on the day of a party.

Folk commiserated with Ma Rimmer on the loss of her shop and her dog.

'To lose a shop and a dog is hard, dead hard.'

'And on Coronation Day an' all. Why, I bet if the Queen knew it'd right upset her day, it would really.'

While Brackley Street was ablaze, Ursula was under it. She was kneeling at the side of the canal. She was cupping her hands and bringing them, water-filled, up to her mouth and drinking deep.

The water's cabbage stench was delicious to her and so cool. Smoke had rasped her throat; the water soothed it, soothed her. Its taste was not unpleasant, only slightly stale, the cabbage was all in the smell. By drinking it, she hoped to poison herself but the crowd was growing and soon they would discover her. It was too slow a way to die.

She knew now that she should not have left Andreas's room but should have stayed with him, fallen on him and let the flames devour them both, but she had been cowardly.

She would have to be brave. It was important to pay for what she had done. She had not done anything to pay back for the baby on the kitchen table or Norah at the foot of the stairs. She had done nothing, been nothing, had merely gone on living and living badly. More needed to be done. Andreas's death would be part-payment and her own would make up the bill. Two deaths for two deaths. She would be quits then, evens. Again she had that feeling of accomplishment.

Head first, like a crocodile, she slid into the water. As she eased her way down, below the splash and bubble of her entry, she could hear a hiss as if a fire were being extinguished, a sweet soft hiss.

The crowd on Brackley Street had grown, strengthened by partygoers on other, smaller streets. Among them was a young Irishman, moon-faced and ginger-haired, with his wife and small boy. He heard the splashes of the desperately buoyant Ursula as she tried to drown herself and failed. He turned to his wife.

'There's a woman down there drowning.'

'Well, go down and save her, you soft mick.'

He had rushed down the steps to the canal. His son, a sullen little boy, bored with the fire, had wanted to go with his dad and tried to tug free from his mother's hands.

'You stay here and look away, our Ayomon,' Mrs Devlin told her son. 'There's nothing you can do to help.'

V

The House of Content

I

The Inquest

A child had been murdered and savagely so. Its mother, hardly a day later, had also been found dead. This much was known and undisputed. What remained unknown, and so much disputed, was precisely how they had died and at whose hands.

It was hoped that an inquest would do what the police had so far failed to do: cast a sharp and unremitting light on these dark events. What little light it did summon seemed only to create more shadows.

The inquest was officially opened at the House of Content. The coroner and jury, all men and all from Radcliffe Park, traipsed through the house uncertain what to look for.

It was the outside privy at which they looked longest. They banged at its sides, inspected its tarpaulined roof, scratched at the whitewashed wood with the studious concentration of prospective housebuyers. Finally, they lifted up the toilet seat and peered intently into its dark and fetid mouth.

They returned on foot up Brackley Street to the Grenfell Gospel Hall where the rest of the inquest was to be held.

It was eleven o'clock, Monday morning, 10 November 1938. The summer just gone had been sultry hot and autumn was barely new but that morning the blue granite paving flags were sugared over with frost and snow was falling all over Radcliffe Park. Feeble flakes without strength or brilliance, they weren't long on the ground before they were the colour and texture of slush.

Outside Grenfell Gospel Hall it was bitter cold but the crowd was not deterred. In buckets of hot coke a woman was baking jacket potatoes and selling them at a halfpenny each. She had also set up a stall with tea at a penny a cup. Business was as good as the weather was bad and many were the pennies she dropped into her brown leather handbag, a handbag in which she kept, along with God knew what else, a tiny puppy by the name of Stock.

If outside was bitter cold, inside Grenfell Gospel Hall condensation fairly dribbled down the walls. The press packed the balcony meant on Sundays for the choir and the general public and ill-wishers filled up the pews and the aisles along the sides.

The first witness was called. Elizabeth Gibbons (Miss), twenty-one, was not a little pretty but thought to have too much neck for some. She worked for the Trench family Mondays, Wednesdays, Fridays, and Saturdays sometimes. She did the cleaning and the washing and helped out her aunty, Mrs Alice Gibbons, with the cooking and whatever else needed doing. She said that Mr Trench did not pay well and Mrs Trench had been dead fussy – the hall had gasped at that 'dead' – but, yes, she had enjoyed her job. She was saving up to get married. 'But I don't know who to as yet,' she added appealingly.

She had arrived at the House of Content at seven o'clock along with Mrs Gibbons. Seven was when they usually arrived and this day had started no different. After lighting the fire for hot water, they had brewed up and had a bit of breakfast. And, no, the kitchen was just as Lizzie and her aunt had left it the previous evening except for four cups and a dirty milk-pan in the sink.

At a quarter to eight she brought out some tea for Pendle the gardener. Pendle and Mrs Gibbons did not get on but Lizzie liked him well enough. He was hosing down the lawn and told her that the hot weather was doing it no good.

'I went round the house opening the curtains and windows. It was then I noticed that the dining-room door was ever so slightly opened.'

The coroner here drew the attention of the jury to the ground plan of the House of Content, which had been chalked up on a blackboard.

Not only was the dining-room door open, Lizzie told them, but the shutters of the middle window had been pushed apart and the sash raised. 'Well, when I saw the door open and the window, too, I thought: Hang about, Mr Trench, he locks up every night without fail.'

Did she do or say anything when she saw the door and window open? the coroner asked.

'I did mention it in passing to my Aunty Alice but she just said: "Well, what of it?" Then she gave me two cups of tea to take up to Mr and Mrs Trench.'

On those mornings that she worked for them Lizzie always took up tea for Mr and Mrs Trench and she woke up Ursula and Miss Matchett, too.

Did she wake them that morning?

Lizzie said she did. 'I took the tea into Mr and Mrs Trench. I said to Mrs Trench, I said, "Shall I wake the child?" but she was dead dopey that morning. There was no sense in what she said other than that she had an awful headache and had passed a bad night. She said yes, to waken the child but that he wasn't in his room but in Ursula's or in Miss Matchett's. She couldn't remember which. So I went into Miss Matchett's.'

Was Miss Matchett awake?

'She was awake but she wasn't up.'

Did she look tired? Did she, like Mrs Trench, look as if she had passed a bad night?

'Oh, no, not at all, she never does. Full face of make-up day or night. Always looks smart, does Miss Matchett.' She said it as though she thought smartness a crime, resentment thickening her voice.

'Anyway, I says to her, I says: "Where's the child?" And she says to me, she says, "In his room," as if to say, "Where else would he be?" '

The coroner pointed out to the jury that the child's bedroom had originally been a dressing-room. It had connecting doors to the two front bedrooms, the Trenches' and Miss Matchett's, and it also opened out on to the landing.

Elizabeth Gibbons confirmed the coroner's description.

'Three doors it has and it's only the size of a big cupboard. And it's got the tiniest little window. So, anyway, when Miss Matchett said he was in his room I said to her: "Can I go in and wake him?" Miss Matchett said yes because he's usually awake by now and scriking like mad. It wasn't like him to be quiet in the mornings. Wasn't like him to be quiet at all.

So I went in and the cot were empty.'

The coroner stopped her there and asked that the cot be brought in.

Edmund Trench's cot, white-painted and pink-coverleted, much larger than one would have expected, about the size of a small single bed, was wheeled down the centre aisle of the Grenfell Gospel Hall like a refreshment-trolley and parked in front of Elizabeth Gibbons.

Explain how it looked, the coroner ordered her.

Nonplussed, she said, 'It looked like a cot. What else would it have looked like?'

Had it been slept in?

She found it difficult to say. 'Yes. . . . No. . . . Sort of.'

Be specific.

'Well, the cot was made up and the coverlet all smoothed out but the pillow wasn't fluffed up or nothing. You could see where the child's head had been, the dent, you know. That's what I meant, yes, no, sort of. The bed was made but the pillow wasn't. So I told Miss Matchett. She was up by then and doing her nails. She said to try Ursula's room and that's what I did.'

Was Miss Trench awake?

'No, because I had to knock on the door twice before she answered. When I poked my head round the door I could see that the child weren't there. I asked her if she'd seen the child. She said: "What? Is he missing?" And I said: "Looks like it." Then I told her about the dining-room door and the open window because I were dead worried by then. So she said to tell Miss Matchett and Mr Trench but not Mrs Trench because, seeing as how she was pregnant, it would upset her. She said to tell Mr Trench she wanted to see him, so I did. Mr Trench said to me, "Wait down in the kitchen," and I went straight there. That's where I stayed until two o'clock that afternoon. I stayed right there through all the fuss and when they found the child and brought it in they laid it out on the kitchen table and I saw that an' all. I felt dead sick when I saw it, I did, honest.'

Was it usual for the child to be moved from one bedroom to another?

Well, it was a bit,' she said sadly. 'He was never a child for sleeping alone. He was a mardy child altogether although he's dead now and you don't like to say. He was spoiled rotten by his mam; a tell-tale, too. He never told tales on me. None to tell. But he ran to his mam for the least little thing and he was scared of the dark. Scared of missing something, more like.'

Grenfell Gospel Hall hissed at Lizzie's words. She did wrong to criticise the child. It would have been all very well to call the other people in the case names but not the child. No badness was wanted about him. Death had not only cleansed him of faults, it had sanctified him.

'He used to sleep in Mr and Mrs Trench's room but he kept waking and Mrs Trench, being pregnant, needed her sleep. Miss Matchett had him most nights, Ursula only sometimes. He rarely slept in his own room. That cot was wheeled about like a barrow.'

She looked sadly at the cot as did the whole of Grenfell Gospel Hall, the people at the back standing up on the pews to do so.

Wheel it away, the coroner said solemnly.

Elizabeth Gibbons, thinking it was an order meant for her, rose from her stiff-backed chair and promptly began to push the cot back up the centre aisle although she had no real idea where she was supposed to wheel it when she got to the back of the hall.

The coroner had not meant to dismiss her but, seeing her go, reflected that she had probably told all. You may stand down, Miss Gibbons, he called after her, but Miss Gibbons was now wheeling the cot down the steps of the Grenfell Gospel Hall and into Brackley Street itself.

The crowd outside gasped to see her with the cot in broad daylight, as shocked as if she had walked out carrying the corpse it had once contained.

'Where you going with that?' a police constable asked her, which made her feel as though she had been caught stealing it.

Mrs Gibbons was then called.

Whereas the niece's buttons seemed to hold back a flood of generous flesh, her aunt, in comparison, was a river in drought, a dust-dry ditch. Darkly dressed, her pinched face a tiny pin-prick of light in the black sky of her best scarf and shawl.

Her lack of affection for the inhabitants of the House of Content was apparent and was a guarantee of honesty. Here was no loyal servant who would paint her employers, scarlet with spilt blood, pale pink with the whitewash of servility. This was a woman from Radcliffe Park. She would speak as she found and what she found was not pleasing.

While, yes, it had been true that she had been employed by Frederick Trench as cook, this was true no longer. She would never enter that house or work for that family again, not as long as there was blood on it and on them. Who would?

Grenfell Gospel Hall murmured in sympathy.

'I feel no badness towards Mr Trench but I want it known I no longer work for him and neither does our Lizzie and she should have said as much when she was up here.'

It was clear that inside this small woman spluttered an enormous motor fuelled by long-term resentment. The coroner and jury leaned forward, expecting revelations.

She had worked for Mr Trench for five years, coming soon after the death of his first wife. As an outsider but one familiar with their ways, she was asked her opinion of Mr Trench and his second wife, the now-deceased Norah.

'He adored her,' Mrs Gibbons said simply but with a look which indicated that it was a mystery to her how any man could have adored Norah Trench.

Grenfell Gospel Hall mumbled in disappointment. They did not want to hear of a Frederick Trench who loved his wife but about one capable of killing her. Mrs Gibbons felt their disappointment keenly, but what could she do?

'He adored her,' she said again, repeating this sad fact.

And the son, the child, Edmund?

'Him, too. Apple of his eye.' Mrs Gibbons could universalise any statement by simply denying it expressiveness. Her flat voice implied that this was the way not only of Frederick Trench but of most men: they loved women to whom they were not suited and valued their sons as the vain value mirrors.

And did he equally love his daughter?

Here Mrs Gibbons was on happier territory. 'They could have been closer,' she said with heavy subtlety.

They had their differences, father and daughter?

Mrs Gibbons paused. There had been something between father and daughter that had looked like distance but that might well have been complicity. She had never been sure.

'Not differences, no. She adored him, that was plain, and he liked her well enough but he never showed it. He preferred the son but most of all he preferred Norah. If there were differences between father and daughter it was because of her. I suppose Ursula was put out because Norah had taken her mother's place and he would take his wife's side against his daughter's. There was always spats between them, niggling little arguments. They didn't get on, anyone could see that, although mostly they were civil to each other – or just about. There may been other reasons for differences between them but none I can put my finger on.'

It was clear that, if these reasons had been fingerable, Mrs Gibbons would have happily offered them up but Grenfell Gospel Hall muttered happily at last. A motive had been found: Ursula Trench had hated Mrs Trench and had killed both mother and child out of spite. To Grenfell Gospel Hall, unrestricted by the need for evidence, it all seemed very straightforward.

And how was Miss Trench with the child?

Mrs Gibbons faltered slightly. Having given the case a little clarity by providing it with what looked like a motive, she was reluctant to muddy it again but she was pledged to speak as she found.

'Ursula and the little lad got on fine. She wasn't mad about him but she often looked after him and gave him sweets and I don't know what else. Even made a rag doll for him once. He thought the world of her. It made his mam proper jealous sometimes because, as I said, her and Ursula, they didn't get on.'

The time came for Mrs Gibbons's opinion of Miss Matchett, sister-in-law to the deceased Norah. According to her, the sisters had been cut from the same gaudy cloth, and pretty cheap material that had been too.

'I mean, she was there to be helping out with the child, supposedly. She seldom did a tap of work, as far as I could see. Far too full of herself for decent work. Anna Matchett's the sort who leaves lipstick on her cup and fag ash on her breakfast-plate.'

Miss Matchett and Mr Trench, how were relations between them?

Dearly would Mrs Gibbons have loved to dish the dirt, dearly would Grenfell Gospel Hall have loved to let her do it, but Mrs Gibbons was not quite able.

'They were friendly, polite. If you're thinking hanky-panky . . . well, there was none of that. Mr Trench thought too much of himself and of his wife, and Anna Matchett was never one to be short of company. It's well known that she's been seen drinking in the bar of the Mansfield Hotel.'

There was Anna painted as a slut and Ursula as a murderess and Mrs Gibbons holding the brush with a flourish. It was such a canvas that the folk in the Grenfell Gospel Hall had queued to see.

Joseph Pendle came next.

A tall tree of a man, spindly and bent, his skin was like bark, his arms like ungainly branches. His was a quiet presence. Grenfell Gospel Hall shushed itself whenever the man spoke, for his voice was low and rustling like wind through leaves.

Pendle's voice betrayed the uneasiness his wooden body could not convey. For a withdrawn soul, unused to public scrutiny, giving evidence before coroner, jury and Grenfell Gospel Hall was an ordeal that, unlike Mrs Gibbons, he was unable to relish. He was aware that he was being studied by them. He was aware, too, that his words were being listened to with an attentiveness they had never before deserved. He knew that what he had to say was important. The reputation of Frederick Trench and his family depended upon his testimony.

Few would have called Frederick Trench a generous man but Pendle was one of them. A retired millhand, Pendle worked the garden of the House of Content. It was not a regular job, nor was he paid a regular wage. Trench gave him gifts of money at Christmas and Easter, and help with the rent at other times. For Pendle this was payment enough. He would have worked in the garden of the House of Content for nothing, just for the sheer pleasure of being in 'one of the few clean places in Radcliffe Park'.

Trench's clothes often came his way and he wore some now: a good dark suit from Lewis's with hardly any wear in it. He was not comfortable in formal clothes but the unfamiliar hang of a new jacket and the choking grip of a stiff white collar were less constricting than the fear of being disloyal to the master who had been so fair to him.

'I come across from Mallet most every day in summer but generally I come when I'm needed. That morning I came near to eight. I didn't go near the kitchen because me and Mrs Gibbons, we don't get on. Her's not the type to be got on with, but Lizzie gives me tea in a mug most mornings she's there. She gave me some that morning, too, and then next thing I know she's calling out the window that the child is missing. So I rushed in although my boots were wet and grassy from hosing down the lawn. I was at the foot of the stairs and I met Mr Trench. He came down the stairs and he said to me, he said, "Joseph," he said, "they've stolen Eddie in a blanket." His face were ashen. Like a lily he was. "Help me," he says, "help find him while I go for the police." '

The House of Content had a telephone. Did you not suggest to Mr Trench that he use it?

It was not Pendle's place to suggest anything to a man like Mr Trench. As for telephones, they were terrible things. You picked them up and little voices spoke in your ear and that couldn't be healthy. They had them in big houses and some pubs but Pendle would have nowt to do with them. He could understand anyone not using a telephone. 'And the police station were only a short run across the park.

'Then his daughter comes down the stairs. Mr Trench says to her, he says: "Ursula, you go help Pendle search the garden." Then he left.'

Would Pendle comment on Miss Trench's appearance and demeanour?

'Pink and uncertain,' Pendle had commented spontaneously and then, pleased with the description, repeated it: 'Pink and uncertain. She was that eager to help her dad and find the child for him, you could see that. She come out with me and she searched about with me. She searched about the lawns and round about the garden tap and I searched about the bushes. We worked our way down until we reached the bottom where the privy and the compost was.'

Pendle paused and then continued with his testimony, his

delivery slow and plodding, as if the story he was recounting had happened to someone else.

'The privy's over by the corner. It's not much used except by me. The girl, Miss Trench, she says to me, she says, "Let's try there," and so we did. It's a bit of a mess, that part of the garden. It's where I keep my compost. There's long grass and weeds there. That morning the long grass was all trampled, not much trampled but trampled. I saw footmarks, too.'

Large or small footmarks?

Pendle could not say for sure. 'I never properly took them in. Smallish, happen; maybe largish, too. I told the girl to stand back. She was in a bit of panic and was twirling about back and forth and worrying about where the child were if he weren't in the house and he weren't in the garden. Then she stops all of a sudden and says, "Perhaps he's in there," and she went quite calm. The door to the privy was open a bit, so I opened it wider. On the floor there was blood, a pool of it, dried out but as wide as my hand. I lifted up the privy seat. It was dark but I could make something white out and I knew what it were right there and then. But I said to the girl to go fetch me a candle or a torch from the kitchen. Well, off she went and I were left there by myself.'

What did he do while the girl was away?

'Me? I did nowt. Prayed, happen. Prayed that happen it weren't no child I saw but a doll maybe. It looked like a doll. But I knew it weren't. I could see blood on the grass and on the compost-heap. All dry it were, but I could tell it were blood. The girl came back with a candle and matches for to light it. She weren't gone but a minute. She lit the candle and held it up for me to see by. I reached down into the privy and I drew up a blanket.'

His mahogany hands re-enacted the scene. He dangled an invisible blanket before coroner, jury and enthralled Gospel Hall.

'It were wet, soaked right through with blood and streaked with shit. Old shit,' he added like a connoisseur.

The coroner asked him not to use such a word. 'Night soil' would do. Pendle said he would but, seeing that no one used the privy at night, wouldn't 'day soil' be better? The coroner said the word 'soiled' would cover the situation. 'Well, it covered the blanket, too,' Pendle replied.

He dropped the invisible blanket on the floor of the Gospel Hall and continued with his story.

'I took the candle off the girl and by its light I saw the child. It were wedged between the splashboard and the back of the vault.' 'Splashboard' and 'vault' were words he had learned especially for the inquest and so he said them proudly.

Asked how the child lay, he said that it had lain on its left side, with its left hand and left foot trailing in the water.

'Stiff it was and cold. It wore a nightdress all soaked through with blood and so ripped about and tattered that it weren't no more than a rag about its neck. When I lifted it up, dripping, its head fell back because its throat had been cut nearly to the neck. It almost came clean off. The girl was upset at seeing it so. She danced about again, dead agitated, but I said, "Calm down," and she calmed down good as gold. Her feet were bare, I noticed, and she was still in her nightgown. She'd come straight from her bed. I said I thought she were very brave and did her father proud and that calmed and pleased her, too. She lay out the blanket and I lay the child in it. I wrapped it up in it and carried it back to the house. By that time Mr Trench and the policemen had come.'

Pendle said how its face had been white as a clean candle except for its mouth which had been all bruised as if someone had hit it but its eyes had been closed and it had looked happy enough. Leastways, he had seen more miserable-looking corpses though none so young. Asked where, he said Somme, Passchendaele, Ypres. He had driven ambulances, you see.

Praised for his evidence and cool tones, Pendle then thanked the coroner and said how he hoped that they found the bugger as done it, to which the coroner nodded, the jury harrumphed, and Grenfell Gospel Hall cheered.

Superintendent Sissons was called to a number of hisses. A face as bland as the moon's, squat and dwarfish, he gave his testimony in a loud voice that crackled with a sense of failure.

He told how Trench had arrived at the station in a breathless panic claiming that his child had been kidnapped. Sissons, his men and Mr Trench had then gone to the House of Content where they arrived just as Pendle was bringing the child into the kitchen.

'He lay the child on the table. Everyone was in the kitchen except Mrs Trench. Her sister, Miss Matchett, said she would slip upstairs and tell her that the child had been found. Trench told her to say nothing but that the child had been found and to keep her in her room. I also told Miss Matchett to phone the doctor but Ursula Trench said that there was a doctor in Park End and it'd be quicker if she fetched him. I told Pendle to take the child from off the table and put it in the washhouse so that when he came the doctor could examine it in peace. I waited for the doctor to arrive. He came immediately. Together we cursorily examined the child's body and then I went to examine the privy. Grass had been trampled and there were footprints. They were found to belong to Miss Trench and a man, most likely Pendle. They were fresh and could have been made when the two had found the body. There was much blood too, some on the grass, some on top of the compost-heap. There was some on the floor of the privy and on the toilet seat. Inside the vault there was a deal of it, too. The child's throat had been cut and it had been stabbed several times, so there should have been more blood and over a wider area but there was not. I inspected the garden thereafter. A small fire lit the day before was still warm. It was raked over but nothing was found in its ashes. There were footprints on the lawn but these were all fresh-made by Miss Trench, Pendle, myself and my men. Pendle having hosed the lawns down that morning, these prints were clear and fresh. No weapon was found on this or subsequent searches of the garden, house or the surrounding area. The canal to the back of the house has been dredged, the park and all the gardens along Park End have also been thoroughly searched but to no avail. A bread-knife is missing from the kitchen of the House of Content. It is fair to assume that this was the murder weapon.'

Had a search of the child's room showed any signs of disturbance?

'Very little sign indeed. The bed was made, tucked in quite neatly, but the pillow was flattened and one of the blankets was missing, the blanket found about the dead child in the privy.'

Asked about the dining-room window and the likelihood of intruders breaking in and stealing the child, Sissons was doubtful. There was a catch on the dining-room window which meant it could only be opened from within. Trench had said that he had locked this window firmly but later had said that perhaps he had not. The gravel underneath the window had not been greatly disturbed.

'I questioned each of the persons present soon after I had examined the corpse, searched the garden and inspected the child's room. They were all very helpful and their stories never varied except for Mr Trench. He was vague, irrational and discursive. He held up the interviews of others, particularly that of his daughter, by rushing in, questioning my conduct, repeating his own suppositions that gypsies or bad men had stolen the child and used him so.'

Mrs Trench had not been interviewed until late afternoon. She had been heavily drugged by Mr Trench and had not been informed of the child's death, only that he was missing. She was close to term with her second child and Trench was taking care that she should not be upset. Sissons thought Trench's actions suspicious and unhelpful. All he could get by way of testimony from Mrs Trench was that her husband had slept by her the whole night through. She knew this was so because she had passed a bad night.

'She said it was her habit to pass a bad night and even with potions her sleep was drowsy and thin. She heard nothing, she said, nothing. She was very upset. I then asked Trench to administer no more potions as I wished to speak with Mrs Trench at greater length come morning. I then left the house.'

He had left the house?

'I left the house. I had two policemen on duty there. One was by the privy, the other by the gate. This last was at Mr Trench's request. There was a crowd gathering there, an unsympathetic crowd.'

Did he ever speak to Mrs Trench again?

'I did not.'

Why?

'She died. She died an hour or so after I left the house.'

Was it possible that Mrs Trench knew more than she had told or had been able to tell?

233

'That was possible,' Sissons assented stiffly.

And that by leaving the house Sissons had placed Mrs Trench in danger?

'It's true that Mrs Trench's death was very unfortunate.'

Unfortunate for Mrs Trench, it most certainly had been.

'Yes, yes,' Sissons said, 'very much so. Unfortunate for us all. She might have had a lot to tell.'

Yes, yes, Superintendent Sissons, perhaps more than you have been able to tell.

Sissons had found no weapon, no culprit, no motive. As his evidence petered out, Sissons's lack of success in explaining what had happened to both child and mother became as clear to him as it was to the coroner, jury and the whole of Grenfell Gospel Hall. His voice paused, plopped and guttered like a gas-lamp going out. Booed, he left the stand and a cruel woman way at the back of Grenfell Gospel Hall yelled out: 'Who's your landlord, Sissons, and how much rent has he let you off?'

Doctor Sartori gave evidence next, a narrow, fleshless man, whose hands trembled strangely. To disguise a faintly foreign accent, he snapped out his words like a dog cracking open a bone.

'I am a general practitioner and police surgeon. I also lecture on first aid, a subject on which I have written many volumes.

'I reside at Park End. I am a neighbour to Frederick Trench but know him neither socially nor professionally. Like me, he prefers his own and his family's company.'

What was then not known but was later to be discovered was that Dr Sartori, besides liking his own and his family's company, was also rather fond of the surgical spirits he used to clean his instruments with. This explained his trembling hands, which at the time were thought to be rather graceful and to be expected of a foreigner.

'That morning, a little after eight, Mr Trench's daughter, Ursula, came to me. She told me that her brother had been found in the privy with his throat cut. She begged me come immediately. I did so. I found the body in the washhouse. I am familiar with pathology from my younger days and was a pathologist for a time. True, it was long ago but dead bodies do not change nor do the ways of looking at them. In this instance, the child's throat had been cut to the bone by some sharp instrument from left to right. All the membranes, blood-vessels, nerves and air-tubes were completely divided. The cut was made by a single sharp incision and with an unhesitating hand. A clean sweep.'

Dr Sartori demonstrated the sweep with a slash of a near-skeletal finger across his own bony neck.

'Peeling away the nightgown I found some twelve stab wounds evidently made by the same instrument. The worst and probably the first wound penetrated through the nightgown, passed through the lining of the heart, fracturing two ribs and puncturing the left ventricle. All the stabs pierced the flesh but none was as deep or as damaging as that which I have judged to be the first.'

Would the instrument used have been a razor, asked the coroner, or a knife?

'A knife I think, definitely not a razor.'

A bread-knife? suggested the coroner.

Sartori answered wryly that a knife capable of cutting through flesh so efficiently would have no difficulty slicing bread.

'The deepest wound was some four inches but it was not the cause of death. All the wounds to the body were inflicted after the child had died.'

The child was then already dead before it had been stabbed?

Sartori nodded sadly that this was so.

Was it dead before its throat had been cut?

'A child of that size would have sent out a gush of blood in one jet. There would have been a quantity of blood of not less than three pints. Quite definitely it was dead.'

If the child had not been killed with a knife, how, then, had it died?

'There was about its mouth and nostrils a blackened appearance. It is my belief that the child was smothered by the pressure of a hand or soft substance over the mouth and nose.'

Would that have been in the house or in the garden?

Sartori could not say.

Had the child been drugged? Why had he not screamed out?

'I cannot say why the child did not cry out. Perhaps the child was gagged to prevent him from doing so. The gag prevented him from breathing and he died.'

Was this possible? Was this likely?

'It is possible and it is not unlikely. He had not been drugged, of that I am certain. I examined the interior of his stomach. In all other respects, he was a remarkably healthy child, finely developed and well looked after.'

How long had the child been dead when it was found?

'Five, no more than six hours. He was quite cold and surprisingly rigid. The skin of his left hand and foot were wrinkled from having been in the soiled water. There were also bruises on the back of its head, the left arm and about his ankles. These seemed to have occurred after death. I believe that the body had been wedged behind the splashboard and this would explain the bruises. There was a small bruise on his left thigh but that was less recent, a day older at least.'

Sartori did not stay in Grenfell Gospel Hall to see how the inquest would be affected by his evidence. He said he had patients to whom he must attend. Back in his Park End surgery, however, he spent the afternoon alone drinking surgical spirits in a cup sweetened with honey.

Trench was called, to much murmuring.

In his bearing, he aimed at looking the soldier he had once been, with shoulders well back and chin forward, but his inner man was stooped. The loss of wife and child lay heavy on him. Grief was already whittling away at his frame. It had pared down his square face, curving and hollowing it, and giving it a shadowed look. He was clean-shaven and smartly dressed but that was Ursula's doing. Trench was past caring about his appearance.

He said he had last seen the child when his daughter had taken him up to his room.

'I kissed him goodnight. I always did.'

He had slept well that night. He had not wakened. His wife usually slept restlessly and sometimes disturbed him but not overmuch and not that night. Lizzie Gibbons woke him at eight. She then returned to tell him that his daughter wished to speak with him. It was his daughter who told him that the child was missing and that the dining-room window had been found open.

He began to cry at this point. He was given water but little time to wipe or still his tears. The coroner was pressing him to continue.

He said that the first thing he felt, together with concern for his missing child, was concern for his wife. She was near to giving birth and had had a trying pregnancy. She was easily upset and his first thought was to protect her. Before he left for the police he gave her a sleeping powder. She usually had some by her bed.

You gave her more than was normal?

'Yes,' he said quietly.

Louder, please.

'Yes,' he boomed and then his voice softened again. 'I gave her three spoons.'

How many normally?

'One,' he said, and hung his head.

You gave her more later.

'One spoonful more at midday. I did not want her wakened or worried. Perhaps I did wrong there. Yes, maybe I did. But it was to protect her and the child, the unborn child.'

Overdosing your wife seems a strange way of protecting her. If she had been in a less drugged state she might have been more help to the police. Perhaps she might not even have died.

Trench covered his face with his hands. 'All this was true,' he said, 'and who knows it better than me?

'I just wanted to keep Eddie's death a secret from her.'

No other reason?

'To give myself time to find the strength to tell her that he was dead.'

Did she ever find out about her son?

'No, thank God. Death took her first and left me here alone.'

Trench broke down again. The weeping was so at odds with what everyone had expected, which had been a show of grief, a shaky lip or a weak voice. These ungainly tears and loud snuffles he made raised him in public estimation. The coroner paid them no heed.

You left the house for the police? You didn't phone?

'I didn't think. I was not in a fit state.'

Was it because you did not wish to be in the house when the body was found?

'Why should I wish that? I had no thought of bodies. I thought my son missing, not dead.'

Then, was it to waste time?

'No! It was a quick dash across the park. The police came quickly, quicker maybe because I was there to hurry them along. No time was wasted in fetching the police but time has been wasted since. They have ransacked my house, dug up my garden, ripped open the body of my son and the body of my wife, refused to let me bury them until all this is over and questioned over and over my family, such as remain of it, my employees, even my tenants. They have given me no peace and not once have they searched elsewhere. The canal was dredged but only that part my garden backs on to, not further up, not further down. Bad men came in the night and killed my child. Now they go free, unquestioned and happy. It is not fair!'

Trench bellowed the word 'fair'. It rang round the walls of Grenfell Gospel Hall and fell on ears previously deaf to pity. No, it was not fair and perhaps there were such things as bad men.

Sissons was called again. Yes, a search had been made of Trench's house and gardens and he had said as much before. Trench should expect such things if people died on property belonging to him. No, there had been no search for 'bad men'. It was an unlikely theory and even Trench could not suggest names of men who hated him enough to kill his son.

'But do I have to know their names?' Trench asked, not unreasonably. 'This man is an incompetent. It's well known and you've seen as much yourself this very day. His investigation has been a mockery and, ay, so has this inquest. No, not inquest, this inquisition! Why have you hounded me like you have? Why do you suggest such evil things about me? You have no right to ask what you have asked or to suggest what you've suggested. Why have you let evil-minded gossip rule the day and Mrs Gibbons to spit poison and dirt at me and my poor family? You have run this inquest disgracefully. I shall sue! I shall sue!'

Here Trench fell to loud weeping once more. He had cried too much; Grenfell Gospel Hall would not allow itself to be impressed by that again. He was taken out of the hall, past a baying crowd, and into a taxi that would take him back to the House of Content. He would not hear the testimony of Anna Matchett nor of his daughter, Ursula.

Anna Matchett wore black. Her tailored suit and tight-fitting cap with black tulle veil were grudgingly admired. A smart woman she looked, and Grenfell Gospel Hall, expecting a trollop, was disconcerted by her.

She looked, someone said, like Joan Crawford, that is, if you could imagine a Joan Crawford with red hair and a thick waist. What she did not look like was a woman born in Mallet nor one who would frequent the bar of the Mansfield Hotel. More to the point, she did not look like a woman capable of killing a child: would she have risked chipping her nail-varnish?

The thin veil that fell over her forehead and which hid her eyebrows from view was dark enough to make the rest of her face chalk-white and expressive of grief. The face had been carefully prepared. She had been up since dawn colouring it in, wiping away scarlet lips, replacing them with coral pink and then wiping that away, too, in preference for some even paler shade. She had dabbed and restored, inked and re-inked, glossed and matted her face to achieve a look of perfect blandness. Make-up no longer accentuated her striking features, it erased them.

Her voice, too, was steady and characterless, as free from personality as its owner was free from guilt. The only thing the voice gave away was that, despite the smart appearance and good deportment, Anna Matchett was most definitely Mallet-born.

She had last seen the child when she had kissed it goodnight. Ursula had then taken it to its room.

His room? asked the coroner. The coroner was easier in his questions than he had been with Trench.

'Yes, his own room. Sometimes he slept in my room. He was afraid of the dark. Sometimes he slept in Ursula's room. Sometimes with his mother but not lately. Norah slept badly even with the powders. Her restlessness would wake the child. So he slept alone or with me or with

239

Ursula. We talked of having a rota, of taking it in turns.'

Was it so arduous a task to have a child sleep in your room?

'No, but if he woke, he cried or wanted attention. He was a demanding child.'

Did he wake that night?

'If he did, I didn't hear him.'

If he had woken, he would have cried?

'He normally did.'

But you heard nothing?

'No, I heard nothing. I slept the whole night through. I had taken some of the powder my sister took.'

Why?

'Sometimes I slept badly, too.'

That night you slept well?

'Yes. Too well maybe.'

She was asked about her relationship with her sister.

'Norah and me, we sometimes quarrelled but never seriously. Sisters do. We quarrelled out of closeness. We were that close, you see.'

Anna held up two entwined fingers to show how close they had been.

And the child? What had she thought of the child?

'A lovely child, the light of his parents' life, mine, too, and Ursula's, I dare say.'

Yet hadn't she called him demanding?

'What child isn't?'

And spoiled? Would she agree he had been spoiled?

'If he was, then it was proof he was loved too much, rather than not loved at all.'

There was nothing in this or anything else she had to say that could incriminate her. Suspicion hovered over her head like a cloud: it shadowed but did not touch her.

Ursula was eighteen that day but far from birthday-bright. Blank-faced with the dull and unrelenting stare of a dead fish on a plate, she gave her name, her age and her testimony in the flat and unreflective tone of one who had learned all three by heart.

She had taken the child up at eight-thirty. She had stayed with him until he had fallen to sleep. She did not go downstairs

240

again but to her own room. The day had been hot, she had had a headache and had been tired. She had gone straight to bed. She had slept the whole night through and had heard nothing until Lizzie knocked on her door to waken her.

'I generally sleep well and am difficult to wake. I know of no one who could have a spite against the child or any of my family. My family is a happy one. The child was much loved and so was Norah.'

Miss Trench's bedroom looked out on to the garden and was above the dining-room. If someone had left or entered the house by the dining-room window, would she not have heard something?

'Sometimes I hear Pendle in the morning. The path round the house is gravelly and crunches but I heard nothing that night.'

It had been Miss Trench's idea to search the privy, not Pendle's. Why had she suggested looking there?

'I can't recall it being my idea. I can't recall it being anybody's idea. We had searched the whole garden. It was the one place left.'

As the last person to have seen the child alive – other than the murderer – and as one of the two people who had found its corpse, she should have been quizzed much longer and to more effect. There were gasps of disbelief when she was told to sit down. She had spoken concisely and there was little left to ask her but some hanging idea of justice demanded that she be grilled more thoroughly. She should have been grilled until she spat and sizzled but, as she stood down and took her place next to Anna Matchett, there seemed no one cooler than Miss Ursula Trench.

As the first part of the inquest was drawing to a close, Grenfell Gospel Hall considered its verdict. Anna's black suit and carefully faded face had won her admiration and lent her credibility. Trench's tears had made him friends where until that morning he had had only enemies. His tears had proved him a grieving widower and bereft father. In comparison, his dry-eyed and ice-voiced daughter looked hard and unconvincing.

The jury would have to go on evidence to decide the cause of death and give what subtle pointers they could at the person they thought responsible for it. Grenfell Gospel Hall did not need to rely on evidence nor concern itself with how little real and conclusive evidence there was.

Could Trench have killed his own son? they asked themselves. True, fathers had killed their sons before, but that didn't bear thinking about too closely. Abraham had been prepared to sacrifice Isaac but only because God had bullied him into it. Even God Himself had only let His son die on the firm understanding that it was just until Easter.

There was Anna Matchett, but it was hard to believe her capable of killing. They could see her killing a lover, perhaps. She would wear a broad-brimmed hat and a wide-shouldered coat. The pistol would be found smoking in her black-gloved hand. The camera would come in close up and her eyes would be milky with tears. The music would swell and the screen dissolve into a flashback wherein it would be explained how the lover had abused this passionate woman and left her with no choice but murder. Then Adolphe Menjou would defend her in court and prove that her lover had been a psychotic with two months to live who had goaded her to murder as part of a bizarre suicide plan. Grenfell Gospel Hall would have liked such a trial. As for child-murder, it was all too messy for a woman like Anna Matchett to commit.

Grenfell Gospel Hall convicted Ursula because she was the most likely candidate and the least appealing. Ursula Trench, fish-eyed and unemotional, the step-daughter pushed out into the cold, had the clearest and oldest of motives. She had killed out of spite.

There would be no trial to follow the inquest. There would not be enough evidence to convict anyone. What was needed was a confession and none was forthcoming. Seekers of legal justice would have to make do with the inquest – such as it was.

The coroner and jury had, finally at least, to play by the rules. They could find no one guilty even if there had been evidence to do so. They could point a finger but needed justification to do so. Murder by person or persons unknown, said the foreman. Murder by person or persons unknown, repeated the coroner.

Neither foreman nor coroner looked at Ursula. Each made a definite effort not to look at Ursula.

In the afternoon the coroner and the same jury met again to consider the death of Norah Trench. Dr Sartori, Sissons, Trench, Anna and Ursula were recalled and a young constable by the name of Hindle also gave evidence. It was as suspicious a death as that of her son's which had taken place not hours before it, but the evidence could point only one way: accidental death.

II

The Evening After

The park became suddenly popular the day the child was
discovered dead. Sightseers sauntered down Park End and
gathered by the park-gates, close to the drive of the House
of Content. A policeman stood guard to prevent the crowd
going up the drive and disturbing the peace of the house's
unfortunate inhabitants. The crowd was jolly but polite and the
policeman most obliging. He pointed to one of the windows on
the first floor, the curtains of which had been pulled. Was that
where they were keeping the child's body? No, the policeman
told them, it was the mother's room. She was near to term,
sickly and, it was said, still ignorant of the little boy's death.

Round the back, at the bottom of the garden of the
House of Content, stood another policeman guarding the
privy against intruders or disturbance.

Anna Matchett came out the kitchen door, carrying, breast
high, a tray of hot tea and some cake for the lovely young
constable who had been so attentive throughout the day.

Ursula, looking out of her bedroom window, saw Anna cross
the garden. Now there was only her father, herself and Norah
in the house. The child had been taken to the mortuary, Mrs
Gibbons, Lizzie and Pendle had left late afternoon and Sissons
had left not half an hour ago, taking all but the two constables
with him. It was the safest she had been all day.

It had been a day of success. She had been so happy.
It had been a job to hide how happy she was. Now she
knew for certain that her father loved her and that she had
guaranteed that love. She thought she would burn up with
such knowledge.

She threw herself on the rose-patterned bed, burying her
smiling face in the pillow. It was no good. She was too happy,

too restless. She was so much aglow with her secret knowledge, her secret power, that she wasn't sure whether it was her or the evening sun that lit up the room.

The police were gone but not for long. It was not over yet. The business had been messy, very messy, but mess had been its saving grace.

She recalled Sissons's expression throughout the day: delight mixed with and finally confounded by desperation. Here was murder. Here in this house, obviously, was the murderer. He knew it but all he had was this knowing and no proof. She recalled how sweaty he had become, so sweaty that the air about him seemed damp.

They had taken Eddie off at noon. He would be lying now on a marble slab, his insides on show. They would not find anything except that he was dead. They would not find out who had made him so unless it really was true that victims retained in their eyes the reflection of their murderer. She had a vision of the child's lids being drawn back like petals. She shivered but remained calm.

The child was dead. Poor Eddie. She was not without feeling. She had watched it grow after all. She had seen it develop from pampered buddha to crawling pig, heard it progress from wailing to gibberish to fully formed words. The more it had grown, the more words it had learned, the more its power and influence had grown. It had been another life, one that had been considered more important than her own.

Searching the garden that morning had been agony. Pendle had been so slow. The time he had spent rifling through privet bushes and the like – as if she would have left the child in such a place! Yet she had admired the man, too. He had been so gentle with the child. He had lifted it up out of the vault as if it had been a tender plant he was pulling out of the earth, shaking off the foul water from its limbs like soil from roots.

When the child had been lain on the kitchen table they had all gathered about it. She was aware that what others looked at in horror she had thought beautiful. Its left hand and foot had been swollen and wrinkled from having been in water and the body had smelt more of being kept so long in the privy than of corruption. The knife wounds on its chest were like little mouths, red-lipped and gaping, but generally the body was white, all blood drained from it. It had, she thought, a faintly waxy look to it. Death had made a candle of it. The black hair slicked back from its skull with privy water was like the candle's greasy wick. Light him, she thought, and he will burn.

Much as she enjoyed seeing the child laid out on the table and the opportunity it gave her of inspecting her handiwork by daylight, she would have wished her father had been spared the sight. Her poor father. He had loved the boy, she supposed. His death would grieve him, haunt him possibly. How strong he had been today, rushing around, interrupting Sissons, ordering the police about, talking all the while of 'bad men' and avoiding her eyes.

Sissons had not believed in any 'bad men'. That had been obvious. He knew it was somebody in the house but could not decide who.

'Is this a happy house?' he had asked her and she had nearly said, 'It is now,' but had stopped herself. After all, it was not yet a happy house. There was still Norah to consider.

The child was dead. That much had been accomplished. Norah remained, a stone over which to stumble unless it was kicked out of the way.

Her father was such a goose with that woman. Drugging her to protect her like that. Tell her, I tried to say, but not too loud – with my eyes I tried to say it but he looked away. Tell her straight, 'Your son is dead,' like when you told me my mother was dead. 'Your mother's dead,' you said, just like that.

It was pathetic to see him trying to bar the police from seeing her. I said out loud, 'It's their job, Father,' and I tried to signal with my eyes, tried to say, 'What can she tell them?' but he was all fluster.

There she was in bed, curtains pulled, big belly, mouth open, snoring. I was that embarrassed for the police and for him, her lying there gob open like that.

'Where's Eddie?' she kept on saying and 'My husband's been with me all night.'

They got nothing from her but that. She looked a right sight. When my mother was ill in bed she was always a lady, always had her hair in a plait, nightie always clean and smooth, even at the end.

She sat up on the bed and inspected the burn on the heel of her foot. She had been barefoot all day and no one had commented. Shoes would have hurt her and bare feet had been convenient when finding the body because it confused the footprints she had made the night before. Last night and this morning the burn had been angry, red and shaped like a rosebud. Now it was less sore, less red, more brown, a withered rosebud.

She got off the bed, pulled back the rug and kneeled down. She looked up to check that Anna was still in the garden, then lifted up a foot of floorboard, delved into the space it made and pulled out a bread-knife. The blade was still freckled with blood, dried now, and there was a crust of blood where the blade met the handle. Last night there had been nowhere else to put it. Later, much later, she planned to hide it in the top of her stockings, the woollen ones that didn't ladder easy. She would walk up Brackley Street and back along the canal and drop it in as she passed. For the moment, however, it was safe. The only danger would be moments like this when, unable to resist, she would take out the knife, this knife, not evidence of murder but of her father's love.

The space underneath the floorboard held more than the knife. It was where she kept her treasures. There was an old brooch of her mother's with a picture of the Sacred Heart and the words 'See how I have loved you'. The clasp was broken and the brooch was unwearable but, like the other treasures, it was precious to her. She picked them out and laid each on the bed: an old comb, a fob watch, a dress pin, a button and the charred remains of a rag doll that had fallen into the fire. There was also a photograph of her father in black swimming-trunks on a beach in Cornwall, a calm sea to the back of him and beside him Norah in a swimsuit. Her father stared back at the camera, his grin strong and happy, but Norah's expression could only be guessed at: her face had been scratched away by Ursula's malicious fingernails.

These and other treasures lay on a bed of white tulle, her mother's wedding veil. She lifted it out, pulled it over her head and sat awhile. It was comforting to sit so, the bedroom all foggy through the veil, but dangerous, too, if someone were to enter or the police to return.

Wisely, Ursula took off the veil but before she put it and the other treasures back under the floorboard she took one more look at the photograph, gazing first at her father in his swimming-trunks and then at the white cloud where Norah's face had been. Ursula held the point of the knife over the photograph's bald patch and then skewered it through.

She heard a sound on the landing, a door clicking open, the shuffle of footsteps. She shoved dagger, veil, photograph and the other treasures back into the hole, replaced the board, pulled the rug back over it and listened.

Someone was on the landing. Father? Anna? The police? She crept to the door, opened it slightly and peered through the crack.

Norah was standing on the landing. Her hair was loose about her face, a nest of snakes. Her nightdress, white, patterned with roses, was wrinkled, rucked up round her pregnant belly, her knees on show.

'Norah?' Ursula asked, coming towards her. 'Shouldn't you be in bed?'

'Ursula, where's Eddie?' Norah's voice was vague and high, quite unlike her.

She looks a mess, thought Ursula. She looks such a mess. Her face was creased and puffy with too much sleep. She had managed to powder her face before coming out. The pink powder had been applied with a distracted hand and without a mirror. It had been flicked over her wild hair and down the front of her nightdress. Powdered her face but not smoothed her nightie or combed her hair: Norah was so vain, so lazy and so vain.

'Where's Eddie?'

'Back to bed, Norah.' Ursula took her arm.

'No!' Norah pulled her arm away as if Ursula's touch had burned it. She staggered to the top of the stairs where she held on to the wooden Welsh dragon in which the banister ended. The dragon was cool, comforting, unlike Ursula.

Seeing her, Ursula thought, Well, this is it, and marvelled at how things fell into place and at her power for making them do so. She had asked Norah to go to bed but Norah had said 'No'. She had tried to save her but Norah had refused to leave harm's way. A dead child, a dead Norah, the stones over which she had formerly stumbled swept away, a smooth path for her and her father to walk upon. He would be so grateful. He would see the point of one more death. He would see that it was done to protect him.

'Now, Norah,' she said as if to a child, enjoying treating Norah as Norah had always treated her.

'Where's Eddie?' Norah spoke as if through a fog in which she was panic-stricken and lost.

' "Where's Eddie? Where's Eddie?" Is that the only song you know? Eddie's dead, Norah, he's dead.'

The fog lifted in Norah's head. Her eyes were suddenly clear and comprehending, her mouth a perfect 'O'. She was about to speak but Ursula hushed her.

'That's right, Norah dear, Eddie's dead. Poor Eddie. And do you know what?'

'What?' Norah managed to gulp.

'You're next.'

Ursula shoved Norah, round and white in her ballooning nightdress, as if she were rolling a snowball. She watched with interest as Norah tumbled down the stairs. Such a racket and a clumping sound she made as she fell.

'So noisy, Norah,' Ursula gently chided her and then ran down after her, jumping over the splayed body where it had come to rest at the foot of the stairs.

Her father came slowly, reluctantly out of the parlour. She heard the door open behind her and his cry of 'Norah! Norah!' Ursula placed the tip of her forefinger on her tongue, licked it, made two strokes in the air and then scored them through. It was a private rite but her father witnessed it.

He came and stood beside her. Norah lay like a Saint Andrew's cross in front of them. Her head was at their feet, eyes twitching, blood running from between her legs as if from a bowl, staining the nightgown, a red circle, a rose, large and blooming rapidly.

Her father said nothing. She looked up at him.

'This is for you,' she said quietly, confident that he would appreciate and accept her gift.

She had heard how cats, unable to understand how their human owners managed to feed themselves when they never hunted, would hunt for them. They would snatch at a sparrow or a mouse with quick teeth and claws, carry it to their owners and, dropping it at their feet, would look up at their owners as Ursula now looked up at her father: Take this. You cannot hunt. I have hunted for you. Eat. Enjoy. The owner would look down with distaste and even horror at this offering, ignorant of the generous impulse it represented. To the owner it was beastliness and a mess on the carpet.

And just as the cat knows by the scolding and the thwack on the nose that it receives that its offering is not appreciated, so Ursula could tell by her father's coldly ferocious stare that she had failed to please him.

'No, this was not needed, not needed at all! You've gone too far! Like last night, you've gone too far. . . . ' He spoke as calmly as he could, although his shoulders and hands were shaking. He would have said more but he heard the kitchen door swing shut. Anna had returned and the young policeman with her.

Trench called out to him: 'Help us, my wife . . . she's fallen.'

If Anna and her constable had returned one second later, much would have been different. Trench had spent the whole day trapped in a part. He had lied the whole day. Deceit had him in too tight a grip for him to break free of it in a moment. Compelled to protect his daughter as she had protected him, he would carry on the lie.

As for Ursula, she had thought to buy his love or at best gain protection from his hatred and had failed to achieve either. The flame that had burned within her throughout the day guttered and died.

'She's dead, sir,' the policeman announced needlessly. 'Don't no one move while I phone Mr Sissons.'

As the policeman shouted down the phone to the superintendent, Trench leaned forward and took his daughter in his arms. He pushed her hair from her ear and whispered gently but through clenched teeth: 'I shall make you pay for this. Pay hard. Pay long. Pay very hard. Pay very long. Your whole life long I'll make you pay. I'll have you burn in Hell for what you've done.'

III

The Evening Before

Norah Trench, heavy with child and grumbling under the weight, lay on the sofa and occupied herself with sighing. Her husband sat across from her in the easy chair that was known as his, one hand stroking his moustache, the other drumming a quick rhythm on his rounded thighs. Anna Matchett sat at the piano which she could not play but the keys of which she touched now and then as if to accompany the flat, tuneless hum she made in her boredom. The child, Edmund, sat on the floor, his back against the sofa. With the paw of his teddy bear he traced the red thread in the rose-patterned carpet. Dressed for bed, he was being deliberately quiet in the hope of staying in his mother's company longer than he was normally allowed.

Ursula sat by the window in a hard-backed chair sewing a new hem on an old skirt. As she pushed and pulled the needle through the red linen, she imagined with pleasure doing likewise to Norah Trench's mouth.

Ursula, nearly eighteen, looked much younger. She had the thin face and the fishy eyes of a miserable child and the petulant manner of a charmless one. Her thoughts that evening were of envy, jealousy, blood, of being overlooked and not belonging – but her thoughts were ever so. In her watery-brown dress, hair falling unfashionably straight over her brow and neck, her body curveless, all corners, she would have been invisible, blotted out by the beige evening light, if it had not been for the bright red linen in her lap through which she plied her needle with such murderous attention.

Pendle had lit a fire in the garden – only a small one to get rid of the rubbish, he had explained to Mr Trench. All evening the air had been dappled with its smoke, peppered with its scents. The parlour was slowly darkening, the beige light becoming more deeply brown and stuffy with the day's heat and the smell of Pendle's fire.

The front of the house caught the sun something cruel, Norah had complained. One could go blind sitting in that parlour on sunny days. It would have been more sensible, if less comfortable, to sit in the cool dining-room which caught the sun only early in the morning but Norah would have none of it. The dining-room was for dining, she said, and the parlour was for parlouring – she thought it was French for passing the day.

Ursula would have sat alone in the dining-room. When her mother had been alive and able to sit downstairs, the dining-table was pushed back to the wall and easy chairs with high backs and wide wings brought in and set about the fire. The dining-room was darkly impressive. Ursula liked to sit reading through the volumes of encyclopaedia that were kept there. Morbidly, she liked to study the illustrations: the veins of the body, the respiratory system, the development of the foetus, the bloody bag that was the human heart. However, it was odd to sit apart, odd to sit alone when your family sat together. Oddness was a crime in Norah's eyes: it was Ursula's natural state.

In the kitchen Mrs Gibbons, in her scarf and shawl, was picking the fluff off Lizzie's jacket before handing it to her along with her final instruction.

'Slice that bread and then cover it with a cloth until they're ready for it. And, ay, take care and slice it thin. She likes it thin enough to see through.'

She was Norah Trench and, according to Mrs Gibbons, skinny bread was one of Norah's fancy airs – one of many. She was all airs, was Norah Trench, but Mrs Gibbons said as how it would take a strong wind to blow the smell of Mallet off her. Mallet-born meant Mallet-mannered and always would be if Mrs Gibbons was any judge.

'I'll go tell them goodnight. You be done for when I'm back.'

Mrs Gibbons muttered as she moved across the hall to the parlour door. The hall smelt of paint and nail-varnish. She rapped at the parlour door, opened it and poked her head round.

'We're off home now, Mrs T.,' she said cheerily, acting the merry servant.

'Oh, are you going?' Norah's voice and eyes were pitiful, as if Mrs Gibbons's going was permanent and tragic.

'There's bread cut for supper.'

'Cut thin?'

'Cut dead thin. I watched Lizzie do it. Goodnight, then.'

Mrs Gibbons's 'Goodnight' was loud and ringing. Four feeble echoes returned it.

In the kitchen Lizzie had her jacket on.

'Have you cut that bread?'

'I've cut that bread.'

'Right, we're off out of here, then.'

The back door slammed but no one in the parlour heard it. Ursula watched as Mrs Gibbons and Lizzie came from the side of the house and crunched their way down the gravel drive. Lizzie smiled up at Ursula as they passed.

Lizzie lived with Mrs Gibbons in a terraced house on Montgomery Road where squalid Mallet tapered into grimy but respectable Radcliffe Park. Mr Gibbons was long dead from his lungs but there was a son who worked in Lewis's as a shopwalker. Evenings he liked to knit, which was not a manly pastime in Mallet. If neighbours called, the needles would be quickly passed to Lizzie who had learned to hold them as if she could use them. Mrs Gibbons said as how her son was sensitive and how he got it from her. He had knitted her a lovely shawl with little matchstick men in clogs along the bottom of it. She kept it for best and had not yet had an opportunity of wearing it. If anyone asked, Lizzie had to say it was her who knitted it because folk already talked about her sensitive cousin. She said how nice he was, how his hands were always clean with long fingers and how, of an evening, between knittings, he would do impressions of Gracie Fields. 'We have a right laugh sometimes,' Lizzie had said.

Ursula looked after them longingly as they turned into the park.

Norah was uncomfortable and let it be known. She lay, splayed out on the sofa, her legs and arms thin pins unable to burst the ever expanding balloon of her belly. There was a thin gloss of sweat on her face, neck and chest. She watched her sister Anna at the piano. It made her feel mountainous, ugly. She had been pregnant, it seemed, for years. She would never be normal again.

'Why do I have to wear this sack?' She pulled at the purple smock, sticky and wrinkled.

'Because you're pregnant,' Anna answered smartly. 'And you'd look silly squeezed into a dress for a normal-sized woman. Anyway, you've other smocks. Mind you, you're fast growing out of them, too. I must say I never thought you'd stretch to the width you have. Do you think you'll ever get your figure back?'

Norah, in answer, burst into tears.

Trench was there immediately, pulling a hankie from his smoking-jacket. He flapped it anxiously before his weeping wife who pushed it and him away.

Anna looked lovely that evening, the cow. She dressed up on purpose, Norah was sure of it. The worst of it was that the grey silk dress, the bodice laced through with frosted beads, was Norah's own. It had belonged to her in the days when her hips had been narrow and she had had a waist her fingers could meet round. Looking down at her belly, she wondered if she would ever have a waist to speak of again.

Anna looked smart. Norah also looked smart when she wasn't pregnant. For the Matchett sisters, looking smart had been a mutual dream while growing up in darkest Mallet. Norah, the eldest, had been the first to realise that if a girl wished to look smart she had to think smart.

Norah may have been Mallet-born but she worked hard at not being Mallet-mannered. From adolescence on, she had devoted herself to looking and thinking smart. She had done her best to coat herself with a varnish of gentility but had been cack-handed with the brush. The varnish was rich in cracks and bits of fluff spoiled the even sheen she so desired.

She had trained as a nurse, not a proper one, she'd not had the brains. A year or two mopping floors and scouring bedpans suggested that this was not the way for a smart girl to get on. She heard about how going private could make you a packet and how qualifications weren't essential. She had looked after a snotty woman with bladder problems and an old man with a prolapsed rectum. The old man said he would leave her money in his will if he could just once put his hand down her pinny. He didn't. The money went to a niece in Scunthorpe who had no need of it. Norah eventually ended up in the House of Content nursing Mrs Miriam Trench.

Norah was praised by doctor, husband and even daughter for her cool ways and conscientious attitude but Miriam had been fast fading and Norah wasn't employed for long. She left the House of Content immediately following Miriam's death but re-entered its doors, past the statue of Our Lady of Lourdes, only a year later, not as paid servant but as mistress, wife to Mr Trench.

The draught from flapping tongues raised quite a few eyebrows. The draught grew to a healthy breeze when nine months to the day she brought forth a son. That the pregnancy had been a painful one was thought only a justice and a result of her being so narrow in the hips.

Norah was happy, or happy enough. With a little bit of effort, a good deal of smartness and a face that with a lick of paint could pass for a doll's, she had achieved not one dream but three: she had a big house, she had married a rich man and she had rid herself of that hideous surname.

'Norah Trench.'

She would say it over and over again as if it were a posh scarf she couldn't leave off putting round her neck, her wrist, her waist, wherever it suited, and it suited wherever it was put.

'Norah Trench.'

She repeated it so often that Anna, unmarried and still burdened by the name of Matchett, could have happily sliced off her sister's tongue with a bread-knife.

'Norah Trench,' Norah would say when Anna came up from Mallet to visit. 'It has a ring to it, hasn't it? Norah Trench.'

Anna said the only ring about Norah was the one she left round the bath.

'And there's my wedding ring, too, Anna. You're not forgetting that.'

Anna was not allowed to forget the wedding ring. Norah

always made sure that the ring caught the light even though, as it was such a slim thing, this wasn't always easy. She was forever passing Anna cups of tea or plates of sandwiches, sliced thin, or pointing at whatever could be pointed at with a carefully angled hand.

'And yet', said Anna, looking at it intently, 'it's a very thin ring as rings go, isn't it? I mean, it's not very big. I suppose, it being his second time round, your Freddie'd not wanted to overspend, knowing how these things aren't always permanent.'

Norah said as rings go it was the best she could want and it fitted round her finger dead tastefully. Anna said it would fit better round her neck and she would oblige if Norah let her. Norah said Anna was a jealous cat but she liked Anna to be jealous. Anna's jealousy was proof of Norah's success.

'And how is that man from the Water Board you were seeing, Anna? Such a pity you didn't settle down with him. He was your best chance so far. There's money to be made in sewage. It was sewage he was in, wasn't it? I am surprised you turned your nose up at him.

It was a rivalry of sisters. There was no badness in it – only the usual spit and venom of two women brought up too close in a house cramped enough to have made Siamese twins of them. Only a year separated them, with Anna, at twenty-five, the younger and more shapely. They had the same round faces and flat features, the same beaked nose and frizzy hair, except Anna's was redder and more tameable whereas Norah's was muddy and more wild.

Anna also had the more generous chest but a bigger bosom had not won Anna a husband. Being smart had done that for Norah, and having a skill. Nursing had got her into big houses and into the House of Content. Anna had no skill. She had dithered and wasted her time. Like her sister, she had the idea that the world owed her something but she was too lazy-minded to make it pay up.

It was envy of Norah's skill and the fruits it could harvest that brought Anna to the House of Content. When Norah was pregnant a second time she had screamed and stamped for more help about the house and, specifically, a nursery maid to help with Edmund. Trench would part with money only if given no other choice. Make use of Ursula who does nothing, he had said. Norah had spat at that. Make use of Anna, then, he suggested. Norah had spat at that, too, but with less force. Anna was family, cheap, and preferable to Ursula. Norah and Anna had talked about it and Anna had said 'Yes' after Norah persuaded her it was a way to get on. Looking after a house, a pregnant woman, a young child would give Anna skills to which she could refer when answering advertisements in *The Lady*. Freddie, she was sure, could be counted on for a good reference.

Whatever skills Anna acquired she used half-heartedly. Being a servant was not her idea of getting on. Still, the House of Content was better than living alone in Mallet, and Norah was her sister after all. The days passed easily enough but their only real interest was in arguing with Norah – a sport to which both were addicted.

'And are you really happy in this house, our Norah? Tell me.'

'I'm pleased to call it mine, yes. You'll not know the pleasure of having a house that's your own, you being single and no prospect of not being so.'

'Well, I don't know, our Norah. It doesn't seem to me you'll ever be at home in this house for all you do it up.'

'You didn't see it when I first came. Gloomy was not the word. You could have looked high and low for a set of decent table-mats.'

'Table-mats? Now, they didn't have them in Mallet.'

'They just about had tables in Mallet. I've long since left that life behind.'

'Yes, you've come a long way and all credit to you. But, as I said, this is a big house.'

'Yes. So you said.'

'A big house and . . . well, our Norah, you're small folk.'

'I'm as good as any.'

'You're as good as me, our Norah, so I know whereof I speak.'

'You know whereof, do you?'

'I know whereof. You're small folk in a big house and it shows. Stands out miles. I'm your sister so I can say it. The only big thing about you is your gob.'

'Gob?'

'Gob.'

'Don't judge me by your low standards, Anna Matchett. *Miss* Anna Matchett. You use a word like *gob* in a house like this, with proper antimacassars and lamps from Lewis's. You've learned nothing from me on how to enlarge yourself.'

'Well, everything's paid for, I suppose. You've no debts and that's a blessing. Then, again, you spend nothing. I've never known a man for keeping his tabs on his money as your Freddie. It can't be easy for you, Norah love.'

Anna had hit on Norah's wound. She picked over the scab delicately but without mercy. Norah may have had a husband but she did not have his wallet and what does a smart girl need a man's heart for if she hasn't got his wallet?

Norah had dreamed of turning the House of Content into a palace of pastels and of herself as a general in charge of an army of maids in white bob hats. She had married expecting those dreams to be realised but found she had to make do with Mrs Gibbons in to cook and not live in, and Lizzie every other day. With so many folk on the dole, Norah had argued, and labour so cheap, it was both good sense and a kindness to employ a servant or two. But Norah was doomed to a life of luxury on the cheap and sly extravagances, of buying tasselled lampshades and half-good linen and sitting tight until the end of the month when the bills came as well as a row with Freddie. Freddie, so loving, so attentive in all other matters, was unyielding in the one area where Norah most desired him to be generous.

Be careful of what you dream for it may come true, thought Norah. The House of Content had come true for Norah and one of life's goals had become instead one of its banes.

Anna's cruelly slow rendition of 'Chopsticks' was not pleasing to Norah. The child in her womb was kicking in time with it.

'Come away from that piano, Anna. You can no more play it than I can.'

Anna ignored her. 'I always hoped as how I was musical. They said as how our mam was when she was a girl. She used to call herself a singer but she was never that. She'd stand up after a few drinks in the pub but only because she was — '

'Anna! Leave that piano alone. You play on my nerves,

you do really, and it's not fair.' Norah's voice was just above a whine and her look was vicious.

Anna slammed the lid down. 'Happy now? You *are* crabby this evening.'

Norah fidgeted on the sofa. 'I am not.' She rubbed her swollen stomach. 'I'm uncomfortable.'

'Would you like my cushion, Norah dear?' Trench asked.

Norah, creaking a little, stretched out her arm and touched his knee. 'You are sweet, Freddie, you really are. If you'd be so kind. Just there, at the small of my back which is where the pressure lies, there's a love.'

Norah had two voices: the Mallet bark she used with Anna and the cracked and honeyed tones she used with the rest of the world, husband included.

Trench kneeled down to arrange the cushion to Norah's liking. Anna looked away, bored with Norah's performance, and caught Ursula's contemptuous stare. For Ursula, her father had lost all dignity with his cushion. Anna, noticing the girl's sharp eyes, wondered if that was what 'looking daggers' meant.

Trench rubbed his cheek against his wife's pretty face.

'Ooh! Your moustache makes me all ticklish, Freddie.' Norah's giggle suggested that the moustache and being tickled by it were more fun than it was decent to say.

Trench stroked his moustache proudly. He rose and stood over her, his stomach the equal of Norah's.

Ursula shivered and wondered how it felt to be made ticklish by her father's moustache or to smooth her hands over his convex belly.

Trench's moustache was as old as his marriage to Norah. He had grown it for her on their honeymoon. She said it made him look younger and, past forty and with a new wife half his age, he knew he had needed something.

'A man should have a moustache,' Norah announced grandly, 'and it is his wife's duty to attend it as devotedly as she would her own coiffure or garden.' For Norah, *coiffure* was pronounced 'coeefoor'; as for attending to a garden, if it was long, thin and green, it was grass, and, if it was long, thin, green with a coloured bit at the end, it was a flower. The garden of the House of Content was her husband's concern. It was the one thing on which he ever spent money without arguing the toss.

'This is Norah in her magazine voice,' Anna told Ursula who had heard it before.

Norah sniffed and carried on. 'One wonders what can ail the wives of men with straggly moustaches. Oral hair — '

'Oral hair! That sounds dead rude.'

'It sounds rude to them as are. And need I remind you my child is in this room, so watch your mouth, Anna Matchett.'

'Oh, I'll not speak again, then.'

'If only that were true. Now, come closer, Freddie, and let me attend to your oral hair. Pass me them scissors, Ursula, there's a kindness.'

Ursula came across to the sofa holding the scissors blade outwards.

'That's not the way to pass scissors, Ursula, and well you know it.'

Ursula turned away back to her seat by the window.

'Was that an apology I heard, Ursula?' she heard her father ask.

'Oh, never you mind about Ursula and me. Now, bend over, Freddie love. You're such a big boy I can't reach and you know I've not to stretch.'

Trench bent close and Norah snipped away at his moustache with the dress scissors.

'Stop smirking, Freddie, or I'll snip that lip.'

Anna lit a cigarette, Ursula pushed the needle into the red linen with increasing firmness, and the child crawled from round the sofa to pick up the silvery snips of hair from his mother's smock.

'You should be in bed, precious heart,' his mother told him. Trench agreed but Norah then protested. 'Oh, but let him stay a while longer. He only wants to be by his mother, precious heart. Kiss Mummy, precious heart.'

'You spoil him, Norah,' Trench forced himself to say.

'She does,' Anna agreed.

Ursula bit at the red thread.

'It's not good for him.'

Trench thought the child hung by his mother more than was manly or wise. Anna said that she had thought the same thing often.

'And who asked you?' Norah flared. 'And must you smoke in my condition and in this parlour?'

'I'm not in your condition.'

'You know very well what I mean.'

'Oh, give over, Norah. You just moan for moaning's sake.'

'Women shouldn't smoke. There's nothing worse. I saw one smoking in Brackley Street. She was that common.'

'Joan Crawford smokes in the films and she's not common.'

'Yes, but not in Brackley Street and not in this parlour where folk have to breathe. Make her stop, Freddie. I'm so uncomfortable and no one understands.'

Norah pulled the child to her and sobbed into its ear, which made the child sob, too. Trench dithered over weeping mother and weeping child, adding shushing noises to the din they made. Anna, nowtily, stubbed out her cigarette on the parquet tiles underneath the piano and Ursula, sewing done, hands in lap, imagined what peace there would be when Norah and her child were no more.

'Norah, Norah, stop crying so,' begged Trench, patting her heaving shoulders. 'You make the child cry more. Eddie, stop those tears right now. Anna, make them stop.'

'She'll stop when she wants,' said Anna wisely.

'No one cares,' claimed Norah, gasping for air and the tears still coming. 'No one understands. Only precious heart cares for his mummy.'

The child redoubled his tears to prove his mother true.

'Anna, help me quieten her down. Norah, shh now, shh!' Trench spoke slowly but could not calm the woman and the child was enjoying his tears too much to want to stop.

Anna was watching her cuticles grow and Trench was at a loss. 'Ursula!' he cried, proof he was at wits' end. 'Do something!'

Ursula blinked as if she could not quite believe the command but, not needing to hear it twice, walked round the sofa, took Norah by the shoulders and slapped her in the face. As slaps go, it was harder than was needed but efficient. Norah was instantly shocked into silence, as was the child who had never seen one adult hit another and so was interested.

'She did that to me this morning,' the child told its mother solemnly.

261

Norah, her own injury forgotten, wits restored, understood exactly. 'Ursula hit you this morning? She hit you?' Norah's voice was iced. On her face was an expression of victorious satisfaction, of one who had long been in search of damning evidence against an enemy and had now found it. 'Tell us, precious heart, what she did to you, and don't be frightened.'

Like his mother, the child loved an audience. He took a self-important pause while he looked up at stunned father, interested Anna and blank-faced step-sister before lisping: 'This morning she hit me. Well, not hit me, pinched me. Pinched me hard.'

Hit or pinch, it was all the same to Norah. 'Well, miss, what have you to say to that?'

Ursula, it seemed, had nothing to say.

'Is this true?' asked Trench. Her father's voice seemed terrible to her but her own voice and expression were models of control.

'No,' she said simply.

'Of course she'd deny it. What do you expect? Eddie darling, show Mummy where she pinched you.'

The child rolled up its nightgown and there on the white chicken flesh of its thigh was a bruise, quite small but perfectly navy.

'It's only small,' said Anna, disappointed.

'The size matters not at all,' answered Norah.

'He must have knocked himself,' said Ursula limply, indifferent.

'Liar!'

'Maybe it's the child who's lying,' Anna suggested idly.

'My child does not lie!' Norah was passionate. 'He tells his mother everything, don't you, precious heart?'

Precious heart grinned at the compliment.

'He's a tell-tale,' said Ursula but without malice, as if it were a sad fact.

Anna felt she had to agree with Ursula there. 'You've spoilt that lad rotten. If he was pinched, why has he said nothing until now?'

'He wanted to tell his mother.'

'Exactly. He tells you everything just like a tell-tale should.' Anna was starting to enjoy herself again.

Norah could not understand how the argument had turned from attacking Ursula to defending Eddie. 'Whose side are you on?' she screamed at Anna.

Anna said in all mock-innocence: 'Sides? I didn't know there were any.'

'Freddie!' Norah was desperate. 'What are you going to do about it?'

Trench puffed himself up to dispense justice but found there was none to give. Deflated, he said weakly: 'What can I do? If Ursula says she didn't do it and Eddie says she did, who am I to believe?'

For Norah, it was simple. 'You believe me!'

Trench, hardly daring to say it, said: 'But, Norah, love, dear, he does tell tales.'

'Well, if he does, he tells truthful ones.' Norah could think of no better reply, believed there was none, and the child set up crying again.

'That child ought to be in bed,' Trench shouted. 'There's another instance of spoiling.'

'Don't you snarl at me, Freddie Trench. I see you tell me off quick enough but you were quiet enough a minute ago when I wanted you to deal with her!'

'Cocoa!' trilled Anna, bored with watching spats, and Ursula, tired of being the cause of so many, said: 'I'll make it.' Then, to tease Norah, she said to the snivelling child: 'Come on, Eddie, I'll make you a milky drink.'

Eddie pulled down his nightgown and trotted after her.

The hall floor, polished that morning by Lizzie Gibbons, was a dark mirror over which she walked with the child in tow. The hall was generally gloomy. Even on the brightest days the sun scarcely penetrated the panels of paned glass that striped either side of the front door. Yet, darkly brown though the hall was, the statue of Our Lady of Lourdes had always glowed white. It stood in the corner by the hatstand, not quite life-sized and, for all that it was made of cheap plaster, somehow delicate and pure.

It had been planted there by Ursula's mother, the late and blessed Miriam, who had carried it (although not personally) all the way back from Lourdes. She had gone there for a miracle but had been disappointed: the statue had been consolation. As a girl, Ursula, transfixed before it, had imitated its praying hands and benignly bowed head. She did so now. The child watched her, amused.

Ursula did not keep the pose long but not because she feared the child's laughter. Nor was it because her own angular body was unable to match what she saw as Our Lady's graceful lines: for her it had been ruined. The statue, which she could not but see as her dead mother incarnate in plaster, had been horribly disfigured by Norah that very morning.

Norah had never liked it and had decided to cheer it up. She and her son had spent the late hours of morning painting it with the child's lead paints. The statue was no longer white. Its veil and gown were petrol blue and its sash a cheap gold. Its face had also been made up: the pious lips a bold scarlet, the drooping lids lavender blue. On the slope of its cheeks were streaks of Mad Pink. Round its neck blobs of scarlet on gold, an attempt at a ruby necklace, made it look as though Our Lady had been garrotted.

Anna had come along to inspect the statue. It was she who suggested that a touch of nail-varnish would brighten up those hands poised in prayer. A coat of Red Admiral had been applied to Our Lady's nails but before it had dried it had dribbled down her fingers to her wrists. Come midday, Our Lady looked like a strangled tart who had worked in an abattoir.

Standing back to view the improvement, Norah argued that just because she was Our Lady didn't mean she was averse to a bit of powder and paint.

Anna had agreed: 'Well, if she was alive today I'm sure there'd be more than a touch of hair-lacquer under that veil.'

Trench had come home and had pretended to be cross and disapproving but had been unable to keep it up. He had thrown his head back and laughed.

Ursula had not laughed. She had seethed silently in her room, the laughter stealing up the stairs to taunt her. She had hid in the white tent of her mother's veil, hugging the charred rag doll to her chest, dreaming of vengeance.

Norah was evil. Norah was pollutant. By desecrating the statue she had desecrated the memory of Miriam Trench as effectively as if she had dug up the coffin and disfigured the corpse inside it. The statue was the very spirit of the House of Content, the centre which held it straight and true. It was a thing to which reverence was due and to which damage had been done instead. In her temple of white veil, Ursula felt the house's outrage at what had been done and trembled for it. She felt the power she had invested in the statue flee from it and enter her bloodstream like a virus.

She had bided her time for half an hour and then had come down to take the child for a walk round the garden. The day was hot, dry and shadowless; the child, as always, easy in her company. At the bottom of the garden she took him in her arms and sat with him in the garden privy. He struggled to get out but she told him struggling made the dark even darker. She sat holding him close, enjoying his terror. He whimpered, begging to be let out; it was dark, it smelt bad and he was scared. She was unyielding until his whimpering became one long continuous wail. Cry on, she had thought, they will not hear you. She took the soft flesh between her thumb and forefinger and pinched it hard.

The child screeched and, suddenly panicking, she thought of Pendle. If Pendle was about the garden, he would hear and he would tell on her. She shushed the child, rocked it, became loving and kind until the child grew quiet again.

The sun blinded her when they finally emerged. The child stumbled back to the house in search of his mother and justice but she caught him before he had run more than a yard. She held him by the shoulders and stared into his tear-swollen face.

'You will not tell on me,' she said. It was not a request but a command.

'I will,' the child had said passionately but, face to face with his attacker, sensing perhaps some power in her that the other adults in his world did not possess, conviction deserted him.

'What has been done to you has been done for a reason. See this hand?'

The child saw her right hand splayed palm outwards in front of him. It was so much larger than his own, clean and white while his were covered in lead paints. Yes, he nodded, he saw it.

'It is a magic hand.'

The child could half-believe it.

'See the mark on your leg?'

The child rolled up his shorts and inspected the bruise that had already appeared on his thigh. He loved the bruise instantly as he loved any scab or cut that lingered when the nastiness of pain had gone.

'It means you are special, chosen, important.' Ursula whispered it like a secret and the child accepted it. It accorded with his own belief that he was precious and unique. 'You will bear that mark until you die.'

The child nodded seriously, completely involved.

'Speak of it to anyone and it will disappear and you will no longer be special or important ever again.'

The child no more wanted to lose this mark than anything else he had been given. It was his.

Ursula moved her hand away and from the pocket of her dress drew out a bag of barley sugars. To the child the sight of the barley sugars in its grasp was proof that the hand was magic. Ursula saw the effect she had on the child. Such power I have, she thought. I should use it more often.

'If you don't tell anyone that I kept you in there, then tonight when you go to bed I'll give you these sweets. Barley sugars. You like them.'

The child did not need to consider this offer long.

The pair walked about and then sat on the lawn. The garden was blurred by a green heat. Dragonflies hummed about them and a white butterfly drew haloes round the heads of Ursula and the child. Pendle came by and saw them and thought how close they were and pretty together.

The child had kept his word. He had not spoken of the mark, only showed it and that didn't count. Nor had he told on her for keeping him in the dark of the privy. He thought himself clever for that and so he was, a clever child, a wise child, a sharp child, Norah's child.

In the kitchen, alone with Ursula once more, the child believed again the story she had told him. He regretted his disloyalty to her but regretted even more the loss of the barley sugars of which he had dreamed all evening.

'Can I have them barley sugars?'

Unusually for him, he made the request almost nervously, as if he hardly dared ask. He was used to having his demands met but knew he no longer deserved the sweets.

'I didn't want to tell on you,' he said miserably.

'Maybe you didn't,' Ursula said. It was not that she had relented, just that her mind had moved on to other, more important things. 'They're under your pillow. I put them there before dinner.'

She sat him on the table and began spooning the cocoa powder into the cups. The child chewed on the thin slices of bread Lizzie Gibbons had cut for supper.

'You'll spoil your appetite for the barley sugars,' she warned him, sounding as if she truly cared.

She poured milk from the covered jug into a pan. In her mother's day there would have been someone to do this for her. In her mother's day there had been a cook, two live-in maids and a woman who came to do the washing. Her father sacked them all two weeks after Miriam died. He claimed the expense was too great and that Mrs Gibbons and Lizzie were cheaper and all that was needed.

The house deserved to be properly staffed. For Ursula there was satisfaction to be had in the knowledge that there were at least some things her mother had possessed that Norah had not inherited but this was an insipid consolation. Norah had the run of the house and the love of Frederick Trench, which was more than Ursula could claim.

She ached for her father's love. She saw it given, freely and unearned, to Norah and to the child. Even Anna Matchett stood within the warm glow of his kind regards while Ursula stood within the cool draughts of his indifference. She wondered if this had always been so and strongly supposed that it had. He had never loved her, daughter to him though she was and love something she had a right to expect.

If her father could ignore her, it was even easier for Norah to overlook her.

When Ursula entered a room, Norah would turn and stare, surprised to see this stranger. Or, more frequently, she would grimace and shiver as if a smell or a chill had invaded the room. Other times, on entering a room and finding Ursula alone, Norah would hesitate, turn and leave, switching the light off as she did so. Ursula would protest.

'Oh, I am sorry, Ursula love,' Norah would coo, voice burbling with the syrup of insincerity, too thick with that syrup to be sweet. 'I quite forgot you were there. So easy to do. In another world I am.'

Ursula wished her in another world, wished her in Hell, and sometimes she said as much.

'Why, Ursula, temper, temper. Come, come, we don't want Daddy knowing what a jealous little cat you are. You know what happens to cats after all. They get put out. You'd not want putting out now, would you, Ursula love?'

Despite Norah's occupancy, Ursula felt that the house was hers. She saw it still as her mother had made it, a fortress of silence and pleasant gloom. Moreover, she felt partnered to it. The same dark architecture that ordered the bricks and joints, defined its perspectives and shadows, answered the joints and sinews of her soul. The house was part of her. It was her fate, her second skin, her prison, her past. It was all the things from which she could not escape. Because of this, Norah's tenancy, irksome and insulting though it was, did not wound her as deeply as did Norah's unrivalled residence in her father's heart.

Ursula did not know but maybe you could buy love. It could not be earned or demanded as a right so maybe it could be bought. Or maybe somebody could owe it you like a debt. She hoped that this was so. She could not endure much longer without it. There had to be someone who could acknowledge her, make her part of life, someone in whose head she could sit and be as close as close can be.

'Is that cocoa done?'

Anna had entered the kitchen. The frosted beads on her bodice caught what little light was left in the kitchen. She bent over the child, kissed and hugged him, snuggling against his neck. The child lay back on the table-top, giggling and kicking his legs up.

'You're dead soft, you are, Eddie Trench, dead soft.' She picked the child up – 'Oh, you're a lump' – and sat him on the stone floor. 'You shouldn't sit him on the table like that and not watch him. He might fall and hurt himself.'

Anna wanted to ask Ursula if she had really pinched the child and why, but Ursula, she had found, was not one for intimacy and the sharing of secrets.

'Which is Norah's cocoa?'

Ursula pointed it out.

Anna put her back to the child so that it could not see what she was about to do and so 'tell' his mother. She undid a small white envelope, poured a white granular powder into the cup and mixed it with the cocoa. It was Norah's sleeping powder and this was how, unknown to her, it was administered. Norah slept badly. She claimed the 'Lump' and the kicking child within it gave her no rest but hated to take the sleeping powders. She said they were ineffective anyway. Slipping them into her late-night cocoas was the best way of getting her to take them.

'Put plenty of sugar in it,' Anna whispered. 'It'll take the taste away.'

She turned and saw the child looking up at her with narrowed eyes, a knowing, suspicious look.

'Well, Master Trench, beddie-boes for you, I should think.'

The child, thinking of the barley sugars under his pillow, nodded.

'Well, Ursula will take you up, won't you?'

'I will not.'

'Oh, be a pet, Ursula. I toss and turn so when I sleep and he sleeps as light as his mother. I'm forever waking him and you know what he's like when he wakes in the dark. Cry, cry, cry. I can't be doing with it. You'd like to go up with Ursula, wouldn't you, Eddie?'

His thoughts were all for the barley sugars. He crawled over to Ursula and wrapped his arms around her legs.

'There, see, I told you.'

'I thought the child was your responsibility,' Ursula said, scowling. 'I thought that was why you were here, to help look after him.'

'Well, yes, that was the plan.'

Anna leaned back against the cupboard and took a packet of Wild Woodbines from her dress pocket. She lit one from the flame under the milk, dropped the empty green packet on the floor for the child to play with and exhaled a healthy cloud of blue smoke. Anna was relaxing.

'Take that pan off the heat and let's have a minute.'

Ursula took the pan off the heat. Little chats with Anna were becoming regular events in her life, ones she endured rather than enjoyed.

'Like I said, that was the plan. It was Norah's idea, of course. I've no skills to help me get on in life and there are all these jobs in *The Lady* that Norah thinks are dead right for me. She thinks I'll get into a big house and marry a rich man. As if! Well, I went along with it but looking after babies and tidying up after folk . . . well, I don't want that.'

Anna flicked her cigarette to get rid of an inch of ash. The ash fell on the child's arm. The child fingered it with interest. Ursula noticed this, noticed, too, with some disappointment, that the child was not burned.

'I know things between you and our Norah are a bit chilly. Well, you're not close and on evenings like this who can blame you? Have you never thought of getting out, Ursula?'

'I love this house,' Ursula said grimly, 'and I couldn't leave my father.'

'And yet he doesn't seem to have much time for you?' Anna considered this fact but not for long. 'You and me, we're not alike. I want to get out. You've never lived in Mallet, so you'll not know what I've known. I want a life better than the one to be had in Mallet or in this house.'

She looked at Ursula as if she might know where such a life could be found. She took a deep drag of her cigarette. 'I don't want a husband – though if there was a rich one going for nothing I wouldn't say no. I think that men are too much thought of. They're not the be-all and end-all, are they? I mean, they bring home a wage, if you're lucky, but I'd rather bring home my own wage. In our street, Malahide Street where me and Norah were born, the men hang about on corners. There's scarcely jobs for them, so there's none at all for me. Good jobs, I mean. I've done my time in factories and shops. That's not what I want. What I want is some of the gravy.'

Anna grew wistful, her voice as languid as the smoke that curled up from her cigarette.

'Some of the gravy or the know-how to get a spoon near it and sip it for myself. Maybe the war'll help.'

What war was this? If there was a war on, Ursula would have heard about it. It was something you noticed whether you were interested in it or not.

'Oh, it's coming,' Anna said definitely. 'That'll wake us up and no mistake. I'm not dreading it, either. Wars are good for women. I had an aunty who said so. She drove a bus in the last one, so she should know. I can drive, too. Well, nearly. I had this fella taught me how to change gears but he wanted to marry me before he'd let me do it while the car was moving. You see, I have had offers of marriage. None that got me near the gravy, otherwise I'd have said "Yes" long ago.'

'Norah thought she'd got the gravy, didn't she?'

'Yes, except that she's finding the gravy doesn't flow so easy.'

'Father's careful with money,' Ursula said loyally.

'Well, there's careful and there's careful,' Anna felt bound to say. 'Still, he married money, too. He had none of his own. Born up in Brackley Street your dad, a shop somewhere.'

'My dad married for love.' She would not let Anna imply otherwise.

'Well, I dare say so did our Norah, but money never harms. A drop or two of the gravy, it lubricates.' 'Lubricates' was a word to do with cars. Anna was fond of words to do with cars. She took another drag of her cigarette.

The child at their feet, bored, unused to being anything but the centre of attention, began to pull at Ursula's laces, fretting and whimpering, the very copy of his mother.

'He's tired. He should be in bed.'

She put the milk back on to boil, pulling the skin off it with a fork.

'I meant it about the war. A fool'd argue about there not being one. April they dug trenches in the park and there's them masks in the hall cupboard.'

Ursula remembered the gas-masks. There had been four of them sent by the Government and none for the child. Norah had had a canary fit when she learned that children as young as Eddie were not to be issued them. Did they think babies and small children not worth saving? For a week it had been a real fear for Norah and the child had cried for ages, too. Everyone

271

had a gas-mask but him and it wasn't fair. Anna and her father had rowed quite seriously about the coming war but Ursula had been unconcerned except when encouraged by the others to try on her gas-mask. Anna had said, 'Oh, quick, take it off! It looks like a death's head, it does really,' and Norah had coolly commented: 'Oh, I don't know. I think it quite suits her.'

Ursula poured the hot milk into the cups and said: 'I don't think about wars and stuff. They're nothing to do with me.'

'But you should think about it. I'm not political, not at all, but I follow the world when it's interesting. I mean, you're part of it, aren't you, the world? It's history. It's what makes you and, I suppose, you make it a little, too.'

'It's not my world,' said Ursula, plonking the cups on to a tray. 'This house and my father are my world.'

Anna looked about her. 'Well, if it is, all I can say is poor you.'

She decided that she hated Anna Matchett – not as much as Norah or the child – but hated her none the less. What right had Anna Matchett to say 'poor you' when all she was was a sponging relative, no better than a lodger, worse than a lodger because she did not even pay her way? She fluttered about the house with her fine frocks and common manner, pretending to understand the world and poor Ursula. Well, poor Ursula's world was a small one, one over which she did not even rule, but it was a world she understood and over which she had a power so dangerous it frightened her to use it.

History was nothing. History was what took place outside the garden of the House of Content. Geography, not history, explained Ursula's world. It was not time, but place, this house, that compelled and determined the lives within it, inspired loyalties, formed character and shaped destiny.

Anna Matchett thought she was so clever but she was a fool. She thought she understood the world and was out to get the best she could from it but her world was too large to be understood. Ursula's world was not. She knew it perfectly. She had known it in its Eden state, had seen it eroded and become a bad land, but she would reclaim it. She would restructure and restore its original geography. It could be done. She could do it. She had, she thought, the power.

Ursula took up the tray and Anna took up the child and followed Ursula into the parlour, which was no longer steeped in evening gloom but lit by two bright and fussy lamps. The windows had been closed against moths and midges but the smell of Pendle's fire still laced the heavy air.

'Ursula's taking Eddie up to bed,' Anna announced on entering the parlour.

Ursula would have protested – she had agreed to no such thing – but her father's praise came quicker than her complaint.

'Why, Ursula, that'd be good of you. See, Norah, she's not that bad.'

Norah harrumphed. 'If I was better in myself I'd take him up but he's such a big boy and I'm not to lift as you all know. Precious heart is too heavy for his mummy, isn't precious heart?'

The child was passed from Anna to Trench, both of whom kissed it, and then he was given to Norah, who accepted his kisses as things she thoroughly deserved. The child was then given reluctantly but without comment to Ursula.

'I'll say goodnight,' said Ursula.

'Goodnight, Ursula,' Anna chimed and – bliss – her father smiled. Norah gave a pantomime-sized shudder as Ursula left but Ursula had learned not to look.

As she carried Eddie up the stairs, she carried also the image of her father smiling at her as he sat beneath the standard lamp, smooth hands on his broad thighs, the veins as blue as the cigar smoke from the cigar he held between his fingers. It was the smile of a man whose love, his daughter felt, was worth earning, buying, getting somehow.

She took the child up to her room and sat him on the bed. It was not yet dark enough to turn on the bedside lamp. Besides, the evening light, tinged with red, gave the dark furniture a rosy edge. She went across to his room to fetch his cot. She wheeled it back to her room and parked it by her bed.

The child was not slow to ask for his barley sugars. Ursula said he could have just one. He sucked it, gormlessly happy, while she made up the cot.

Eddie said he wanted to spend a penny.

'Only a penny?'

The child nodded and Ursula took him along to the toilet. She rolled up his nightgown and held him over the toilet bowl.

He did not like to use the chamberpot and was too small to piss perfectly into the bowl. Ursula held him by the shoulders and, as he pissed noisily and happily, wondered what kind of mess he would make if she were to smash his head against the porcelain.

Back in her room, she prepared herself for bed. The child watched with lazily narrowed eyes as she slipped out of her brown dress and pulled on her white nightie over vest and long knickers.

She was not sure if it was wise to inspect her treasure while the child was still awake but a glance out of the window at the evening sky, scratched red with the setting sun, told her it would soon be dark. She would not have done so on any other evening – the child was sure to tell Norah in the morning – but she knew tonight that it did not matter. The child would not tell. She knew it almost as a certainty.

Shoving the barley sugar from side to side in his mouth, the child watched as Ursula lifted the short stretch of floorboard and pulled out the brooch, the comb, fob watch, dress pin, button, photograph, scorched rag doll and yard upon yard of white tulle veil.

Eddie thought little of her treasures and fingered each one dismissively as she set them out on the peach-coloured quilt. The photograph of his father he failed to recognise but the rag doll pleased him. Its burned appearance gave it charm. He liked it and, as with everything he liked, he wanted it.

'You like the doll?' she asked him, holding it in front of his face just as that morning she had held out her hand.

Oh, yes, he liked the doll.

'And the veil? Do you like the veil?'

The veil entranced him.

She threw it up in the air. It hung for a moment like a cloud above their heads and then fell, settling on the bed like snow.

The child was enchanted. He had wanted the doll and now he wanted the veil. He wanted both.

Ursula smiled, enjoying his greed. He didn't understand that she was not sharing her treasures with him but allowing him to witness them. To satisfy his greed, however, she handed him the doll and once again threw the veil up in the air.

The child giggled, raised his hands and opened wide his mouth to catch at it as it wafted lazily down. He fell back on the bed with a sigh as the veil softly covered him.

Ursula sat on the bed, her back against the pillows, and took the child in her lap. She made a tent of the white veil. The late sun touched it and tinged it ruby.

The child fell to sleeping, his breath warm and rhythmical on the crook of her arm. His expression was restful, even blissful, and so, too, was Ursula's. She looked down at the rag doll, blank-faced but for two embroidered lips shaped, as were Ursula's own in a smile of mischievous complicity.

Norah wittered on, her voice rising and falling, a knife cutting slice after thin slice of stale bread. Trench listened to it as if it were birdsong.

She grumbled about Ursula, the pinched white thigh of precious heart, accusations, malicious and unfounded, of precious heart's tale-telling, the heat, the smoke, the lump, how the baby inside her would never get born or, if it did, would be the death of her, and how she would not sleep that night, she knew it for a fact, how she never slept any night or slept proper anyhow, and, oh, how it was all too much to bear but bear it she would because she was a martyr, she was really. When Anna told her it was time to take her sleeping powder she grumbled about that, too.

Anna left the room and then came back with a glass of water which the sleeping powder had turned milky.

'Drink it up in one go, Norah, and then finish off that cocoa to get rid of the taste.'

Norah took out her hankie and wiped the lipstick from her mouth, something she did before drinking anything. Marks left by lipsticks were so common, she had observed, looking piteously at Anna who was forever leaving marks like red admirals on the best bone china.

Trench liked the dainty way she dabbed at her mouth, liked, too, the thought of women with their made-up faces. Miriam, his first wife, had worn no make-up and had said that if a woman wore muck on her face it was because there was muck on her soul. Poor Miriam, he allowed himself to think,

275

make-up wouldn't have done her much good; no wonder she was so set against it.

Norah, complaining all the while, drank down the milky sleeping draught – 'It'll do me no good' – and drained the cocoa.

Anna took the glass and empty cups back to the kitchen.

'You'll feel better now,' Trench assured his wife.

'If I do, it'll be a blessing,' Norah said sadly.

'You're bearing up well, my love.'

'Well, Freddie, that's thanks to your support.'

Husband's hand met wife's and kisses were blown until Anna returned.

'I'll not sleep a wink,' Norah claimed again.

Trench laughed. 'Nonsense, you snore fit to beat the band.'

'I do not. I never snore. And must you smoke that cigar! It makes me proper nauseous. You know it does.'

Trench threw the butt of his cigar into the empty fireplace. Norah, pacified, lay back on the sofa. Dark stains formed under her arms, her mouth grew slack and her eyelids heavy. Presently she slept.

Anna shook her shoulder.

'Time you were in bed.'

'No,' Norah groaned. 'Not yet. I'll not sleep a wink if I go up too early.'

Anna woke her three more times and each time Norah protested that it was still too early and, no, she had not been sleeping, just resting her eyes for a spell.

In a silence broken only by Norah's bubbling snores, Anna sat by the window smoking cigarette after cigarette and Trench in his chair worked his way through cigar after cigar. The smoke lingered about the lamps and veiled the parlour in a blue fog through which they watched the dozing Norah and, from time to time, each other.

An ormolu clock on the mantelpiece chimed tinnily on the hour but too softly to waken Norah.

At eleven, Anna tried again.

'Come on, look at the time. It's far too late and I'm wanting my bed an' all.'

Norah agreed that it was late. 'You'll help me get dressed, won't you? It's such an effort when you're my size. Everything's an effort. I'll not sleep a wink tonight, Freddie, and you'll not, either, with me tossing and turning beside you.'

Trench kissed his wife. 'I'd not have it any other way. I'll be up after I've locked up. Goodnight, Anna.'

'Goodnight, Freddie.'

Dressed for bed, Norah made to go for the door to Eddie's room. She wanted a good-night peek at precious heart.

'You'll not find him in there. He went up with Ursula, remember?'

'Poor precious heart, so scared of the dark. Like you were once.'

Anna fondly remembered her childhood fears and how, in the bed she had shared with her sister, she had clung to Norah, glad that there was someone older and unafraid in whose protective arms she could hide.

'I don't like Eddie being with Ursula,' said Norah. 'He should be with you. God knows that's why I asked you here.'

'Well, he is as a rule but Ursula's giving me a rest for the night. I thought I'd have a lie-in tomorrow.'

'I don't trust her.'

'That's nonsense. Eddie loves being with Ursula.'

'I don't know why. She does nothing to earn that love. I don't trust her, Anna, I never have.'

'Shush now, Norah, just sleep. You've more than one child to worry about and you need your rest.'

'Sometimes I think it'll never get born. Sometimes I think I'll die before it happens.'

'That's common, fears like that.'

'I often have fears. Sometimes I think I'm fat and lumpy and moaning all the time and that Freddie won't love me and I can't help feeling as I do.'

'Shush, Norah. Freddie loves you, I'm sure of it, and you'll be fine. Everything's fine. Sleep now.'

Anna turned off the light.

'I'll not sleep a wink,' Norah called after her, but as Anna slowly closed the door she could hear Norah's breathing come deep and low.

She passed by the child's room and then opened the door to her own. She reached for the light-switch but swore instead. She closed the door quickly and in the dark moved towards the foot of her bed.

Downstairs, Trench locked and bolted all the doors after checking that the windows were securely fastened. Such fastidiousness was almost a ritual with him. In the dining-room he made sure the catches on the sash windows were drawn and looked out into the garden. It was a clear night, the sky not black but, as ever over Radcliffe Park, faintly brown washed over with navy blue. Moonlight fell like chalk-dust, powdering the trees, the carefully sculptured bushes and the iridescently green lawns.

No life is pure success but what purity and success Trench enjoyed were enshrined in the garden of the House of Content. Money he had, property he had, a wife he loved, a son, a daughter, another child to come, but the garden was the one thing he possessed without qualification, compromise or deceit. It was something he had earned.

Old Man Hewitt had told him it was to be his special kingdom. It was the old man's particular gift to his son-in-law.

'Miriam'll do what's wanted to make the house looked lived-in but the garden's your domain.'

Hewitt had less than a fortnight left in him when he said that, the cancer chewing away at his throat. He hacked and spat out the words, pink saliva lining his toothless smile. Trench silently accepted the old man's gift and the conditions on which it was given.

He had been born no better than the old man; it was one more reason why the old man had wanted him. Frederick Trench was the son of a decent couple who kept a newspaper shop by the canal bridge in Brackley Street. His childhood and youth were happy but undistinguished and the pattern of his adult life well and truly set. He suited Radcliffe Park and was ignorant and uncaring of what lay beyond its smoky skyline until, all of twenty-one and after a drunken night with his pals, he joined up in the summer of 1915. Apart from four months in a hospital in Dover suffering from mortar wounds, and two months extended leave in Portsmouth with a nurse he had met in Dover, he spent the war either at the front line or seldom more than two or three miles away from it.

He wrote to his parents but never visited them. Their world of early-morning newspapers and shop-counter civilities, the solid buildings and hard cobbled streets, had grown unreal to him. It was separate from the world in which he fought, a world of mud and rats, rubble and fire, male companionship and human debris. To both his horror and his pride, he found that it was a world in which he flourished and the life he led in it was a charmed one.

To remain not only alive but relatively unscathed was only slightly more miraculous to him than his rise from private to company commander. By 1918 he had some two hundred men in his charge. He gave or denied them leave, listened to their complaints, bullied them into acts of bravery, wrote to their parents when they died, even helped bury them if they died with their bodies more or less intact or in places where it was convenient to dig a grave. He would, in later life, know money, respect, even power over tenants and influence over councils, but his soul would never hum again with quite that same feeling of accomplishment.

Proud of his position and seeming invulnerability, he was also numbed through with self-disgust. He was horrified at the part of him that could shoot down enemies as if they were no more than tin ducks on a funfair shooting-stall, the part of him that could lie in a ditch watching a rat scurry over his belly or use the corpse of a man he knew well as cover from gunfire and all the while remain, in essence, unmoved and unpitying.

His military career ended with the war. It was made clear to him that the war had provided him with a social mobility that peace and the return of the *status quo* would now refuse him. He was of the wrong class. He spoke with an accent fellow-officers and superiors found comic and incomprehensible. There was nothing for it but to go back to Radcliffe Park.

Radcliffe Park, unaltered by war, was as unreal to him as the Martian landscape of craters, lime and mud had once been. He found the newsagent's boarded up and his parents dead of pneumonia. He found also a letter from Old Man Hewitt, the landlord, informing him that he had kept the property vacant – at some cost to himself – because he had not wanted the young hero to return to find himself without home, family or occupation.

Trench tried to grieve for his parents, plan for the future, renew friendships and learn to be what he thought of as human again but some of his humanity must have dribbled away, spent itself like blood from a severed limb, soaked into the mud of the battlefield. He was a cup half-filled.

Another letter came from Old Man Hewitt, wanting to know what was to be done with the empty shop. The tone was less sympathetic but he invited the hero to come talk with him at his home, the House of Content.

Trench knew the House of Content well enough. Since coming home he had passed by it every day on his way to the park. The park was where he knew some peace and he visited it each morning. Half had been given over to growing vegetables for the war effort but mostly it was well-kept grass and the flowers were preciously bright. Gardens, he thought, were wonderful inventions. Walking in one was like floating in a green bath. It washed away the grime of war and left him clean and refreshed for the short time he was there.

Although he was no longer entitled to, he wore his uniform to the House of Content, sensing it would impress the old man. Nothing had been said or implied in either of Hewitt's letters, but Trench knew this was no ordinary interview between tenant and landlord. If it had been as simple as that, he would not have been invited to the House of Content.

The old man was dying. This was immediately evident. His face was pared horribly thin and he had lost all his hair; his bald skull was patterned over with an embroidery of veins that bulged painfully. He extended a cold hand, the fingers almost pure bone, the skin dry and flaking. When Trench shook it he did so gingerly, as if afraid that too firm a grip would leave him holding a palmful of dust.

Across Hewitt's throat ran a triangular gash through which his Adam's apple poked. He spoke through burps and gurgles, his mouth frothy with spit. His speech was a hideous noise that made others flinch, but Trench had heard worse sounds. He had even seen men in worse condition than Hewitt, although they had usually been dead.

'I take it you don't want to stay on in Brackley Street.'

Trench said the old man was about right. Being a newsagent was not what he wanted in life.

The old man chuckled approvingly, the dribble falling like tears down his chin. 'Then, what *do* you want in life?'

Trench was hard put to say what he wanted. 'Something good.'

The old man seemed satisfied with the reply. Words came painfully to him. He dragged up each syllable as if he were drawing it from a well inside himself. He announced his intentions without preamble, persuasion or subtlety. He was going to give Trench a job. He would make him rent collector for properties in Radcliffe Park, Mallet, Humsey and some shops and storehouses in the centre of the city.

'Not rent collector,' he burped out, correcting himself as quickly as he could. 'Manager.'

The newsagent's would go to a young couple by the name of Rimmer.

'Wife has a club foot. Ugly woman. Sings a lot.'

'And where will I live if they live there?'

The old man had no need of words to answer that. He waved his hand and looked about him: Trench would live with him in the House of Content.

Hewitt then dismissed him and told him to return the next day. This was not to give Trench time to think but because he was too tired to continue speaking. Words were hard-earned currency and he could only spend so many a day.

Hewitt offered to ring for Miriam, his daughter, to show him out but Trench had said there was no need. As he left the house he did see the daughter, a fleeting ghost turning up the stairs.

He walked about the park and urged himself to think over what Hewitt had said but thought came as reluctantly into his head as speech had come to Hewitt's tongue.

He sat a while by the duck-pond and skimmed stones across its glassy surface. He was thinking how it would soon be winter and the park no longer green when he heard a clumping sound and then felt what looked like a claw take hold of his arm. It was the daughter, Miriam.

'You're coming to live with us and manage rent for Father.'

She sounded as if the decision had already been made. Her voice was a whistle, sharp and tinnily genteel. She stood no taller than his elbow, her back slightly crooked, one leg rimmed round in a calliper, her face a round white plate from which two over-large eyes stared out with too great an intensity to be attractive: an ugly woman, but a rich one.

'I've seen you walk by every day this fortnight or more. You walk here often. It was me who pointed you out to Father and it was him who told me how you stood. He's ill. You can see that. He wants things settled. He wants me settled. You know what that amounts to?'

She looked away, ashamed.

He did not answer but offered to walk her back to the House of Content. She took his arm and limped alongside him until they reached the drive. A lace curtain shivered as they came into view.

'You've no coat on,' he noticed.

'No, I just rushed out after you. I've been following you.'

They stood a while looking at the ground. Miriam studied his soldier's boots, black and glossy as mirrors, and he the red weals where the calliper bit into her ankle.

'I picked you out, Mr Trench,' the woman told him, eyes still cast down, a raspberry blush staining her skin from the neck up. 'But it's you as really chooses. I've watched you pass by and once before, in the park, I nearly stopped you but I knew that'd not be proper. Anyway, I knew I had no need. I knew Father'd take up the matter for me. It was him as sent me out here now. "Go after him," he said. "Court him." As if I could.'

She stroked her thigh, the ribs of her calliper visible through the white cotton frock.

'I'm sickly, Mr Trench. I'll not live long.' She made it sound like a promise.

She limped back to the house, entered it and closed the door without looking back at him.

Trench stood at the gate. He stared up at the house. Its brick had a scrubbed look to it, a rich red that looked as if the grime of Radcliffe Park would never dare coat it. Its windows gleamed, the paintwork freshly done, a yellow shocking to the eye, but it was the gardens he remembered. At the front they were a riot of reds and blues, gaudy and insistent, cheap and violent, but at the back he had seen long lawns of green velvet and bushes carved out of jade.

He turned and went home to pack.

The old man's death did not postpone the wedding. The bride wore mostly black out of mourning, over which she draped a small avalanche of white tulle veil. Her flowers were also white, as were her stockings, silk, laddered by the calliper.

They honeymooned in France but it was not the same country in which he had fought. It had become truly a foreign land and so repellent to him. They stayed mostly near Lourdes. Miriam went every day to bathe her leg and soak her arthritic claw. At night he buried his face against her neck and did his husbandly duty, the calliper standing to attention at the foot of the bed, beating out the time to his passionless strokes. Miriam appeared grateful and not unmoved by this activity. He used to hold her down by the wrists, which she thought passionate and masterful; in fact it was to stop her scraping his back with her claw.

She became pregnant with Ursula and nearly died giving birth. Trench stalked the hall of the House of Content, praying she would make good the promise she had once made him. The midwife called him up and said how well his wife had done. She handed him his child wrapped in a counterpane.

He looked down at its red face, wrinkled and blotched, and waited for the shock of hot iron on his soul that would brand him a father. It did not come, although he willed it passionately. Nothing in him melted so as to form a bond with the child.

The moment passed. There was to be no reprieve from inner numbness. The child was just a child. It had failed to save him. Its raw peeled look reminded him of a body he had once fallen on in Normandy.

He gave the child back to the midwife, who returned it to its mother's arms.

'I'll call it Ursula,' Miriam managed to moan. She said it as if the name were a curse she was forced to bestow upon it.

'Ay, you do that,' Trench had said. The child was Miriam's to call what she liked.

Everything was Miriam's, everything. He owned nothing of his own, although Miriam was kind enough to let him act as though he did. She had only the vaguest of interests in money. She seemed barely to realise the extent of her wealth. Trench, however, knew it intimately. He managed it with the same devotion he displayed in cultivating the gardens of the House of Content. Miriam was happy that this was so. It was for this her father had chosen him. It left her free to meditate on life's misery and to continue on the slow merry-go-round of sickness and discomfort she had ridden her whole life long.

Her resolve weakened as did her body until the only thing she wanted in bed was an easy death. Trench took to visiting the bar of the Mansfield Hotel or sometimes a pub in Petergate where there were rooms up top and ladies in the snug. The ladies were usually clean even if the rooms were not.

The doctors said that there was a great deal wrong with Miriam Trench but what really ailed her was a poor attitude. She had been born to wealth but not good looks. She had social standing but a poor constitution. She thought the world had short-changed her and sickness was her way of retiring from it. Once she had found herself first a husband, then a daughter, she had lost interest in them. She gave neither the same attention as she gave the cancerous growth in her stomach which finally killed her.

A slow succession of nurses passed through the House of Content, Norah Matchett being the last and the prettiest. It was 1933 and Trench had had fourteen years of his deal with only the pleasure of counting the money and none of the pleasure of calling it his own.

Norah became Trench's ideal, his object of long-repressed desire, because she came at the right moment, made herself available, and was Miriam's exact opposite. Where Miriam was crooked, sad-eyed and his social superior, Norah was as flat as a board with a face as shiny and bland as a doll's. Also, like him, she had not been born to money or a big house. She could make only a poor but enthusiastic pretence at gentility. He loved Norah for her lady-like airs because she fell so short of breathing them in naturally.

Miriam died. The death, although sudden, was no surprise. Only the daughter, Ursula, looked troubled by it.

Norah left his employ and it was arranged that they would not meet for some nine months at least. The ban was her idea. He had suggested the occasional evening-running-into-early-morning in a room over a pub in Petergate but Norah was firm. She realised that a woman bedded by a man in a pub in Petergate would never be bedded by that same man in the House of Content. She had learned something from the incident of the will and the prolapsed rectum.

With Miriam dead and Norah biding her time in Mallet, here now, in Anna's words, was Trench's chance to spoon up the gravy. However, at a private reading of Miriam's will – only Trench and a solicitor were present – he discovered that the gravy-boat had landed in a port other than his own. The money, the policies, the properties, the House of Content, its furnishings, its gardens: everything was Ursula's or would be when the girl reached eighteen.

It was a costly business to bribe the solicitor to tear up the will and allow instead another to take its place, one written before Ursula's birth, the one Miriam had shown him on the eve of their wedding, the one for which he had sold his life away. There was no moral struggle. Guilt at cheating his daughter did not weigh upon him as hard as his outrage at being cheated by Miriam: that is, until the deceit had been accomplished.

No one ever questioned Miriam's legacy to him. It was common gossip that it had been his price for marrying a cripple, but once the money was securely his it grew heavy and unmanageable in his pockets. He was haunted by the fear that his crime would be uncovered, that the girl would find out and, in her wrath, make him account for every penny spent. He knew her so little and understood her even less that he expected her to act as he would have done in her position.

Trench never did enjoy the wealth for which he had first sold himself and then stolen. Every coin spent was stamped with guilt, every note creased with bad conscience. Poor Norah suffered the most and never knew why. She had married a rich man to improve her station and would never know why the gravy-train had halted just outside.

The nine months spent without Norah were nine months spent with Ursula. He had never needed to confront the girl before. She had always been Miriam's child, Miriam's familiar. He had watched her as a child, clumsy and eerily silent in his presence. He had almost despised her. She had failed to do what he had expected a child to do: save him, refresh him, commit him to life. Sometimes she seemed hardly a child at all, so quiet and watchful. He strongly suspected her of being a spirit strangely mingled with good and evil, haunting the House of Content.

They spent their evenings together, father and daughter, winter evenings, the parlour lit by fire. He would fantasise about Norah, the smooth planes of her belly and thighs, the tiny breasts that made his hands feel so large when he held them. He imagined her sitting astride his lap, her body naked, her hair hanging over her face, his tongue circling her nipples, his fingers scratching at her back, the pair of them sweating, gasping in time as he thrust deeper into her, a hard and unrelenting rhythm. As his imagination inflamed him, he would grind his buttocks into the cushions of his easy chair. He would close his eyes and a groan would come unbidden in his throat. The sound would wake him from the dream. He would look across to see his daughter, watching. He would cough and cover himself with his hands, thankful that the scarlet glow of the fire disguised his flushed appearance.

She was only a child after all. What was she now thirteen or was it fourteen? She wasn't to know what he had been thinking. She was far too young to interpret the lusty mime of his hips.

He saw her naked shortly after that. He opened the door to the bathroom just as she was stepping into the bath. Her body was a stick, all bone, the ribs protruding, nipples as round as her shocked eyes. The flesh was white, the hair between her legs shockingly black.

He closed the door immediately, blustered through a brief apology, went to his bedroom, pulled open a drawer, took out one of his dead wife's handkerchiefs and masturbated into it.

Norah! Norah! he commanded his imagination. Norah came. Norah dressed. Norah in long knickers and nothing else. Norah in the kitchen late at night when it was dark and he ramming it into her – more violent in his fantasy than he would ever have dared be in life. Norah naked. Norah pleading. But at the height of it not Norah but Ursula, veiled in steam, beckoning, legs wide open, inviting, pleading, Ursula!

He could not quite believe what he had done and so chose to forget it. He was unsuccessful. He could throw the hankie, dry and stiff with stains, into the parlour fire but he could not burn away the memory of his desire. It was as if once a thought had entered his mind it could never be dislodged. His mind played with the occasion like a cat with a ball of wool until he was hopelessly entangled by it.

Evenings alone with the girl, the parlour shadowed red and black by the firelight, he would forsake his easy chair to share the sofa with her. They talked comfortably together although her chatter bored him. It was not her conversation that interested him but the line of her throat, the fresh perfume of her adolescent body, the memory of its barely formed breasts and white untested flesh.

He took to his bed earlier so as to avoid spending time with her. Seeing him leave, she would always look sad; sometimes she would not even wait for him to go before crying. She would run across to him, ignore his stilted attempts to repulse her and wrap her arms around his waist, her hot tears melting his starched shirt-front. Her mother was dead, she would remind him. She felt alone and did not wish to be alone, a horrible feeling. He would pat her head tentatively as if afraid her hair were a mass of wires sizzling with unearthed electricity. His other hand would wander with daring slowness down her long back before he held her away from him and told her to be a big girl, a grown-up girl. Daddy, too, was sometimes upset and Ursula would best help him by being grown-up. She wanted to help her daddy, didn't she? To his own ears every word he uttered sounded thick with repressed lechery. In answer, she would look up at him and nod seriously, her eyes showing more understanding than Trench found comfortable.

One night she appeared by his bed. In the darkness her nightgown glowed. She looked like a ghost drawn on a blackboard. She mumbled apologetically, said how upset she was and lonely, frightened of the dark, of the House of Content and life without her mother. Trench did not turn on the light by his bed but kept the room as dark as the inside of his head in which, for the moment, he had extinguished all thought or principle. Instead he raised the blankets and the girl slid in beside him, magnetised by the warmth of his bed, his body and his desire.

She did not encourage but accepted what was done to her and her pleasure in it seemed slight. She was dry, stiff but biddable to his will. He ran his fingers down her body as if it were a piano. She shivered, made ticklish coughs and groans but no music. He kissed her, hugged her, explored her body gently but with relish, put his cock between her two cold, uncertain hands and then between her thighs but refrained from entering her. Ironically, as if it would somehow excuse or qualify his wrongdoing, he concentrated his mind on Norah, the true engine of his desire.

Trench taught himself to see the episode as a period of sickness. Lust was a fever into which he had fallen and that one night was its crisis. Morning came and with it the manufactured conviction that he was cured.

He rose, bundled up his clothes, left the girl sleeping and dressed in the narrow dressing-room that annexed his room. He waited for her to come down to breakfast and when she did he told her he was to marry Norah. He acted as if this one announcement would inoculate them both; him from the return of the disease, her from possible infection.

The girl seemed hardly to react at all. The knife in her hand did not hesitate even slightly as it cut through the butter.

'Norah who?' she asked, although she knew full well.

'Norah Matchett.'

'Oh,' she said simply, as if that were all that could be said.

Neither mentioned the incident again. It was as if it had never occurred. None the less, it continued to smoulder like fire hidden under ashes.

Trench had never been easy in his daughter's company. He had treated her always with cold and irreproachable politeness but to the indifference he had felt towards her since birth was now added fear. There was always the possibility that she would 'tell'. Once married to Norah, Ursula's continued presence turned his life into a dark pond only thinly covered with ice over which he had to move most carefully if he were

288

to avoid drowning. That was why, in confrontations between Norah and Ursula, such as the one that evening over the child's pinched thigh, he avoided taking sides. He dithered whenever possible, pretended ignorance, powerlessness or neutrality.

Norah occupied his heart but not fully. There was always a part of him that remained untenanted. Like the House of Content, there were rooms in his heart that were locked and left unused. When handed his son there was within him that same absence of feeling as when he had first held his daughter. Having expected this, he did not blame the child and acted the proud father.

The war which had so cauterised his emotions still had the power to haunt him. Not a few weeks before Chamberlain had met Hitler again, Hitler wanted bits of Czechoslovakia and it looked like Chamberlain would let him have them. Trench wished Chamberlain well. Anything that avoided a war had his backing. Anna Matchett laughed at him. It was all a sham and a waste of time, this giving away bits of Czecho-whatever-it-was, and it looked as though Anna was right. Not a few days later parts of the park had been dug up and turned into trenches. Gas-masks had been issued.

'See,' Anna had said, 'I said as much, didn't I? If there's no war this year, there'll be one the next.'

It was clear that she was looking forward to it but he trembled and grew angry. He frightened himself with images of Radcliffe Park levelled to mud and rubble, the House of Content a charred shell, the skyline blood-red with fire and bodies lying, broken and burned, all down the length of Brackley Street.

Norah told him to be quiet because he was upsetting her and only Ursula seemed convinced by what he said. Her eyes glistened as he described Brackley Street aflame but her eyes always glistened when she heard him speak with anything like passion. Her excitement was repugnant to him.

Anna Matchett listened politely enough. Freddie was her brother-in-law and rarely made a speech so she let him have his say, but added that it was all exaggeration and he was an old woman for talking so.

'That's white-feather talk, that is, and I'll tickle you with one if you don't change your tune.'

Afterwards Anna waited for him on the landing when

he came up to bed. In the dark she said she was sorry for speaking down to him like that.

'I mean, Freddie, you know whereof you speak, you being a veteran.'

'All men my age are veterans near enough,' he answered.

Her voice disturbed him, so soft and seeming to speak of things other than what she said. He was disturbed, too, by the dark and her closeness. He could feel her breath on his face.

'You're so quiet about things, Freddie, as a rule. You never know what you're thinking. It never shows.'

Her hand grazed his waist lightly, almost accidentally, hard to tell in the dark.

'If I'd been in a war like you, I'd wear medals all the time.'

'I've medals. In the drawer I've medals.'

'I'd have you wear them, I would, all the time.' She rubbed a line above his left breast where the medals would hang if Anna had her way and then she let her hand fall slowly down along his stomach, circling his groin, scratching at his trousers playfully with her long nails.

She led him to her bedroom door and through it to her bed. He was about to fall on her, the mattress wheezing, but the sight of his son's cot pulled him up.

'It's all right, risk it. He won't wake up if you're quick and quiet. Go on, Freddie, you know you want to.'

He was quiet, his mouth chewing on the quilted counterpane to stifle his moans, and quick, too, buttoning himself up and leaving without a goodbye as soon as he was done.

The child in his cot stirred, came near to waking but slept on.

It had been on Trench's part spontaneous but not on Anna's. She didn't think Freddie irresistible, although she could tell that he had been a handsome lad once; nor was it because Freddie was rich: she knew what money he had could never be got easily. Spiting Norah had given it spice but nor was that the reason. The reason was gravy.

Trench, she knew, had property all over and, no doubt, every now and then, one of them shops in the centre of the city fell vacant. There was ever such a smart shop just by Lewis's that Anna thought would make a lovely hat-shop or beautician's, or a shop just for cosmetics and perfumes: Anna had not decided which yet.

Her seduction of Frederick Trench, so effortlessly done, was a business manoeuvre. If, when the proposition was put to him, he turned it down, she would threaten to tell Norah. Either way Freddie Trench would give Anna her taste of the gravy.

For Trench the whole business had been a small earthquake: unexpected, dangerous and, the danger over, quite thrilling. Anna was his sister-in-law and now she was his mistress. Norah had not been particularly active and sex had only ever been the price a woman paid for a husband and a wifely routine. Now pregnancy made her quarrelsome. She was not averse to his kisses, the odd hug, but she could not abide being lingered over.

Trench had respected his wife's feelings but had felt restless. The memory of Ursula in the bathroom recurred too often in his mind. He found himself thinking of that and of the night he had pulled her into his bed. These were not pleasant thoughts and Anna came to him at the right time. An alliance with his sister-in-law was not a clever one but it was safer than thinking of Ursula.

It helped that Anna was so like Norah in the face, made it less of a deceit somehow. It helped, too, that Anna was rounder, heavier-breasted, more 'mistressy' and, although more glamorous than Norah had ever been, more coarse-natured.

What he would have liked would be to linger over Anna's body but this had not yet been possible. If the child was in her room they had to be quick and quiet. The pantry, the kitchen table, the outside privy, the parlour sofa, they were all too cramped or unpleasant and there was always the danger of being caught. The unused top floor of the House of Content would have been most practical but Anna said that she wasn't going to do it on bare boards for anyone. Only on a night when Ursula could be persuaded into keeping the child and Norah conned into taking double her sleeping powders could they lie together safely. Tonight they would, for the first time.

The doors had been locked and bolted, the windows had been checked, the child was with Ursula, Norah, though come morning she would deny it, was sleeping thickly, and upstairs Anna was waiting.

The unlit stairs reminded him of that first time with Anna. The darkness together with his thumping heart also reminded him, curiously, of the trenches. He half-expected the whoop of a shell to sound in the garden and the carpet to turn muddy under his feet.

He stood on the landing and listened for sounds of wakefulness from Norah or from Ursula. None reached him but he waited a while longer to make certain, the delay only increasing his anticipation of Anna naked between sheets.

He slowly opened her door and edged into her room.

'Freddie. Come in quick and don't turn on that light.' Anna's whisper, sharp as a knife, cut through the darkness.

The moon shone through the curtains; there was just enough light to see by.

'What's the cot doing in here?'

'That bloody girl of yours wheeled it in.'

'Is the child in it?'

'Of course he is.'

'Well, wheel him out into his own room.'

'I can't. The door to his room's been locked and the door on the landing. I can hardly wake Norah by pushing it past her, now can I? Ursula's done this. She's done it in spite. I knocked on her door when I found it in here but she didn't answer. I'd have said something if she had.'

There was now nothing to say and nothing to be done with the cot but to let it stand where it was. Defeated, Trench sat on the bed, his back to Anna. Anna sat with her arms round her knees. Both looked at the cot and the sleeping child like two disappointed cricketers watching the rain that had stopped their play.

'That's our bit of fun spoilt.' This had been the night Anna had hoped to put forward her proposition. More than fun had been spoilt.

'I was looking forward to this,' he told her sulkily, his lips pouting. Anna thought he looked the spit of Ursula when he did that but she said nothing.

'There'll be other times,' she said, but he was not to be easily consoled.

'We've done it before like this.'

'Like what?'

'The first time.'

'You were quick and quiet then.'

'I'll be quick and quiet now.'

'Well, I don't know.'

'Please, Anna.'

Anna reckoned something up in her head and then nodded. She supposed it was best to keep him sweet. She lay down, snuggling under the sheets, but Trench stayed as he was, his back towards her, watching the child.

'Take your nightie off.'

'You said quick and quiet.'

'I want to see you.'

'Seeing me won't make it quick and quiet.'

'Take it off.'

He heard her sigh, the bed creak, and the static snap and rustle of her nightgown as she pulled it over her head. He turned from the child to see Anna kneeling on the bed. He got up and slowly pulled back the curtains.

The light of the full moon rushed over the room like a wave. The child squirmed, moaned slightly, and Anna threw her head back in delight as the light silvered her body.

'Marvellous,' was all he could say. She looked to him like a woman in his head when his hand was around his cock and he was away and wanking it, all breasts and flesh, red hair and warm shadows.

He came over to her but she pushed him away.

'Now you, Freddie. Fair's fair.'

He hesitated not because of the child but because he had not been naked before a woman since a boy in front of his mother. With his wives he had kept his pyjamas on and with the women in the pub in Petergate he had opened his pants no wider than was necessary. Anna lay back, spread her thighs and that decided him. He pulled off slippers, shirt, vest, rolled down trousers and long pants and stood naked before her.

'Was this from the war?'

Anna leaned over and traced the patch of burned skin that ran down Trench's leg from his hip to his knee. It was pink and puckered like a long lip.

'It's a burn. From the war. And here, too.'

He turned. A map of Australia in creased pink covered his lower back.

'Mortar fire,' he explained.

'Does it hurt much?'

'Not any more. Not this long while.'

'Does Norah ever touch you there?'

She traced out Queensland.

'No.'

'Does she ever touch you here?'

'Sometimes she holds it for me,' he said, looking down. 'If it's weekends or she wants money for things from the shops.'

'Does she ever do this?'

She did to him with her mouth what Norah had never done and what he had never asked her to do, what the women in the pub in Petergate offered to do for the money he was unwilling to give. He regretted that particular meanness now as he watched Anna's head bob back and forth and felt her tongue sliver up and down his cock. He dug his hands into her rich pile of hair, hot and dry, kneaded it like dough, making the grips fall from it and ping on to the linoleum below. He kept an eye on the child and half a mind on the women in Petergate he had been unwilling to pay. Free was better, though.

'Don't you mind?'

'Mind what, Freddie?'

'The germs.'

'What germs?'

'Norah says —'

'Norah? She's never done this, has she?'

'No.'

She kissed her way up over his white belly to his chest.

'Does she ever do this?' she asked between nipples.

He shook his head, pleasure paralysing his tongue.

'Did Miriam?'

He shook his head again.

'Did Ursula?' she asked and covered his mouth with her lips before he could reply.

Both gave sideways glances at the cot and made a mental

note to remember the child. Perhaps the note was too hastily scribbled or they forgot to read it; the child did not occur to them again.

Anna mauled and urged and Freddie heaved and piled with an abandon he might have dated pre-war and the way Anna threshed and rallied back it seemed almost like a battle. Engrossed in each other, they forgot the child, forgot Norah, forgot Ursula, forgot the towel to put under Anna's buttock to catch Freddie's spillage and prevent staining the sheets.

Norah was only two walls away and sleeping hard: she would not hear them. It was not likely that Ursula was on the landing, her ear to the door, but the pair of them had an audience of at least one: little Eddie Trench gazed at them through the bars of his cot, politely waiting for a break in the action before reminding them of his presence.

Whatever they are doing, the child thinks, they should not be doing it in the dark. They should not be doing it in front of him and they should not be doing it without his mother. He knows what they are doing is wrong because they have woken him. Waking him is wrong, naughty even. When his father, gulping like a goldfish, slivers off his Aunty Anna, Eddie stands up in his cot and tells them that he is going to tell his mother.

Trench sits bolt upright but it is Anna who is nearest and, in her shock, lashes out at the child with only the thought of quietening him in her head. It is the shock she feels that makes the blow so strong. The child falls back to avoid the blow and hits its head on the corner of the cot. The cot shakes and almost topples over but Anna has the wit to catch it and pull it back.

Trench watches, numbed.

Anna watches, equally numbed.

Both wait for the child to cry, which it does, loud and strong in misery. He yells for his mother he knows is two walls away and so must be made to hear.

Anna grabs at him, covers his mouth with her hand, but the child's cry is hardly stifled at all. She panics, picks up the pillow and presses it down on the child's face and the child's cries become instantly a moan, a buzz as of a dying fly against a window-pane. The child struggles, begins to drum its arms and feet against the mattress. In the moonlit quiet of the room it sounds like thunder.

'Hold him,' Anna tells Trench. Her voice is urgent and hard.

Trench holds down his son's arms and legs. In the moonlight he compares his large hands, pale, flecked with dark hairs, with his son's quivering limbs. The longer he holds them the less they quiver until they are completely still and the room is quiet again except for Anna's heavy breathing as she continues to push down on the pillow.

For Trench, breath, like thought, has been suspended all this time. He exhales now. The air has grown chill. He realises he is naked but for his socks and that Anna is also naked. He realises his nakedness in the way Adam must have realised his when he stood guiltily before God.

The cry does not wake Ursula. She has not slept. Her eyes gleam in what moonlight sneaks through the curtains and penetrates the snowfall of white tulle veil in which she has decked herself. She sits upright in bed. One hand scrunches up the rag doll's head, its blood-red 'O' of a mouth twists into a silent scream. With her other hand she turns the doll's body round and round so that its neck becomes ever more tightly wound. The fabric is old, rotten with age and weakened by fire. It cannot withstand this murderous pressure and it rips at the neck with a sound that is like lips parting from a kiss.

She hears it rip and relaxes her grip. She holds it up by its few strings of hair and dangles it. In the smoky gloom of moonlight through veil, the doll is a silhouette. A black shadow, it twirls and untwirls. Its stuffing begins to fall gently in her lap. Her mouth curves into a smile and her head fills with the sound of wings beating against glass.

*

The child's cry wakes Norah – or half-wakes her. She moans and stirs. The child often cries in the night but now that Anna is here she has trained herself to ignore it. Her hand travels to the other side of the bed in search of Freddie, meets only a coldness and withdraws. She does not open her eyes to see the undented pillow, the tucked-in sheet. She supposes him to be calling on nature and this makes her smile. How nice it is to have a husband who preferred a cold walk across the landing to disturbing his wife with the sounds of the pot under the bed being dragged out and noisily used. It is considerate of him. It is genteel.

She turns and snuggles more deeply into sleep.

The child lay unnaturally straight. The pillow still covered its face but nothing could hide the fact of death.

Father and aunt stood over the cot, each wishing that Time would stagger back and so erase what had been done, but although Time has many tricks this was not one of them. Instead they waited for some saving thought to come into their heads. None came.

Murder, quickly and easily accomplished, drained them none the less. Speech, when it finally came, was as sluggish as the thoughts they were intended to express. They spoke numbly and without emphasis, sleep-talking.

'Oh God,' Trench said at last. 'What have you done?'

'What have we done?' Anna, unable to answer it, merely repeated his question, a dull echo, but with one significant alteration.

Trench did not argue but hung his head, accepting mutual responsibility.

'We may', said Anna slowly, 'as well get dressed.'

Yes, one could not think when one was naked. Clothes would bring on thought and getting dressed was something practical.

Trench put his clothes back on and Anna the dress she had laid out for morning, a dress that was velvety blue and pleated from the waist. They took their time. To hurry was to panic and they did not want that. Each bent down before the dressing-table mirror, Trench to straighten his tie, Anna to smooth out her hair. Neither seemed to recognise their own reflection. Moonlight made their faces quite bloodless.

Finished, they sat side by side on the bed, their backs deliberately to the child.

'What we've done', Anna said, choosing her words with difficulty and with care, 'was an accident and no one's fault. It was never intentional and we must neither of us ever speak of blame.'

Trench nodded. It was easier and best to agree with Anna.

'But we can't let anyone know because no one would understand.'

She spoke to him as if he were a child and this made him think of the child, his child, the dead child. He would have wept then but tears would not have come.

'We can't say what we were doing in this room. We can't say we were together. Because they'd hang us for that sure as anything. They would.'

Anna's hand played about her throat with an imaginary noose. She fingered it like a necklace.

'The child was in his room. *His* room. I asked you to unbolt his door from your side and you did that. Then I went to bed. And you went to your bed. And men came into the house while we were sleeping and they killed him.'

'What men?'

'Bad men.' Anna knew that it sounded weak but what other story could she tell? Desperation made her say it with conviction, at least. The imaginary noose drew a little tighter round her neck but Trench was nodding.

'Yes, bad men.'

'They take him out of his room. . . . '

'How did they get in?'

Anna floundered. 'I don't know. We'll think about that later.'

'They take him out of his room and out into the garden and they kill him.'

'The garden?' Trench, for the first time, sounded grieved.

'Yes, they take him out and they kill him.'

'Why?'

'Why's not a question we need answer,' Anna snapped. 'We'll not be expected to answer. Bad men kill all the time and the world's a violent place and no one knows why. And when

298

they ask us why we can say we don't know. Who'd expect us to know?'

Anna's voice had become a whine, the copy of her sister's. The sound of it caused Trench to cry. Tears dripped down his nose and hung from his chin. 'Norah, Norah, Norah,' he moaned.

'Bugger Norah. It's us in trouble. Us.' By 'us' Anna meant 'me, me, me'. A weeping man was no help to her. 'We've not the time to spare for tears. Cry tomorrow or next year but not now or we will have something to cry about. Take up the child.'

Trench sat there still.

'I said, take up the child.'

Trench took up the child and wrapped it in a blanket. He had lifted the child many times before. He expects it to curl its arms around his neck, rest its face against his shoulder, but the child is as floppy as a rag doll. Its limbs dangle, its head lolls back over his arm, its mouth is a black 'O' and from it no sound comes.

Anna leads the way, he follows. The landing is dark. The floorboards and the stairs creak painfully. Their footsteps ring like bullets. The child's head knocks against the banister rails like a stick in the spokes of a moving wheel.

At the bottom of the stairs he lays it down on the hall floor to give his arms a rest. The tarted statue of Our Lady of Lourdes stares down at him mockingly.

Anna Matchett, a Mallet-born Lady Macbeth, hisses at him to hurry, chivvies him on through the kitchen, unbolts the door and follows him through it after searching the drawers for the bread-knife.

Trench is halfway across the lawn by the time Anna catches up with him. They head for the privy because it is at the very bottom of the garden, a leafy place and dark, but they move towards it with such grace and speed it is as if it were a place long set aside for the disposal of dead infants.

Trench puts the child gently on the grass, its head resting on the foot of the compost-heap as if it were a cushion.

The canal is beyond the garden wall. Trench has some idea that it is the canal where the child will be placed to rest. He makes to climb the wall but before he does so the moon, hidden by the one cloud in the otherwise smooth and navy sky, resurfaces. The white walls of the privy glow in its light, the garden is softened into sculptures and planes of green mist but the child looks flat, almost a photograph.

Anna hands him the knife.

'What's this for?' he asks. 'Isn't it dead enough?'

'If bad men take a child they don't kill it nicely like what we've done. All soft and with a pillow. Bad men use knives. You must make it look like murder.'

'Nicely . . . all soft . . . look like!'

Anna has not the patience to argue over vocabulary.

'Now's not the time for talking, now's the time for doing. Do it, Freddie, do it. Do it quick and quiet or somebody'll come, somebody'll see.'

He takes the knife. He expects it to look strange in his hand but, no, it looks at home. It looks as if it belongs in his grip and as though it were a knife never meant for bread but for flesh.

He had once had a knife and he had used it often. Its blade had been no longer than his finger, yet with it he had sliced through uniform, burned skin and muscles to retrieve equipment from dead soldiers.

'I've done this before,' he tells Anna.

Anna is not interested. She stamps her foot, wanting it all over and done with.

'Just do it. Do it again if you've done it before but just do it.'

Trench undoes his tie, rolls it up and puts it in his trouser pocket. He takes off his shirt, folds it, lays it a yard or two away, and begins to take off his trousers. Anna, who has turned away, looks back and asks him what he's doing.

'There'll be blood. I don't want it on my clothes.'

Anna understands and is pleased to see at last a little wisdom from him. She nods and stands back a little further.

He is naked now. He kneels down, pulls away the blanket and with his left hand shields the child's face as if he does not want it to see what he is about to do. With the point of his knife, he draws circles in the air above its chest and considers where best to make the first cut. He tries not to think of the child at all but to imagine it is a yard of cadaver in the mud of a battlefield and himself an officer doing his duty. He presses the knife into the child's chest but too gingerly. He only scratches at it. A circle of blood stains the child's nightgown, a tiny circle like a small rose. It is not enough. He is too delicate. He must act like the bad men. He must stab and stab.

He raises the knife, both hands on the handle, and closes his eyes as he prepares to rain down blow upon blow.

'What are you doing?'

The voice surprises him. He drops the knife. It hits the ground. He looks down at the child. Its mouth is open but it has not spoken nor has Anna.

It is Ursula who has spoken. She is standing behind Anna. Moonlight makes a halo of her hair.

Dead child and naked father: two fantasies long cherished, suddenly made real. Such power she had – nothing was beyond her.

That night as the child lay in her lap under the veil she had contemplated its murder. It had not been an idle, fitful contemplation but a precise imagining. It could be done and she could do it, but what would be the cost? She would have gained nothing by it and lost everything. Such an act would exile her from the House of Content and from her father's presence.

She had pulled away the veil, put Eddie back in his cot and wheeled it back into Anna's room. By locking both the doors in Anna's room and on the landing she ensured that the cot would stay by Anna's bed. Later she would hear Anna knock on her door and swear at her for being so spiteful but by then Ursula had been intent on other things.

What she wanted to do could not be done alone. In her room, aware of her weakness, her inability to change or control the geography of her world, she had called on God, Our Lady, the Blessed Miriam and the House of Content for help. They heard her call. They answered and rewarded her fidelity. In her temple of white veil she prayed to them and as she prayed she listened until she heard the child's cry slice through the night and knew instinctively that it was dead.

The cry would, of course, be unheard by Anna although she lay only inches away, neither would Norah nor her father hear it. It was a sound to which only her ears were attuned: the special noise of a soul being ripped from the child's body and flung into the fires of Hell where she had wished it.

She relaxed, lay back and let the veil slip from her face.

In the morning, she expected, Anna would wake and find the child dead or Lizzie would come in with a cup of tea which she would drop with a scream. Tomorrow Ursula would have to act the sorrowful sister and be as shocked as everybody else but her sorrow would not be too extreme. She had to reserve her strength after all. Norah would be much harder to kill than any child and Norah was next.

She had not been prepared for the sound of her father – unmistakably her father – coming from Anna's room. She could hear Anna, too. She heard their soft tread on the landing and then the creaking of stairs. She got up and pressed her ear against the door. The sounds came from the hallway now. She opened the door and stepped out on to the landing. Muffled by distance came the rasp of bolts being drawn back. The kitchen door, she guessed.

She went back to her room and pulled back the curtains, a cool draught from the open sash window chilling her legs. She looked out at the garden. The embers of Pendle's fire still glowed a faint orange beneath its covering of ash and the moon illuminated the garden. The light was a dull pearl and yet the lawns, the shrubs, the cloud-headed trees were quite lime. She saw her father marching across the garden, a blanketed bundle in his arms. Anna was hurrying after him.

She left the room without a thought for slippers or dressing-gown and moved swiftly through the darkened house and out on to the moonlit garden to see her father imitating Abraham and Anna looking away, her hand about her throat, pretending not to be there. She spoke, surprising them both, and her father dropped the knife. Now he was crouched down in search of it, one hand cupped over his genitals.

Her father thus, the child thus, so much she had imagined but not exactly in this way. It was like seeing the back of a piece of complicated embroidery on which she had worked with long and intense dedication: what had been carefully stitched and precisely detailed became, when turned over, a mess of loops, stray threads and knots; the composition was still familiar but blurred, ragged and in reverse.

She had only the vaguest idea of how her father had come to kill the child and in what way Anna was involved but she realised instinctively and without hesitation that they had been instruments of her will. They had acted out the drama she had composed in her head but evidently they were still in need of her direction.

'I'll help you,' she told her father. 'Give me the knife.'

Anna gasped but Ursula read gratitude in her father's shocked expression. He looked so pathetic searching blindly for the knife and his belly creased comically when he crouched. The sight touched her.

After all, she thinks, it is because of me that he is here. Now he needs me as I have needed him. Love, she saw, could indeed be earned or owed you like a debt.

Trench pulled away the blanket from the child to cover up his nakedness.

'No,' Ursula told him. 'Leave it. Spread it out so I can lay him out on it.'

Trench did as he was told and then stood back. Ursula studied the knife and then the child. As she did so, Trench edged round her to join Anna. They stood hand in hand, each not daring to speak, not daring to think.

The blade was a good one. Her father had chosen well. The child was already cold, its flesh grey but its mouth looked badly bruised. She pulled her nightgown over her head and then took off the vest and long knickers and threw them to Anna who let them fall to the ground.

Ursula kneeled down and lifted the child on to her lap. She was like a marble madonna as she cradled it in her arms but she was thinking of another statue, the plaster Our Lady of Lourdes that this child had helped to desecrate. She remembered in particular the ruby choker Norah had painted about Our Lady's neck. What would Norah think if her precious heart were to wear a similar necklace.

Holding the knife in her fist, she ploughed a clean line along the softly yielding flesh of the child's throat. Blood did not spurt out as she had expected but oozed thickly in the knife's wake, covering the child's body, soaking the bib of its nightgown and covering Ursula's arm, breast, thigh and a little of the blanket. More blood dripped thickly but slowly on to the blanket as she dangled the child by its legs. She looked across at her father and at Anna who was looking away.

Unable to express his horror and pity, Trench's face was a blank page on which Ursula read only admiration. She also mistook his silence together with Anna's still-turned back as an indication that more was required from her.

She lay the child back on the blanket. Its head lolloped backwards, loose as the rag doll's had been after it had been drained of its stuffing. She felt no repulsion, only disappointment because the child was dead and so could not be hurt or dishonoured except in memory. The body it had left behind was merely litter.

She remembered her father's position. She took the knife in both hands and brought the knife down again and again and again. The blade did not go deep after the first few blows. Obstruction – ribs and things, she supposed – prevented depth but she found a steady rhythm in her stabbing that was pleasant and hypnotic.

'That's enough.' It was Anna who spoke. 'That's done it enough.'

Looking down at the bloody debris, Ursula supposed that, yes, it probably had.

'Now what?' she asked, wiping her hands on a clean corner of the blanket.

'Now leave it and let's get back to the house.'

'Leave it?' Trench asked, his voice low and confused. 'There on the grass? In the cold? Throw it over the wall. Into the canal.'

Ursula picked up the child by its head first, but its neck tore dangerously, and then by the arm. But she thought better of it and laid the child back on the blanket.

'The canal's a bad idea. People use it as a short cut to Brackley Street. Suppose someone on an early shift finds it?'

'Well?' Anna whined. 'It's got to be found, hasn't it?'

'But not before we've cleaned up.'

Ursula was unsure as to what, apart from herself, needed to

be cleaned up. That the real crime had taken place inside her head she did not doubt. The inside of her head was a safe place and she had no need to worry over it. However, the crime had also taken place elsewhere. What she had imagined so precisely had been enacted by others. Her thoughts had been projected into the real world like a film on a screen and had left real shadows.

'We don't want it found until we're ready for it to be found. We have things to do and stories to invent.'

She looked about for a place to put the child; the privy seemed to her the most obvious, fitting and secure. She barked at Anna to open the door and lift up the seat.

'Why me?' asked Anna, who thought she had done enough that night.

'Because I've got blood on my hands.' Ursula held her hands out for Anna to admire.

Anna did as she was told and Ursula wedged the child behind the splashboard but allowed its arm and leg to dangle prettily in the fetid water. She dropped the blanket in after wiping herself down with it as best she could.

While Ursula was busy arranging the child, Anna picked up the knife. It was clammy with blood and warm from Ursula's grip. Repelled, she threw it to the other side of the garden. It landed on Pendle's fire. A cloud of grey ash rose like applause.

'What did you do that for?' Ursula scolded. 'Do you think it'll melt and leave no trace? Do something useful. Pick up our clothes. There's no blood on you. Go back to the kitchen and wait. I'll have to get the knife now. Father, help me wash.'

Anna, glad to get away, walked back to the house. She felt calmer now that she had something practical to do again; Ursula was in charge, not her. Anna wanted as little responsibility as possible.

Trench followed his daughter like a mute slave. With a snapped branch from a privet bush Ursula pushed the knife away from the smouldering fire towards the garden tap. The tap leaked and the ground around it was soft and damp. The knife hissed quietly as it was shoved along and Ursula's bare feet left clear prints.

'Tomorrow I'll have to come out in bare feet to look for the child.'

Trench nodded.

'Wash me down, Father.'

He turned the tap gently round and the hose attached to it slowly thickened and snaked into life. The water, no more than a soft trickle, fell over her body and mixed with the smeared blood to make rivulets of pink.

Daughter held father's eyes all the while until she stood shivering but clean, white in the moonlight, as white as the statue of Our Lady of Lourdes in the hall of the House of Content. One day that, too, would be wiped clean.

'Last time it was dark and you could not see me. There was blood left on the sheets. I had to wash that, too. Remember, Father.'

He remembered and the line of his mouth trembled.

On their way back across the lawn, he noticed she was turning to look at the back of her leg.

'What is it?' he asked.

'I don't know. I must have burned my heel on the fire, though I don't remember how.'

In the kitchen, skin damp and shivering still, Anna inspected her for blood, found none and wiped her down with a tea-towel.

'It's from the dirty washing. I thought that better than using a clean one.'

Ursula nodded approvingly. 'Put it back when we've done.'

Anna, orders received, nodded back.

Ursula and Trench dressed and Anna made tea.

'There's not often a time when tea's a redundant drink,' Anna said. It was so like what Norah would have said that Trench broke down. Anna handed him the tea-towel to wipe his eyes. She murmured consolingly but her face showed her impatience. Ursula, too, was impatient to continue. Tears spent for Norah were time wasted. She called her troops to order.

'Well, Anna, tell me, what was your plan?'

'We decided bad men came into the house.'

Ursula tutted.

Anna shrugged her shoulders. 'I know, but what else could we say?'

'What bad men?'

'Do we need to know that?' Anna flustered. She had been through this with Trench.

Ursula thought for a while and then agreed. 'You're right. Bad men'll have to do. Better a story with loose ends than one that's all neat. How did they get in?'

Anna had not thought. 'Through the door,' she supposed.

'Which door?'

'The back door, this door here, the kitchen door.'

'But it was bolted.'

'Perhaps he forgot to bolt it.'

'He wouldn't forget to bolt a door.'

'Well, he might have.'

He looked as if he might have forgotten his own name. He stirred his tea round and round until it splashed into the saucer.

'I'd not forget to bolt a door,' he said finally, 'but I might forget to check a window.'

'Well done, Father. A window. The sash window in the dining-room. You forgot about it or didn't notice it.'

'Yes, I saw that the window was closed,' he said slowly, feeling himself into the part, 'but I forgot to check if the catch was on.'

'They came in through the dining-room window,' Ursula said. 'They crept upstairs and into Anna's room.'

Anna wasn't having that. 'Oh, yes, and I'm lying there and I tell them: "Go ahead, don't mind me." I'm not having that. If we are rearranging the past, why can't the child be in its own room?'

Ursula grudgingly supposed that the cot could go back into the child's room.

'That's very gracious of you. It's all your fault it was in my room in the first place. If you'd kept the child in your room none of this would have happened.'

With this Ursula did not argue nor did she care to. Of course it was her fault but not in any way that Anna could have understood. Anna worked at a level of malice and spite whereas Ursula mined a deeper, richer seam.

'Shall we stop arguing and go on planning?' she suggested brightly.

Anna tutted and Trench said nothing. He would let the women do the planning. When he talked he would talk to Anna. He avoided even looking at his daughter. He did not dare. She frightened him.

'Right, these bad men come up the stairs. Dead quiet they are. Eddie is alone and sleeping in his room. No one knows any different.'

'Oh God, I've just thought.' Anna said, slapping her hand over her surprised mouth.

'What? What have you just thought?'

'Norah knows he wasn't in his room.'

At the sound of his wife's name, Trench hung his head and softly repeated it.

'I told Norah last night that he was with you.'

'Did Norah go into his room?'

'No.'

'Then, that's all right. She only thought she was with me.'

That was Norah dismissed. It was pleasant to dismiss Norah so easily. She must do it more often.

'Yes. Now, where were we? The bad men. The bad men take him downstairs.'

'They'd have to smother him first,' said Trench, a small boy sitting with the grown-ups. 'He was smothered with a pillow.'

Ursula narrowed her eyes. So that was how it was done.

'Very well, then, he was smothered. They smothered him to keep him quiet. We all know that he'd have cried out otherwise.'

Anna and Trench nodded in sad agreement. Yes, Eddie would definitely have cried out if wakened by strangers and in the dark.

'They take him down the stairs, out by the back door – we must leave it unbolted – and then out into the garden where they did what I did to him just now before hiding him in the privy.'

'I can't see the why of it. Any of it,' Trench complained.

'But that's the beauty of it. There is no why. No reason for it. It'll be that much harder to trace back to us.'

Trench could not understand Ursula's explanation. He looked to Anna who was no help.

'I've tried explaining it to him,' Anna told Ursula, 'but it was no use. Men, they're just thick. Can't you see, Freddie? If the child was killed by us, then we'd have left it how it was. We wouldn't have done to it what we've just done.'

'But we have. We did. We cut its throat. We stabbed it and left it in the dirt. Or she did. Her.'

'Yes, but to make it look like murder,' said Anna, patience draining from her.

'But it *was* murder!' he shouted.

'A professional murder's what I mean. His father wouldn't cut its throat. His sister wouldn't stab him again and again. But bad men, they would.' Anna could not make it clearer. She was about to give up. She nearly said, 'We'll talk about it in the morning,' but morning would be too late, she realised.

'Do you understand better now, Father?' Ursula asked him gently.

Trench looked away and sighed. Perhaps he would soon wake up. It would be dark and Norah would be lying right by him, snoring in his ear.

'Yes, I understand. I suppose I have to.'

This settled, Anna felt she could express her doubts.

'This story of yours, Ursula, about the bad men and how they set about doing what they do; don't you think it's all a bit too weak?'

Ursula shook her head. 'Not as weak as all that. It's messy, that's all, and messy is good. It's a kidnap gone wrong. They smother the child to get it out of the house but only to quieten it. They get outside and see it's dead. They get angry and so they do what they do to the child and they throw it in the privy. These bad men, maybe they're not bright and it all goes wrong on them.'

Anna said it was still a weak story and adding motives for the bad men did not strengthen it.

'It's the only story we've got and it'll have to do. It's like this evening, isn't it? The pinch? Eddie said I pinched him. I said I didn't. His word against mine. You all knew I done it but you couldn't prove it for certain. Well, this is like that and this time it's not his word against anyone's because he's dead and he's got no words any more. We have to speak for

309

him. We tell them it's the bad men. They might say, no, it's us. They might know it's us – or one of us – but they can't prove it unless we confess. And, anyway, maybe we'll be believed. People get killed every day and no one knows why or how. People die in houses and rooms and wars and hospitals and there's no one to blame so let's blame the bad men.'

The speech was for her father. He was looking at the future as if it were a dark tunnel down which he was too afraid to walk. She wanted her words to light his way.

Dark things certainly occupied him but his most immediate concern was not for himself but for Norah. Come tomorrow he would have to tell her that Eddie was dead. 'Oh, Norah,' he moaned again.

'Yes,' Anna agreed, 'Norah.'

Norah, Norah! Was there no other tune for them to sing, thought Ursula but realised that Norah was indeed the next problem to be overcome.

'Drug her. Keep her sleeping the whole day if you can. Never mind what folk say. Keep her sleeping and undisturbed. If she wakes and they want to talk to her we can pass off what she says quite easily.'

She knew it was only a temporary solution. She had in mind a more permanent one but kept that quiet for the moment, confident that a saner father would see the sense of it. (Anna she did not worry about.)

'It's two o'clock,' Anna said needlessly when the tinny chimes of the ormolu clock were heard from the parlour.

'So it is and we've not half-planned what we're to do. Come morning, we'll let Lizzie find out that the child's missing. We have to wait for her to do that. Father, you'll go straight for the police when she tells you. Don't use the telephone, go across the park. It'll take longer that way; not much longer but you never know, we may need the time. Anna, you stay upstairs if you can and make sure Norah's undisturbed. I'll go search the garden with Pendle and look for the child with him. I have to do that,' she explained to Anna, 'because I left clear footprints by the tap. We stick to our story of bad men and our uninterrupted sleep. We heard nothing. We saw nothing. We know nothing. Father, there's the sash window to be left open, and once you've done that don't dawdle in the dark but come straight back. Anna, wash these cups and saucers and put them away.'

Both Anna and Trench did her bidding. This girl who had been thought of no account directed their actions like an empress.

'And what'll you be doing?' Anna asked peevishly.

'Sitting here,' Ursula answered smartly. 'Thanks to you throwing that knife in the fire I burned my heel. See.' She showed Anna the red mark on her foot. 'I'll put some butter on it. It'll be all right.'

'Yes,' Anna agreed. 'Burns don't last long. They heal up soon as look at them.'

Anna washed the cups and saucers while Ursula, her heel attended to, wiped them dry and returned them to the cupboard.

Anna, alone with Ursula, grew nervous. It seemed to her that it was not she but Ursula who had killed the child. By taking charge of the situation, she had also taken responsibility for it. Ursula seemed as glad to receive that responsibility as Anna was glad to give it.

'It's like this evening,' said Ursula, 'when I was making the cocoa and you were yapping away. You're quieter now, I notice.'

'Well, a lot has happened since,' said Anna.

'You were on about war and the world and I said this house and my father were my world. It's for him I've done all this and gladly. I'll hang for him if need be.'

'Why?' asked Anna. For the first time, the noose about her neck was loosened. Anna would never wear a noose. It belonged to Ursula.

'Maybe he'll love me now. I've done something to deserve it. He owes me.'

Ursula was convinced of this, Anna less so but she said nothing, free of the noose.

Trench returned from the dining-room.

'Have you opened that window?'

'I've opened it.'

'Right, shall we go through our stories again?'

Neither Trench nor Anna wished to do so but Ursula would not be disobeyed.

'Last night I slept by my wife. I did not wake and heard nothing. When I discovered that my child was missing I went for the police. When I returned, my child had been found. It is my belief that bad men came into the house and stole my child for money and somehow he was killed.'

'Try to put a bit of passion into it, Father. It sounds like you're dictating. Now you, Anna.'

Anna was all conversational ease. 'Well, last night I slept alone. I don't know about you. When I discovered that little Eddie was missing I stayed by my sister, Norah. She's pregnant and not to be upset. When I came downstairs I discovered. . . . Shall I go on?'

'Some things we'll have to play by ear. What's important is that we all three agree. We saw nothing. We heard nothing. We know nothing. If all three agree about that we may be thought guilty but we'll not be found guilty. I can see neither of you wants to hear me practise my story but that's all right. I'll get by. I'll find it easy. I think it's best we go to bed now. I'll take some butter up for my foot and I'll take the knife, too. I've a place for that.'

'And where's that?' Anna wanted to know.

'Somewhere where it'll not be found.'

'Which is where?'

'Behind a veil. Goodnight, then.'

It seemed right that each should kiss the other, shake hands and wish each other well for the morning but the kisses given to Ursula were dry and passionless and the handshakes limp and without amity.

Ursula left, bestowing on her father an especial smile that he refused to notice.

Trench and Anna were left alone in the kitchen.

'A hard night we've had of it, Freddie, and worse to come.'

'I think she's evil.'

'Ursula? No, not evil, misguided and doing it all for you.'

'But the pleasure she took in it.'

'Well, I can't deny that she seemed to be enjoying herself more than she ought. Perhaps she is a little evil but she's saving your neck, Freddie, and mine, too, I suppose. You must see that.'

Trench could see only a naked Ursula, darkly splattered,

312

holding the child up by the leg, exultant and powerful.

'Anna?' He grasped her arm. 'We two did a bad thing but we did it without ill-will, out of panic and I don't know what. We weren't to blame. We were powerless and not to blame, I see that. I think I can see that. But her? She did it out of badness.'

Anna agreed as she would agree to anything which minimised her guilt.

'We'd not have gone through with it,' Trench went on, believing every word. 'I'd not have had the strength to use that knife on my own child. We'd have given up and gone back and owned up, wouldn't we?'

Now that this was no longer possible, Anna agreed that this is what they would have done.

'She's done this, not us, and now we're stuck with it.'

Anna was worried by this. 'But, Freddie, you do see that this way is best. This way we might be saved. You have to see that. You have to stick by what's been agreed.' Anna felt the noose that had been relaxed while Ursula had presided tighten once again. 'You have to stick now. You can't not, Freddie, you can't not.'

'I suppose', said Freddie, 'we'll be punished one way or another for what was done.'

'But you will stick?'

'Ay, I'll stick for one reason, I'll stick for Norah. I can't have her knowing that she's married to the man who killed her son.'

'That's it, Freddie, stick for Norah.'

'But, Anna, promise me?'

'Promise you what?'

'Promise me you'll not leave Norah alone with Ursula. Promise me.'

'Promise,' said Anna, who saw no need for such a promise and so gave it easily. 'Now to bed, Freddie, to bed.'

✳

As he slips between the sheets Norah's warmth envelops him and its bliss deepens his guilt.

Norah will be devastated by the child's death but she will not suspect him of it. If she does, he can count on her silence.

More than a marriage vow binds Frederick and Norah Trench. It had been Norah who had measured out and served Miriam's medicine after all. If she does think the worst she cannot inform the police but what she could do, would do, is stop loving him and that he could not bear.

That night he sleeps but thinly. He fights images of dead sons and naked daughters by conceiving great plans for Norah: holidays, servants, a new house, a separate bank account. He dreams of pound notes, bonds and tenancy agreements, and drops of blood seeping through them like rosebuds opening.

A cold night Anna Matchett has of it. She looks to the future but cannot find it. She fears there may not be one or that if life does go on it will always be a looking-back-over-the-shoulder business and she has never been one for doing that. Her conscience is unmarked. She will fight to keep it so. It is the only sensible thing for a smart girl to do. She deserves to get by, to get on. She deserves it because . . . because . . . because.

Ursula in her room does not go straight to sleep but will have no difficulty in doing so. She chooses not to for the moment.

She has pinned the veil on her head. She wears it like a bride. She kneels. It is as if her room is suddenly a cathedral and her bed an altar, the rag doll under her pillow the host in the tabernacle. Her hands join in prayer. She prays for forgiveness, to give thanks and for companionship's sake, and then she rises, sits on the bed and inspects her heel.

The burn is small but painful. It stings to touch and throbs powerfully. It is oval-shaped and ochre-red. It is like a rose – the only flower the green garden has given forth all summer.

She climbs into bed and sits upright, bolstered by pillows, her veil intact. The dawn begins to grain the darkness with silver chards but from under her veil the room is seen as if through a fall of snow. The birds will sing soon.

She pushes the veil back from her face and looks ahead for a while. Her gaze is abstracted and dull but suddenly it sharpens. She looks down and then across at your thumb as it holds down this page and then she looks up at you.

She prepares to speak. She has no nerves. Her voice is one that Ayomon Devlin would recognise – clipped and delivered from the side of her mouth – but Devlin is not here to listen to it, only you.

'So.

What was it you were expecting?

Not this.

Or maybe you were.

I did believe it was me who killed the child and that Father and Anna . . . well, they just did my bidding.

I know better now.

It was just the coincidence of it, me plotting it all out in my head and them doing it.

That coincidence came from God. I have always felt under his gaze and, at certain times, I have felt something of his power. That night I had the power, and the power it was good. Neglected and lonely for so long, it was nice to feel so special. And, yes, of course the power was good. Look who I prayed to, to get it.

Killing Norah, that was all me. I don't deny it. Not a clever thing to do. It cost me my father's love which is what I wanted all along.

All I ever wanted?

All I ever wanted was to love life and for life to love me back. I wanted respect and the knowing that I belonged but all I ever got was a reputation.

Reputation was why I went up to Brackley Street the night of the riot. It wasn't to refresh my soul but to get noticed and keep my name alive because all I had was a name. I never planned on being burned. Well, you wouldn't, would you?

Memory's an unreliable thing. It stops and falters and even lies. Imagination can fill the gaps quite well, so well you forget what's true and what's made up. Who knows what's true? I don't know anything for sure or not really.

I don't know about motives. What makes you do a thing, it's something short and intense. It hasn't got a name. Motives are what you call it when you're trying to guess what it is.

You can't trust nothing.

315

Not even this, what I'm saying.

Who'd trust me?

The only safe place is in your head and that's not too safe a place no more.'

The dark lightens. She becomes a girl again, a tired girl who has had a hard night and who will have a busy day, a girl who needs her sleep. She has her strength to conserve. She has things for which that strength will be much needed.

Sleep comes quickly and she dreams not of blood but of roses, red roses falling from Heaven, a shower of red roses that touch earth, grow icy-white and burst into flames. She dreams happily about the flames. They lick at her legs, her arms, her face, rough kitten-licks but pleasurable. These are flames that do not burn but purify. This is a fire that devours itself and her with it. It leaves behind only smoke, the memory of fire, a veil of rich smoke through which nothing can be seen or even guessed at.